About The Author

Andrea Jutson is a w ... . She has written tw ... t medium James Paxt ... t work on a third. In her career, ... a bookseller, journalist, collections librarian, book buyer and journalist again, and once spent almost a year selling tickets at a heritage site in London. She now works at a public relations agency, and lives in South Auckland.

This edition published in 2018 by Williams & Whiting

ISBN 9781911266822

Williams & Whiting (Publishers)

15 Chestnut Grove, Hurstpierpoint,

West Sussex, BN6 9SS

Also by Andrea Jutson from Williams & Whiting

The Darkness Looking Back

For information about these and other books

published by Williams & Whiting

go to : www.williamsandwhiting.com

SENSELESS

ANDREA JUTSON

Williams and Whiting

Prologue

BY RIGHTS WEDNESDAY night should have been quiet. Fucking typical, thought Paxton. So much for easing him into his working week. Instead of the usual moderate midweek crowd, there was a fortieth birthday and a full house of binge-drinking insurance brokers getting louder with every shot. The drunker they got, the cruder the names of their cocktails. He'd already been over twice after complaints at the few other tables, but he might as well have been passing pamphlets on Jesus. Preaching wasn't welcome in a bar. Now he just shut up, poured drinks, and wondered why the hell he was still there.

He watched as a woman lurched for the ladies', on heels not designed for drunks with a weight problem. Warmed your heart, really. Change the scenery, but people always stay the same.

He couldn't say he hadn't asked for it. You didn't leave your home country blissfully free of connections or qualifications and just expect to walk into steady, well-paid and, God forbid, halfway *respectable* employment elsewhere. He'd left England five years ago. Auckland was more like home than anywhere he'd visited, but with the advantage of thousands of miles in between, and a much better weather forecast on almost any day of the year. It was a logical end point to his travels. Being in the middle of nowhere, it was too damn expensive to leave.

At last the bar puked out the birthday girl and her inebriated colleagues. Paxton finished wiping things off and started counting the coins.

'Oi, James. See you tomorrow.'

Adam Suasua was waving as he headed for the door. Adam was one of the other barmen at Anubis and probably Paxton's best mate in this country. Or any for that matter. The rowdies never bothered him. If he got any more laid-back he'd be a corpse.

Paxton jerked his chin in acknowledgement. 'Yeah. Unfortunately.'

'Hey, James?' Adam had turned around.

'What?'

'How can you tell if a plane's full of Poms?' Adam grinned. 'When the engines are off but the whining's still going ...'

Paxton's raised middle finger got only Adam's back. Smart bastard. But it was a depressing thought. With some people, the longer they were away from home, the more English they got. Soon he'd be saying 'I fink', watching *Coronation Street* and apologising to whoever wrote off his car. Yeah, like hell. He owned an ageing Nissan Sunny. No apologies necessary.

It was after midnight by the time he finished the cash-up. The job came with off-street parking, which on the weekends was always a godsend, but midweek in winter the carpark was deserted except for him and Brent Palmer, the bar manager. His footsteps echoed flatly on the tarmac, their sound swallowed by the vastness of the dark. But Paxton was beyond being afraid of the dark. That was one of the many reasons he'd had to get out of Britain. It wasn't that he thought there was nothing out there. He knew there was.

He took his usual route home, along Patteson Avenue and the houses winding down to the waterfront. The radio had been the latest thing to pack up in his imported turd on wheels, but as it had only ever run on Japanese frequencies it wasn't really an issue. He made do with the silence.

Perhaps this was fate.

He was never sure later whether he'd have noticed the dog if there had been other distractions. Although the roads were relatively empty at this time of night, the movement of a black dog in the pitch darkness might have gone unmarked. The street lighting was nothing short of abysmal. It was almost like driving through a tunnel; that same feeling of being cut off from the rest of the world, nothing to do with the narrowness of the street. But there, just at the edge of his headlights, Paxton saw a dark shape move into the road, right in the path of his car.

He instinctively slammed his foot hard on the brakes. *They* at least seemed to be working. The car stopped dead with a force that rattled his teeth in his head, and left him unsure whether he'd hit whatever it was. Paxton closed his eyes for a second, trying to sound less like an asthmatic, then edged closer to the kerb and parked. With shaky legs he climbed out of the car.

The black dog was wheeling uncertainly in the road, as if it had been spun in circles and was trying to find its bearings. But whether it was dazed because of him or something else, Paxton couldn't tell. It trotted a little way up the hill then paused in deep confusion, shifting its feet, its movements never ceasing. All the while it whined softly to itself.

It's frightened, Paxton realised suddenly. But what on earth could have scared it so badly?

He could make out a collar on its neck, and dimly he formed an idea of grabbing the dog and dropping it off if there was an address. It was clearly someone's dog, a pet that would probably be missed and greatly mourned if found flattened in the middle of the road. Patteson Ave was steep and poky and full of near blind corners, a twisting death-trap for unwary drivers, or black dogs who might stray into the road just around an unlit corner ...

He prayed there was more than a number on the tag. A mobile on his income was an unwarranted luxury. Determining to get this over with, he stepped in the dog's direction.

Instantly it started barking, for a moment shorting all of his senses, except the one marked Flight. Thoughts of an easy apprehension vanished. Inwardly cursing, Paxton crouched until he was on the same level, trying not to topple over from fatigue. He focused on the dog, a black Labrador all eyes and bared teeth in the dark. In a low voice he spoke to it, soothing, willing it to be calm.

Quiet, dog, I'm not going to hurt you.

He remained crouching there for a minute or so, until the barking gradually ceased. The lights in the houses nearby stayed incuriously off; Neighbourhood Watch had gone to bed. Finally the dog grunted, then began to whine again, almost a moaning pitched low in its throat. He should have been a better interpreter. Gently running his hands over its coat, Paxton checked for tenderness, but nowhere on its body were there any signs of damage. An unlikely hit-and-run then. Abandoned maybe, but highly improbable in the early hours of morning. There was no tag. Christ.

He straightened, feeling every muscle in his legs, and groggily tried to consider.

But the dog seemed to have decided without him. Calmer now, but with an air of purpose, it loped up the hill again towards a small reserve. Lacking the capacity for independent thought, Paxton wearily trailed after it. Some external force was pulling him forward. There was something very, very wrong, but the dog wasn't talking. Ill at ease, he saw it enter the reserve. The park was even darker than the street, without the benefit of light. There were no houses here on the northern side of the reserve, only a Girl Guide hall with windows that were now black and empty, just like those in all the houses at the far edge of the park, suddenly horribly distant.

You're fucking mad, James. A woman was murdered in a park not far from here. Go home before you fall down and embarrass yourself.

With a building sense of dread he watched his feet ignore him. He walked deeper into the park, descending behind the dog into the hollow sloping down from the road, skirting a play area with its deserted swings hanging silent in the darkness. It loomed up on his left, more sensed than seen. Somehow sucking in all the light. He stumbled a little on the uneven ground, which was hummocked in waves, contoured like a rolling sea frozen into place.

Suddenly an explosion of noise shot ice into his stomach, fixing him immobile to the spot. It was barking; high-pitched to the point of madness, unnerving, repeated without pausing for breath. It came from the Labrador. Its whole frame was rigid with terror, ears retreating into its head. And Paxton knew why he had come.

A body lay sprawled on the grass, soaking in its own blood, a dog lead twisted savagely round its neck. Paxton knew without checking that the man was dead.

Because the past had returned to haunt him.

Chapter ONE

MY NAME IS Mark Bradley. Please listen, something awful has happened. You have to find my daughter. You have to tell her I love her. And — I'm sorry.

Oh Lena ... I'm so sorry ... I've really ballsed up now, haven't I?

You see, I couldn't sleep. I often get that; I needed to clear my head. Stupid fool. I never take the pills. And now look — it's lights out permanently. If only I'd known ... But that always comes after, doesn't it?

But what really makes me angry with myself, utterly furious in fact, is that I never saw who did this. I could kill myself.

Ha. Now there's a laugh! ... Oh God. Christ, Lena ...

Sorry. It's just ... I've been trying and trying to think, but I never saw his face. All I saw was him beating me, with a pipe, over and over. Then tying the lead around my neck, and kicking Glen. He had dark hair, I think, dark ... But I couldn't say how tall he was; he was all bent over, wasn't he?

Arrghhh! Bloody useless. You won't see me on CSI. Still, the police don't usually get witnesses to their own murders, do they?

But please — would you tell her ...

Just tell her this, that I didn't feel a thing. I was gone before the second blow fell. I felt nothing. I want her to know that. But I'm not leaving her either. Not until I know she's safe from him.

Please — find him. Find whoever did this and make sure he's locked away. I beg you. If you don't I swear I'll never sleep again.

'I swear,' said Paxton.

He blinked as he came to himself. Hastily he looked around, a futile reflex he could not prevent. He couldn't see his own feet in the darkness, but he knew he was alone. He was still alive.

The Labrador had vanished. Softly he called, 'Glen. Glen!' He whistled. 'Here boy! Come!' There was the faint scratching of nails on concrete, but the dog would not come back inside the park. Paxton couldn't find it in his heart to blame him. He felt sick. He couldn't look at the body beside him, or the dark puddle of blood around it. Suddenly he felt the urge to put space in between them.

He turned, sprinting for the house across from the reserve, and pounded on the door a bit louder than he meant to. He waited, almost pacing, till it opened.

'Hi, I'm really sorry, but could I please use your phone ...?'

HE waited for the police with Glen. The woman who answered the door had been understandably horrified at this pollution of her neighbourhood. (House prices had been soaring.) And there were two kids peeking blearily down the stairs. She'd invited him to stay for a coffee, reckless of the caffeine. Coffee or no coffee there'd be no more sleep tonight. But Paxton had refused. He needed to think, and he couldn't do that while making small talk with an anxious young couple. The husband had come down before long, and was pressing him for the details.

In the end Paxton went to his car and turned on the heat, with Glen on the seat beside him. The dog was calmer in his presence. He couldn't say the same for the neighbours, if they knew what he had done.

When he was a small boy back in Shropshire, his aunt told him that she hated their new magnolia. A valid opinion, except that his aunt had been dead for six years. Shortly after, the magnolia followed.

That was only the start.

Little James Paxton often talked when there was nobody there. He embarrassed strangers with personal details, he never cried when his pets died, and his imaginary friend was a bit more convincing than most. It's not common for them to teach you snatches of Latin.

Soon he had learned to keep quiet, which came as a great relief to his parents. Even his closest friends never suspected there was more than the usual abnormal about him. Until he'd gone on a class trip to Wales.

One of those historical visits. He and his mates had, like typical fourteen-year-olds, been fooling about swapping speculations on the lesbian old ladies of Llangollen. Not for them the more politically correct view of harmless Florence Nightingales. He'd been enjoying himself immensely until Ruthin Castle.

The 'castle' these days was boring, just a typical Victorian excretion-cum-hotel hosting period banquets. In the winter there were medieval discos.

The ruins behind it, the original structure, seemed equally unfulfilling. His history teacher had spittled on about curtain walls and barbicans and baileys amid a pathetic crumble of masonry that resembled less a fortress than a rock garden after years of neglect. It was more weed than wall.

Then like Lady Macbeth they'd walked the ramparts, in search of the infamous Grey Lady's grave. The local guide told the students her history. Wife of the steward of Ruthin in the fifteenth century, she had beheaded him with an axe after discovering his amour with a younger woman. Other versions had her chopping the rival. Whatever the truth, she had been executed, and shamefully buried in unconsecrated ground. Her ghost was said to walk there to that day.

There was the usual outbreak of joking, but for once James wasn't joining in.

He could feel her.

It began as a creeping sensation in the pit of his stomach, an awareness of nature mis-stepping. His senses reached out, probing, while at the same time another part of his mind shrank desperately away. Small points of light fixed him, the natural play of sunlight on leaf and stem, but suddenly grown entrancing ...

He couldn't move. The cold increased, until his limbs felt like rods of ice despite the sun that was baking the stones. He could no longer feel his heart beating. Only sadness, deep sadness and anger, that overwhelmed and took from him the power of speech. It was another who spoke through his mouth, and stopped all his class-mates in their tracks.

Shame! I have been twice forsaken, first by him and then by those who punished me. I am she who was done wrong and yet those wretches punish me! Twice betrayed, twice damned, and yet the shame lies not with me!

The voice rose to a frenzied shout, echoing in the horrified silence.

GOD ROT HIS BONES!

NO one sat next to him on the bus on the way home. He might as well have had a damp patch spreading from under his pants. Classes were the same story for almost a week, until a periodic crackdown on truancy created a shortage of chairs. Even the teacher had been pale and shaken. Sometime later they told him that he had had some kind of seizure that sent his body into spasm and made his eyes roll in his head. His breathing had been laboured; they could see him drowning before their eyes. They were all afraid he was going to die. But this was quite some time later.

In the meantime the subject, like James, was carefully avoided. He was the weird kid after that, and he learned to cope with playing alone, like Darren who played chess with himself. Among other things. The tension eased with time, but the caution was never fully erased. You like to think you have no secrets from your friends. But you like to think the possibility exists.

The cruel thing was, James was not a mind-reader. He was, as his grandmother told him, a medium like she was. The freak gene that skipped merrily through the generations had come to rest in him. To use his gran's terms, 'A blessing or a curse, there's stuff all you can do about it.'

He'd always known he could talk to dead people, but it wasn't like that kid on *The Sixth Sense*. You sort of got used to it when it was all you'd ever known. A bit like being short, in a way. It was something you hoped to outgrow, but the day came when you realised you never would. Besides, the spirits didn't tend to come splattered in blood or other gory details. They were forces left over from the living, and most living people didn't walk around with six-inch exit wounds gaping through their kidneys.

Through spirit and intuition — some said they were the same thing — he could learn a lot about people, more than they themselves might know. But it wasn't like he knew their every thought, or even wanted to. What other people made of lunch was hardly worth discovering. To listen to voices in his head without a break would drive him mad. He might as well be suffering schizophrenia. Long ago he'd learned to close off from it all, to use his gift only when he had to. It was just that sometimes he wasn't given the choice.

Like now.

What lay in the park steeped in blood was more than just a body — his name was Mark. And he had asked for Paxton's help. The words stuck in his head, desperate and sorrowing, like a Miserere: *You have to find my daughter. You have to tell her I love her.*

And then there was Paxton's own promise, to find the dark-haired man. A rash promise it seemed now, yet he was damned if he could have said otherwise. Mark's self-accusation had torn acutely at his mind. *Oh Lena, I'm so sorry.* Even the victim was guilty.

But there was another thing Paxton couldn't overlook. He knew Mark was not the first.

He'd felt that as soon as he'd come across the body as if the stench of evil was rising from the blood. Whoever had done this had done it before, and his taste for it was only increasing. Sheer love of murder, of the power, was indelibly stamped on his work. Beyond that Paxton knew nothing, but his knowledge of that was enough. Destiny had just shat on his doorstep. His only hope was that the police would clean things up.

A couple of uniforms were first on the scene, arriving in a matter of minutes. Clearly fresh from handing out sloganed keyrings to drivers on the waterfront. Today's anti-speeding initiative, tomorrow's recycling collection. But they were trying. They parked up behind him and rapped on his window. Paxton obediently got out, immediately wishing he hadn't. He could almost feel his bollocks shrinking in the absence of air-conditioning.

'Hi. You the man who called in the incident?'

'Yeah. He's over there.' He nodded towards the park, but the dark huddle was invisible from this distance.

'There's a dead man in the park?' The constable's manner was deadly formal, somehow driving it home to Paxton more than anything else had so far. Other people were taking it seriously. This was real.

'Yes. I couldn't see much, but his head's been bashed in.'

'You're sure he's dead? Did you check?'

'No. But I'm positive.'

The other one, a woman with short dirty-blonde hair, looked at him strangely, exchanging a glance with her partner. Paxton instantly wished he'd shut it. 'You didn't touch anything, did you?'

'No.' He thought it wisest to say no more.

They swapped glances again, then the woman nodded. 'All right. Crime squad'll be here shortly. Stay here, Mr ...?'

'Paxton.' They waited.

'James Paxton.' He almost cringed at how Bond it *didn't* sound.

'Right. We're going to cordon off the area, but we'd like you to stay here please. They'll need to ask you a few questions.'

'Sure.' Already Paxton felt the night was going to be the longest of his life. He got back into the car.

He'd just sat back down when another car drew up with a second pair of coppers. They bypassed the minor congestion at the kerb, pulling into the lay-by directly beside the reserve. Plain clothes — the crime squad. Paxton debated simply winding down his window to conserve heat. What the hell, he hadn't thawed yet anyway. He got out of the car.

Crime squad were talking to the constables. As he approached, the detectives glanced over. The blond, tall bloke with the glasses seemed to be the one in charge.

'Evening, sir. Thanks for notifying us of this, but if you wouldn't mind waiting here for a moment.'

At scenes like this, the dead took precedence over the living. Specs shone a spotlight over the grass, tiptoeing with almost balletic care in a wide arc around the body. Detective number two followed almost exactly in his footsteps, disturbing not a blade more grass than was necessary. The two uniforms started sealing the spot with incident tape as the detectives bent over the body. They unbent fairly quickly.

'Well, he couldn't get more dead.'

The tall one's words carried further than he'd intended in the hush. The other one was silent, switching off his torch. Paxton sent up a private prayer of gratitude that he hadn't been carrying one. The man's fresh-faced buoyancy had vanished on viewing the body, along with all the colour in his face. By the looks of things his stomach contents were only with difficulty kept from following. You could get hardened to most things, but mutilated corpses were unique.

In preference to studying the body, the younger man returned to Paxton. He stuck out a hand.

'Hi. Detective Constable Stirling.' They shook hands. Stirling already seemed to be recovering. Someone at least was benefiting from the freezing air. 'Bloody cold out here, isn't it?' he said.

Paxton liked him instantly. He was a young guy, probably about the same age as Paxton, with fair hair and a firm grip. Most likely he hadn't graduated from plain constable long.

'At least one of us isn't feeling it.' He added a quick deprecating smile, to show disrespect wasn't intended. Stirling gave a little grimace.

'Must have been a nasty shock, coming across him like that. How did it happen? Strange time for a walk in the park, never mind the weather.'

'His dog ran out in front of my car. I went to see if I'd hit it, and it led me in here.' He shivered involuntarily, not sure of the cause. 'If I'd known what I'd find, I'd never have gone.'

He considered how sincerely he meant it. He noticed that Stirling turned his head towards the car, observing the dog in it. The senior detective was approaching them now, and Paxton shot a sudden glance at Stirling.

'Am I a suspect?'

'Want me to read you your rights?'

'Thanks, but I've watched enough cop shows.'

'Similar drill. You are not obliged to talk, you have the right to consult a solicitor, anything you say may be used in evidence ... but I really *would* prefer you to say if you saw a car speeding away from the site, or a suspicious-looking bloke with a hood on taking a walk with his cricket bat.'

Making light, to wash out the shadows. And the image of a man whom all the king's horses and all the king's men ...

The big blond detective reached them, rubbing his hands together mantis-fashion, though whether from cold or excitement Paxton couldn't tell.

'You taken a statement?'

'Mr Paxton — Detective Rees. I'm just in the middle of it, Tony.'

'Better not interrogate him too much. Sergeant's bound to be here soon.'

'What's the bet he arrives before the ambulance?'

Rees snorted. Then he cocked his head as his ears picked up a sound advancing up the road. They all lost interest as it was identified as a subwoofer, attached to a bright green Subaru WRX that was almost visibly vibrating from the bass. *Loud enough to wake the dead*, Paxton thought. But the dead were already awake.

The WRX slowed as it caught sight of the cop-mobile, going to a near crawl as the headlights picked up the crime tape and the circle of people on the footpath. Then the constable with the tape waved it on, and it accelerated off up the hill.

'Bloody boy racers.' Taxpayers spent millions on improving tolerance in the services. Nice to see it wasn't going to waste.

Another vehicle approached, more sedately, and the cops craned their necks hopefully towards it. It was a four-wheel drive. The sort Adam called a Queen Street tractor. It pulled into the lay-by and a weedy-looking man in a brown leather jacket jumped out, followed by a cameraman. The driver pointed a remote at the 4x4. It armed with a loud beep, seeming somehow more offensive in the stillness than the low thumping of the stereo.

'Shit.' Rees swore under his breath. 'The media.'

Stirling looked as if someone had just dropped a wet one. 'Why the hell would you bother with an alarm at one in the morning, on a deserted road with a bunch of policemen in front of you?'

He turned to Paxton.

'Best if you don't say anything to him just yet. He won't like it, but we haven't had a chance to go through it.'

Paxton watched the man's approach with a wonder mixed with distaste.

'How'd he find out about this so quickly? Do they hang round your headquarters or something?'

Stirling shrugged. 'Scanners. Probably monitoring North Coms, where all the emergency calls go through. It's illegal, but it's not a good idea to arrest one. Specially with a camera ...' His gaze settled balefully back on the news crew. 'Bloody sad at this time of night.'

'Must not be enough on TV ...'

'Evening, Detectives. Doesn't sound like good news. Except for us, I mean.' The reporter wore the smutty grin of a pervert in a convent.

Rees sighed. 'Please stand clear, sir. We're in the middle of an investigation.' He went to radio something from his car. In retaliation, the cameraman started filming the street.

In the usual pattern of all things happening at once, an unmarked police car braked next to the kerb, the ambulance behind it, bathing the scene in red lights like a macabre disco.

'Good job he was already dead.'

Stirling said it in a mutter, but Paxton heard. He smiled. Stirling saw him, and looked a bit abashed. 'You didn't hear me say that.'

Four detectives got out of the unmarked. Three came over to shift about in the cold beside Stirling, while Rees went to meet the detective sergeant, joining up with the ambulance men. They stepped gingerly out to the corpse, one after the other playing follow the leader. After a brief discussion the DS came back, leaving Rees and the ambulance man who'd accompanied them with the body.

He stood for a second taking in the post-incidental debris. Early forties, with regulation thinning hair and the pale, sagging features that suggested physical retraining was long overdue. He displayed the sombre expression reserved for the presence of the dead, whether at a murder scene or a funeral. He glanced back out at the looming shadow that was Rees with displeasure.

'The bloody cheek of him. He might have left it for me. Serves him right, I've put him in charge of the body. He can damn well stay with it all night, for trampling up the crime scene.'

Stirling was looking a little deadpan. Paxton didn't feel the need to drop him in it.

The DS turned to one of the other men behind him. 'See if the Eagle's available for a fly-over, would you? You can't see anything in this light.' The detective nodded and returned to the car. 'The rest of you, get talking.'

He pointed to the houses along the southern edge of the park, none of which even now had lighted windows. Silently the coppers trudged off.

'And who's this?' The DS looked at Paxton as if he didn't expect him to be capable of answering himself.

Stirling nodded respectfully at Paxton, once more slipping into policeman mode, which Paxton found amusing.

'This gentleman says he found the body when a dog ran out in front of his car. Went to take a look, and ...'

The DS fixed glinting eyes on Paxton.

'You left your car at — what was it? Midnight, in a poorly lit street, to follow a dog?'

Paxton instantly felt like a moron. He had a way with words. If not with people. Paxton wished he'd been left with the DC. He said, 'That's right, Sergeant ...?'

'Gardner. Detective Sergeant Gardner.' He didn't offer his hand. 'And you are?'

'James Paxton. I thought I'd hit him. The dog, I mean.' The bastard had him acting guilty within three damn minutes.

'How'd you know it was *his* dog?'

Paxton was momentarily thrown. The truth was out of the question. 'I just ... assumed. He had a dog rope tied round his neck, and the dog looked frightened.'

'You're English, I take it.' There was something about the way he said it that implied: *figures*. 'What were you doing out this way at this time of night?'

As if Paxton had deliberately taken a wrong turn at Piccadilly. 'I work at Anubis, on the waterfront.' He added, with a bit of emphasis, 'I was going home.'

'You know the man you found?'

'No.'

'See any other cars in the area? People?'

'No.'

Even monosyllables were wasted on this arsehole. The detective from the car reappeared. 'Eagle's out in Otara, Sarge. But we can get dogs out.'

'Shit ... All right, if that's the best we can do.' He turned abruptly back to Paxton. 'That your car parked over there?'

Paxton followed his glance and nodded warily, caught by surprise.

'So once you saw the dog was OK, why did you follow it into the park? It's a bit of a walk. You didn't *see* the body from the road?' The casual set of Gardner's features was a threadbare cloak for his blatant scepticism.

'I ...' Paxton didn't have a follow-up, as bankrupt of answers as Gardner.

'No special reason, then?'

Now he was really pissing Paxton off. He wore an almost knowing smirk, thinly washed over with deference. Stirling was frowning, seeming troubled, but he remained in his place. Gardner tossed out yet another question, with a sudden keen glance.

'Nothing more you can tell us about what happened?'

'No.'

Less assurance than he'd aimed for. He was rehearing the sound of Mark's pleading inside his head.

The DS seemed to see right through him, unable to reconcile the figures and therefore rounding up. He gazed at Paxton a moment longer, his face unsmiling, then turned to Stirling with a dismissive air.

'Get his details.' Then to Paxton: 'Thank you, sir. You've been a great help.' He strolled off towards his car, pulling a mobile from his pocket. The other detective was still using the radio.

Stirling seemed rather apologetic as he took down Paxton's stats. Paxton pitied him if he had to work with this rubber tit. More cops had arrived — photographers, SOCOs in blue overalls, and a bleary-eyed man with pathologist written all over him. Paxton saw the TV man chatting with the husband from over the road, while the cameraman threw a jealous look at the police photographer ducking the crime tape. Finally the neighbours appeared to be taking an interest. He noticed a tall man wave hello to the bloke talking to the reporter and stroll over to join them, nodding and gazing into the park, hands thrust casually into his pockets. There was a porch light on in the house right next to the park, and a trio in dressing gowns and slippers were shuffling down the drive directly opposite, rubbernecking at the pile-up of police cars.

Paxton lost no time in leaving. The reporter was drifting in his direction while the DS wasn't looking, and he wasn't much relishing the idea of another interview, especially one for TV.

He gave the scene the once-over as he got back in his car. The incident tape effectively shut him out from everything; unwanted, unthanked and under suspicion. Cops were swarming Mark's body like maggots, picking it for evidence. He wasn't a person to them. Paxton supposed this was only proper. Still, *he* wasn't really a person either, apparently. Now he knew how a woman felt. All the time they'd been together he'd sensed Gardner staring at his chest. Envisioning a row of numbers across it. Before he went to bed he was tempted to shower.

The worst of it was leaving Glen. He was already in the back of a police van. It felt like a betrayal. The dog had already lost his owner and very nearly his wits, and now he faced the rest of the night in the cells.

Not that there was much of it left. Difficult to believe that less than two hours ago he'd been driving this same road home from work, thinking the night was already over. For Mark it was. But only in a manner of speaking. In another sense this night would stretch on for eternity. Paxton didn't like to dwell on the thought, but didn't know how to dismiss it. For the lack of a radio, all he could hear was voices.

THE comforts of home provided little in the way of a distraction. Paxton lived alone, in a two-bedroom flat in an area that estate agents flattered as the Kohimarama border, but which actually meant Glen Innes. It was close to work and the beautiful Tamaki Drive waterfront without actually being a desirable address. The people two doors down had a collection of gutted car carcasses on their lawn. Fortunately these were less of an eyesore now that the grass concealed most of them.

Paxton didn't mind where he lived. His street was pretty quiet in the scheme of things, and he'd lived in far worse. Until *now* it had seemed fairly safe, a cocoon almost against the reality of what he was, but tonight admittedly changed everything. If he'd been much of a drinker he would have brought out the tequila, but it tasted like stale piss and he didn't need a drink problem on top of everything else. The latter not his own, which made it worse. He didn't need a drinking problem on top of everything else. Wine was more his style, and far less messy, but it hardly did the job at times like these.

Without bothering even to brush his teeth he got into bed and switched off the light, but sounds and images kept flashing through his mind, preventing sleep. A dark shape darting into the headlights, the screech of the tyres on the road, the black dog rigid, almost screaming with terror, the body lying on the ground doused with blood, its grisly necklace biting too tight into the flesh. And finally, the words, which kept him awake till dawn:

Please — find him. I beg you. If you don't I swear I'll never sleep again.

Chapter TWO

'GO AWAY! *PLEASE* ...' Lena listened to the phone ringing for about the eleventh time that morning, no longer up to anything but whispering at it to stop. 'Just sod off, goddamn you ...'

She was now hunched in a ball on the sofa, a mug of tea stone cold on the table beside her.

The doorbell had started the ringing. They'd canvassed from house to house until somebody, a neighbour with a Samoyed, had recognised Glen and his collar from walks. She'd pointed them to Mark's house, where the key from his pocket had opened the door. Lena had gone down to the morgue to make the ID official. She had driven there herself, insisted on it, though once she'd arrived she couldn't remember how. Even being told of Glen, of the key, of Mark's absence from the house, couldn't make it all real. There was still a chance, a small one but she hung on, that he was alive, that the victim wasn't him.

The sight of her father's body, cleansed of the blood and somehow all the more pathetic, was a knife in her gut. You can prepare for something all you like, you can tell yourself for years that it will happen, but the pain, whenever it comes, is still unavoidable. The proof of ongoing infidelity, the death of a cancer patient — you don't grieve less because it is expected.

But *this* ... this was an avalanche.

What would have been invisible at night was made cruelly plain in the stark chapel. Under the unbeautifying lights of the morgue he was pale and oddly shrunken, as though a vampire had made the wounds and sucked the blood from his whole body. Scattered across his cheeks was a horrid mass of blotches from where the blood had settled as he'd lain face down on the ground. Just above the shroud a small sliver of neck was exposed, bruising tattooed an ugly purple upon the livid skin.

Lena could only look for a couple of seconds before turning away, burying her face in her hands and bursting into sobs. She knew, because she'd asked, what was under the sheet draped over his scalp. The morgue assistants had done their best, but there was only so much they could do. Whoever had murdered her father had not stopped with the fatal blow, contenting themselves with the kill. They'd kept hitting, as if in a blind rage, until the skull was crushed and misshapen from the attack. Then in a last act of spite they'd added the noose, the lead that would once have been attached to Glen's collar.

The questions came next. The same as the ones in her mind, given voice by the sergeant, Gardner, as he scrutinised her every facial tic. He'd probed her attentively for a reaction at the first sight of her father, brutalised steak on the butcher's slab. Do you know of anyone who might have wanted to harm your father? Can you think of a motive for this sort of attack? But her father was — had been — an optometrist, hardly a judge or a cop or a crim. This brutality made no sense. None of it did.

'Can I get you something to drink? Would you like to sit down?' This was the female constable who had accompanied her. Despite being sent to offer feminine support, she was a picture of discomfort in the face of tears. Gardner had vanished as soon as the questions were finished. Lena shook her head, not at all eager to prolong the experience. She forced herself to speak. 'No, thank you. I want to get home.'

The constable tried hard to conceal her relief, but seemed determined to fulfil her duty.

'Are you all right to drive? You've had a nasty shock; I'm more than happy to take you if you like.'

Lena shook her head again, privately agreeing with her, but she was damned if she'd let anyone treat her like glass.

'I need to be by myself, thanks.'

Next the woman tried offering her counselling, along with a personal recommendation of pills, but by now Lena was turning everything down on principle. All she wanted was to be alone. As, thanks to some well-adjusted credit to the community, she now was.

She took a last backward glance at her father on her way out, but the morgue attendant had already covered his face.

No matter; she was not likely to forget.

SEVERAL times that day she found herself staring at Glen, wondering exactly what he'd seen. At others she was thankful he couldn't tell her. She'd seen a little too much to be comfortable with the information.

Disbelief had faded as soon as she visualised the injuries, then in its place came nausea and rage. She'd tried to call her mother, but there was never any answer. It was the middle of the night in Europe but she suspected there was no one home. Elke Raeder was her father's ex-wife, and had long ago gone back to her native Switzerland. Since her remarriage to a businessman and Lena's acquisition of half-siblings, the lines of communication had almost broken down. Even so, it would have been a comfort for Lena to feel she still had family. If her family had been answering her calls.

She left two messages, and gave up the next time the machine answered.

The phones at her end were temporarily silent, for which she was grateful. Ringing work had been a mistake, necessary though it had been. People knew she lived alone, and they couldn't bear the thought. Why could no one simply text-message, like they did for everything else? A nice, impersonal SORRY 4 YR LOSS!. It was about all she was up to right now. They'd given her the week off. More if she needed it. She was tempted to never go back, never go anywhere ...

She lay down on the sofa, cushioning her head on the armrest, and let her eyes close. In the darkness under her eyelids her father's face appeared, neatly underscored with a ring of purple. And then, inexorably, the imagined image of his scalp, with a clarity sharp as razors. The tears came flooding back then, and washed it mercifully away.

The sound of the doorbell was a shock. She had to physically focus, almost as if she were coming out of anaesthesia. Glen rushed to the door on cue, tail waving madly. Lena lay there for a moment in stupid surprise, blinking, then in one movement pushed herself up-right. Perversely, she was grateful for the intrusion. It meant she'd be obliged to start acting human again. She felt a little ashamed of her orgy of grief on the couch; like she'd been a toddler throwing a tantrum, instead of exercising the self-control expected of adults.

She dimly ran through the list of possibles as she went to the door. Better not be her landlord. Dogs in the house were strictly verboten. But it'd be someone from work probably, with flowers. Or maybe the police, although they ought to have called. Which made her wonder guiltily if they had.

Bugger them anyway. Especially the constable.

My aunt swears by St John's Wort whenever she's feeling a bit rough. Jesus.

When she opened the door, however, her visitor was no one she recognised. He was just above the average height, slim, with hair the colour of chocolate and a distinctly uneasy expression in his brown eyes. Like her, he was wearing jeans. She put him at about thirty. Whoever he was, he didn't look like a cop. At the sight of her he almost took a step back, and if possible looked even more uncomfortable, which only added to Lena's misery. No doubt her face looked like she'd been washing in acid.

'Can I help you?'

'Hi. I'm sorry to burst in on you like this, but — are you Lena Bradley?'

'Yes. I take it you've come about my father.'

Phrased wearily, it wasn't a question. The stranger looked apologetic, but seemed oddly encouraged by her response. He said softly, 'Yes. I met him last night.'

Lena froze, her pupils dilating with shock. Torn between contempt and cold fear. He looked back at her with a hint of pity, then looked past her to the muzzle snuffling at the crack in the doorway.

'Hello, Glen. All right?' Pieces began to fall into place.

'Wait a minute. Are you the one who found him — the guy who reported the murder?'

Paxton nodded. 'I'm James Paxton, yeah.'

He didn't say he was sorry, but Lena felt it anyway. Without thinking, she held the door open.

'Come in.'

GLEN gambolled around the newcomer, inhaling his scent, apparently fully recovered from the trauma of the previous night. The world's shittiest guard dog — had he greeted his master's killer with a lick to the hand? Rolled over for a belly-scratching? Only Lena had seen him moping, but dogs grieve in different ways than people. Watching James Paxton pat him she was suddenly reminded of something.

'How did you know his name? Are you one of the neighbours?' Paxton hesitated, which struck a false note. She felt a trace of the fear returning.

'I think I'd better introduce myself. Properly.'

He started pacing around the room, tension soaking from him like sweat. Psyching himself up for something. Lena could feel her alarm growing, wondering now whether she had made a mistake letting him in to her lounge, and if the police had, in letting him go. Vivid was the old adage about the first to the scene of the crime. He glanced her way then and noticed her expression. Suddenly he gave a sheepish smile, which softened all his features.

'Sorry. I didn't mean to scare you. You must be thinking you've let a madman into your home.'

'You forgot the axe-murderer part.'

His smile vanished instantly. 'Yeah.' He looked away for a second, then returned his gaze to her steadily, something questioning in his demeanour. 'I've been trying to decide whether to trust you. I'm sorry if that sounds a little rude but, believe me, when I explain you'll understand.' He gave a harried laugh. 'This is *not* the sort of thing you raise at the bus stop.'

She gave him an uncertain look. 'You weren't at the park to ... meet men? Were you?'

Paxton's jaw dropped. 'No! *God* no! ...' He grinned. 'Even if I were gay, the view from the carpark at work is *way* more romantic.'

Lena let out a giggle before she could help herself. She cut off abruptly, surprised at herself. At how good it felt.

Paxton too seemed surprised, and visibly relaxed. His next question came out of the blue.

'Do you believe in ghosts?'

Lena was taken aback by the conversational dogleg. Where the hell had that come from? But Paxton was already moving on, more assured now.

'A lot of people would have difficulty believing this, and I don't blame you if you don't either. It's a lot easier to believe there aren't dead people hanging around us.'

Lena shivered. He looked straight at her, his eyes never wavering from hers. 'But sometimes there are.'

'What are you trying to tell me? Are you saying that my dad is around the house somewhere? Rearranging all the towels?'

She was getting angry in her discomfort. 'Because I don't bloody —'

'I knew the dog's name was Glen because Mark told me.' There was a long pause.

'Ohhhhhh ... My God. I don't believe this. My dad is murdered by some psycho in a park, and now I'm comforted by a man who talks to dead people!' She gave a bitter little laugh that came out like a sob. 'For Christ's sake, what did *I* do?'

She waved an arm towards the door, her voice unsteady as a drunk's. 'I don't mean to be rude, but could you possibly throw yourself out? I'm a bit distracted at the moment.'

Paxton didn't budge. 'Your dad took sleeping pills. Or rather, *didn't* take them.'

Lena's mouth dropped open. 'What?'

'He said: *"Stupid fool, I never take the pills."* He said he often had trouble sleeping, but he never took the pills — he took Glen for a walk instead.'

Lena stared at him in silence, for a frozen moment incapable of a reply.

'And he asked me — begged me — to tell you that he loves you, his daughter Lena, and he's sorry he's had to leave you.'

He stopped then and shook his head, wondering. 'The poor sod was *blaming* himself for being murdered! I've never met anyone so polite, not even when they're alive.'

Tears were crawling down her cheeks, her face contorting like melting plastic. Paxton could see her trembling with the effort of keeping it in. The previous night had been nothing to this. He kept his eyes on the carpet, hating himself.

'All the time he kept saying, "I'm sorry. Oh Lena, I'm sorry." He wanted me to say that he didn't feel anything, and he wouldn't leave until he knew you were safe from whoever attacked him. Whoever this was — this wasn't his first time, and I'm afraid it won't be his last.'

He glanced up at her, and had to steel himself to go on. Lena was breathing raggedly, her eyes jammed shut, biting her fist to keep from sobbing aloud so hard she had nearly drawn blood. Paxton turned his eyes away again, to the visual blandness of the cream-papered wall.

Wretchedly he said, 'I really didn't want to hurt you this way, but — it was what your father asked me to do. I couldn't sleep last night. I kept hearing his voice in my head.'

She said nothing. Paxton sighed, feeling drained beyond anything he'd ever known before.

'I'm really sorry. I shouldn't have ... I should have at least waited, I wasn't thinking.' Awkwardly he eased towards the door, muttering in a fog of self-loathing. 'I'll leave you alone now. I should have done in the first place.'

He had his hand on the doorknob when she spoke. 'What else did he say?'

He started, caught off guard, and turned to face her. She had stopped crying and was looking full at him, scraping away her tears with the back of one hand. He could see the teeth-marks imprinted across her knuckles.

'Did he say anything else to you? Did he know who killed him?' He heard the desperation ring out in her voice. This was, if anything, worse than before. He shook his head.

'I'm sorry. The attacker came at him from behind. He was berating himself for not knowing.'

'Are you sure? What did he say *exactly*?'

Paxton tried to make his brain function, something that was presently giving him trouble. 'Ahhmmm ... I think, something about, "What a bloody useless witness. They'll never have me on *CSI*." I remember him mentioning that.'

Astonishingly, Lena laughed. It struck him then that she probably laughed often. It suited her.

'Dad did watch *CSI*. He used to try and be all scientific and medical, and I kept reminding him he was only an eye doctor and hardly a pathologist.'

There was a brief pause, as they both remembered the circumstances. She sat down, and Paxton did likewise. The pause drew out painfully, until Paxton smiled at her gently.

'What was it that made you change your mind?'

She looked down at her hands, embarrassed. 'Sorry about that. It's just —'

'Extremely common. Believe me. If I were you, I'd have twisted my balls off.'

That drew a smile. She looked at him, her blue gaze curious and open for the first time.

'You knew about the pills. You were bang on; I always had to nag him. He preferred walking. At *three a.m.* sometimes; it worried me sick. He couldn't read, he said, or then he'd just be thinking about the book.'

She was quiet for a second, then looked up again and smiled at him tentatively.

'But after that, it was what you said about him apologising. He did it all the time. Some sort of guilt mechanism after the divorce. He always *tried* to be there for me. I guess that this really would upset him.'

'Take it from me, it did.'

She smiled again, sniffing and wiping her nose on her hand. 'Urgh, I need a hanky. Excuse me.'

While she was out of the room, his eyes went back to Glen. *Glen!* Stupid name for a dog or a human. He raised his voice. 'If you don't mind my asking, why did he call his dog Glen?'

'It's actually short for Glenfiddich. His show name is Ashby Single Malt.'

She came back into the lounge. 'The sire was from Scotland, and the breeder was doing a theme.' She rolled her eyes.

'What's his brother's name? Famous Grouse?'

'Wow, you really *are* psychic.' Speculation crept into her countenance, and he inwardly squirmed. 'That's what you are, isn't it? You'd have to be.'

Paxton hated the term psychic. Not only did it have an essential similarity to other words containing the same prefix, but it made him think of crystal-ball gazers and charlatans who went ohh-hmmm. As it was, he didn't much like 'medium' or 'whack job' either.

'For want of a better word, I'm a medium. That's what my grandmother liked to call it, and she's the only one who ever really understood it, including me.' He put up a hand as she seemed about to say something. 'And before you ask, no, I can't read minds, and I don't do parties. I can talk to spirits, is all. Personally I'd just have wanted not to be crap at football.'

The corners of her eyes creased up as she tried not to laugh again.

'Just my luck, to be Derek Acorah without the ball skills.'

'Who's Derek Acorah?'

'Never mind.'

He found himself wondering about her.

'Can I ask you, does your mother know about this?' He caught himself, embarrassed. 'Sorry, I don't even know whether —'

'It's all right. She lives in Zurich; *she's* not dead.' The nicely resigned tone not quite ringing true. 'Though for me she might as well be. She walked out when I was five. I spent a few years in Switzerland with her later — Swiss schools still have their snob value, you know — but ...' She trailed off and shook her head. Her voice took on a bitter cadence. 'It was two years before she bothered to contact me. For two years I almost thought she was dead.'

The phone rang then, startling them, and Paxton listened as Lena limply rehashed her day, her shoulders slumping. Another sympathy caller; she'd probably had dozens already. Jesus, how did she cope? He'd have ripped the phone out before going through all this. And she couldn't be older than twenty-five; her ponytail made her look like a schoolgirl, a sweep of wavy dark hair that didn't match the image conjured up by a Swiss heritage. Her eyes, though — they were Aryan enough, a blue-grey made more intense by the shadows hollowed out underneath.

Standing there, he was assailed by a rush of pity. Without his realising it, the regret had gone.

When she hung up, she looked so exhausted that Paxton felt he'd be heartless to stay longer. Much as he realised he wanted to.

'I should really be going. This is all — a lot to take in.' He waved an arm ineffectually, trying a smile that came out as a grimace.

Her smile came out much like his own.

'Yeah.' Then she added, slowly, 'Thanks for coming, and for doing what Dad wanted — in spite of me. I'm sure it can't have been easy for you.'

Paxton shook his head. 'Nah. I've always enjoyed watching girls cry.'

He was rewarded with another fleeting smile, and felt an unexpected kick of pleasure in his gut. Immediately, his defences shut it down.

'Well, take care. Fingers crossed the police find out who did this, soon.' Nice. All the wit and personality of an accountant. He almost winced.

She nodded, her eyes dropping. 'Thanks.' She followed him to the door without saying anything. This time he hadn't even reached the door handle before she blurted, 'Can I have your phone number?'

Paxton would have given anything to be able to analyse his feelings at that moment. That couldn't be relief, now, surely. A knot of panic crystallised in his stomach, at the same time as he found an agreement coming out of his mouth. He waited while she scanned hastily round for a pen and paper with a determined confusion that was oddly touching. Finally she located a ballpoint and grabbed an old circular from the mess on her coffee table, tearing a page from it.

'Right.'

She scribbled down the number he gave her and they stood there uncomfortably for a moment, having gone through the customary drivel already. At last he said, 'See you.' And with a brief smile propelled himself away.

He glanced back as he was getting in the car, and saw her wrestling with Glen in the doorway. He did a quick wave and watched her try to reciprocate, keeping a hand on Glen's collar at the same time and virtually getting yanked off her feet. He sniggered, unable to help himself, turning his head away so that she couldn't see.

Still, something in the set of his shoulders must have alerted her, because her lips seemed to be forming the word 'bastard' as he drove away.

Chapter THREE

HE KNEW HIS anonymity was blown when he saw the journos around the tables. Piss and the press were traditionally tight, but there were far too many in this bar, on this night, for it to be a coincidence. Some perched on stools like alcoholic buzzards, necks crooked over their drinks.

As he approached, in his regulation bartender blacks, the same necks bent in his direction with predatory interest. He'd met enough journalists in his time to recognise the signs. The flickering eyes, reminiscent of crims on the run, which signalled that they were on the pull for someone. So far they might have been particularly clueless sociopaths, looking for a loose skirt to drool on, but there were other tokens. The giveaway notepad in front of one; the fact that someone else was filming the bar on his phone.

It was the idiot with his press pass on the bar that finally tipped him off. It was a homemade one; the Kiwis weren't big on credentials. The staff were eyeing him like a wino who'd lost control of necessary functions.

Fuck. Had to have been Gardner behind this. Who else could have tipped them off?

The one at the bar hailed him as he took his place behind it. 'Are you James Paxton?'

When Paxton failed to reply, he turned to Paxton's colleagues. 'Is this the man I was asking about?'

The other pen men were approaching now, drawn to him like flies. Brent noted Paxton's implacable silence and sighed, seeming divided between his training in hospitality and his desire to evict them with boot-marks.

'Look, as I said before, this man has a job to do, and if you're really desperate to talk to him you can do it in his own time. We've already ascertained you're not the cops, and I'm not paying him good money to stand around yakking with the paparazzi. Even if you are buying meals.'

The only section of the paper Brent ever read was sports, except the TV columns when sporting events were on. Working with him during an important rugby match was like sticking a hand in a jammed lawnmower. Once he'd almost punched a punter who'd distracted him from the bar TV while the deciding try was being scored.

But the reporters were calmly unfazed. If not certifiably safe in a public place, there were at least plenty of witnesses. There were four by this time, bolstering bare cheek in numbers. Pack mentality, Paxton thought. Five minutes later they'd be ripping each other's throats out to get the most juicy story. No doubt they all thought he was guilty as sin, but what was the risk of murder compared to a brush with fame? He was sorely tempted to scare them all shitless. Stare at them and leer, while slowly slitting lemons. *Slice. Slice*. Or pour a Bloody Mary and dip his finger in the red. Lick it deliberately, savouring the taste. Staring all the while. Possibly with a few drops on his chin for extra impact.

But he knew that in the end it was hardly constructive. They were bound to paint him as the biggest threat to society since Osama bin Laden, and he didn't need to bring the cops down on him harder, let alone all the publicity. At least none had come armed with a camera from *One News*. Best to give them what they wanted, or what they thought they wanted, and keep the ensuing storms to a minimum. Some of the customers clustered round the bar were already staring.

Next up was a long-haired young man wearing a jumper with fraying cuffs and at least a week's facial regrowth that failed to cover bad skin. Typical journalistic arrogance. They felt no need to impress anyone. It was always the other way round.

The young reporter pulled out a gold Parker pen with an all-over pattern of fingerprints. 'Hi, I'm John Merchant from the *New Zealand Herald*. I'd just like to ask you a few questions — won't take a minute.'

Everyone called it the *Herald*. When Merchant lovingly recited its full name, Paxton knew what a cunt he was dealing with. Where else would he be from, the *Sydney Morning Herald?*

Bullshit Merchant was speaking, without waiting for an answer. 'I've been informed that you came across the victim of an attack last night.'

Paxton noticed he avoided the word murder. As if Mark's skull had been pulped by manslaughter.

'I was wondering if you could tell me in your own words how exactly this came about. Could you *describe* what happened to me?'

Nothing's happened to you yet, Paxton thought. *But it might.* Briefly he wondered if anyone ever called him Nosey Parker, on account of the pen and the enormous excrescence sprouting from the middle of his face.

He shook his head at Brent to say don't worry, then addressed them all. 'As my manager has already explained to you, I'm not in a position to talk right now. But if you're around after my shift I'll talk to you then.'

Pointedly turning his back, he walked away to serve a blonde with far too much make-up. The journos were obliged to return to their seats, nursing their drinks like a grudge. He could feel them glaring at him periodically throughout the long evening. He was willing to bet some had started their day before six, but they'd be damned if they left and got scooped. He didn't finish until midnight. For once it put him in a good mood.

That was until he remembered Lena. The thought made his spirits plummet instantly. If they were on to *him*, no doubt they'd also be harassing her. What were her views on the murder? How was she feeling (devastated, elated, numb, homicidal)? Did she want to watch the attacker burn at the stake? All the thoughtful questions calculated to interest the reader, and finger open the wounds of the bereaved till they screamed.

'You all right, James?'

The question at his elbow startled him, quiet as it was. Adam was standing there, a look of concern on his face that told Paxton his own expression must have been frightening.

'Did they tell you why they wanted to talk to me?' he asked.

'No. Just said to tell them when you came in. So what did you do, get busted for molestering or something?'

'It's *molesting,* you dumb coconut.'

'I told you you needed a girlfriend.'

Adam didn't mind being called a coconut. Paxton had picked it up from him. It made up for Adam calling him Pommy. He'd only called him Pommy Paxton *once* ...

Adam was born in Auckland but his parents were from Samoa, and he enjoyed slipping into Island patois when he was out for a laugh. It was like a Scottish accent; somehow it made people twice as funny. But Adam didn't seem in the mood tonight. Paxton's vibes must have been catching. Paxton poured a couple of beers, generating a bit too much head in his haste, then managed to return to his friend, who was lurking in a corner of the bar pretending to slice limes.

'Put the knife down before I tell you.'

Adam glanced at him, with a half-smile of astonishment. 'Man, this must be bad.'

'It is.'

Adam's smile faded.

'I found a dead body last night. On Patteson Ave.'

He went on without stopping, as Adam's pupils dilated with shock. 'It was pitch black and a dog ran out in front of me; I was terrified I'd hit it. So I got out to investigate and it led me into a park. This man was lying there, his head totally bashed in, and I got the hell out to call the police.' He didn't feel like explaining the rest, even to Adam. He said merely, 'It is *not* something I'm extra keen to talk about, I'll tell you that now.'

Adam plainly believed him. So absorbed was he in what Paxton was saying that a sudden request for a Guinness made him crush the lime he was still holding. Juice dripped onto his shirt.

'Ah, shit! Sorry, sir. Just the one, was it?'

THE bar was getting full; there were no more opportunities to talk. And Paxton's triumph whenever he caught a glimpse of a reporter was tempered by a twinge of distress for Lena. There was no time to worry about anything, but he seemed to manage it constantly anyway, despite feeling like a complete prat. He was attracted to her, no question about that. Not only was she startlingly pretty and, beyond a doubt, gorgeous after a few hours' sleep and the use of a hairbrush, but she was funny, and ballsy — and, in short, there was not a chance in hell of his taking it further. She reminded him too much of what he was trying to escape, back home in the past. He cursed himself again for so readily giving Lena his number.

Anubis closed at midnight, and the reporters were banished to the street to await Paxton. Brent wasn't about to let the bastards camp out in his bar. Paxton was grateful. The night was particularly cold. He knew he shouldn't have felt that way about journalists — after all, he'd aspired to be one, of a sort — but possibly that had something to do with it. Throughout his travels he'd earned the occasional bit of cash writing travel articles for anyone who'd take them. The *Herald* had once printed a spec piece of his on Lake Tahoe and reduced it to the size of goat piddle. The by-line had also read James Paxman, confusing him with the BBC's Jeremy. Somehow the flattery was lost on him.

Still, better Paxman than Beadle.

Despite taking their time over the cash-up, at last Brent and Paxton finished, and Paxton was at the mercy of the newshounds. Their manners were Antarctic, like the weather, gaining nothing from collective sleep-deprivation and the youngest's incipient hangover. They'd all be too late to get this interview into the morning's papers. He was far too shagged for this.

Merchant laid in with a vengeance, pissing his earlier politeness to the wind. He'd been interrupted mid-cigarette. 'Is it true that you are so far the only person placed at a murder scene, thus making you in effect the prime suspect?'

'Yeah,' said Paxton.

That threw them for a second. Unfortunately no longer. The next to speak was Tubby Tim with the rat's arse goatee, from the *East and Bays Courier*. Paxton had some acquaintances there, who were regulars, but Arsebeard wasn't one of them.

'So, can you tell us *exactly* what happened?'

'No.'

All four of them blinked.

'I wasn't there for the murder. All I did was find the body.'

A vein throbbed in Merchant's neck as he choked back whatever he had been about to say. They stood with pens poised like the most unpalatable breed of varsity student, the ones who sit at the front and become analysts. Paxton wondered if they really expected him to come out with a confession, and what they would do if he did.

Yes actually, I am a sadistic maniac. And by the way, is that ballpoint pen sharp?

It was almost depressing to tell them the truth, which he did in as few words as possible. The abbreviated version naturally, omitting the part that would keep him in headlines for months, and probably, he thought sourly, in psych wards. Again he thought of Lena, and hoped fervently that she had been spared this. Futile hope; grief sells.

Now it was Press Pass's turn. 'What were your feelings on discovering the body?'

Paxton simply stared at him, until all of them looked away. 'Any further questions? I'm rather tired, as I'm sure you are too.'

They actually seemed relieved, especially the one who'd been pacing himself with bourbon and cokes. They thanked him insincerely for his time and rapidly departed. Now that it was over, Paxton felt like his marrow had been substituted with lead. After last night and the endless day that had followed it, his systems were all sparking out. In this state he'd be luckier to make it home than Sonny Jim Beam.

On his way he passed the park, and he resisted looking in. At the next intersection he noticed that his fingers were clenched tight round the steering wheel. The drive home from work had lost its sweetness for a very long time. Guilt snagged at the back of his brain like a twist of hair caught painfully on wire. He'd promised Mark that he'd find the killer. For all his gift it was impossible, a task well beyond his means, yet knowing this did little for his conscience. Much as Gardner had irritated him he couldn't help wishing him luck, for his own peace of mind.

You didn't help my daughter. You lied.

LIAR!

For the hundredth time he wished that New Zealanders tipped barmen properly, like the Americans had. You couldn't buy a car stereo with a few mingy drinks, and he was desperate for Prodigy, cranked up loud.

He pulled into his street, noticing the car parked outside his house instantly. Not a reporter, surely. And he would hope that the cops were somewhat more subtle in their methods of observation. Then recognition hit, and he slumped back in his seat. It was a blue Honda hatchback, and he'd last seen it in Lena's driveway.

God no. Not again.

He slowed, quickly debating whether to just keep going, past the house and looping back to the beach. Then her car door opened, and he knew he'd been seen. He could still have gone on, without stopping, but somehow this would have been worse.

Reluctantly he turned into his driveway and killed the engine. Lena was waiting for him as he got out of the car. As he drew nearer he saw she appeared as exhausted as he felt. Her skin looked crafted from eggshell.

'How long have you been waiting?'

'Going on four hours.'

'Christ.' He let out a long, slow breath. He looked at her a moment longer, feeling again the deep pull of sympathy. *Why* was his compassion still functioning at one in the morning?

He heard himself say, 'Come inside. It'll be warmer.'

As they stepped into the lounge he was uncomfortably conscious of the shabby furnishings; the second-cheapest sofa on offer at Furniture City and the 21-inch sitting directly on the stained beige carpet. And not much else. The dishes from breakfast and lunch were still in the sink, just out of view.

'It's not very exciting, sorry. GI chic, minus the striped net curtains.'

She didn't seem to notice. 'That's all right. I've had enough sensory overload for one day.'

The light from the exposed bulb in the ceiling should have had a soft focus effect, but instead showed up the ghastly pallor of her face. She dropped on to the tiny sofa as if it had suddenly developed a force field. Incredulity surfaced in Paxton's mind.

'How on earth did you manage to find me? I'm not even in the phone book yet.'

'I used the website.'

Clever, James. 'Oh. Forgot about that.' Auckland wasn't London, despite a similar sprawl. Among fewer than two million souls, there couldn't be too many J Paxtons living near Patteson Ave. And — of course, she'd already had his number.

She smiled at him, warmth glowing through her tiredness. 'It's been one hell of a day.' She looked a little embarrassed, pulling her hands into her sleeves like a child. 'Look, I'm really sorry to just come round like this. It's well after midnight for Christ's sake, I wouldn't blame you if you'd locked the door and phoned the cops. But — well, I tried calling you and couldn't get any answer, so I came on the off chance you'd be home soon. Didn't realise you'd be quite *this* late.'

'I work in a bar.'

'Oh. I was beginning to wonder about you.'

Paxton gave her a cynical smile. 'Look at this place. More Social Welfare than social butterfly. Does it look like I can afford to have a life?'

'One like mine you could.' He raised his eyebrows. 'I teach schoolkids after hours.'

'Oh? What do you teach?'

'German and French. At a private language academy. It's only a few hours a week, and I avoid the major hells of the education system.'

'I thought you said your classes had kids.'

She laughed, and for all the sheer Monty Pythonism of having her in his lounge in the early hours of the morning, socialising over a murder, he was enjoying himself.

'You must be thinking I'm desperate, stalking you,' Lena said. 'It couldn't have been further from my mind.' *Liar*.

She was studying her lap. 'Before I came round I dropped in on the police. They were all very confident, don't worry about a thing, ma'am, but they haven't got a clue. No witnesses, no murder weapon. And forensics takes ages ... I realise it's early days yet ...'

He understood. He'd spoken to Gardner.

'I'm sure they're more than capable. They've already got a strong suspect.'

'Congratulations.' This obviously came as no surprise. Clearly she'd spoken to Gardner as well.

'Do they know I've talked to you?'

'No — and I'm not going to tell them.'

'You'd probably go straight on witness protection. If they have that in New Zealand.'

Lena smiled. 'In Munich once I got asked if we had cars.'

'Should have said no, but our sheep have learned to be fast.'

Laughing, she said, 'At least you're not that bad in England.'

'Thinking you're just a rugby-mad sheep-shagging backwater famous only for a handful of singers and film stars? No; we reserve that for the Welsh.'

She laughed again, which turned into a yawn. She got up, the effort it took almost defeating her.

'It's way past your bedtime, and *mine* for that matter. I should go. Thanks for —'

'For listening to you piss around the question?'

She blinked, gazing up at him in surprise. There was a faint smile on his face, but his expression was meaningful. Too knowing. Her eyes fled to the corner. Paxton noticed there was a spider's web in it. Finally she said, 'They said they were appealing for witnesses — it'll be all through the papers tomorrow. This morning, that is. But ...'

'Ah. I knew you didn't come here for the décor.'

It burst out of her like an eruption. 'Can't you tell who the murderer is? Didn't you say you knew he'd done it before? I mean, you spoke to my dad, you can pick up so much that ordinary people can't ...'

The pain was like being burnt.

'I can't. I wish I could, believe you me, but there's a limit to what I can do. Some people can tell you anything about what happened without even going near the place, but unfortunately I'm shit at all that.'

He babbled on to fill the silence that fell. He felt like he'd slapped her. 'See, there's various kinds of abilities. Clairvoyance, the famous one, where you can actually see images of things. That's something I *can't* do. Then there's clairsentience, which is basically like intuition, or smelling lilacs in the room or even just this tingling at the back of your neck. I get that a little bit, and the more I develop it the stronger it gets. But what I am mainly is clairaudient, being able to hear voices, which I don't admit often as you can imagine.'

He ran a hand through his hair and sighed. 'I'm supposed to have a spirit guide who tells me things, but we're not exactly on speaking terms. I've spent many many years putting him on mute. It was hard enough getting the other kids to play football with me. Plus they all thought my gran was a witch.'

'I'm sorry.' It came out softly, in absolute contrition. She blinked, her vitality fast fading, and he saw tears gathering at the corners of her eyes. Shit. Awkwardly he pulled her into a hug. He caught the faint waft of shampoo, and tried stolidly not to bury his face in her hair. She leaned against him heavily, lacking the energy for hysterics, tears sliding silently down her face. Then all at once he heard her voice from near his shoulder.

'I was thinking if he wasn't the first, you might pick something up somewhere else.'

He loosened his hold, leaning back to look at her face.

'There aren't that many murders in Auckland, surely. If it *is* a serial killer, you might be able to trace his signature at another site.'

For a moment he was speechless. 'Bloody hell.'

She took one look at his expression, and suddenly snorted. As Paxton gaped like a broken fly, she collapsed into giggles. She clamped a hand to her mouth in a vain attempt to stop herself, almost sobbing again with laughter. She dropped her head on to his chest, helpless, and her giggles came out muffled against his shirt. Paxton shook his head, unable to hold back a grin.

'Jesus, woman, there are cockroaches softer than you.'

He could feel her shaking with laughter. After a moment she calmed down and let go of him, wiping the residue of snot and tears from her face. The rest had soaked into his shirt.

'The look on your face ...' Her smile dissolved. 'It's a lot to ask.'

'And as I told you, I mightn't find anything.'

'Then you're just the same as the cops.'

'Point.' He considered her carefully for a second. 'If I refuse you'll be here at *two* tomorrow morning, won't you?'

'No.'

He could see she meant it. She resembled a wraith. Hollow eyes like sinkholes. If he refused her she wouldn't have the strength to keep pushing.

'Go home. Get some sleep.' He gently took her elbow and led her through the door. 'Then call me tomorrow.'

Chapter FOUR

THREE A.M., AND she was dead on her feet. If she didn't stop working overtime at the hospital she'd end up as one of the patients. She shouldn't really have taken the four hours' leave — didn't sound much, did it? She could have stayed on. But tonight was exceptionally quiet in the unit, for once. After the hellish week she'd had she'd have ended up sleeping anyway. Much nicer on her own pillow than upright in one of those hospital chairs. A stretcher would have been more comfortable.

She fought back a minor surge of guilt. Gloria Tan had been brought up to regard refusing work as anathema, and there was a chronic shortage of nurses. Most of her colleagues had been poached by the UK, where at least you could keep a straight face at the wages. At this precise moment Gloria was finding it hard to walk in a straight line. Fatigue — the worst form of intoxication.

She headed into Countdown, which at Greenlane was 24 hours. A godsend given her shifts. The carpark was virtually deserted at this time of night except for the cars of supermarket staff and the crew from the McDonald's opposite. How anyone could face food of such gut-bogging awfulness at three in the morning was more than Gloria could imagine.

HE stuck to the coffee. He sipped it slowly as he watched the intermittent lights of the traffic passing along Great South Road, hearing the hissing exhalation of tyres on the motorway just beyond in the other direction. Night, devoid of the chaos and rush of daylight, was the optimum time for thinking. There was space to fully absorb all the details, or conversely to let the mind wander. He was often up at this hour spinning fantasies and analysing ... and observing. During the daytime this was one of the hubs of Auckland existence, but now in the wee small hours it was almost idyllic. Private.

He'd sat here for a bit just taking it in. The calm before the storm. As Gloria entered the supermarket he stepped out of the shadow of the restaurant, strolling easily over to her car. His eyes performed a brief flickering survey to make sure he wasn't being watched. But there was nobody else in the carpark, and Great South Road was bordering on empty, except for a few returning club goers who were only keeping an eye out for breath-testing checkpoints. Who, even of the living dead who'd served him more than half an hour ago, would have picked him from any other customer buying McMuck?

No one would notice.

He studied the white Mirage, clocking the a+ sticker in the window. The logo for the Auckland District Health Board. So she worked at the hospital. If she hadn't been wearing a long coat he'd have spotted her uniform straight away. And at three in the morning she wasn't likely to just clean out the bedpans.

Well well. Fate *could* be a bastard.

GLORIA didn't take long over her shopping, having had little to do. Just a can of deodorant and a bunch of stuff for tomorrow's lunch — marked-down bread rolls from the previous morning and a king-size bar of Cadbury's that found its way into her basket. Self-medication. She rather liked the peace of shopping so late, without the crowds that almost invariably clogged the aisles at other times of day, like on those posters of cholesterol-choked arteries. She exchanged an obligatory moan with the checkout assistant about the hell of working the night shift and carried her small cache of groceries outside.

The carpark was floodlit, illuminating everything in sickly light. The big golden M shone out like a beacon to weapons-grade food. Not another soul to be seen anywhere. She set down her shopping next to the car, wondering as she fumbled through her handbag for the key whether she should use the interval to make a start on the chocolate. The next moment the thought was chased clean out of her mind.

'Help.'

It came as a grunt, so laced with pain that her senses caught immediately. It was coming from the direction of the side street that ran behind the carpark. Gloria squinted anxiously into the darkness, but still she could see nothing. Outside the reach of the lights her eyes were useless. Then came a faint groan of agony, almost beyond the limits of hearing. Now that her senses had sharpened she could discern laboured breathing, catching acutely at intervals. All her instincts cried out against it.

'Where are you? What's happened?'

A heavy pause, then, so softly she had to strain to hear: 'Over here. I can't ... breathe ...'

Without consideration Gloria abandoned her shopping and half-ran towards the voice, spurred on by a surge of adrenaline twice as effective as chocolate. She crossed the narrow raised patch of dirt and scrub that divided the carpark from the street, and her eyes fell on a crumpled figure beneath one of the trees. Surprisingly young and fit-looking for someone in this kind of trouble. His ragged breathing grew louder as she approached, as he struggled to raise himself up on an elbow.

'I think ... it's my heart ... it's like this iron band ...' His voice was already failing, tapering to a high whisper when she hushed him, bending over his body.

'Ssssh. Listen to me. Listen. Can you feel any tingling in your fingers? Like pins and needles?'

His reply was a bare husk. 'Yeah, and I'm so cold. So cold ...' His eyelids began to droop, and Gloria dropped to her knees in panic, grabbing for his hand.

But he grabbed her first. In a blur of movement faster than thinking, he yanked her wrist to pull her off balance, then lashed an arm around her neck like a whipcord. Her eyes bulged in her head in shock and pain. And a split second later, fear. She tried to fight him, digging at his arm with claw-like hands, but her nails were kept pitifully short for work and he seemed to feel nothing beneath his jacket. It was like scrabbling at iron. On her knees she was helpless, unable to run or even to kick, held down by the tremendous crushing weight of his grip.

Now the frantic gasps for breath were coming from her, but the hands upon her body were not there to revive ...

He kept his arms around her throat for longer than was necessary, even when she pitched forward like a glassy-eyed ragdoll. He found that he was breathing almost as hard as before, when it had all been an act. He could still feel the warmth of her on the sensitive under-side of his arm.

Wild excitement rose within him as it registered that she was dead. Never before had it been this intense. The prostitutes had been easy, in life and in death, both of them literally gagging for it. No one would miss them; a couple of sex games gone sadly awry. Then it had been private, indoors, and while the foreplay was mildly interesting the aftermath was frankly anticlimactic. Stupid bitches — the second one had thought he was charging up extra. Until the foul ciggie breath ebbed from her body.

But this one, like the one before, was different. Sure, he could hardly strangle someone calmly to death during a game at Eden Park — unless it was particularly close — but this was as public as it got. There was something almost elemental about extinguishing a life in the open, luring them to their death like a hunter stalking game. This was the real thrill. And his execution was a stroke of pure genius, sizing up the clues and selecting an appropriate strategy.

A woman with a health board sticker on her car, shopping at three a.m. Had to be a nurse or a doctor, coming off shift.

Risk and release.

He couldn't wait to do it all again.

Chapter FIVE

'WHEN QUESTIONED ABOUT his involvement in the killing, Mr Paxton denied all knowledge. "All I did was find the body," he said. Police are appealing for further witnesses.'

'What did you *do*?'

'Fuck ... *Wankers*. I should have known this would happen.' Paxton had the grace to look ashamed. 'I was a *little* unforthcoming ...'

'Just a little.'

A small grin appeared on his face, irrepressible. 'I made them wait outside in the cold until after midnight.'

'Bloody hell, no wonder!'

'Well, it was Brent too!'

Never underestimate a reporter with a vendetta. Paxton had learned his lesson. The murder was all over the radio. Hangover Man had never said where he was from, Paxton remembered. It hadn't made the front page of the *Herald*; the All Blacks' latest thrashing was more tragic news. However, they'd managed to squeeze in a few quotes on one of the inside pages. Merchant must have been more enterprising than he thought. Couldn't have got this for anything less than tongue-swapping with the chief sub.

They were sitting at Lena's house, just Paxton and Lena, reading the morning's post-mortem. It was cosier at her place, without the suspicion of rats behind the walls. Though as small as his, her flat was a little newer, and the kitchen area got all the early sun, which burnt off some of the chill. They sat with tea at the small dining-table, the paper spread out between them.

'Serves me right for baiting the press, I guess. No sense of humour unless it involves politicians spanking each other in Parliament.'

'Did that happen back home?'

'Anything's possible. We made Cliff Richard famous.' He nodded at the phone on the bench, which had been disconnected from the jack. 'And I'd watch who you criticise for being obstructive.'

Lena grinned slyly. 'Whoops.'

Paxton laughed, letting his tea cool in the mug in front of him. He was falling like a whale without a parachute and he was utterly helpless to stop it. God, he fancied her. And for once, his essential peculiarities didn't seem to be getting in the way. He had no idea how Lena saw him, with his crap student's job and his rodents' dosshouse, only that she seemed to need him. That was rapidly becoming less and less of a problem.

'You haven't given an interview to *Woman's Day* yet?'

'No.' She didn't say that she was terrified of the phone ringing. Unplugging it had not been defiance, but fear. She tried not to hate herself for it. 'Can't say I've been tempted. Maybe the exposure'd help find Dad's murderer quicker, but I'm not too excited at sharing page space with Kim Kardashian and her arse.'

'Celebrity lifestyle not to your liking? Don't worry, you wouldn't get anywhere near Kim. You'd be in with the local news, somewhere in the middle just before the I'm-too-fat-to-fit-in-the-shot-let-alone-a-bikini diets and overpriced tat for cellulite.'

'For someone single and supposedly straight, you're scarily well informed about women's magazines.'

'I know they have pictures of women.'

Her laugh was nothing like a Swiss schoolgirl's. 'Dirty sod.'

Afraid of saying something he'd regret, he navigated the conversation on to a safer tack. 'Did you mean it about trawling round the other murder sites for a vibe?'

'Only if you want to.' She was serious.

Paxton wanted to all right, trying not to feel like a sick bastard for being so happy at the idea of visiting the places where people had met violent deaths. The skies were closing in and a frigid drizzle had started to spray down outside, so he drove back home for his coat. Appealing as pressing close under a tiny umbrella was to Paxton, Lena had insisted on the coat. She was already struggling to cope with a murder; dealing with a suicide as well wasn't on the agenda.

Just as he'd collected his coat from the detritus at the back of his wardrobe, there was a knock at the door. *That was quick*, he thought automatically. He went to let Lena in. But what greeted him when the door opened was markedly less attractive. Gardner, with Stirling a step behind. Paxton marvelled at the impeccably bad timing. Gardner caught sight of the coat in his hand.

'Sorry, is this a bad time?'

His voice carried the unmistakable conviction that if this was the worst of all possible moments, Paxton would still find a way to make time. Or suffer the consequences.

Paxton sighed, feeling his spirits evaporate like spilt aftershave. 'How can I help you, Sergeant?'

'We'd like you to supply us with a bit more information, if it's convenient. There's a few more things we'd like to know.'

A voice suddenly flashed through Paxton's conscious, verging on clairaudience. *Mis-terr Aanderrson* ... Agent Smith from *The Matrix*. The thought of the balding, doughy DS doing karate was risible. He couldn't waste a blow-up doll. If Paxton hadn't been so fucked off he would have laughed. He noticed Stirling didn't look happy. Paxton sensed that he'd come along to censor the proceedings.

'Just let me call my friend and tell her I'm not coming.'

He let the cops wait in the lounge while he took his cordless into the hall and rang Lena on her mobile. It was the only phone she still had working. Paxton was cautious with his language, knowing the detectives could hear every word from any part of the house.

'Hi, it's me. Look, I'm really sorry, but I'll have to take a rain check. I've got a couple of cops sitting on my sofa.'

'What?'

Paxton wondered whether the expostulation had carried into the lounge. 'I'll call you back when I'm done. Hopefully there'll still be time to do something then.'

'Yeah …' She seemed at a loss for invectives to throw at them. Paxton was heartened by the response. He drifted back into the lounge. Damn. The couch was going to reek of bacon. Although in Gardner's case brimstone seemed more likely.

'Can I get either of you a coffee?'

'No thanks.'

Stirling spoke up. 'I'll have one. Milk, no sugar, thanks.'

Gardner said nothing, though Paxton saw the corners of his mouth pinch. This at least ought to be entertaining. As he brought the coffee, Gardner sat with hands folded on his lap; the expression on his face Paxton recognised from their previous encounter. *I don't trust you, and if you slip I'll be on your throat before you even hit the ground.*

'Can I ask you what you were doing last night?'

'Working. Until at least midnight.'

'And after that …?'

Paxton paused, watching Gardner's face. 'Being interviewed about the murder.'

Gardner continued to gaze back at him, a sphinx without a clue. No twitch of guilt. 'Contacted the paper, did you?'

'No. I was rather thinking you must have. Often leak witnesses to the press, do you? Hoping it'll soften them up?'

Gardner reacted with a supercilious stare. 'I don't need to resort to such tactics.' His mouth lifted arrogantly. 'There may be leaks on the force, but usually you find it's the neighbours.'

He looked at Paxton as if he were dog shit tracked on to the carpet. Mortification struck Paxton with a thump as he remembered the man from over the road. He'd been chatting eagerly to the TV guy at length. Incautious prat would have spilled the size of his own knob to a rep from the media. He felt like a clot for revealing so much to the man and his wife in the first shock of discovery.

'So when did you finish with this interview?'

'Can't have been later than one — I was home by quarter past.' Again Gardner kept his mouth shut. It would have been self-evident to a parsnip that he was hiding something. Something Paxton definitely wasn't going to like. The suspicion was obviously mutual. Stirling swallowed a mouthful of coffee, with a sideways glance at his superior.

'Been listening to the radio lately?'

'No. I've been out all morning, and the one in my car is busted.'

'Then you won't have heard. There was a second murder last night.'

Paxton went still. As his face went blank, his mind started spooling frenetically. Could this be what Lena was looking for? And then, a fraction of a beat later: *My God. He's killing them off like ants.*

He heard himself ask, shaken, 'Are you sure it's the same bloke?'

Gardner spoke, with seeming reluctance. He was clearly not rapt with Stirling for snipping off his jollies so soon.

'Wouldn't like to say at this stage.' He refused to elaborate. The less information given, the more likely the offender will give himself away. Paxton read it plainly in his thoughts. Psychic ability wasn't necessary when dealing with this cunt.

'I didn't do it, and I didn't do it the other night either. I was — like Mark — in the wrong place at the wrong time.' He meant it to sound firm, but it came out merely weary. He looked at Stirling. 'What happened?'

Stirling glanced again at Gardner. 'Can't give away all the details, but we found the body of a woman in Greenlane. A nurse at the hospital. You could learn as much by switching on the news.'

'Where was it exactly?'

'In the street behind the Countdown carpark. She was doing some late-night shopping.'

'And does my alibi put me in the clear?'

Gardner took over. 'The woman bought articles from the supermarket well after the time you're covered for. As far as I'm concerned, we can't rule out anyone yet.'

Paxton caught Stirling's eyelids drooping in what looked like disgust. The sergeant's complacent little threats were as portentous as a fart in a high wind.

'Do you think your arrival home would have woken the neighbours?'

'Not likely. But you'd have to ask them that.'

'Oh, we will, sir. We're pretty thorough.'

Paxton could have given him several other words for it. Instead he got to his feet. 'Well, I'll let you get on with it, shall I? Hope I've been helpful.'

Gardner only smiled, and held out his hand. Paxton shook it, wishing he could crush it into dust.

'Solid grip.' The sergeant's voice was light, but Paxton was willing to bet his words were laden with meaning.

Stirling spoke from near the door. 'Thanks for the coffee.' He raised a hand in farewell, with a smile at Paxton.

Gardner's smile oozed insincerity, accompanied by a pseudo-friendly nod. 'See you again.'

Paxton had no doubt he would.

LENA had already set out from her place when Paxton's call came through. Not in the mood to turn back, she found herself driving onward regardless. Keeping an appointment made in secret with her unconscious, she wound up at the park. One of many in the area, but it would always be The Park to her now. She halted the Civic and sat for — she had no idea. Time had passed beyond measuring. Not yet forty-eight hours. Not even two days since it happened. The impossibility of it all stopped her breath. She'd kept pressing on in so much of a hurry, blurring his loss with movement. Sitting still and letting it all catch up was like stopping on train tracks.

She dreaded the funeral; it was set for tomorrow. The mere arrangement of it had been sheer torment. The mundane and shattering picking up of the pieces, sorting out wills and personal effects, was something she had tried hard to avoid. She'd pushed on past it, eagerly chasing closure, but that wouldn't really come until she'd faced what lay behind her. She fooled herself that she was moving on, but without the trial of empty rooms and packing boxes she wouldn't truly qualify. Real life was still on hold.

She got out of the car and wandered slowly through the reserve, marking the faint traces of the crime circus's occupation. Flattened grass. Though the ground was fast turning to a swamp she could still make out the holes where the tent had been erected over her father's body, in anticipation of the rain. She looked closely with sick fascination for stains, but if there had been any the rain had rinsed them clean. That was a relief. No doubt the neighbours had all made the visit, avidly trampling the grass while they denounced the blight upon their backyard. She could see one of them watching now, a face framed in a window across the road, attracted by the car and the umbrella. Turning her back, she stood where she thought her father might have lain, trying with every ounce of will to receive a sign.

Nothing. No shift beneath her feet. No hairs raising the flesh on her arms, no rush of warmth and recognition, no whisper from behind some invisible screen. The world was a blank. And the biting cold was only from the rain, puddling on the dirt. Whatever voices spoke to James Paxton, not one was calling to her.

The skies were grey and heavy as concrete, pissing down harder as she drove. Appropriate under the circumstances. Passing up the hill, she caught a glimpse of a car containing a couple of familiar figures descending well under the speed limit in the other lane. She peered over hastily as she went past, meeting the eyes of the bloke in the passenger's seat, whose face muscles slackened in an instant of realisation. That shit Gardner and his partner, she was certain. She'd seen the other one when she'd cornered Gardner about his progress. Gardner had had him bring the coffee.

Just then her mobile went off. She looked back over her shoulder, and saw the younger one was doing the same.

'Hi. They've gone.'

'I know, I just saw them.'

He sounded confused. 'Where are you?'

She hesitated. 'I've been to the park.'

'I see. You OK?'

'He didn't tell me anything.'

Paxton said nothing.

'I know I shouldn't … I don't know what I was expecting. It's not like I've ever showed signs of psychic ability, I don't know why I ever thought …'

'Hey.'

'But I did think there was a link ...'

His voice was gentle. 'Just because you can't hear it doesn't mean it's not there.'

'Anyway. I'd probably have shat myself if anything happened.'

'That's called contaminating a crime scene.'

He'd ambushed her into a laugh. She heard the crackle of her breath in the receiver. 'Hey, what did the cops want from you?'

'A confession.'

'Whaaaat! This is just getting ridiculous.' She glared at passing cars. 'Flaming Nazis, there's no evidence to tie you to anything.'

'No evidence to the contrary either.'

'I'll speak to them. I'll tell them I'm sure you —'

He interrupted her. 'Thanks. But I'm not certain it'd do any good.'

'Interfering with a witness or whatever?'

'Whatever.' There was a pause, and she imagined he was nodding at the other end. 'I'm proved to have been at the scene of the crime, the only one to have been so far, and knowing that I've been to see you would practically give the sergeant an orgasm. He's dying to pin everything on me, and after you requested that your name not appear in the papers, how on earth would I have known how to get hold of you? And for that matter, why the hell would I? Unless I wasn't such a stranger to your dad — or you — as I'm pretending ...'

Lena fell silent as the sense of it sank in. They'd both look complicit. She remembered Gardner's eyes at the morgue, piercing her skin as if he could see beneath.

Paxton went on, his voice betraying something of interest. 'But there is something I can take out of this.'

‘What’s that?’

‘They told me there’s been a second murder.’

Lena sat electrified in her seat.

‘So I suggest you get here quick.’

Chapter SIX

STIRLING SAID NOT a word to his boss about seeing Lena Bradley pass their car. Correctly he surmised that she had been to visit the scene of her father's death, and he respected her privacy. He doubted Gardner would give a dog's bollock anyway. Both detectives stared at the park as they crept by, a visual reminder of their failure so far.

'What makes you so sure Paxton did it?'

Gardner glanced over at him, his lips pursing in disdain. 'Who said I thought he was guilty?'

'Come *on,* Sarge. I've seen skinheads be more open-minded. The moment we heard about the nurse you were desperate to have another go.' Stirling could never imagine calling Gardner by his first name. Not as a mere DC. He'd have bet anything Gardner was sorry the New Zealand Police had all but dispensed with the 'sir'.

'He still hasn't adequately explained what he was doing there in the first place.'

'You saw the dog. He was afraid he'd run it over.'

Gardner snorted. 'It's a pretty thin story. No one else has been placed at the scene, and there's something he's not telling us. You aren't going to tell me you think he's entirely straight?'

Stirling paused. 'Noooo ...' He hated to admit it, but he was sure Gardner was right. Still, he took exception to the older bastard's attitude. It was well known round CIB that the sergeant was angling for *senior* sergeant. Even so, to Stirling it was a poor excuse for scalping the first head that popped itself up, just for another trophy to dangle from his tool belt.

'When you've had a bit more experience like me, you'll realise that the only time you can take a witness at face value is ... Whoops. I guess there isn't one.'

'Suspicious old sod, aren't you?'

'I'm a detective. It's the reason they're paying me.' He turned a baleful eye on Stirling. 'You'd do well to remember that, Mother Teresa. You can't just give people the benefit of the doubt. Or you might as well be back in uniform, letting girls with big tits off traffic offences.'

'You still don't have a motive.'

'I'm working on it.'

Stirling bit back an expletive. 'You're not convinced he did the other one as well, are you? We kept him up till two the morning before, barbecuing him over the first one!'

Gardner seemed reluctant. 'I'll agree there are discrepancies. I'll leave it to Graeme and Tony to decide.'

Graeme Kirkpatrick was the detective sergeant in charge of the Tan case, and Tony Rees was assisting. He'd had a hell of a week.

'You know the statistics,' Gardner continued. 'How often are murderers completely unknown to their victims?'

Stirling remained resolutely silent. They had something called the policeman's ABC: Accept Nothing. Believe Nobody. Confirm Everything. Stirling didn't know why he trusted James Paxton as much as he did. Usually in the presence of Gardner he kept his mouth shut; respect for one's elders and all that. Plus there was only so much smug condescension anyone could take without smashing cartilage. But instinctively he felt that Gardner was wrong. Unjust he was used to, but it was the wrong part that rankled. Whatever Paxton was holding back, Stirling didn't think it was guilt. There was simply no reason, as far as he could discover.

'Why in Christ's name would a man bash in an optometrist, or an optician or whatever he was, and wait round *with* the dog for the cops? It's not like he even fabricated a decent alibi. It's far too obvious.'

Gardner sneered. 'Andy, you know as well as I do there are people out there who can gun down entire families, then call it in, sob for the cameras, and go for lunch without even washing their hands. That's why we have *serial* killers — because some psychos have the ability to fool even their closest relatives until eighty-six bodies are found piled in the basement.'

Serial killers. They were back to Gloria Tan again. Stubborn git.

Stirling couldn't be buggered prolonging the argument.

Instead, his mind ran over the same question all the way back to headquarters. *But if Paxton didn't do it — who did?* It reminded him, oddly, of a nursery rhyme. This little pig, going why why why why, all the way home ...

'WHAT happens if you can't feel anything?'

They were walking across the tarseal, weaving between the parked cars and the shoppers with their trolleys. Paxton shrugged. 'Not sure. It's up to you.'

'We'll cross that bridge when we come to it.' She refused to think about failure. It would have started her thinking about other things.

A small knot of people stood at the edge of the carpark, gesturing idly, facing the street behind. As the only view was of the carwash up the road, it could easily be assumed that this was where Gloria had died. The usual vultures were out for a vicarious thrill, the best of human nature on display. Slaying-spotters. At the sight of them, Lena paused. She felt slightly uneasy even adopting their behaviour. It didn't sit right. Death was a private thing. Only of course Gloria hadn't died on her own. The remembrance of this drained some of the bile out of Lena's stomach.

Paxton's gait slowed as they reached the circle of tragedy tourists. There was nothing to see, but without being told he knew where to go. There was death here. The air almost stank with it.

There was no grass on the verge, only a strip of bare asphalt beyond the wizened assortment of stalks that passed for greenery edging the carpark. As Paxton scoped out the street behind, the irony bit hard. If she'd been murdered during office hours, Gloria's witnesses would have been the staff at the national office of Habitat for Humanity, plus inquisitive little pre-schoolers at the childcare centre just opposite.

Look, kids, here's what happens when you watch too many bad shows on TV. See, sometimes they don't get back up again ...

But had she gone? He stepped a little to the left of the rest, beside a small naked tree, feeling the details come to him in bursts of intuition. A dream without the images, where twisted unreality is merely accepted as fact. A woman, going to help. Someone lying beneath the tree, in pain, deception emanating from him like foul brown smoke. There had been a trick, some trap had been set, and the woman had walked straight into it, snared before she had a chance to resist. She'd been petrified, scratching thrashing choking insane with terror. But he'd showed her no mercy. He'd strangled her to death. Yes. Most definitely *he*.

'It's him.'

He said it so only Lena could hear. She was already at his side. He sensed a sort of uncomfortable awe coming from her as she looked at him. Putting a distance between them.

'Did you speak to her?' Her voice was low, but her eyebrows were halfway to her hairline.

'No. She's already passed on. But I can tell what happened. It's pretty potent.'

He related everything he'd read, thinking as he did so how utterly useless it all was. He now knew what had happened, but he still had no idea who the killer was, or what in the hell he was going to do next. What was he supposed to do, wait until the next murder and show up again, like a sick as shit groupie?

'Are you not able to … channel her or something?' Though she tried not to show it, Lena was clearly disappointed. Once again Paxton was astonished at the nature of human belief. People were the world's worst sceptics, but once confronted with a little evidence they expected you to walk on water, and turn it all to chardonnay to boot. Bless her. He wished he could share her belief.

He let out a breath, at least sharing her frustration. 'Errrrmmm … Spirits don't just hang around all the time. For the most part they leave the earthly plane. Or something like that; it's difficult. Your father clearly felt he had some unfinished business, so he stayed on, but I imagine Gloria didn't have such a strong tie.'

'But I thought mediums were supposed to be able to talk to spirits. Isn't that what people go to you for?'

'Yeah, it helps when you've got them there. Often souls queue up to talk to someone they were close to, but they don't know me from a bar of soap. She's got no reason to contact me.'

'So …'

He could see what she was thinking. 'I'd really need to get in touch with family, yeah.'

Lena stared at him, her mind obviously working furiously. Then she seemed to catch herself. She blinked, looking suddenly repentant. 'I'm so sorry. I can't believe I'm doing this to you. I must seem like the most ungrateful bitch; I keep making you do all these things, and here I am going, "Oh, where's the killer then?" Like I expected you to pull him out of your arse or something. I know it doesn't work like that.'

'Now there's an image.'

She broke into a sunny smile. 'This has to be worth a few drinks. But wait — shit. You're a bartender.' She shook her head, self-mocking. 'Yeah, let's go celebrate at work.'

'Pass.'

'God, I'll never repay you.'

'I haven't done anything yet.'

She stared at him. He shrugged. 'Lot of Tans in the phone book. How were you planning on doing this?'

'You serious?'

'I'm up to my neck in it now. I've come across two murders, and the police suspect me of both. Might as well humiliate the wankers. Do a good deed for society.' He gave a crooked grin. It was wiped away in a second when she leaned over to kiss his cheek.

'I'll never make a crack about whinging Poms again.'

Paxton forced himself to leer as was proper, and no more. No mean effort. His face wanted to split into little pieces. Nice and restrained. And all this for a poxy kiss on the cheek. Christ, he was almost thirty.

Yeah, and you've never had a girlfriend. Your so-called gift has a shitload to answer for.

IT was Lena's idea to go to the hospital. The idea seemed to horrify her even as she put it in words, but alternatives were slim. They stood in the impersonal reception area, full of potted plants, multi-lingual signs, grease-printed magazines, waiting patients, families. Nurses much like Gloria would have been.

'God, I feel sick.'

He caught her eye. 'You're in the right place.'

Both were whispering, not merely out of respect for their surroundings. A receptionist in her early forties was superintending the filling out of a form, hampered by the fact that she didn't understand a word of the Niuean content. With an English translation she was struggling to guide the patient, an obese poster-boy for coronary care with a sinus problem, through the dense medicalese. Harried, she was glancing around for help, but no one else seemed to be Niuean. Finally the comedy sketch was over, and Lena was on.

'Hello, are you here to visit a relative?'

The receptionist was eyeing Lena's bouquet, a stark bunch of lilies and white tulips. Grossly short on tact for a hospital. Lena hesitated, and Paxton gave her a mental prod.

'Actually, I just came to bring these. I heard about what happened to Gloria Tan, and ...'

The receptionist's misgivings vanished abruptly. 'Oh yes, wasn't it awful? Why anyone would want to *do* such a thing to such a lovely woman! I just can't believe it — none of us can!'

Paxton was relieved. He wasn't quite sure what they'd have done if Gloria Tan had been a bitch. Lena shook her head.

'I couldn't believe it either. She was so good when my dad was in hospital — she made sure he had everything he wanted, and she was always ready to talk whenever he got lonely. He said it made all the horror he was going through bearable.'

The other woman's face was lined with compassion. 'Did he ask you to bring in these flowers?'

Lena considered the sterile industrial flooring for a beat too long. 'No. He died a short while ago ... But yes, I did it for him.'

Paxton wanted to put an arm round her then. Instead he kept his eyes on the clock hanging on the wall behind the desk, and counted off the seconds.

'Oh, I'm so sorry.'

'Is there any way of passing my sympathy on to her family? They must be so devastated. I've just lost my father, but this must be a thousand times worse.'

The receptionist, deeply distressed, fossicked through her records.

'Oh, we still have her address. And thank you. It's so lovely of you, what you're doing. I'm sure her parents will really appreciate it.'

Paxton saw Lena swallow. She turned her head away.

'Here we go. I'll write it down for you.' The receptionist scribbled it on a memo pad, and tore it off.

'Give them my regards too, won't you? We've started a card and a collection, but tell them Yvonne thought she was *such* a lovely girl, and that my thoughts are with them.'

'Will do, Yvonne,' said Paxton. 'Thanks.'

As they were leaving they heard her call one of the passing nurses, and point them out. 'Those people brought flowers for Gloria. She cared for the lady's father when he was in hospital. He's dead too ... Poor thing. Isn't it a shame?'

LENA remained mute as they drove from the hospital car park. She had let Paxton drive. She clasped the paper in her hands, automatically shredding it without even realising. Hearing, Paxton glanced over.

'Oi! That's the address you're ripping to pieces.'

She started, and abruptly put it on the dashboard. 'Sorry.' She already had a just passed away weight on her conscience, but it was small fry compared with what was to come next.

Paxton sent her a brief look. 'As long as they don't call you a lunatic, count yourself lucky.'

Lena looked across at him in surprise, suddenly reminded that Paxton had done it all before. In her guilt, she'd forgotten. She felt a new respect for him, remembering how she'd treated him like crap. How far her beliefs had stretched in a short couple of days.

He was looking amused. 'I know you think you're Mata Hari at the moment. And I can't say I enjoyed that much either.' He cracked a rueful smile, his eyes becoming more serious. 'But it's all for a good cause. Eh?'

After a moment, she returned the smile, with gratitude.

They fell silent as they exited the motorway near Gloria's place of death, muscles relaxing only one they were safely amid the nonstop car yards of Great South Road.

A well-preserved old villa near the Harp of Erin, off-white painted green around the windows. Garden neatly kept, though not much to look at in winter.

Lights are on, but nobody's home. It popped from nowhere into Lena's mind. Though it was daylight and no lights were on anywhere, the blinds had the same effect. They were pulled wide open, but it didn't feel like there was anyone living inside. Lena suppressed a shiver, and told herself it was the shock of stepping into the air.

They'd driven here without a thought as to whether there'd be anyone here when they arrived. In some way the visit was like ripping off a plaster — less painful if they caught their quarry by surprise. In practice, it would still be excruciating. They left the lilies in the car.

A woman answered Paxton's knock, somewhere in her mid-sixties and barely reaching Paxton's shoulder. Lena wondered if she were really as old as she looked, or if the last twenty-four hours had brought all the years slamming down upon her at once. The woman's hair was still black, but heavily shading to grey and white.

'Yes?'

Of habit polite, but highly suspicious. Clearly she'd been interrupted this way before. Paxton took the floor.

'Forgive us for disturbing you like this, but are you Mrs Tan?'

'Yes. Is this about my daughter?'

Different accent, but déjà vu of the ugliest description. The well of grief beneath the dead façade was all too horribly plain.

'It's about finding who did this,' said Paxton.

Mrs Tan stared. Thought it over, her eyes watching both of them carefully. Then she nodded, just once, moving aside to let them enter.

The interior was as immaculate as the front. Carpet meticulously vacuumed, the only sign of clutter the figurines and photos on the mantel. Paxton tried not to look at them too openly, peeking at them with fatal curiosity as they followed Mrs Tan into the lounge. One picture in a small silver frame was of a young woman in a nurse's uniform; the same woman who appeared more than once. Flanked by both parents in a graduation gown, alone, as a child ... The murdered woman now had a face. Pleasant to look at, though not quite pretty, but easily imagined smiling over a sickbed, just as it was smiling everywhere over the fireplace.

They wouldn't have a photo of her now, of that smiling face baring its teeth in a strangled grimace, bloody bitten tongue lolling the colour of a bruise from the stiff frozen lips. Dark eyes staring and cold as marbles.

The sofa was the tint of puce that could have been described as blood-purple. Once seated, Paxton and Lena each waited to see who'd crack first. Paxton had the experience, and Lena the motivation. Neither really felt it was enough. Finally, Paxton gave in, seeking refuge in politeness.

'You've got a lovely place. Been in it long?'

The caution eased for a moment. A place with exposed wires and batts leaking from the ceiling will still get some sort of response from its owner. 'Almost twenty years. But in New Zealand, about forty years. Since we came out from Taiwan. Before this we live in Mangere.'

A decidedly lower-rent suburb, thanks to the constant influx of foreigners into the neighbourhood. Not to mention domestic passengers, charter and freight, all of it thundering incessantly overhead.

'My name is Mary. May I ask who you are? Are you friends of Gloria's?'

Paxton took a breath. 'No. I'm James Paxton, and this is Lena Bradley. Lena's father was killed a few days ago as well. And we believe by the same man who killed your daughter.'

She stared at them, hardly believing it. Her eyes went in astonishment to Lena, with a look of doubt. The thought of more death, more grief, seemed to overwhelm her. 'Your father was killed too? And — and by the same person? You know this?'

'We'd like you to help us find him, if you can.' Lena said it gently, trying not to alarm her just yet. Though that was surely not in the too distant future.

'How?'

Paxton and Lena exchanged glances, but fortunately Mary Tan was already rising, ignoring the silence.

'Wait a minute. I'll get my husband. His name is Frank.' She disappeared. They heard the disembodied jabbering of voices somewhere down the hall. Frank didn't seem to be at home to visitors. But after what seemed like hours, there came the sound of a door closing and footsteps creaking on the ageing floorboards towards them.

Frank Tan was barely taller than his wife, though his hair was substantially greyer. His dark eyes were well-lined with age. He said nothing as he sat in the solitary armchair at one end of the room, merely nodding in acknowledgement of their presence. The wordless expectation made everything worse. Lena's stomach was beginning to shift again.

Mary seemed as edgy as they were. She glanced almost fearfully at her husband. 'He never misses work. About three days, in forty years. Even when Gloria was born. He left from the hospital.'

Frank still said nothing. Over his shoulder, he smiled beside his daughter in her gown. The silence stretched on.

Paxton wondered whether the sofa was really as uncomfortable as it seemed, or whether it was just him. Felt like he was sitting on pins. Seeing there was no chance of help, he plunged in.

'I don't know if you've heard of psychics — or mediums. People who can speak to those who have died, and pass on messages?'

A swift look between the couple. Frank grunted, and his wife nodded slowly. Paxton could feel the suspicion doubling, hostility descending like low cloud. He willed himself consciously not to fidget. Lena's fingers were digging into the aubergine padding.

'Miss Bradley contacted me because I have the ability to communicate with the spirit world, and thus have the potential to gain information about the killer.' It came out horribly stilted. He couldn't bring himself to tell the truth in its entirety. Trust was still a long long way away. Lena looked a little surprised, but left the talking to him.

Frank Tan spoke, his enunciation slightly quaint like his wife's, but angry as hell with it.

'What makes you think my daughter was killed by the same man who kill your father?' His eyes burnt furiously into Lena, singling her out as the weaker party. She shrank into the seat, gripping it tighter. 'Eh? Why you want to disturb the dead? You want information, you should go to the police.' His arms waved menacingly as he spoke.

'Pardon me, sir, but the police have no idea. And we *all* want to know who's doing this, to stop him doing it again. I know what I'm suggesting sounds ... disrespectful. But we're trying to help other people who might suffer the same horrible fate as your daughter. And her father.'

He turned his head toward Lena. She looked dazed and miserable. Totally out of her depth. But the next moment she opened her mouth, surprising him.

'I laughed at him when he came to me. He was recommended — by a friend — and I tried to throw him out of my house. I was angry, just like you.' She focused on Mary, who so far had said nothing. 'But he convinced me that he really can speak to ... the dead. And if Gloria saw who did this to her, as my father sadly did not, then we have a better chance of catching the murderer.'

Their faces were clean of expression. Silent as death.

'Don't you want justice for your daughter?' Paxton knew as he said the words that it was hopeless.

'I think you had better go.'

This was Mary, who after a hasty glance at her husband got up and walked quickly to the door. 'Thank you for your concern, but we do not believe in that kind of thing.'

She stood with the door firmly open. Frank was shaking his head, muttering to himself. His eyes were hard as toffee as he watched them go.

PAXTON stole a glance at Lena as they stumbled down the concrete drive. Her eyes had filled with tears that were hanging on for dear life.

'Hey.' He placed a hand on her arm. 'Nothing to get worked up over. To be honest, I sort of expected it.'

She stopped at the car and covered her face with both hands. 'Idiot! Stupid, stupid, *stupid.* I should have listened to myself, I should have *thought*, instead of going barging into some people's home and trying to invade their privacy! My God, what did I think I was doing?'

She was sobbing by the time she reached the end. Paxton gently freed her face from her hands and pressed it into his shirt, rubbing her back.

'You've got to realise that most people aren't receptive to all this stuff. I've learned that the hard way. This was always going to be a long shot — and I shouldn't have let you do it. I should have said something.'

He was swallowing back guilt like cold chunder. His rationale had been woefully absent at the prospect of Lena's company. Not to mention her gratitude.

Lena pulled back, shaking her head. 'Even if they had been willing ... It's too soon. Hell, their daughter was murdered last night. It's still raw. *God*, what an idiot I was. A fucking selfish idiot. Oh, and as well as a fraud!'

'Yeah, you still owe me for the flowers.'

She hit him. Not hard, and on his chest, but she did it again. Then she laughed feebly, her face still incongruously wet with tears. She wiped at her eyes.

'Sorry. I'll try to stop crying on your shoulder. It's getting to be a habit.'

'There are worse things.' Much worse. But he left that unsaid. He looked at the flowers in the front seat. 'You're damn well going to use them too, you know. I paid a fortune for them.'

'Christ. I'll pay you back!'

'Excellent. You can start by getting lunch.'

She gaped at him. 'You're actually hungry?'

'It's almost three. Aren't you?'

'Starving.' She said it in a tone of wonder. Amazed to find that she was. 'What do you feel like?'

'Surprise me. As long as it's not with McDonald's ...'

'You come from England and you're concerned about crap food?'

'You're half Swiss and a female. Shouldn't you already be carrying chocolate?'

She gave him the finger and got into the driver's seat. As she twisted the key in the ignition, she cast him a look.

'James?'

'Yeah?'

Her voice was sincere. 'Thanks.'

Paxton smiled. Most pointless thing she'd said all day.

Chapter SEVEN

'BEFORE I MET you I wasn't even sure about ghosts. I've always thought of myself as open-minded, but I wasn't going to be suckered into anything without evidence.'

'I've always been a sceptic myself. Sort of hard to avoid the life after death issue, so I concentrate on chucking shit on UFOs, conspiracy theories and organised religion.'

'And sightings of Elvis.'

Paxton grinned. 'I saw Saddam Hussein going for sarnies in Barcelona once. Either him, or one of his chubby decoys. Fatty ordered the full toastie and chips combo and kept refilling his drink.'

'The way you're going you'll be joining him at Weight Watchers.'

'My shift starts in a couple of hours! This has to do me for lunch and dinner.'

They were sitting in a small but busy café in Newmarket, with their backs to Broadway. Paxton forked in another bite of his panini. He'd also got a wedge of lemon tart, a mini savoury and an enormous latte lined up in front of him. He noticed Lena tracking their disappearance with her eyes. Her plate was already empty.

'I've never been the type of mystic who goes on about chakras and crystals and all that bollocks. Fine if you believe in that sort of thing.' He held up both hands. 'But just because for some strange reason I have this gift, it doesn't mean I have to start using crystal balls and looking for portals into other dimensions.'

Lena snorted.

'Believe me, I've met these people.' He grinned. 'I horrified all of *them*. It's worrying enough trying to make rent let alone make sure all my spiritual planes are in alignment or anything.'

'Bit wasted on you, all this, isn't it?'

He shrugged. 'Probably explains why I'm not very good.'

'Yuh. Lesser people don't get their bodies invaded by scorned husband-killers from the 1400s.'

Service was slow, and they'd managed to get in a lot of talking. Paxton tended to be shy, by nature as well as by experience, and talking about himself ranked up there with scrubbing the Anubis toilets without gloves. But the conversation flowed so easily with Lena; Paxton savoured it while it lasted. After the mourning. The morning after. Didn't they amount to the same thing?

'You ready for the funeral tomorrow?' He said it quietly, aware he was spoiling the mood.

'I guess.'

'I realise you'll hardly be looking forward to it.'

'Actually, in a way I am. It's another step you've got to go through, isn't it? Towards putting this all behind you.'

'Like today.'

She groaned, rubbing a hand across her eyes. After a moment she said, 'I was trying to use other people — like I've used you — all to pursue my own revenge against this bastard. I feel terrible.'

'Don't. If I was worried about being used, I wouldn't be here. But I think you have to ask yourself, do you want to stop this now? Think about what it's doing to you, and think *very carefully* about whether it's worth it.'

She fiddled with her coffee cup. 'I certainly wouldn't be visiting the family next time. If it ever happens again.'

She met Paxton's eye. No doubt about that. He'd sensed pure evil. She pushed the subject aside. 'Will you come? To the funeral, I mean.'

'Ahhhm ...'

'You don't have to! I just thought you might like to —'

'No, it's not that. I'd love to. It's just that the cops often keep an eye out for this sort of thing. On the basis that murderers are often known to their victims. Or that the fuckwits like to gloat.'

'Of course. Sorry. I forgot.' She moved on to the sugar pourer, twisting it slowly round on the table.

'No, listen. I'll be there.'

'But —'

'They've still got no proof. And for all they know, I read about it in the paper, in the Dispatches column. Just act like you don't know me.'

AS it turned out, caution was unnecessary. The police already knew. Graeme Kirkpatrick came marching in to Gardner's office, his five o'clock shadow looking more like half past ten, and a tomato sauce blot over his growing gut. He was a good cop, but he tended to be rather excitable.

'Ray, I've just got off the phone with Frank and Mary Tan. I was just ringing to follow up, and they told me they've had a visit from Mark Bradley's daughter.'

'What!'

Kirkpatrick savoured the kicker. 'And you'll never guess who else. Your mate Paxton.'

Gardner virtually started, his chair creaking abruptly as he whipped forward.

'How the *fuck* ...?'

'Preston or something like it, she said. She couldn't quite remember. Didn't ring any bells with me. Dark hair, dark eyes, slim, about average height, blah blah, so far so useless. And they told me he was English. They've been here long enough to tell. Well, by sheer luck Tony came past and heard me talking. When he heard *that* it clicked, and got me to ask. And bingo.

He's claiming to have communicated with the spirit of Mark Bradley.'

Gardner's jaw plummeted so fast it almost dislocated. 'What, like one of those 0900 psychics?'

'Apparently, yeah.'

'Bloody hell ... We've got him now!' He smacked the desk with the flat of his hand, his eyes snapping in triumph. 'I *knew* it! He was hiding something from the start!'

'But why would Bradley's daughter want anything to do with him? How did he find her, for starters? It doesn't add up.'

Gardner looked up at him, saying nothing. 'She's in on it too, do you reckon?'

Gardner frowned at his in-tray in perplexity, his avenging energy dimmed. 'It's totally out of left field. If the usual domestic motives were to blame, then why the hell would they do in Gloria Tan? They could hardly get will money out of *her*. Unless she was a witness ...'

'Nope. Nowhere near Mission Bay at the time of the first murder. She was on shift.'

'Bugger.'

'Still circumstantial, Ray. You're going to need better than this if you're going to charge him. Or them.'

'We need ESR to bloody pull finger and get us some proof.' The Institute of Environmental and Scientific Research handled all the forensics testing for the police. It wasn't the FBI. Or even a glossy TV version. Thanks to the bog of work, results took weeks, and quite often months.

'It would help if you had a murder weapon.'

'Don't need one. I know he did it. Why else would he still be getting involved? Something's bloody fishy, and I'm damn well going to find out what.'

At that moment DC Stirling walked into the cramped office. Picking up on the tension, he swivelled his head between

Kirkpatrick and Gardner. He was thankful Rees wasn't in there as well. He doubted he'd have had room to breathe.

'I miss something?'

Gardner smiled, looking cheered. 'Your golden boy's just been found talking to the murdered woman's parents. Says he's a bona-fide psychic.'

Stirling blinked. 'Who? Do you mean James Paxton?'

'That's right. Says he talked to the ghost of Mark Bradley — now *that's* something he didn't pass on.'

Stirling looked bewildered. Kirkpatrick felt rather sorry for him. Gardner wasn't one for letting people down gently, or for grace in victory.

'Still think he's perfectly innocent then? He's been running around with Bradley's daughter.'

Another surprise, but Stirling handled it well. In a flash he was reminded of the phone call during their visit — the unknown person Paxton had to cancel when Stirling and Gardner turned up on his doorstep. Then a second image, of Lena Bradley grabbing for her cellphone in the car on the way to the park. Two disconnected events, that were suddenly fused in his mind. He held his tongue, and counted to three.

'Don't suppose you've considered he still might be telling the truth? Just because he's in touch with the victim's daughter doesn't mean he's the killer. He might have felt a connection with her, seeing as he found the body. Would have been almost as much of a shock to him.'

'But how would he have found her?'

'Same way he tracked down the Tans, I guess. Why don't you ask him?' Stirling shrugged. He didn't know what it was about the prick. Faced with that pasty mug he'd have stood up for Manson.

'You think he's a genuine psychic? Could have located her that way.' Kirkpatrick looked intrigued.

'You're bloody joking, Graeme.'

'Just exploring options.'

'I've had enough. One more hint of shit like this, and I'm hauling him in.'

Chapter EIGHT

ACCORDING TO MAORI tradition, rain at a funeral meant the gods were weeping for the dead. Paxton wished they'd heard of the Brit stiff upper lip. His trousers were getting soaked. True to an Auckland July, the rain was bucketing down. It was just a short distance from his car to the church, but he was wet through by the time he arrived. He'd looked at the slightly overcast sky and left his umbrella at home. Should have known that was just asking for it. Fortunately Mark had elected cremation, so there wouldn't be any need to shiver over a graveside.

The service was in a Presbyterian church on Remuera Road, Auckland's nearest answer to Harley Street. Mark's clinic had been just along further, sandwiched between an oral surgeon and a chiropodist. Paxton pressed his way through the throngs of well-dressed mourners clogging the entrance, inching from foot to foot like a penguin through the crowded foyer. A couple of women were handing out programmes, or whatever they were called. The term didn't seem quite appropriate, but he didn't know what else to call them. He took one, wanting to reach into his pocket for change, feeling like when he was last at the theatre. Except that today the performance most definitely wasn't live.

What was it actors said after a tough evening? *Hideous show, that. I died.*

He studied the face in his hands, grainy and nothing like its original colour, but still recognisably human. Now he had a face for the voice. The smile looked stilted and vaguely uneasy — Mark seemed as little at home in front of a camera as Paxton, who much preferred to be behind it. The hair was dark, like Lena's, and still impressively thick along his forehead. Mark hadn't died of old age. Didn't even look fifty — unless it was an old photo. But the haircut was all too horribly recent. Paxton suspected the picture had been taken this year. He tried to look at it objectively, and couldn't. Not handsome and not plain, not the kind of face you could ever imagine hating enough to smash so many times ... But whoever it was hadn't gone for the face, he remembered.

He turned the pamphlet over. A religious verse was printed on the back. He scanned it for half a second before turning it back over, looking for some resemblance to Lena. The pickings were disappointing. Where his nose was quite large, hers was finer, more delicate, and even the shade of his hair looked darker. Her cheekbones and her mouth also seemed inherited from her mother. Only the eyes gave it away. A pair of unusually kind-looking eyes, laser-printed to hell but which maintained some inherent spark of good humour. He stared down at them a moment longer, drawn in by the resemblance. Then he craned his head round for Lena.

He finally spotted her in a talking group of people, mainly women he didn't recognise.

Then out of the corner of his eye, he saw someone he did. Or rather two someones, weaving towards him.

'Well, well, well, Mr Paxton! Fancy seeing *you* here.'

Paxton realised he'd been incredibly stupid. 'Should have known you would be.'

Christ, he bloody knew it. Gardner and Stirling, plainclothes in fancy dress. In his suit Gardner would have been even more of an Agent Smith clone, except that it was an embarrassment round the waist, with as much style as a flasher's mac. He wondered whether the suit had seen much action since 1980. Appearances didn't seem favourable. For the man wearing it, definitely not. The dark material heightened the office-boy pallor of his face, raising doubts as to whether the corpse had employed an understudy.

'Still, it's not such an unexpected pleasure,' Gardner went on. 'We learned just yesterday you were acquainted with Mr Bradley's daughter.'

Congratulations, thought Paxton. Contradicted yourself in three sentences. Favourite yet again for Twat of the Year. But the news was another unpleasant jolt. He ought to have realised that the Tans would bring it up.

Warily he said, 'I felt sort of responsible. I mean, I'd just found her father dead; I couldn't help wanting to see that she was all right. I know how I'd feel in her situation.'

He hadn't seen his father in five years. He loved his dad, but ties were limited to a phone call at birthdays and Christmas. All of a sudden he felt a twinge of regret.

'And you've seen her more than once?'

Paxton shrugged noncommittally. 'I guess, what with the shock, we had something in common.'

Gardner paused, something very nasty under his tongue. Paxton knew what was coming.

'They tell me ... you're presenting yourself as a psychic.'

'That's because I *am* one.'

'Gave a reading for Miss Bradley, did you?'

'I don't do seances — if that's what you're wondering. Summoning up Princess Diana with dribbly candles and all that. I just talk to the ones who want to come, as and when they do.'

'Then do me a favour and get an answer to this one. Why the hell did you think you could go around interfering with a police investigation?'

What investigation? Paxton almost gagged on the question. Gardner was getting very in his face, which would have been unpleasant even at the best of times. The air of menace was unmistakable, the sergeant's face twisted with contempt.

'Intimidating family members — or prying for information. You take your pick. Whatever you're doing, you're one step closer to needing a damn good lawyer.'

Beside him, Stirling shifted his feet uncomfortably. 'Sir, this is a funeral ...'

'Never mind, Constable. Your boss doesn't respect the living, let alone the dead.' Paxton was furious, struggling not to commit the crime he was accused of after all. He kept his voice low, a hiss of sheer rage, so as not to disturb the mourners. Some were rubber-necking anyway.

'I'm trying to help a woman who's lost her father — you know, the one whose funeral you're crapping all over — and while I admit I made a mistake in contacting the Tans, that makes me a fool, not a murderer. If you object to my methods, fine. I won't be doing it again. But *don't* go drooling on me for something I didn't do, mate, because it makes you look twice the bloody fool ... Enjoy the funeral.'

Even as he walked away he knew he'd been unwise, but he'd have defied Christ to turn the other cheek. The expression on Gardner had been worth it. He'd even picked up the ghost of a smile from Andy Stirling.

Then without warning the air thickened, his neck prickling with a draught that was not of the wind outside. Paxton froze, then relaxed. To think he'd believed he wouldn't know anyone else here.

Well, that adds class to the whole show. A bloomin' emperor penguin with a badge. If you chucked him an anchovy do you think he'd bugger off?

'Hello, Mark,' said Paxton softly. He carefully went to stand beside a large arrangement of flowers, in a corner where hopefully no one would notice the schizo holding a conversation with empty space. He felt the presence following, invisible at his back.

I've been watching you. I've seen you with my daughter. And I want to say thanks. You've been marvellous. I really mean it — thanks a lot, James. You're a good man.

Paxton changed the subject. 'You haven't remembered anything else that might help?'

The tone altered immediately. *No. I'm sorry. I've tried so hard. But — nothing. There just isn't anything to remember.*

The answer was expected, if disheartening. Paxton stared desolately at the flowers. After a spell Mark spoke again.

Never thought I'd get to see my own funeral. Wonder what Brian Perry's doing here? My God he's packed it on.

'Don't you believe in the afterlife, then? I thought that's what Christianity was all about?' Paxton automatically used the present tense, forgetting it no longer applied.

What? I don't — Oh ... Do you mean the church? No, I've never believed in all this turn up Sunday or burn up someday rubbish. Jury was out on religion, mind you, but I never did the faithful, God-fearing, church on Sundays thing. Good choice, though. My ex is Catholic. She'd be bloody pissed off if she knew Lena had gone hardcore Presbyterian for the whole service. Should have told her I wanted a black Mass ...

Paxton heard the strain in his voice despite the laughter. Mark was fading. Paxton knew it cost Mark as much to talk as it did for him to listen.

'Speaking of Lena ...'

Yes. Thanks, you can pass on a message. Tell her not to worry. I'm fine. And don't you worry, either. There's no way the penguin can finger you. If he does, I'll haunt the cretin's office. Bugger up the coffee machine ...

The drowsy dynamic of the room shifted, as the stragglers began taking their seats. Paxton saw Gardner and Stirling take a place standing at the back. He sat at the end of the row opposite, feeling their eyes on him. Very faintly, the voice arrived in his head, draining away to nothing.

James! And tell her she looks beautiful.

The hymn, one Anglican-raised Paxton was unfamiliar with, drowned out any possible response. Not that Paxton was disposed to make any.

His gaze rested on Lena, right at the front near the organ. Her hair was pinned elegantly up off her face, giving an unrestricted view of her profile. She was dressed not in black but in green, which happened to be Paxton's favourite.

Thankfully it was a very short service. Lena had known her father well. Eulogies were given with a minimum of tears, though the heartfelt words of colleagues and friends revealed to Paxton how much Mark had been liked. His best friend was a man named Colin Davenport, a greying bloke running to fat, with the bewildered, devastated air of a Father Christmas who'd had all his presents flogged on Christmas Eve.

Lena's speech was brief, witty, and to the point.

'My dad was an optometrist; he always used to hassle the people who left it ages in between visits. "You'll have been wondering what all those bumps off the front of your bonnet were, then."'

There was a collective howl of laughter. Lena went on. 'But I guess, Dad, there are some things you will *never* see coming ...

'He was the most giving, the most warm-hearted, and at times the most embarrassing man I have ever known ... and no matter what — *no matter what* — he always tried to be there. For everyone, but especially for me, and it hurts like hell that he'll never be there again.'

Her voice wobbled, and she took a minute to steady herself. 'But he didn't raise me to fall in a heap at the first sign of trouble, and I'm going to do him proud. I know *he'd* be proud if he could see you all here today. Missing your Saturday golf.

Going to church. Wearing heinously uncomfortable outfits … All because of him.'

She paused, and glowered at the coffin. 'Yes … You're very pleased with yourself, aren't you?' The congregation roared, and there were a few claps. Paxton grinned to himself. Lena's next words were simple.

'We may never know who did this. I know that. So instead of hate, focus on love. For the man who died, the man we all knew, the man who took his dog for a walk at midnight because he was too damned stubborn to take the pills in his drawer.' She gave a watery laugh, crying for real now. 'God bless you, Dad. I'll miss you.'

She got off the dais to fervent applause, having left half her audience in tears.

The funeral ended shortly after. An old friend of Mark's who frequented the church had picked out the hymns that bookended the service. Paxton noticed that Lena wasn't singing along either. At the final reading she stood with her head bowed to the floor as the words echoed through the room.

Do not stand at my grave and weep: I am not there. I do not sleep …

FUNERAL food was laid out at the back after the service but, aware of Gardner and Stirling's scrutiny, Paxton sedulously avoided Lena. He saw them go up to her and say a few words of condolence, but though civil, she didn't seem eager to talk. He saw Gardner peer at the sympathy register, gazing penetratingly down at the names scrawled there by mourners, as if able to pick a crim's handwriting. Paxton concentrated on his cream cake and the crude pastelled renderings of Jonah being eaten by the whale that were Blu-Tacked to the walls. The one nearest him contained a giant blue blob with teeth that came out of a great white on growth hormone. Jonah was somewhere in the bottom of the picture, indistinguishable without close observation. Paxton's own memories of Sunday school amounted to roughly the same thing. All so hard to swallow now. Unlike Jonah.

The crematorium did not offer food, and the turnout was markedly less. The weather was still rather foul, though at least the rain had stopped. Gardner and Stirling did not make an appearance. Lena was still encircled by those same people from the funeral. Paxton supposed they were her friends. He hovered in the background, never coming near enough to speak. Groups of strangers made him uneasy, and at all events he wanted Lena alone. He saw her glance his way on a couple of occasions, and once she smiled, but she seemed to understand his discomfort and didn't wave him over.

And how do you know her, James?

Oh, I found the body. Police still think I did it too. See, I've got no alibi to speak of as such ...

As he hovered he caught scraps of talk from passers-by, most of it genuine sadness at the loss of the departed, but some were getting a black kind of thrill out of the murder. Paxton spotted one of the guys from the park, the neighbour's friend who'd been chatting to the reporter, standing close to Lena. She was laughing at something he'd said.

Paxton scowled. Probably had a deal going with the television networks, he thought with dislike. An inside scoop on the funeral. God, some people were bastards.

At last they all left. Lena waited as Paxton strolled up, and they turned and walked together across the waterlogged gravel.

'Nice speech,' he said. 'Best I've ever heard, anyway.'

She looked quietly pleased. 'Thanks ... And thanks for coming. I saw you at the funeral, but I never got a chance to say hi.'

'That's OK. But you should have got someone to edit your guest list.'

'Huh?'

'Some people are ghouls. You know that guy you were just chatting to?'

'You mean Jason? Do you know, he saw the cops come the night Dad died?'

'I know, I saw him hobnobbing with the press. I can't believe some people ...'

'What, you think he was after my story?' Lena scoffed. 'Come on, he was really lovely!'

'Yeah, and he's probably selling your nice little chat to TV3. Did he ask if you're on to the killer?'

She laughed again. 'You should have met him; you'd have got on really well. Turns out he was a patient of Dad's as well. He's been going to him since he was a kid. He felt so bad.'

Paxton tried to dredge up some sympathy and couldn't. 'Yeah, well. I had other friends to talk to. This is what I meant about your guest list. Gardner and DC Stirling came to say hi.'

She gave an angry frown. 'Sorry. If I'd seen them earlier I would have thrown them out. As it was I didn't notice until everyone was going to their seats. Vultures. They didn't threaten you again did they?'

'No more than usual.' He decided not to worry her with the truth just yet. Not really the appropriate time. 'Was the cremation your idea, or your father's?'

Lena looked amused. 'Dad's. My mother is —'

'A Catholic.'

Lena stared at him, her brow creasing. 'Did I —?'

'No. That was Mark.'

Now she was positively gawping, her words tumbling over themselves. 'You've spoken to him again? Was he at the funeral?'

'He saw you. Said to say you looked beautiful.'

Lena look stunned for a minute. Tears started forming in her eyes. She fiercely blinked them away, grimacing. 'No no no! You're going to think all I do is cry. I do it every time I see you. Every. Damn. Time! And this makes twice today.' She pulled out a tissue with a deprecating smile. 'God, I'm such a girl.'

Paxton considerately watched the path as she blew her nose. 'He's fine. He said to tell you that too. He's proud of you for the Presbyterian idea, but he wishes you'd thought of a black Mass 'cause that would *really* have pissed off your mum.'

She gave a laugh. 'Poor Mutti. She's really not so bad. And not so Catholic, or she'd never have divorced him ... Truth be told, someone offered to arrange it, and I wasn't in any state to say no.'

She walked along in pensive silence for a few moments. Then she glanced down at the funeral programme she still held in her hand. She crumpled it up along with her tissue, and threw them into a bin at the edge of the car park with palpable relief.

'Bloody *awful* photo ...'

Paxton grinned, and she grinned back at him. They were already at her car.

'D'you want to come back for a coffee? Or some tea? Whatever you feel like.' Paxton was twice as chuffed as he'd heard Mandy? Sandy? ask the same question and get turned down flat.

THE spare room, currently overflowing with bouquets and cards, had been empty for eighteen months now, ever since Lena's friend and fellow student Theresa had followed her authentically German boyfriend to Stuttgart. For Paxton, it held all too uneasy echoes of Lena's mother. *Auf Wiedersehen*, pet. That made three. A mother, then a best friend, then, in a no less final way, Lena's dad. Paxton had run from everyone he loved in England to come here. Lena had stayed right where she was, and everyone had abandoned her.

'So, did you never go to university?' Lena asked him curiously. 'You haven't said anything about it.'

'No.' Paxton shrugged, not elaborating. Now that his own past was up for discussion his enthusiasm vanished.

'Why not? It's not like you don't have the brains. You probably know a lot more than I do.'

'Lacked a proper sense of vocation, I guess. Even though that means I've spent much of the last decade behind bars ...'

'*Why?* It's such a waste!'

'Good way to see the world, though. The work's unchallenging — albeit sometimes to the point of brain death. Been through most of Europe, America, Australia ...'

'So why did you leave in the first place?' That brought him up short.

'Ahhh ...' Paxton sighed. 'There were a number of reasons.' He could see her curiosity grow and morph into concern at the look on his face.

He set his coffee down on the table, pressing the tips of his fingers together. 'Let's just say, there was one incident that tipped the scales on my unpopularity a bit ...'

His head went down without him even being aware of it.

FREAK ...

'I'd rather not talk about it. Some things are better left buried ... I'm a psychic — finally I've learned to admit *that*. But I never wanted to be a therapist.'

Lena took a breath, but Paxton was saved from the inevitable by the bleep of her mobile phone as a text message came in.

The signal reminded him to check his watch. He did a double take, getting out of his seat.

'Shit. I've got to go.'

'Oh bugger, I forgot you were working.'

She looked positively crestfallen. Paxton was delighted. At the same time as he opened his mouth to say, 'Do you think I could —?' she was already saying, 'Hey, can I —?' Both of them stopped and giggled.

'Do you think I could meet up with you sometime even if nobody's been murdered in the previous twenty-four hours?'

'It would make a nice change.'

He waited, and she said, 'They've given me an extra week off work. So ...'

'Well. You know where I live. But if you could do your stakeout on the lawn next time — that way I'll fit in with the neighbours.'

She blushed, laughing. 'Sorry.'

He smiled at her teasingly. 'You really are your father's daughter.'

She smiled back at him, genuine warmth without archness. Suddenly teasing was nowhere on his mind. They were standing very close. The warm floral smell of her perfume was worlds away from the funereal blooms in the church that morning. *It* was very much alive. He couldn't breathe. Without remembering presences or personal history, not even a 'sod Mark' in his brain, he bent his head and kissed her.

When he caught his breath, he said, 'Clever man, your dad. You do look beautiful today.'

He was horrendously late for work. And fuck if he could have cared less.

Chapter NINE

'BASTARD. GETS AN idea into his head and won't let it go. He's worse than a pit bull. But *they've* all been outlawed in this country.' Andy Stirling huffed down on the sofa with a bottle of Heineken, to hell with the weather. 'Wish I could cut bits off *his* scrote.'

'Have a nice funeral?' His wife Nicola stood over him, her arms folded, and a tolerant grin on her face. She was an ironic, easy-going woman with immense patience regarding her husband's duties. Even as a regular uniformed plod taking lumps from drunks with weapons, coming home black-eyed and bleeding, and especially now they kept him so often from home. And lately, in such a foul temper. Stirling left it a bit before replying, swilling his beer round in his mouth.

'Chief suspect turned up. Didn't expect *that*, I must say.'

'And that's pissed you off with Gardner?'

A frustrated expression settled on Stirling's face. He paused again, looking up at her. Feeling he was pleading his case. 'He's such a nice bloke! I *know*, what the fuck am I doing with a badge, but I just don't believe he did it. Even if he is a bit of a flake, what with all this psychic business. Dunno what that's all about. But there's something I can't put my finger on, if only I could bloody *think* what it was ... Frankly, I don't know what to think.'

He took another swig from the bottle, pissed off with his boss, his job, and for the sake of it everything that had ever crossed his path. Particularly as the beer wasn't chilled. Nicola sat on the arm of the sofa. At times like these, she wasn't the counsellor but the confessor. All she had to do was wait.

'He's roping me in to his little crusade against this guy, but the facts just don't fit. Apparently he's been matey with the victim's daughter, which sounds a bit suss I grant you, but I can't see any motive. We've done all the checks, it's not like she's hard-up for cash.'

'So why are you so worried? There's nothing you can do about it — if Gardner can't find the evidence, there's no way he can convict this guy.'

'I am worried, because bloody Gardner is a wanker to work with and is making my life a misery, not to mention this other bloke's ... Fucking acting like Dirty Harry with a carrot up his arse ...' He stopped, raising his head towards her. 'And because somewhere out there the guy Gardner *isn't* chasing is going to kill again. And keep doing it until Gardner realises he's after the wrong man. This is a serial job.' He shook his head. 'You can add gross negligence to the harassment charges. Plain as peanuts, Nic. That's not going to look good for the force, and it doesn't sit too well with me either.'

Moodily he swirled the bottle, which he noticed was almost empty. 'Try going to someone's dad's funeral, and practically getting involved in a stoush with one of the guests. Some days, Nic, I feel like a total shite.'

'And some days you get lucky.'

He tilted his head up at her, consideringly. 'It's been a while.' She smiled. 'Yes. It has ...' She was moving towards him. He quickly sculled down the beer and put down the bottle.

For a few particularly enjoyable moments he lost all recollection of anything else. But the thought returned as she broke from the kiss to pull him to his feet and down the hall, and remained lodged in his brain like a bullet, even as she slid her hands under his shirt, exploring tantalisingly lower. Distracting him from the task at hand, so to speak.

But there's something you have to remember ...

ALL the time he was on the treadmill he was thinking about the kill. The adrenaline rush had nothing to do with exercise. It had everything to do with murder. He'd tried it all, the sex, the drugs, the gym, but there was nothing like the release. Christ, he was almost getting hard. Again. The thrill of it was straining in his pants.

A hard-bodied blonde on the rowing machines provided his excuse, glancing with admiration in his direction. Dumb bitch. Little did she know.

The problem was, he was getting so addicted he almost went into withdrawal between hits. He knew he had to slow it down. The double killings of Wednesday and then Thursday night were too fast, too soon, though admittedly Wednesday had not been expected. Thursday night he'd been planning for ages; he'd picked out his location, gone back several times to check it was safe. Or as safe as murder could get, without being provincial cricket. But Wednesday ... had just fallen into his lap.

Lacked a bit of style, sure. The lead had been a lame attempt to make amends for the haste of the job. A gift from the dead man's hand. On the whole he thought he preferred strangulation. A little bit more personal, not to mention more of a challenge. Still, it was early days, and he'd long ago learnt not to turn down an opportunity whenever it came in his way.

What a buzz to see the whole thing in the papers. The vital statistics in print. Optometrist, late forties, male — but he'd realised *that* much — discovered with his dog in a park near Mission Bay. A random tragedy, they called it. The wrong place at the wrong time, murder by pot luck. Or Russian roulette, more like.

The dog had been even easier than he'd expected. Almost as dozy as the sluts he'd done in first. Cocking its leg off-lead on a tree, miles away from the target. Not a sound as he'd thumped its master, and one good kick had sent it hauling arse in fear. If it had stayed he'd have been tempted to add it to the tally.

Never mind. He was going to do it again. And this time, like the last, he was planning it all in advance. He wiped the droplets of sweat lining his lip, licking at the salt. Tasting almost the tang of blood.

He moved on to the weights. He was good at those — after years of effort, he should have been. Upper body strength was crucial, to the pleasure if not the work. Tonight he'd fantasise about wrapping those muscled arms around another throat. Thrashing out his plan of attack, one he'd tried before without success. He never slept much anyway; sleep was for the fags who couldn't hack the pace. Sleep was when you were vulnerable, and easy prey he was not. Never would be again.

No more uncles creeping into his room, moving his hands where they didn't want to go, fiddling and stroking and breathing hard and telling him it was all a precious secret. Don't tell, will you? You're a mate. I can trust you not to tell.

He hadn't told. He'd learnt.

He too could keep a secret. He too could get away with it. In fact, he could get away with murder.

On Monday he'd get away with it again. But someone else ... wouldn't be getting away at all ...

PAXTON woke Monday morning feeling exorcised of the ghosts of the previous week. So far, nothing from the police. On the other hand, plenty from Lena. On Sunday she'd arranged to meet friends, the ones from the funeral who'd so pissed him off. But now his feelings were distinctly more charitable. Sunday might have been theirs; he had her all of Monday. Strictly in a figurative sense at this stage, more was the pity. Lena had been very interested as to whether her father was watching her all the time. And where he went when he wasn't. Paxton did his best to answer her questions, not understanding half as much as he would have liked himself.

He stretched now, remembering their last goodnight …

Still, all of yesterday he'd had this restlessness gnawing in his stomach, which he couldn't trace back to any special source. Now his mind returned to it, it came creeping back. One purge wasn't enough — these demons were legion. He was thankful he'd never taken to those sorts of dreams that ended in screaming and trips to the map.

You'll find the body … *there*. Oh yeah, and *there*, 'cause its head's been whacked off by a guy with an axe and an ugly tattoo …

Prophetic visions were not his style. But all the same …

He got into the shower, soaking in the steam and the warmth of the water, and it was still there, drumming on him like the spray, that relentless impression of tragedy tiptoeing nearer. Something wasn't letting him be caught by it unawares.

Don't think it's over yet. We've scores to settle, mate. You never listened, but oh you will now …

He finally shut off the water and grabbed for his towel, shivering in the blast of cold air. No bathroom heater in this cheap rented crap-house. Might as well have hosed himself down outside. He dressed quickly, head down, ducking it, but the fear was a schoolyard bully. Not put off by such girly tactics.

He couldn't afford a subscription to the paper, but a stereo in the house he couldn't have done without. He switched the radio on to his usual pop-rock station, having never bothered to learn which ones had the news. On all other days, it was boring as shit. The morning DJs went through the usual hit-and-miss skits while he toasted his breakfast. The prank callers paid by the stations, the one obligatory song in half an hour, the sad-arse phone-ins from the public.

'Hey, Daniel, my missus is wild with me 'cause I gave my Coruba to the dog. What's that all about?'

And finally, the news.

'Great news for Kiwi film-makers — the government has agreed to allow further tax breaks for overseas investors looking to produce films in New Zealand. A spokeswoman for the New Zealand Film Commission has hailed the incentives as a welcome boost for the national industry, and there are predictions of substantial spin-offs for the local economy ... And are you a freak in the bedroom? A poll, conducted in Sweden, has revealed that eight per cent of all respondents prefer to —'

Shag goats in the shower? Paxton couldn't have given a toss. He hit the off button. It didn't seem his intuition had been gratified either.

Which only meant it would hang around until it was.

STACEY Ryan was not in the mood this morning. She was hung over from the party that had blended in to a few hours ago at her best friend Karen's flat. A couple of Archers, a lemon KGB, God knows how many glasses of bubbly ... And she was due behind reception at eight. The sun had barely risen, and now here she was doing an anti-clockwise circuit round the Panmure Basin, like every other morning of the year. At least, when she wasn't snowboarding down at Whakapapa with Matt.

Poor Matt. The piss-poor weather had meant a crap dandruff of snow and ongoing whiteouts. She hoped he wasn't looking for other diversions while he was down there, with no one to instruct. In snowboarding, anyway ...

Her head was pounding even harder than her feet. It was an addiction, and she probably needed help, but at least her thighs looked good. Confident in her model's body, with the carefully retouched blonde hair, she didn't worry so much about the less than stunning effect of her face. She needed to get up early for her run to allow enough time to do her make-up after.

At this time of day she was almost alone on the trail, except for the one solo dog-walker who'd nodded hello as she passed. She liked that. Out on the streets most people would just totally ignore you, but here everyone was friendly. The basin could do that to you. Even in the early dawn it was gorgeous. The tide was in, lapping round the mangroves and covering the unsightly acres of roots and muck. The sky wasn't rose pink, for once, hopefully meaning the days of shit weather were over for a while. The misty pale light was coming up lemon over the horizon, picking out the houses and trees on the opposite bank and flowing out across the water. It was nearly enough to make Stacey snap out of her hangover. It was soothing, nothing harsh enough to attack her bloodshot eyes and do damage to her head. The air was crisp and a little too cool, but her temperature was rising now and she scarcely even noticed.

Almost halfway, coming up to the little railway that ran by the lagoon in the summer and odd weekends.

A guy was there doing his stretches, from one of the exercise boards set up by the council to assist unimaginative health nuts for whom simply jogging wasn't enough. Stacey did them sometimes, but there was no way today. Not with the way her skull was splitting along the seams. She nodded to be friendly, catching his eye. Actually, he was kind of cute.

'Hello.' He was smiling, looking at her with a curious intensity. At her low v-neck and long legs. Checking her out. And she wasn't even wearing foundation. *Eat that, Matt*, she thought in triumph. *Maybe it doesn't matter if you screw round after all ...*

'Hi.' She slowed, bouncing on the spot, and he finished his exercises and joined her. 'Beautiful morning, isn't it?' She was a lot more enthusiastic than she had been. His hair was straight and dark, set off by amazing hazel eyes, brown rippled with green, beneath dark brows. Not half bad.

He turned his face up to the sky. 'I love this time of the morning. There aren't all the people to get in the way.'

She laughed. 'Yeah.' He jogged on, and she sped to catch up, giving him a sideways glance as she pulled even. 'Have I seen you around here before? Your face looks familiar.' She was beginning to remember. Once or twice she *had* seen him, doing his rounds of the basin. Then he had been sweating a bit from the exercise, but he looked cool as a cucumber now.

Climbing the uneven path that rose steeply above the basin, sheltered by the hardy native trees that raised fingers to the tidal spray all along the banks. A thick stand of them obscured the path from anyone below. Suddenly Stacey noticed he wasn't beside her anymore.

Her next thought was: *Oh my God, I'm going to die.*

The toned arm she'd admired from a distance looped around her neck. Like a harmless vine suddenly become a boa constrictor ...

Tightening inexorably in a noose that cut off air, and sound, and life. The hairs upon it were prickling, goosebumps pimpling the skin as the arm beneath flooded with adrenaline. She opened her mouth soundlessly, fighting to force breath first outwards to scream, and then, in a panic, to suck it inwards, to her aching lungs ...

But nothing came. Her eyes gaped wide in disbelief. Desperation. All the while struggling against him, a fish in a net. Realising she was just as helpless.

She couldn't scream, couldn't breathe, couldn't bite him, her chin forced up towards the sky that had looked so beautiful. The hem of sky brushing the hill was the yellow of an old bruise, rapidly draining of colour.

A whisper came in her ear, mocking. *Such a beautiful day.*

The curiosity she'd felt when she saw him, of what it would be like to have his body against hers, had now been cruelly answered.

Funny. She felt nothing at all ...

HE dragged her, down low, keeping her invisible to the growing trickle of cars on the opposite shore. The eastern suburbs were waking up. He slung her body into the shallow mud-coloured waters of the Tamaki Estuary, off the main track most people took. Only diehards and dog-walkers would find her along this part of the inlet. Swimmers went to the pools next door, where the pollutants were at least limited to piss and chlorine.

That had gone well. Even smoothly. And for what it was worth, he had even got to know her. Rather briefly, it was true. It wasn't as if she was that great at talking. She was beginning to get on his nerves; just a dumb blonde with Barbie doll tits. He'd heard more original conversation coming out of something with a pull-cord. The fact that she'd been out of breath hadn't helped. But he liked it. It added a new dimension. A bit like picking up a new skill in a computer game. Jacking the play up a notch.

Yes, he'd definitely try that again.

Chapter TEN

STIRLING WAS SCROLLING through the Internet, on the computer his colleagues in vice often used for checking out innocuously-named porn sites in the surfing logs of suspected paedophiles and upstanding schoolteachers. Little Miss Naughty was not just a cartoon ... It was supposed to be lunchtime, sometime round about two, but he'd barely made a dent in his ham sandwich. He was doing some research on psychics.

'Good sandwich, mate, or is the meat on the screen a bit juicier?' An unusually intelligent remark from a passing DC with crooked teeth and a worse haircut.

'Piss off, Scott.'

'It's just that you look so engrossed ...'

'Don't worry, I've bookmarked your page. Russian mail-order goats, wasn't it?'

He didn't really feel better about being caught visiting Ley on-Line — only $80 for an online reading — than he would have about being caught jerking off in front of kids. His nature, and even more, his training, had brought him to believe that whatever couldn't be substantiated by evidence was grounds for scepticism.

As to James Paxton ... Brick wall every time.

'Leave your naked girlies, Andy, and come with me.'

It was Gardner, looking even grimmer than usual. He'd sprung from out of nowhere, like the wicked fairy in a crap Christmas panto.

'What's up, Sergeant?'

'This way.' Gardner was tight-lipped. Matches your arse, Stirling thought.

With a sense of dread, he got up and followed the DS from the room. He brought his sandwich with him, eating fast.

Something in his boss's manner told him he wouldn't be too keen on finishing it afterward. Instead of his office, Gardner led him further down the hall, to the briefing room. Equally airless as windowless, at least it had more space. Something for which Stirling was thankful when he noticed Rees and Kirkpatrick were already there, waiting inside with a few others. DI William Woodward was standing at the head of the class.

Stirling knew then, before the first words were spoken, what they were going to be.

'We've got another one.' Woodward nodded at Stirling as he took a seat. 'Found face-down in the Tamaki Estuary, right by the Panmure Basin. Woman noticed her as she went along the path, and saw her hair. Looked too much like hair to be weed, she thought, and went down to have a look. Not something she'll be keen to repeat in a hurry. Corpse was pretty fresh — the murder took place this morning, but even so ...'

No one looks good fished out of a river.

'As cause of death appears to be strangulation, judging by the trauma round the throat, it's highly doubtful our witness was involved, being seventy-six years old.'

'Mainly out, she said, to exercise her bowel. I'm surprised she even saw what she did with those magnifying glasses she wears.' This was Detective Sergeant John Blundell, who had been the first plainclothes on the scene. He was a wiry little man who wore glasses himself. Stirling had worked with him a few times, and liked him OK. Methodical, if a bit uncreative.

'And the victim?'

It was Woodward who answered. 'I'm coming to that, Graeme. Young woman, thirty-one. Abandoned car at the scene, ID inside confirming her as one Stacey Ryan. Last seen very early this morning, leaving a friend's party, but she'd had a change of clothes since. Flatmate confirmed she liked jogging round the Panmure Basin. John and I thought she'd have been pretty tough to catch if she'd run. Looked like she lived in the gym, judging from the photos.'

'Yeah,' said Blundell. 'Looks like exercise can be a killer. Not for me, doing laps around the basin.'

'So why the big team of us here, sir? Can't you handle it?' Young DC Sean Coleman, who'd been at the scene. He'd been out of uniform even less time than Stirling. Not long enough to know you didn't rub Gardner up the wrong way, even by accident.

Gardner's lip curled as he answered. 'Because if you've been living on Planet Earth for the past week or so, Detective, you'll have realised some of us have been busy on murder inquiries. Both of which bear a strong resemblance to the incident in question. Sorry, or were you here for an interview at the caff? Down the hall, son, don't be late.'

Stirling realised his teeth would get blunt if he kept on like this. He consciously unclenched them.

'Sorry, sir.' Coleman quietly died in his chair, in the midst of his peers and superiors.

'All he's missing is a blue shirt for that vacant expression,' muttered Gardner. Then he realised: Woodward was wearing his inspector's uniform. 'Sorry, sir. No offence.'

'No worries, Ray. Must say, it goes well with *your* tie.'

Gardner looked down. Unluckily, the shirt he'd put on that morning was sky-blue. Stirling held down a grin. Rees didn't bother. It helped to be six foot four.

Woodward continued the briefing without further asides. The customary stuff; there's a probable serial killer on the prowl, we have to work together if we're going to nail him, no dicking around, fellas, this guy is sick. More grunts were being drafted in to help with the legwork.

'And you're so sure the first murder is part of this?' Kirkpatrick looked merely curious, wanting to hear his opinion.

They'd found bugger all on the Tan case. No clues, no witnesses. When you're desperate enough to drive through McDonald's at three in the morning, chances are you're not at your most observant. That applied to those who worked there as well.

Woodward looked at Gardner. 'Ray?'

'I think it's a fairly good bet. There's the dog lead from the Bradley case: the same fixation with the neck. And sure, the victim was male, while these later two are female, but how often is there a totally flawless pattern? I'd say he's honing a technique. Makes sense. Same — apparent — lack of motive, same window of time, early morning. In roughly the same general area ...'

For once, Stirling was inclined to agree. The same smell of twisted, ruthless malevolence surrounded all three.

'Copycat?' The detective who'd been the last man in charge of Stacey's body, throwing it in because it sounded good.

'The first corpse had barely cooled before they rung in the second. I hardly think that's a reasonable option.' Gardner cleared his throat. 'I'm positive the murders are linked, and I've told the DI that's how we're pursuing them at the moment.'

Woodward nodded. 'Ray's OC of the serial inquiry from now on. Operation Werewolf, for fairly obvious reasons. Anyone comes up with *any*thing on *any* of the cases, it goes back to Ray. All right? So let's bloody get out there and do it.'

Detective Inspector William Woodward was a no-nonsense kind of bloke, but one whom Stirling respected immensely. In private they called him Wooden Willy. Kick him anywhere and he wouldn't flinch. Straight as any copper on the beat. He was also bloody good at his job. This was another incentive for finding the killer. If they didn't, soon, there'd be some very serious questions asked.

Stirling caught up to Gardner as he strode down the hall. He could see the DS just about rolling his tongue over his shiny new promotion, as if he could already taste it.

'So, you still think Paxton is guilty?'

'Haven't interviewed him yet. But I will.' Gardner was smirking nastily. That same impulse to contradict him, no matter how irrational, rose up like bile in Stirling's throat.

'Do you want me to come with you?'

Gardner shrugged. 'If you like. Trying to get a reprieve from the hangman?' The smirk was back with knobs on. 'Anyone would think your missus ought to be jealous ...'

Stirling clamped his lips shut, knowing it was more than his job was worth. Though it was sure as hell worth more than they paid him. Gardner rolled his eyes in disdain, somehow contriving to look down his nose at him despite being fractionally shorter.

'Come on, Andy! The man's first on the scene of a murder, with a *very* poor excuse for a story, and he hooks up with the daughter of the victim and goes round probing the *other* family, tarted up like a psychic! Digging for dirt on the corpse, if you please! He's implicated at every bloody step.'

When Stirling said nothing, he hissed in disgust. 'Maybe it ought to be you in blue, Andy. You haven't got the balls for DC.' He opened the door to his office and stalked inside. 'Despite all the damn evidence, you still think I'm barking up the wrong tree.'

Stirling was suddenly inside the doorframe, wedging the door back open before he could shut it. '*What* did you say?'

'You heard me. You haven't got the balls —'

'No! No ...' Stirling would sort him out later for that, but for the moment his mind was distracted. He was jiggling like a toddler needing a wee. '*Barking!*'

'Well, to be quite honest, Andy ... I wasn't going to say anything ...'

'Dammit, Sarge, could you just listen!' Even that level of restraint was almost the death of him. 'Think about it! Bradley had his dog when he was attacked. Even if it's a crap guard dog, how was the killer to know that? Wouldn't you be afraid the dog would take your head off, or at the very least bark? Just think about it — if the dog started making a racket, there'd be neighbours all around to check out the problem. You'd be caught up to your elbows in blood. Guilty as a priest in a porn shop. And he didn't even bother to take the dog out ...'

Gardner's gaze was fixed on him. He said softly, 'What's your point, Andy?'

He knew full well. He was evil as fuck, but he wasn't stupid. 'Either our murderer was a Class-A moron ...'

'*Or*, he knew his victim.' Gardner regarded him thoughtfully. 'He knew the dog wasn't going to be a problem ...'

'I *knew* there was something. I knew it!' Stirling shook his fist for emphasis, parking on Gardner's desk. 'It's been bugging me for days. Believe me now, Sarge? Paxton couldn't have done it. He didn't even meet Lena Bradley until after.'

Gardner exhaled, a pitying look fogging over his face. 'Oh dear, Andy. You had me impressed there for a minute.'

'Eh?'

'A bugger in black leather spattered with bone chips, holding a chainsaw dripping blood, could look you straight in the eye and say, "Sorry, bro, dunno who carved up all them fuckers over there, eh?" And ten to one, you'd give him the number for trauma counselling and a sit-down with a nice cup of tea. Christ Almighty, Andy!'

Stirling stared at him in disbelief. 'Look —' *you fucking radio-controlled piece of shit*, 'I know when I'm being lied to, all right? And —'

'All right, Andy, let's go. Let's see how he talks himself out of this one. And if he can't ...'

Stirling played along tiredly. 'You're hauling him in.'

'See? Even *you* got that one.'

'THIS constitutes fucking harassment, you know. If you had even half a leg to stand on you'd be charging me and dragging me down to the station, not constantly trailing from my arse like stuck bog paper.' Paxton was sick of humouring their mindless-as-hell mind games. Although in the context of Gardner, 'humouring' was a huge misnomer.

'Mind your language, sir, all we want is a few quick questions.' Very much the aggrieved man of the law. Upright. Upstanding.

And up himself. Paxton wanted nothing more than to shut the door on that false whitewashed facade, with its eyes like two hard currants in an undercooked bun.

'Right. You can ask them from the doorstep.'

'Sir.'

Stirling said it softly, in a tone that could have been warning, reproach, apology or all three. Again, Paxton felt sorry for him. He too was obliged to co-operate. Toe the line or have his toes trodden on ...

He stepped away from the door, pointedly calling back, 'Another coffee, Mr Stirling?'

'Uh ... not today, thank you, Mr Paxton. We won't be staying long.'

Paxton looked over his shoulder to see those sunken currants glittering with rage.

Stirling continued calmly, 'Just a few quick questions, like the Sergeant said.' He didn't dare smile at Gardner, keeping his features neutral.

Take that, you bastard.

The cut-price sofa creaked as the cops sat down. It was the only seat in the room, so Paxton remained standing. At least he was on the right level.

''Nother murder, was there?' Paxton kept things simple.

'This morning. Mind telling us where you were?'

'Mind telling me why you're asking?'

'Just answer the question, please, Mr Paxton.'

'Home. Depending on when, either in bed or in the shower. Hang on, and I took a couple of minutes to have a crap ...'

'Watch your attitude, Mr Paxton.' Gardner's voice was sharp; he seemed to have a temper permanently idling just below meltdown. 'Unless you have some very good witnesses willing to testify in your favour.'

Paxton had had more than enough. 'What I don't understand is why you're constantly on my arse — excuse me, *bottom* — when all I've done is report finding a body in the park. I mean, what do you do when little old ladies have their bags pinched? Check it wasn't a set-up and the bag wasn't stuffed with P? Dozens of sweet-looking pensioners could be running drugs in between bingo tournaments! Shit, why don't you infiltrate rest homes? Do a crack-down on these bitches?'

Gardner was positively snarling. 'That's your alibi, is it? You were home.'

'From knock-off last night until now.'

'Anyone to verify that?'

This was frustrating, but it had to be admitted. 'No. As you very well know, I work late. And I don't exactly drop in to the neighbours' every week for a chat and the loan of some flour. Have you seen number 24? They're in the manufacture of high-grade pharmaceuticals!'

'So no one can confirm your whereabouts.' No one said it. So it just sat there.

Again.

'Well, *one* of the neighbours might have seen something.'

'We'll ask them.'

Correction, Stirling thought. I will. You'll be kicking your feet up in the car.

Gardner was growing almost chatty. 'And this psychic business of yours, Mr Paxton. Care to explain a little bit about it?'

Of all topics, Paxton's least favourite. 'Right, yeah. I see dead people. Well actually, no, I just hear them. Doesn't have quite the same ring to it, does it?'

'So you've spoken to the victims, have you? Either of them told you who dunnit?' A grin was smeared all over his face.

Paxton answered shortly. 'Mark Bradley, I have. But the attacker came from behind. He didn't see anything until afterwards, and even then not much. Besides which, it was dark.'

'And Gloria Tan ...?'

'Nothing. I never spoke to her. Her parents refused to allow it, and I respected their wishes.'

'And what did Miss Bradley want with you?'

Paxton was relieved he didn't seem interested in how they had come upon Gloria's address. He kept his words formal; a proper statement.

'I came to offer my condolences ...' He gritted his teeth, bracing himself. 'In accordance with Mark's request. She seemed intrigued by my ability and wanted to see if we could trace the killer by the same method. Part of the grieving process, I guess. I couldn't blame her.'

The truth, no more, no less. But Gardner wasn't interested in that either.

'Oh really? So you'd never met before you found Mark's body?'

'No.'

'And you'd never met Mark?'

'No.'

'So why did *he* speak to you and not Gloria?'

Paxton could feel his sap rising, and tried to tamp it down. 'It doesn't work like that. I can't just dial up the spirit hotline and natter away to whoever I want. They have to *want* to talk to me, there has to be some sort of link. And Gloria had already gone.'

'And why did Mark want you to find his daughter?'

'Because he was afraid for her. He wanted to reassure her — that was the sort of man he was.'

'And all this you know only through communicating with him ...' The sceptical smirk widened. 'From beyond the grave?'

Paxton stood up. He was fucked off with the attitude and the circular questions. From both reporters and cops who'd need a microscope to find their own dicks.

'Are you going to charge me?'

Gardner looked nicely startled. 'Why? Got something to confess?'

Paxton just shook his head, his tongue sticking with filth.

'Well. We'll be getting along to the neighbours' then.'

Stirling spoke up seriously. 'Sure none of them could vouch for you?'

'Sorry mate, but I'm a wee bit shy, and I've been in the place all of six months.'

Now Gardner looked interested. 'Oh? And where were you before that?'

'In a couple of rental places around here — and before then, I was travelling round the country. Longest I stayed anywhere before this was Wellington. Arsehole of a place. Only flat surface was the airport out. But I was there a few weeks. Name reminded me of home.'

He immediately felt a twat for admitting it. Like admitting to taking cuddly toys to bed. Though truth be told, they *were* the last things he'd had in his bed.

Gardner and Stirling were looking confused.

'Wellington's my home town, sort of. It's part of Telford. Near Shrewsbury.'

'Oh — like the biscuit.'

Paxton was getting resigned to that. At least he wasn't from Worcester.

'Thank you, sir,' said Stirling. He seemed anxious to leave. 'Sorry to bother you again. We do try to be thorough, that's all. We all want this murderer found.'

Paxton could have made a retort, but it wasn't the constable's fault. Gardner turned suddenly, as if something had just occurred to him.

'Did Mr Bradley's dog bark when you found him?'

Paxton stared. 'Barked his head off. He was spooked. Scared the crap out of me for a moment. Even the people across the road said they heard it.'

He saw the DC throw Gardner a look. The sergeant's face curdled. He turned back to the door without saying another word.

Paxton abruptly remembered. 'By the way, where *was* this new murder?'

Stirling answered him. 'Panmure Basin. Or just about. She was dumped in the estuary.' The DC stopped, choosing his phrasing. 'But I would advise you, sir, not to go asking around. Leave it to us.'

This time it was unequivocally a warning.

Chapter ELEVEN

'DAD WAS KILLED by a *friend*?'

'Or at least someone he knows. I dunno — it's a possibility. I've been thinking it over, and that's the only reason I can come up with for why they'd be interested. How many people do you think would know your dog's such a softy?'

Lena looked chilled. Just when she'd thought all was clear, another fall of rocks to pick her way over. Trying not to tumble into the abyss ...

'I wondered why they wanted to know. I told them Glen doesn't usually bark at strangers, unless they ring the doorbell. But if Dad was threatened I'm sure he would have.' She looked at the dog, who was lying with his head on his paws, looking incapable of anything more energetic than scratching himself. She said, half to herself, 'His best mate was a guy called Colin — Colin Davenport.' Paxton vaguely remembered him from the funeral. His eulogy had been very convincing.

'I don't see him bumping Dad off. Christ, I mean ... he runs a firm that fixes and sells computers. And who are the other suspects? A bunch of optometrists!'

Paxton agreed. That was a bit of a problem. There might be a few sharks and heavy breathers among the fraternity, but how many optometrists could you visualise terrorising a community? It was like suspecting the Girl Guides of ritual sacrifice. Mind you, the girl down the road in Telford had been a total bitch. He wouldn't have put ritual killings past Megan Lindsay.

Ju-ju Jimmy, Ju-ju Jimmy,
Pushed his granny down the chimney,
After that
He skinned the cat,
Then ate them both with steak and kidney ...

Lena bit her lip, in a different past. 'I've been gone from Dad's a couple of years now. I admit I don't know everything any more. But I saw him pretty often — I spoke to him almost every day. To the best of my knowledge, no one, absolutely no one, had any reason to kill him. I've been through all this in my mind so many times!'

Paxton sighed. Any more dead ends and he'd start knocking walls down. 'He didn't owe money? Didn't get promoted over anyone? Didn't shag anyone else's wife?'

Lena snorted. 'He didn't shag his own wife. Why do you think I'm the only child?'

'All right. So who would know? Do we go and interview his colleagues at the clinic?'

Lena considered this. 'Mmm. It's the only way I can see ... But I can't, I just can't suspect either of them of doing anything. The only thing is they might have a few clues as to who'd bear a grudge.' She made a face. 'God, this feels so Agatha Christie.'

'Hell of a lot safer in Auckland than a small English village. Johannesburg has nothing on St. Mary Mead. Cesspool of violence and depravity. Full of sex-crazed crack-hos in twinsets.'

'Don't tell me ... You've read all eighty-odd.'

'I read a lot as a kid. Was either books or the bloke in the tunic. Interesting fellow, Septus ... but not much into riding a bike.'

Lena was looking at him strangely. 'You kidding?'

Shit. He could have bitten off his own tongue. Here was the reason he was still a virgin at twenty-nine. He could probably add a while on to that. 'Nope.'

He looked elsewhere, not caring to see her expression. 'Bloody hell.'

He said brusquely, 'Haven't seen him since I was eleven. Or anyone else, thank God. For some reason kids can see a lot more than we can. They're not smart enough to stay ignorant.'

'So —'

He cut her off, dismissing the subject. 'Shall we get a move on? You'll have a busy afternoon.' Today Lena had finally decided to sort through her father's effects.

In any case the afternoon had already been ruined. Whatever he'd been planning, romance was no longer on the cards. Yet again the tarot figure of Death loomed up to raise a bony finger at the spook.

THERE were no ghouls prowling round the basin. Few but the neighbours knew of any crime; a blessed silence that couldn't last long. This one would make tonight's news on every channel. The local media had Stalin backwards. One murder was a statistic. Many were a tragedy — and therefore, a story. Despite the police media blackout, the whispers were already doing the rounds of the newsrooms. *Serial killer on the loose. Three dead — that we know about. Oh my God, we've finally become like America.*

The graduation of New Zealand society to grown-up status could be measured in the nature of its crimes.

For Paxton, the media hush extended to the shores of the basin. He stood there, the toes of his sneakers jutting over the water, feeling nothing but stupid. 'Not here. Stirling said she was found actually in the estuary.' Lena trailed him along the path, to where one track split off to follow the Tamaki Estuary.

The imagery was beautiful. Here, at the crossroads, Paxton had his epiphany.

Bursts of chatter broke in on his consciousness, scratchy and faint like a radio a couple of points off the station.

Such a beautiful day ...

He said ...

The event was set into the mudflats like a swearword on a concrete path. A violation for every part of the earth.

Information came roaring at Paxton, gushing, a high tide of it overflowing the banks.

He said aloud, 'She was with him — they were talking. It was like they were friends. But no, that's not right. He was familiar ... but she didn't know him.'

He kept his eyes on the scummy brown waters of the estuary, not looking for Lena's reaction.

'I'm sensing this trust. More of an interest, really ... I'm getting a warmth. No feeling at all of something bad going to happen.' His voice changed. 'And then — shock. Fear, overwhelming ... *Oh my God, I'm going to die, I'm going to die ...*'

He clutched at his throat, severing the connection. He stood for a moment, catching his breath. Trying to will the hairs on his arm flat.

His neck felt like it had been crushed in a vice. He blinked, glancing over his shoulder. Lena looked shaken, and he could see coming from her that desire to run, that terrified itching at the balls of her feet.

Still rubbing his throat, he muttered, 'And she did ... He strangled her.'

He grimaced a little at the memory of the choking. It was the first time he had ever known anything like it.

'Are you all right?'

Her body language was jerky, wrong. She seemed more in need of comfort than he did. It was a common enough response. He did have the longer experience.

'I'm fine. Just a little off balance. That's never happened before.'

'What hasn't?'

'That feeling as though I were being strangled. My air was cut off, it was horrible. The woman, whoever she was, was trying to tell me that's how she died ... Gave me the willies.' He stared at the ground trying to shake off the residual unease.

'You're sure you're OK?'

'Yeah.'

Lena looked doubtful, thoroughly unsettled by the violence of his reaction. A beat, then he raised his head, lifting his arms out wide and letting them slap down at his sides. 'Come on, let's go. She's too weak to talk, and what she knows isn't worth all the trouble.'

He started along the path, taking the fork that led back to the car park.

'You're sure?' She caught herself, horrified. 'I mean, I don't want you to —'

'No, I'm all right. Really. Nothing I couldn't handle. But honestly, she didn't know who he was. Just some guy.'

'But what about that feeling ...?'

'The warmth? Yeah, there was that.' Paxton frowned. 'Strange. Not in any way threatening.'

'You don't think —? No.'

'No, what?'

She went on, tentatively. 'She was attracted to him? Would that cause it? Must be strong to be strangling those women. And if he were a twenty-stone stranger she'd be unlikely to trust him. I bloody well wouldn't. Stands to reason he's got a nice body. I mean, if he's not threatening, and she's seen him before ... Probably he's been jogging round the basin before, a bit of a fitness freak.'

'Bit of a lady-killer, you mean?' He said it without thinking.

She didn't smile. 'Not *just* ladies, James.'

'No ...'

He'd be bloody glad to get out of here. Attempts to lighten the atmosphere were merely waving sticks of incense through toxic smoke. Now that he'd found it, death hung heavy from his neck. He was extra conscious of every swallow.

He shifted into gear and drove out of the small parking area. Away from the scene suddenly everything was much easier, including his breathing. He reckoned without the traffic. As he moved out of Lagoon Drive he braked sharply to avoid being sideswiped by an Auckland driver in a van at the Panmure roundabout, a more likely site for violent death than the one they'd just visited.

'Fuck me *sideways*! Crazy bastard.'

Lena exhaled through her teeth, swearing under her breath.

But all the tension was dispelled like magic. When their pulses had returned to normal, she smiled at him with a trace of sympathy.

'Throat feeling better?'

'Yeah.' He grimaced again. 'Just thankful she didn't get savaged by wolves.'

'Or she wasn't killed by a kick in the gonads ...'

Paxton struggled not to grin. 'Didn't know chicks had those, actually.'

'A lot you don't know ...'

SOME years previously Ray Gardner, then mere DC Gardner, had been chummy with a fellow detective by the name of Chris Hallam. They'd made the switch from uniform at almost the same time, and the shared head-ons with the brass at the top and the unexpected rigours of the job had given them a sort of kinship. It's difficult to come across a rape victim, smacked senseless and left for dead, festering in her own shit, without forming some kind of bond. Especially when the call-out is from her eight-year-old kid. Being the eldest.

Hallam was a dedicated copper, thorough and bull-headed and tireless, and Gardner had admired him for it, seeing many of the same qualities in himself. But Hallam had long since left Auckland's CIB for the swishier digs of the Met in London. Another instance of the brain drain that Gardner deplored.

However, it had its uses. Now whenever he needed a hand with something outside his jurisdiction, Hallam could always be relied on for contacts and advice. And once again, he'd delivered.

'Bless you, Saint Christopher, bless you ...'

Gardner looked at the email filling the screen, muttering to himself in what almost amounted to awe. Hallam had pulled a few strings with an acquaintance in the West Midlands police, who had got on to a mate from Shropshire who just happened to live in Paxton's old local ...

This was police co-operation, if you liked. Pint politics. No red tape required. All the usual channels neatly bypassed and the real dirt raked into the open.

And Gardner had to admit, there was dirt. He clicked his mouse down the page. Hallam's source seemed to have derived some enjoyment from his task. There was quite a story.

Neighbours had spoken of an uncommunicative boy; if not exactly a Nigel No-mates, then something very close. Few real friends. Quite a few stories witnessed first-hand, and many more of the 'I heard down the pub' description.

I heard down the pub, that Paxton boy calls up demons ...

Nah, love, that's rubbish. Talks to himself a bit, but ...

Sumthink funny about him, all right. Wouldn't want to be alone with him in a dark room, if you know what I mean.

Confirmed by several, all reliable types, the story that someone's dead granny had passed on a message that Kirsty had better stop messing about with that Clark boy and stick with Mike because if she kept on like she was with both of them she was bound to get herself up the duff shortly and Justin Clark could never support them both with that bleedin' drug habit of his ...

Five-year-old James had reduced the neighbour's girl Kirsty to tears of humiliation, though at the time the boy had said he didn't even know what it meant. Simply a matter of reciting verbatim the blank verse filling his head. It was just one example of many. As Paxton had grown older the stories grew more far-fetched but less verifiable, except for the one involving his entire class, corroborated by a retired schoolteacher. Gardner took his hat off. *That* was creative. Centuries-old murderesses? Not bad for a kid of fourteen.

And finally, the straw that broke the camel's back.

Paxton had never been a typical Shropshire lad. Never conformed to any type at all. That was precisely the problem. He wasn't the cosy, tea-and-biscuits old gran of a medium like Doris Stokes, who went on the telly. Nor did he set up like a proper psychic and offer readings at fifty pounds a pop. He didn't belong to any associations, or give demonstrations. He didn't even own a tarot deck. Instead he kept himself private, and refused to say what he knew. There was no way of knowing what went on inside his head, behind those dark eyes.

But Cheryl Nichols had always batted down the scoffers. They never dared mock him in her pub.

Gerroff home and see to your own crystal balls. They'll have fossilised by now, from lack of use ...

They were colleagues, and seemingly good mates. Paxton had also got on well with her husband David, who always dropped by the Cock's Head for lunch. Until the day he simply dropped dead ... He'd built up her faith, her dependence, while she was at her lowest, going on some spiritual power trip until she was unable to wipe her backside without the guru's say-so. Then cruelly he'd thrown her off. In front of a full house of witnesses, shouting, when she'd laid a hand on his arm. She'd lost her balance, ploughed straight into the wall. And then he'd done a runner while she sat there, weeping fit to burst.

He claimed she was stalking him. That it was her fault he'd had to leave for the restaurant in Wolverhampton; harassing him at work, leaving endless messages, turning up everywhere he went. Funny, then, that the word FREAK had been spray-painted on *his* lawn. Cheryl Nichols had been well liked round Telford; they all said she'd changed since the day she started consulting James Paxton. And not for the better.

In all his years on the force, Gardner had come across dozens like her. Gang bitches and battered wives, or just the frightened victims of emotional terrorism, so brainwashed by the tyranny they'd come to believe in their own need for it, their own deserving of yet another thrashing to keep them in line. So thirsty for acknowledgement they were grateful for abuse. Some of the bruising was internal, nothing on show, but that didn't make it any less brutal.

Voices had spoken up for and against James Paxton, but Gardner knew which ones to listen to.

Psychic, no. He didn't believe in that shit. Psychological issues, most definitely. Paxton fit all the criteria for one sick piece of filth.

That Bradley girl was in some trouble.

Chapter TWELVE

CURRIE JACOBSON KNOWLES was in a multi-storey building on Shortland Street, one of those old and now very trendy locations downtown. The street was known throughout the country thanks to a dire local soap. *Shortland Street* cut everyone's grass — styling itself on *ER*, naming itself after *Coro Street* and generally being an equally big pile of crap. Paxton never heard the boast 'something million viewers can't be wrong' without an incredulous snort.

Unlike the telly drama, the solicitors' had taste. From the antique but perfectly maintained lift in the foyer downstairs, to the muted green carpeting of the offices themselves, everything spoke of money.

Paxton remained seated in one of the plush-covered chairs as Lena got up to meet the solicitor. He felt uncomfortable intruding. It was a little like sitting in on someone else's colonoscopy. You were kind of surplus to requirements and not really enjoying it any more than they were.

'I'll wait here if you like.'

'It's OK. Not like I've got anything left to hide, is it?'

Paxton glanced at the table beside his chair. The choice of magazines was between *Hello!, The Cut* golfing monthly, and *House and Garden*. He got up.

Mark's solicitor was Duncan Knowles, the usual dry old stick of a solicitor Paxton couldn't imagine a metre away from his desk. Dental-filling-grey hair, what there was left of it, too many dinners he hadn't had to pay for sitting round his waist, and specs that shrank his pupils to pinheads. But his eye was kind enough as he condoled with Lena over her loss, and he got down to business with an admirable directness Paxton would never have expected from anyone trained in the law.

The will itself was straightforward. A painting to Mark's ex-wife, a good one he'd bought for her birthday. The same one he'd refused to send on to Switzerland when she'd phoned up to ask. His share of the practice equally to his two colleagues, Phillip Vaughan and Ngaire Alexander, who would be notified in due course. The remainder to Lena. He hadn't been the sort to patronise golf clubs, or swing them, and he'd put in donations to the charities regularly during his life, so he was buggered if he was doing it after his death as well.

Lena could almost hear his declarations in her head. She wondered, briefly, if James would be able to.

But nothing, anywhere, to suggest anyone might have had a motive for taking his life.

Try as she might, she couldn't believe it. She pictured genial old Phil Vaughan and sweet, rather serious Ngaire, happily married to a well-off accountant with three kids. The idea of their ordering a hit was ludicrous. Like contemplating the arrest of a homicidal Care Bear. Her mind wouldn't quite twist round it. And as for the other murders … The word kept popping up: *senseless*.

'Well, all the best, Miss Bradley. Get in touch again in a few days, just to let me know how things are going.'

'Thank you, Duncan. I appreciate it.'

'Nice to meet you, Mr Paxton.'

He shook hands with faultless good manners, the family solicitor who would never, on any occasion, presume to use first names. The shelves of binders probably swung out to reveal a bed set into the wall.

Lena was quiet on the way back to Mark's. Staring out the window. Not caring that she was now considerably richer. Yesterday, her hands had clung to the objects she was supposed to be packing away, her eyes going distant as she recalled memories which Paxton could never share. From time to time she'd give a sigh. Those little cries of delight or regret that told him he might as well be in the next room: they were not aimed at him.

'Oh, look! The knight from Prague! I'd forgotten we even had him!'

For years it had been her house too, these things had in part been hers. Now they were solely hers. It was a huge weight to suddenly find dumped in her lap.

Today was more of the same. He wrapped newspaper round whatever she told him to, packing it carefully away in marked boxes, and made her tea every few hours. Reminded her to drink it when she forgot.

He glanced at the clock and his stomach gurgled as if by reflex. Six o'clock, and they hadn't stopped for lunch. Two seconds ago he hadn't noticed; now all of a sudden he was ravenous.

'How about we take a break for a bit? D'you fancy Chinese?'

She glanced up, almost guiltily, from a pile of faded paperbacks she seemed more intent on reading than packing. 'Um ... yeah. Good idea. What do you want, fried rice?'

'I'll grab a couple of things. I'm famished.'

'OK. I'm easy, I'll eat anything.'

'Including half of mine. Next time we go to a café I'm ordering two lemon tarts.'

She gave a laugh, sheepishly ducking her head.

'"Ooh, I might just have a taste," she says ... Knew I shouldn't have offered you any.'

She raised her head again. 'You still here?'

He left her in the middle of the living room floor, in a sea of newsprint. Away from the house the solitude was extreme. Paxton drove on auto-pilot, sunk in memories of his own.

The spaces outside the shops were full when he arrived. Paxton slowed, wavering. He could easily have parked on the street. Instead he flicked his blinkers off and kept going. Back to his own place.

Was it too early? But then, they'd always been early risers. A civil servant and a schoolteacher. He could have used the phone at Mark's, but he'd have felt somehow heartless, using the phone of a dead man to make toll calls. Having the estate pick up the tab for what he really should have done long ago.

Twelve hours' difference — he literally was on the opposite side of the world. The arse end, if you asked Alan Paxton.

His dad answered. 'Hello?'

'Dad.'

There was a pause, not owing to the time lag from Britain.

'My God! And it's not even my birthday! Cath, love, it's James.'

There was so much astonished delight in his father's voice, clear as a bell through the satellite, that Paxton almost cried. There was popping at the other end while his parents mucked about with the speaker.

'Hello? Hello, are you still there?'

'Hi, Mum. Didn't wake you up, did I?' He smiled at the anxiety in her voice. He doubted either of them could work the DVD player with him gone. Netflix would scare them witless.

'Oh, don't worry about that. Time we were getting up anyway. Oh love, it's so good to hear from you! Nothing's wrong, is it?' The anxiety was back, and made him smile again. A touch of ruefulness in it this time. Worry often marked Cathy Paxton's attitude when it came to her son.

'Er ...' To be honest, he hadn't really thought what he'd tell them. The contact had been enough. 'No. No. Just thought it was high time I gave you a ring, that's all.'

'Are you still in Auckland?' That was his dad. 'Or have you decided that's as big a hole as Wellington?'

'Which one?'

'Arrr! The one you're talking out of.'

His mother cut back in, seizing her chance to talk.

'Did you get that job you were going for? Some sort of pub, wasn't it? I remember you telling me about that when you rang on my birthday.'

Christ. It *had* been a while. He'd been at Anubis nearly six months.

'Yeah, I got it. Place is called Anubis. It's not too bad, actually. Better than most places I've worked. I've even made a few friends.'

'That's great, love!'

'Met a girl, too ...'

And it all came out. About Lena. Not about the circumstances surrounding their meeting. Just that she was gorgeous as hell, funny, and had just lost her dad in an accident. As much as he could he kept the details to himself, not willing to remind them too strongly of the awkwardness when he'd left.

They'd tried to understand, given him their love anyway despite all the stares and the silences, but the fact was he was an embarrassment. Always the granddad who broke wind in company. Or the cherub-faced tot who looked up the vicar's dress in church. Like his mother's mother, dearly loved but not without pain.

They were thrilled about Lena, though. Probably also that he wasn't gay. He'd taken his time about it. They wanted to talk to her next time. Especially his mother. He had his sister to thank for already stoking her grandmotherly instincts. She'd be flocking over to Walthamstow shortly, perching over the crib with hand-knitted booties and dolls' dresses like a buzzard in reverse. As he'd known it would, it came.

'And Natalie's well. Due in a couple of weeks, now; I can't get over it. Where's the time gone?'

'Mmm.'

'She and Hamish are so excited. I haven't been to see them for ages; money's a bit tight at the moment. But I'm going to stay with them in a few days, just till she's on her feet again. She's told me it's a boy!' Not the dresses, then. Hopefully. 'Hamish is over the moon ... Have you talked to her at all?'

'Rang her on her birthday, same as you. Say hi to her and Aimless.'

As a kid his older sister Natalie had threatened to bash his head in if he ever 'used his powers' on her, although that didn't stop her asking about blokes. A pity she hadn't asked him about her current husband. A wanker if ever there was one.

Hamish worked for a construction company. Made an all right living, but he was a man's man, with his one eye fixed firmly up his buttocks. With the proverbial builder's crack he could probably see you coming *and* going. Paxton had said that to his face once, and just about had his taken off.

Hamish had no time for girly poofs like Paxton, who didn't even support Arsenhole. And once Natalie had told him about the other things her brother did, that was it. He made one or two cracks on the subject, proudly displaying his ignorance, then hardly had another word to say to him. Paxton could see Hamish tense whenever Paxton came into his presence. How did one act around a nutter? Wasn't going to be like one of those epileptics, was he, going into fits and dribbling all over the floor?

The increased distance suited Paxton just fine.

But there were just the two of them, him and Nat, and she'd only been a bitch during puberty, same as every other bloke's sister. She didn't deserve Hamish. Cocky Cockney cunt. Well, that was slightly unfair. Hamish was from North London. But two out of three wasn't bad.

'Um ... Sorry to end it like this, but Lena's expecting me.' He didn't say he was only supposed to have popped out for a takeaway. 'But, what with everything going on ... I wanted to talk to you. It's been good to hear your voices.'

He meant it. And felt worse when both of them thanked him so gratefully for calling, saying nothing of how long he'd left it without even passing on his new number.

'Take care, son. Good to hear from you.'

'And send us photos of this Lena, won't you?'

'Doubting my word, Mum?'

'No, I'm not, no ...'

'Just make sure *you're* in the photo too, son.'

'Thanks.'

'And the Loch Ness Monster ...' Paxton hung up.

Chapter THIRTEEN

FASCINATING THING, THE Internet. For the one fee per month you could tap into a seething vastness of knowledge that in decades past would have been totally beyond reach. Somewhere on the net there were doubtless instructions on how to get hold of anthrax for your biological nuke-making kit. Some were probably even in the same alphabet. He hadn't looked. He no longer needed weapons for the games he liked to play.

The screen went blank as he shut down the computer. Six o'clock and time to go. He rubbed his eyes to rid them of the itch. Hours of nigh unblinking concentration played havoc with his contacts, which the glare of monitors and fluorescent lights only made worse. He didn't keep the normal nine to five, and knew few who did. One of those cultural myths, along with the nuclear family or true love. But these days he liked to save plenty of time in the evening for recreation. A man had to have a hobby. For most men the length of the country it was rugby. He too liked blood sports. It was just that his tastes were a little more refined. In fact these days there was no need for blood at all. If he played his cards right.

He walked out of the building, nodding goodbye to the few people who acknowledged him. Computer geeks most of them; wouldn't say hi unless you gave them the Vulcan salute. Wankers. He couldn't believe who he worked with. Come to that, they probably wouldn't either ...

One bonus of the job was the free parking. He liked that there was a space reserved for him. It seemed appropriate. He bleeped the alarm and slid into his car, a red HSV that almost made the earth tremble when it was started. He could be subtle when the situation called for it — but otherwise, why bother?

Pulling straight into rush-hour traffic, blending in with the other how-big-is-my-dick-mobiles — of which quite a number were driven by women — he headed for the gridlock of Symonds Street. Between five and seven the street was a virtual carpark, but for all that it managed bursts of loveliness, edged on both sides with mature plane trees that were green and shady in summer, and breath-taking even as they choked the gutters with bronzey leaves in the autumn. They wrecked the paths with aggressive roots, caused countless pedestrians to slip unwarily arse over tit on a slick of sodden leaves, and yet for all that they commanded the respect of age and beauty, standing still even though the villas that once stood among them had long since been built over, moved out or converted into obscure academic departments.

The university was Symonds Street's main claim to fame now. The University of Auckland, New Zealand's largest, boasting tens of thousands of students. The campus was peopled with anonymous, badly-dressed drones, fleeced like sheep for fees and plodding with oversized backpacks to their dull-as-shit lectures and labs.

But one, a very lucky *one,* was due for selection. With a very special fate in store ...

On the corner of Symonds Street where it flowed down the hill into Anzac Ave stood St Andrews, a lovely faux neoclassical relic of Presbyterianism from the Victorian era. Doric columns and a tower from the front, from the side a humbler block of bluestone. Recently, even more startling changes had rumbled its bastardised stones. Regular services were now conducted in Indonesian.

The buses that stopped alongside it were not quite so regular, as he remembered from his own university days. Even at night there were always a few students loitering late with cellos in their body bags and trumpets from the School of Music nearby or, more sadly, PhD students who'd stayed after hours to work on theses on the lives of the poets. The sort from Athens, 3000 BC.

No point offing *them*, he thought. They'd probably fucking thank him. And if they didn't, they were already socially dead.

In front of Classics and History, both Ancient and Modern, a small carpark lay in the shadow of St Andrews. Staff and permit-holders only; it was unfortunately locked, a bar pulled across and padlocked. However, next to it was a discreet little driveway, which led down to the church offices tucked back from the road. Yellow 'No Parking' notices were painted all over it. But at this time of night, who cared? As he pulled in behind a skeletal tree he had a sliver of Symonds Street in view, a bench smack bang in the middle of it. He killed the lights and waited.

He'd stopped off at the Subway up the road earlier, and whiled away the time with a foot-long and a Sprite. Watching arrivals and departures, much like the people who picnicked at the lookout by the airport. But not as damn sad. Watching was a lifelong habit. First to see how others acted, an exercise in mimicry for the boy who wanted so much to be the same. And now, when it had all become so easy, just for the sheer fun. Old habits died hard. Not like people. Who wanted to be the same now? Going nowhere, just like everyone else, the same patterns, the same lives, the same pathetic little boxes. Who had the power now? Bureaucrats in grey suits, doing nothing more exciting than driving tractors up the steps of Parliament?

What a boring country this was. Where a parking ticket was an act of terrorism. He wasn't fucking going to be a number. Just another Kiwi from a tiny island adrift in the Pacific where the minds were even smaller.

Even the minds of the cops. Thick fucks. Hadn't got a clue. He was out of *their* reach.

Now and for the rest of his life, people were going to *fear … him …*

At half-past eight, when all was dark, and the buses had thinned to an incontinent dribble, a young girl walked towards the stop on the corner. He could see her in the glow of the streetlight. She held a thin black case in her hand. Clarinet? Flute? He had no idea. Could have been a grand piano for all he knew or cared. But she was alone. That was what mattered.

With limitless patience he waited with her for the bus, watching as she shivered in the cold. Stamping her feet, shoulders hunched, though this could have been from the enormous bag she'd rapidly dumped on the footpath. Several buses passed, causing hopeful peering every time, until she slouched back onto the seat, disappointed and increasingly huffy. That mesh seat had to be cold in the winter.

He observed it all from the warmth of his own car. He'd been here hours already, and he had all night. You didn't gain anything by losing your head. And if failure should hit, you chalked it up as a lesson well learnt. And you came back later, confident that it would never happen again. But also better than anyone else.

Her hair was a shade of brown bordering on auburn, with a subtle gloss of red not lost even in the washed-out streetlight. Possibly dyed, but if so it was a very natural effect. It hung to shoulder-level, straight and smooth, hues within it changing ever so slightly in the small movements of her shoulders. It swung forward as she ducked her head to check her watch, coppery highlights rippling like running water. Didn't go with her top, the colour of old nails rusting to nothing.

Presently he saw her stiffen, and gratefully haul the bag back onto her shoulders, grasping for the case. The right bus at last, illuminated sign flashing up Glen Innes, via Panmure. His comfort zone. Well, he'd be fucked. A sign of another sort.

She stuck out a hand and the striped white bus veered into the kerb to let her on. A frequent public transport user; she had a card. She sat somewhere near the middle, a silhouette in the window. The bus blinked to move back into the lane proper, cutting across the nose of a Legacy when it didn't slow.

Typical pride of Auckland Transport at the wheel.

Without haste, behind the Legacy, a red HSV joined the traffic.

HIS absence had been noticed after all. Lena almost leapt on him when he came through the door with the barbecue-pork fried rice and a curry. He didn't think it was from hunger, or any more flattering motive. The house was suddenly too full of memories, and all too empty of life. But not for Paxton.

Stronger than ever he felt Mark's presence in the house, like a cold spot in the room where the sun never reached. Yet, perversely, there was a sort of warmth to it. If Mark was watching Paxton in his house, playing boyfriend to his daughter, fingering his things, there was no hostility in his reaction. Oddly it felt like a blessing. Paxton tried not to take it too literally. Might just be a case of raging wishful thinking buoyed up by the hormones.

He'd come in in a good mood, half owing to the conversation with his parents, half to the smell from the Chinese. Lena topped it off by planting a kiss on him, almost making him drop the containers.

'Hooray. I'm starving! But didn't you have problems getting that past Customs?'

'Eh?'

'Where did you go for that? The Golden Duck, Beijing?'

'Sorry. Queues were out the door.' He took the food over to the table, which was already set. He wasn't a journalist, but thank Christ he could still fabricate a story like one. 'And there was some rugby club do on. Had to wait for them to cook up about ten lots of nasi goreng and noodles, plus a whole shitload of chips and spring rolls and wontons. Surprised they didn't fucking clean out the kitchen before *I* got through.'

Lena laughed. 'As long as there aren't roach heads instead of mushrooms, I'm willing to eat almost anything.'

He was reluctant to tell her the real reason he was late. Not that he was so macho he'd hate to destroy his image. Little Jimmy calling home to his parents. *You* won't die too, Daddy, will you? But right now it would have seemed insensitive. And to explain it ...

Might as well admit it. He felt like a fool.

She slid her arms around his neck, trapping him against the table. 'Should have bought some wine, to celebrate yesterday.'

Paxton was puzzled, but nevertheless pleased. 'What for?'

'A very special occasion.' Her eyes twinkled at him. 'For the first time since I've known you, I didn't cry in front of you.'

'Damn. Must be losing my touch.'

She kissed him again, longer this time, and Paxton was tempted to let the Chinese congeal in a chunk on the table, or better yet, swept onto the floor ...

However, given the location that probably wasn't wise. Mark was still there, just out of reach. An optical illusion in spirit form, sliding away whenever he focused too hard. If he'd been worried about poor taste before ...

Lena's stomach rumbled, nailing the coffin. Paxton grinned. 'Well. Nice to know where I stand.'

'Yeah. Between me and the curry.' She let him go and moved round to pile up her plate. Looked like the only hot action he was getting on the table required a knife and fork. But just now he didn't care. He could murder a curry.

SHE got off at a stop in Ellerslie, the only one who did. Now was the tricky part. How to follow without being seen? Couldn't be done in a car. Crawling at ten kilometres per hour was not only conspicuous as hell, on these busy streets it was asking for road rage. He parked by the kerb, and got out.

Casually he strolled after her, another pedestrian on his way home. The gush of blood swelling his veins was a high, the likes of which made cocaine seem like Diet Coke. Everything was heightened, everything. Senses, pulse rate, breathing.

Anticipation.

He knew no one would ever have known it, watching him. He'd always had a gift for that, and he'd practised to make it better. That inscrutability. That never showing what was going on in his head. No matter if it would have made your flesh shrivel.

She turned into a side street. She was going surprisingly fast, with a quick step reminiscent of held-off panic. Or a little kid, getting up in the middle of the night, and not being quite tall enough to reach the light switch ... Off the main road the street lighting was patchy at best.

All at once she stopped. A creamy yellow, slightly peeling wooden house in a quiet street of them, with a concrete path leading to the road. The cheaper end of Ellerslie. He made a note of the street number: 32. She unzipped the front pocket of her bag and let herself in with a key. Nobody home.

As he slowly walked past, with an uninterested glance at the door opening, he saw the mess through the gap. Student flat. Or bloody hopeless parents. A light came on in the lounge; the flat-mates had gone out without closing the curtains. Must have left before it was dark. Papers littered the room, and a bottle stood empty on the table. Then she pulled the drapes, and he saw nothing more.

That meant she could see nothing of him.

His attention lit on the letterbox. Circulars sprouted from it like weeds. A rusting old tin — with no lock. It was dark on the street, and the lamp posts were all on the opposite side. Keeping his eyes on the blind windows of number 32, he inched up the flap. Listening with bated breath for the screech of metal. Before it could come he slid his fingers inside the crack. The tips of his fingers brushed paper.

A little bit wider ...

A thin squeak as he pushed it too far, but in just a split second he'd whipped his hand free and departed. Vanishing into the dark like ... an assassin. He smiled. Probably not many assassins drove off in a Holden.

When he got back to the car he tossed the letters onto the seat beside him. He'd look over them when he got home. The one with the university crest. The ones from the bank. The handwritten one, most interesting of all.

And he'd try to find out who was about to die next.

PAXTON was getting restless again. After dinner Lena had gone back to her sorting, making piles of things she'd like for herself and things she was mentally matching up with others. Fortunately Mark hadn't been the hoarding type, or she'd never have fitted it all into her own tiny broom closet in Glendowie.

Her father's place was an old spreading wooden house with a latticed gable window below a sharply sloping roof. Mark had bought it as a peeling, DIY investment more than twenty years ago, and had since resisted subdividing for infill housing as so many others had. Now fully restored to patrician elegance, it sat on a rising slope well back on the property, its gardens stretching roadward — to have subdivided would have meant losing the light and the view. There was a flowering cherry on the front lawn, and the whole huge section was marked off by a low brick wall. It had been too big for the three of them then.

Even more so when there were only two. But when the divorce came through Mark had still refused to sell. He was stubborn, and he'd already dug in his roots. And Lena would of course want the space to invite friends to sleep over. Though in the event, it was rarely used for that purpose.

Thanks to Lena's split childhood, in limbo between New Zealand and Europe, Paxton had learned she'd had very few friends. That at least he knew about. Yet another thing they had in common. Accounted for a lot of that independence as well as the closeness between father and daughter.

Lena was lingering over a bent-edged *Chronicles of Narnia*, received through the post at her Swiss boarding school and later kept here in trust till she got a bigger house. Her head was bowed so that her dark hair was brushing the pages.

At that moment it struck him. Mark was everywhere, filling the air, more potent than fried rice or — God help him — the curry. And seeing as he was here, why not ask him? If anyone was owed money, or he'd pissed anyone off, surely the best authority was Mark himself.

Quietly he crept from the living room into the hall. Lena, engrossed in *The Silver Chair*, must have assumed he was going to the littlest room at the end of it. She didn't even raise her head.

Mark's bedroom was the last on her agenda, a sanctum yet to be raided. Paxton pushed open the door and went in, with utmost caution easing it to behind him. He didn't want Lena to hear. Mark's presence was strongest here, beating out from every surface.

Paxton hadn't tried to summon a spirit in a very long while. Since leaving England in fact, or before, if you considered that for months prior to that he was avoiding Cheryl like a penny in a pub urinal. Still, you never quite forgot how. He ought to know. He'd tried.

The air now seemed expectant. Waiting. *Mark* wasn't being summoned. Quite the reverse. Paxton glanced down at the bed. It hadn't been made since the night Mark had left it. The police hadn't touched it, and neither had Lena. There hadn't seemed any point. It would have been sacrilege. Rumpled from sleep that wouldn't come, covers thrown back, left to cool by a body that never returned. The imprint was almost there, a crease outline of the dead.

Deliberately, Paxton sat on it. Mentally crossing his fingers. 'Slob.'

The air said nothing.

'You have your priorities right, don't you? Hovering round the bloody canapés at your own damn funeral, but you can't even make your bed! There's poltergeists neater than you, mate.'

The mattress jiggled. Or had he fancied it? He paused and his breath quickened. He looked down at the ground. Made his words purposefully softer.

'I can see why you loved her.'

I know you can, you sod.

Paxton smiled. 'You were the one who told me to take care of her.'

I'm just bloody grateful I didn't ask you to mind the car as well.

Paxton glanced at the door. To his relief, Lena hadn't come bursting through. Wondering why he was talking to himself. Or suspecting that he wasn't. He felt guilty not including her — again — knowing she'd want to be present. But if there was nothing, he equally didn't want to upset her. A little hope was worse than none.

He got straight to it, not wasting time.

'Did you hear what we were thinking, then? About who might have done it?'

I'm only human, James. If I were to list everyone I'd ever pissed off, you'd be hearing the end over my side. But ...

His voice was a map to his emotions. Made richer by amusement, now it became thinner, more tired. There was a distinct hesitation. The words came out slowly, dragging from him. Somehow gaining more weight.

I didn't borrow money from anyone. However — I did lend some.

Paxton pinned his eyes to the wall.

'Who?'

But he'd never —

'Who?'

Colin.

Paxton stopped. 'Your best friend Colin?'

I told you. It's ridiculous. But —

'He's never mentioned this to Lena.'

And that's just it ...Colin's so scrupulous. We used to call him Tin Bum. He wouldn't even cross the road without the lights. It's unlike him not to try to pay it back, even if it isn't to me personally.

'How much, Mark?' Paxton's tone was sharper than he expected.

Um ... The voice tried to sound offhand and failed dismally. *Ten thousand.*

Paxton sat rigid. 'Shit.'

He said he was having business difficulties. Needed capital ... something. He was my best friend. I didn't really ask.

'Too polite to, weren't you?'

Mark was silent. Paxton didn't want to believe it either.

'Colin.' The fat man in the charcoal suit, the magnetic killer of the eastern suburbs. It didn't wash. And Mark wasn't exactly your East End geezer and pro knee-capper. Might have strained relations for a bit if the loan had been lost, but he couldn't see just cause for murder. Not unless there was a desperate mind, lost control of reason ...

He realised he had a handful of duvet scrunched in his fist. 'That's a big chunk to be keeping from Lena.'

I don't begrudge him the money. If he's in trouble ... He's been a good friend.

Paxton tried to think. He couldn't really blame Colin. If he'd been in the same boat, wouldn't he have been tempted to do the same thing? Suddenly, an interest-free loan becomes an interest-free gift ... But a whole ten thousand dollars.

'I think we'd better talk to him.'

Maybe he's just waiting for the right time.

'Maybe he isn't.'

Chapter FOURTEEN

'WHAT DO YOU think? This for Cuddly Colin?'

She lifted one end of an ornate rug, a Turkish kilim in dark red, black and gold. Impressive but a little vivid in the morning sun, which pooled in the middle where the sides curved in as she held it. Paxton gazed at it, then back up at her face.

'Ahmmm ...' He tried to blink away the golden scrolls burned temporarily into his vision.

'Honestly, he loves it. He was always admiring it whenever he was over. Said once it reminded him of *Prince of Persia*.'

Paxton smiled. 'Once a computer nerd ...'

'The only game I ever played was Patience. I sure as hell don't want it. Anyway, my lounge suite's burgundy.'

'If you're sure.'

'I'm really not sure about any of this, James.' She sighed, snapping her end of the rug like a sheet being folded. A billow of dust arose from it, sparkling in the light.

She'd been thrown when he told her, small blame to her. Colin was her godfather. She'd known him all her life. At the same time, however, she'd been intrigued. Another mystery to solve. Curious, how an ordinary if rather empty life could suddenly catch fire in tragedy. Survivors rising like a phoenix from the ashes, made stronger like tempered steel. Mixed similes that only meant there'd be hell to pay later when it all hit home.

Today they were taking Colin a pretext. Here's that rug you liked, Colin, and just out of interest did you kill my dad? All in such delicate phrasing that Colin need never know. Unless, of course, he was guilty.

'Well, I certainly don't think he did it. Any more than you do, or your dad. But to date it's the only lead. I'm starting to wake up in cold sweats that Gardner will have my arse regardless, to hell with the evidence.'

'Tell him it's taken.' She ruffled his hair. He smiled.

'I can just imagine what that cunt is saying about me. Probably got some checklist he downloaded from the FBI website. Let's see.' He ticked them off on his fingers. 'Loner — *doesn't talk to neighbours*. Two, trouble with authority. Three, pathological liar. Ooh, delusional tendencies — *does* talk to dead people. Umm ... What else? Fascination with violent crimes ... Pommy bastard ... Doesn't think sun rises from my arse ... Hell, let's face it, Lee, I'm toast.'

She laughed, shaking her head. 'He can't. It's just not reasonable.'

'You're telling me there's never been a miscarriage of justice in this country?'

It unsettled him when she grimaced. 'Arthur Allan Thomas. The Crewe murders, in the seventies. Locked away for ten years, till they proved he was totally innocent. They made a movie about it.'

'Well that's encouraging.'

'Is there still an obligatory cavity search when they take you to prison?'

'Yeah, cheers for that.'

'Don't worry, honey, I'll drop by with ointment occasionally.' He grabbed her, sniggering, and kissed her, as was her intention.

The rug was still draped on the floor and he caught his toe on it as he shifted his feet. Irritably he looked down at it, its gaudy colours offensive.

'Bloody carpet. Don't know why Dad bought it.' Lena bent and started rolling it into a tube, scroll pattern inward. 'I'll be glad when it's gone. It'll all be worth *that*, if nothing else.'

Paxton watched her, frowning. 'Colin owes you an explanation at the very least. Common courtesy.'

She glanced round from her squatting position and had to balance herself on the roll of carpet. She bit her lip, her eyes troubled. 'It really isn't like him ...'

'Yet another thing that doesn't make sense. I'm beginning to think it's a sign.'

AT least they had the element of surprise. Colin glanced up from his computer and caught sight of Lena, and blinked as though he'd got a shock off the keyboard.

'Hello, Lena! Good to see you! How've you been getting on?' A man who really deserved the term bearlike, big and shambling, cute in a clawless way. His manner was just the right combination of surprise, delight and fatherly concern as he got up to greet them. Only in the depths could Paxton see the fear. Naked, animal and red raw. Oh yes, he was frightened all right. Gates slammed behind his eyes, and his guard was up, all before he'd got his hands off the keys.

In Paxton's experience this was a *very* bad sign. Usually it meant that the person didn't want their head read by the Witch-boy of Wellington. From someone who'd never even heard his reputation, it didn't bode well at all.

If she'd noticed, Lena didn't show it. 'Hello, Colin. Thanks for the flowers; I must phone Bev and thank her too. As for me — well. I'm coping. You know.'

'He'd be proud of you, Lena. I know I said that on Saturday, but I meant it. He always has been proud of you. Don't know how many hours I've sat through, listening to all your achievements.'

Lena grimaced. 'Sorry about that.'

'Don't be. He's been very lucky with you.' He was sincere, real fondness filling his speech.

Lena hastened to change the subject. 'Have I introduced you to James? We haven't been going out long, but he was at the funeral.'

Colin looked pleased, as an uncle would be for a favourite niece. That wariness was fading from his eyes, still present but less. He was relaxing in the familiar routine of small talk, regarding Paxton with jovial interest. Paxton was struggling to maintain his detachment in the face of such genuine friendliness.

'No, can't say I *have* seen you before. Nice to meet you.' He held out a hand to shake, his face utterly open and guileless. 'How'd you get to meet Lena?'

Straight to the hard questions. Paxton wished they'd tried the same on him, as a pre-emptive strike.

'Mutual friends.' It was the easiest lie to invent, rolling straight off his tongue. He didn't even blink.

Colin didn't appear to notice. 'Speaking of which ... I had the police in here a couple of days ago. They were going through a list of Mark's friends — wanted to know all the usual details. Don't think I was much help. I mean honestly, what on earth could I have told them?' He looked awkwardly at Lena. 'But I don't need to tell you that, do I? Must have been awful for you.'

Lena gave a rapid shake of her head, to ward off his compassion. Paxton could almost see her internal wince of guilt. Sympathy at this time was of all things unwelcome.

'We've brought a present for you, Uncle Colin.' Lena beamed cheerily, reverting to childish playfulness. She stepped out of the office to fetch the carpet, which was leaning against the wall in the hallway.

As she hauled it through the door she said, more seriously, 'If you don't want it, that's all right. It's just that I think Dad would want you to have it. I remember you saying you liked it, once.'

Colin looked aghast as he saw the corner of crimson flapping open at the top. 'That Persian carpet of Mark's? You're not giving *that* to me? You can't!'

'It's yours, if you want it.'

He took the roll from her, rapt. 'I don't believe it. Thank you very much!' He unfurled it a little to gawk at it. 'Are you sure you don't want it? It's a fabulous carpet ...'

'Bit too fabulous for me, I'm afraid. Wouldn't go with any of my crap.'

'Thanks a lot. I'd love it.'

Then as Paxton watched, the dazed look was shot with a flare of guilt. He wondered if he'd imagined it. Colin's admiring grip on the rug loosened considerably, and he seemed all of a sudden eager to put it aside.

'Thanks for bringing this in, Lena. I really appreciate it.' He was drawing their visit to a close. 'You take care, eh? If there's anything you need, just give us a call. Okay?' He hugged her with affectionate sympathy.

He really seems like a nice bloke, Paxton thought. *Except for the lying.*

He studied the fancy computer system with its oversized monitor bunged on the top, the shelves in what looked to be solid hardwood, and the pile of wireless gadgetry on the desk. Also in hardwood.

'You seem to be doing well.' He gestured offhandedly at the rug. 'You could just about get away with that in your office.'

Colin laughed, surprised. 'We've been doing pretty well, yes. Don't know that I'd waste a thing like this on work, though.'

Lena didn't miss Paxton's intent behind the greasing. 'So, all other things aside, business is great for you, Colin.'

Paxton watched his reaction carefully. But if he felt any guilt at the question, he'd suddenly become a hell of a lot better at hiding it. His face lit up like a Cuban cigar.

'We're expanding into Perth within six months, Sydney and Melbourne are doing so well. Like here we're keeping the Australian operation to the big centres, but we should really start to rake it in once we branch out. Profits are just skyrocketing.'

Corporate speak. Paxton would have yawned if it hadn't been so interesting. So Colin wasn't in trouble. Which meant — what? He looked at Lena, who flicked him a glance out of the corner of her eye. Doubting him?

The expression on her face never altered.

'Really? That's strange. It's just that my dad was worried about you — he said something about Anztec being in difficulties just before he was killed.'

At the sight of Colin's face, Paxton went cold.

The transformation was disturbing. Colin blanched, the friendliness vanishing on the instant. The rug, so to speak, was whipped from under his feet. He looked like the detectives had done when they'd stood over Mark's brutalised body.

'He did.'

Not a question. The guilt, the alarm, had come back full force. There was no doubt now. Lena looked ill, staring transfixed in revulsion at Colin's face. She and Paxton stayed silent, letting the vacuum fill itself. Colin stammered a little as he rushed to oblige them.

'Yes, well, true, I did need a wee bit of capital to help with the expansion. Infrastructure and all that, costs a lot to set up.'

He was meeting their eyes again now. Paxton stared back at him impassively, giving him nothing. *Detail's convincing. Shame the general plot is full of shit.*

'But financially we're fine.' He gave a dry little laugh. Like a dry cough. 'Strange that he should mention it at all, really. How ... how did the subject come up?'

A Nazi war criminal sitting in Nuremberg, Paxton thought. *That's who he reminds me of*. Deny or die. The skin on Colin's hands was a little too tight as he rested them on his knees. His smile just a bit too strained.

Lena looked at him dead on. 'He lent you money, Colin. Ten thousand dollars. And you told him it was for your business. You told him a lot of shit, didn't you, Colin?'

Colin gaped, a tiny sound of protest escaping in reflex. Then he shut it again. His silence spoke volumes.

'*Uncle Colin*.' Her voice was singsong, bleeding contempt. 'Tell me it's nothing to do with why my dad was murdered. Tell me the reason you conned him out of ten grand isn't relevant.' She stared at him, her eyes blistering. 'Though I'm not sure I'd believe you anymore.'

'Lena, it's not like that! It's not like that at all! Believe me, this is the last thing I would ever have wanted ... He was my *best friend*.' He was almost trembling, his cheeks flushing red.

'What do you know, Colin? What exactly happened to my father?'

'I don't know anything! It was an accident — a horrible accident, Lena, a tragedy, but believe me I know nothing about it. It's got nothing to do with the ten thousand dollars!' He gave a horrified laugh that held no amusement. 'Do you think I would murder my friend?'

He was in such earnest that Lena and Paxton were thrown. But the techie did protest too much for Paxton. And he'd just admitted it — he knew about the money. Why the guilt? That *fear*? He was surprised Colin didn't have a stain running down his trouser leg.

'Shall I tell you how I really met Lena, Colin?'

Colin looked at him, bemused.

'I came across Mark's body.'

Colin's expression went blank with shock.

'And he urged me to get in touch with Lena.'

Colin stared, his eyes going between Paxton and Lena. 'I don't understand.'

'I'm a medium. I can talk to the dead — and they can talk back.'

Terror streaked across his face, bold as brass on the exposed surface. For a moment his breathing had stopped. Looking at him, Paxton could believe that the heart had also.

Colin said hollowly, 'That's how you knew!' His voice might as well have been a whisper. 'I told him not to tell. I felt ashamed ...' He looked away for comfort towards the vibrant-coloured rug. No comfort there. His eyes were on the move again, seeking an anchor.

'Why didn't you go to a bank? It's what most people would have done.' Lena sounded disbelieving, condemning.

'I couldn't!' He seemed aware of how lame that sounded. 'Shareholders and things — doesn't inspire much confidence in them, does it, when the business is borrowing heavily?'

'Ten thousand dollars? That's nothing for a business this size! You could have added it on to a loan. Companies must do it all the time — you said you were expanding, for Christ's sake!'

'Yes, but ... We'd already borrowed up to the hilt. I mean, I'll get it all back, but ...' He was in a corner, and he knew it. He gave a shrug, arms wide open, struggling to claw back lost ground. 'It was stupid, what can I say? It seemed the easy way at the time.'

'Thank Christ I don't invest in your company.'

Paxton shook his head in disgust. 'Cut the crap, mate. You're lying harder than a bald man on a stone pillow.'

Colin raised his voice. 'Well if you've already spoken to him you know the truth, don't you? You don't need to ask *me* anything!' In his eyes was a miserable fatalism, like a sick old man in a nursing home. Seeing death coming, scared as hell, and still railing against the inevitable.

'Humour us.'

'I've done *nothing*! I didn't hurt him. I didn't *want* to hurt him. And if he told you that he's lying!'

'You've told us more than he has, Colin.'

Colin stared at Lena. 'What?' He looked back at Paxton, his mouth frozen open. 'You mean he didn't —?'

'Oh yes, he did. He told me he'd loaned you the money. But *as of this moment*, he still hasn't told me who killed him.'

'He doesn't know?' Paxton saw the hope returning.

It was time for a little inventive deception. Seemed to be catching. Paxton couldn't raise the tiniest little flag of guilt. 'I'm sure he does. But the dead are just the same as the living. Shock affects them just as it does us. *At the moment* he can't remember. But once it wears off ...'

Colin was grasping the corner of his desk, relief in the lines of his face. 'What if he doesn't remember? He might never be able to tell you.'

'Eventually he will. Anyway ...' Paxton shrugged. 'If he didn't see it, someone else will have. 'Sa big place, over there. Maybe his grandmother was watching. Or his second cousin ... Who knows, I could ask them *right now* ...'

'Get out.' He was gasping. 'The flaming cheek, you coming here and accusing me ... I should have you up for libel.'

'Slander, Uncle Colin. Libel's the one in writing.'

'Eh?'

He gazed at her, as if not recognising who he saw. 'What's gotten into you, Lena? What would Mark say, if he could see you acting like this?'

Paxton said, 'Why don't we ask him?'

'Get out!' Colin exploded, suddenly shouting. His panic was hammered so deep it had hardened to something like rock. He grabbed the rug, slamming it against Paxton's chest. 'Take this damn thing with you, I don't want it! Just get out, both of you, or I'll have a trespass notice served on you.' He raised an arm pointing at the door, his kindly face flushed till it almost matched the rug. 'Go on, get out!'

They left. Paxton's heart was thumping against his ribs, and Lena looked ashen. He took her arm and realised she was shaking.

They sat in the car, speechless, for several minutes.

Chapter FIFTEEN

HALF AN HOUR later Paxton wiped slobbery hands on the sofa cushions, reason slowly soaking back in. Next to him Lena was stroking Glen on the head, looking infinitely more collected.

'You OK?'

She gave a wry smile. 'I'm sort of getting used to this by now.' He picked up her other hand, and she leaned her head against his shoulder.

'Do you really think Colin did it? Even now?'

'You don't, do you?' She lifted her head, looking up at him astutely.

'Even now ... No.'

'Because of my suggestion that that murdered girl could have had the hots for him?'

'Well, that did stagger me.'

She smiled. 'I could have been wrong.'

'True. But my instincts aren't. Much as I hate to admit it, I have to acknowledge my senses are there. And there's no way your Cuddly Colin is the man I sensed at the park, or either of the other two places. I don't care if that jogging girl was as blind as a bat and flipping desperate to boot ... There's just no chance Colin was the one she was lusting after.'

'Well that's a relief.'

'But at the same time ...'

'What the *hell* was that?'

'Exactly ...'

Lena gazed into space. 'I spilled red wine all over his carpet once. A full glass, just about. I was running through the house, *shrieking* at the top of my lungs, chasing Marcus, and I bumped into the coffee table and sent it flying. I was beside myself. And all he did was laugh, tell me "accidents happen", and send me upstairs to watch TV.' She was deep in thought. 'Never *once* have I seen him lose his temper. That was ...'

'Scary?' He wasn't about to argue.

'But — This is driving me insane; we keep coming back to it! Why? Why on earth would he lie about the money? Guilt was written all over his face. And he just did his nut!'

Paxton nodded. 'Mmm. I could see it from some people. That righteous anger at being accused. Met more than a few on the job. Shtone-shober drunks and cutlery-nappers; they get their knickers horribly in a twist and march out with their handbags clinking. But someone like *him* ... He's a teddy bear. He wouldn't get angry, would he, he'd just get horribly confused and hurt.'

'Yes! That's it, that's exactly right.'

'Innocent people don't look like he did. Like a frog, slapping himself down at a table and realising the menu's all in French. Almost croaked when I said I'd speak to Mark ... So even if he didn't do it, he frigging well knows who. Or at least why.'

'But in that case — where in Christ's name is the connection? Dad, yeah OK. But a nurse from Greenlane and a fitness fanatic in Panmure? Where the hell do they fit in?'

'Unsatisfied customers?'

'Hardly.' She let out a heavy sigh, resting her head back against the sofa. 'He's always been an absolute sweetheart to me; that's what I can't get over. He always threatened to swap his son for me whenever I was round there.'

'The one you were chasing through the house?'

She gave a disparaging grin. 'Little shit.'

'Have you always acted that way around males?'

'Not that one. Weird little creep. No wonder his father wanted to swap. They've always had to keep an eye ...'

Her eyes widened. 'Shit ...'

Paxton felt himself tense in his seat.

'No ...! I should have flaming realised ...'

He watched her go inside herself, turning over the facts like suspect pieces of fruit.

'Marcus is my father's dead loss of a godson. Mark: Marcus. Colin and Bev thought it was cute.'

'Yeah, all right.'

'Didn't do the name any favours. He's only a couple of years older than me, and he's always been a total git. The reason I was screaming through the house after him was because he flicked a bogey at me while I was reading and it stuck in my hair. While I was distracted, trying to get it out, he nicked my book and chucked it out the window.' Even after this length of time, the anger still boiled up when summoned. 'He was a total *arsehole*.'

'And you think he might be the reason your father died?' Paxton tried to sound gentle, but couldn't help his scepticism showing. 'Sounds like a pretty typical boy to me. At your sheltered little girls' school in Switzerland you might have been spared this, but plenty of highly respectable men spent their formative years wedging their mates' undies up their cracks.'

'Ohhhh no. I haven't finished.' She wriggled round to face him on the sofa, and he could feel the excitement flooding from her body. 'When he was sixteen or seventeen, young Markie started sticking his pocket money up his nose.'

'Ouch.'

'Well. He might have smoked it, but inhaling is the general idea. He's a smart boy; his parents never actually caught him, but we all knew. Was trying to blame his bloodshot eyes on his contacts, but as Dad was his optometrist it was pretty hard to keep that one up. Dad said he'd never seen pupils that dilated.'

She made a face. 'His dad tried to persuade me to hang around more; said I was a good influence. I was back in New Zealand for good then, not just for holidays. But luckily for me he was always out. At nightclubs — underage, he used to boast to me; I can still see his foul little smirk. Or wherever else he went with those dodgy friends of his. Can't say I was overly concerned.'

'Wait on. So you think Colin was borrowing drug money from your dad to give to his own son?' Paxton's voice was high with incredulity.

'That's the bit I can't figure out. I'll confess, there are still some aspects of it that won't fit, but when you think about it ... See, Colin's wife Bev's almost as much of a softy as he is, but even she'd had enough in the end. So ultimately she read him the riot act —'

'Marcus?'

'Sorry, yes. Not Colin. And anyway Bev told him if he didn't sort himself out he was out of the house, and forget about maintenance. *That* put the wind up him a bit — no matter how spaced out, he never lost sight of his chances. I suppose it helped that a couple of weeks earlier a buddy of his had smashed himself up tanked to the gills on alcohol and various other substances. Marcus didn't want to be lumped in with *that*.'

She looked reflective. 'Never liked to be seen as stupid, Marcus. Dunno why, it always made him maddest when I insulted his intelligence. He'd go ape-shit. Tried to strangle me once when I called him an idiot.'

'He *what*?'

'Yep. Always good with his hands, was Marcus.'

She met his gaze, knowing she'd caught him. He was rattled. 'Go on.'

'After that, he cleaned himself up. Apparently he stopped doing drugs, his grades went through the roof, though he'd never actually been failing in the first place. It's *weird* — even when he was supposed to be spinning out, the level of control he always had … The other guys were caught, grounded, suspended, expelled, arrested. But never Marcus.'

'How does that work? Are you sure —'

'Positive. He even offered me some. "Angel dust for little Angelena".' She imitated him in a smug, sneering tone that instantly had Paxton's knuckles itching.

'Nice …' He looked up at her curiously. 'That your proper name?'

She scowled. 'No. Just his pathetic attempt at humour.'

His mind was skipping ahead. 'What's he look like, this Marcus?'

'I'll come to that in a minute. What's more important, he may seem to have gone all on the straight and narrow now — he works in IT, bit like his proud dad — but he's got money that doesn't come from Daddy or his techno-job. He's gone from being a druggie to a dealer.'

'*Colin's* son?'

'It's probably why. Can you imagine? He never even had any bedtime. Not even when he was four!' She shook her head. 'I will say, though, he's only little league. Just does it for a bit of extra cash, never enough to bring the cops down on his back. At least that's what he told me the last time we met. That was a few years ago now.'

Paxton was lost in thought, considering the implications.

'You see now why I thought he could be our guy? If Colin were protecting *anyone* …'

Paxton's voice came out brisk, almost sharp. 'Dark hair? Would you say he was good-looking?'

'He's got the dark hair, he got that from Bev. And … well, he's not my type, but plenty of women go for him. He's got kind of a man of mystery, dark and dangerous thing about him. Last time I saw him he looked like he hadn't shaved in a week. He's tall, like his dad, and he's always had a nice body. Athletic. Looks like he goes to the gym. You know.'

Paxton could sense her discomfort. He wasn't sure he liked it either.

'But he's a prick! *Arrogant.* And a real chauvinist.'

'Someone who'd kill strange women just for fun?'

She hesitated, watching Glen stretched out asleep on the carpet. 'I don't know ...'

'But Colin thinks *he* does.'

Chapter SIXTEEN

PAXTON STOWED THE Wither Hills, his favourite sav blanc, in the wine rack, before stashing away the eggs and the milk and the bacon and all the other assorted bumf he'd carted back from shopping. He was hoping to avoid a repeat of last week, which had seen half his supplies chucked out in the rubbish, considering how little he'd seen of his house during the week. All things going well, he was aiming to share half the Wither Hills with Lena, in celebration of a job well done. Or at least to take the edge off one cocked up ... Colin was best left to chill. He'd be better dealt with tomorrow, when his defences had softened a bit. Another day to soak in the fear. Then they'd hang him out to dry.

The longer he played with the puzzle, the more he could see of the picture. A drug dealer. Somehow desperate for money. The man who lends it to him when his own father won't give more. A *nurse*, who works in a hospital, with access to drugs ... Yes! And a young blonde, who seems to enjoy the odd bit of recreation. It was paint by numbers, and all he was missing was a few of the digits.

Paxton went into his bedroom and stripped to change into his work uniform. Cheap black pants, black shirt with an alcoholic logo, which though hot as hell in summer, managed to look stupid all year round. Especially with his Midlands in winter complexion, which his colouring returned to by default within seconds of tanning. Once, during a blackout at the bar, Adam had suggested distracting the punters by using Paxton's face as a dartboard. 'Face it, mate, it's the only thing still visible.' Paint a couple of rings round his eyes and he could have stood in for a panda.

Still, Lena seemed to like it.

No matter how bleak the week, that was the bright spot in it. How had a gorgeous chick like that ever gone for the likes of him?

Whenever he searched for the answer, he gave it up as hopeless. Years of trying to explain himself, meeting looks that were blank or disdainful, the hasty excuses, or worse, excited invitations back to the flat, to tell the future ... Most blokes would have foreseen a pair of knickers on the floor, and a fling with a moderately tall dark stranger. But, to his own sorrow, Paxton wasn't one of them. Just his luck to be shy as well as psychic. On paper he was as creative as you liked, but in the flesh he was just too damn honest, and tongue-tied. And cursed, with a grandmother who'd told him never to use his gifts for his own gain. Hard to get too excited with his gran's visage at the front of his mind, crisp and shrivelled as an overdone roast. Even after she was dead. Particularly after she was dead.

You reap what you sow, just mind you that. Don't think you've heard all there is to tell, boyo. You've not spoken to everyone yet ...

Outside the light was failing. He'd already shut the curtains while he was stripping, and he had to switch the light on so he could see to find his uniform. It didn't exactly stand out. As he picked up his shirt he noticed a thread trailing loose from the left sleeve, and he yanked at it mercilessly. The fabric gathered, making a fetching ruched sleeve, while the thread stayed put. He swore.

He got the scissors and hacked the thread off, flattening out the damage. At least it was a crease proof blend, which was about the only thing to be said for it. Paxton hated ironing, unless there was something decent on TV he could watch while he did it. There very seldom was. He spent three minutes on his hair, his teeth and his boots, and went out, a walking advertisement for Stolichnaya.

He passed the park as he drove down Patteson Avenue. A week tonight. He shook his head with the wonder of it.

'Evening, Mark.' Although he knew Mark wasn't there. But the twinge of conscience still was. He prayed that Mark's godson was the killer, if only so he could move on and enjoy the bastard drive.

Even now, if he was in the dark long enough, that voice would come back to him. Distressed, trying to keep calm. The panic overwhelming, because death was no longer a horror to be expected — it had already come.

Please listen, something awful has happened. You have to find my daughter.

Even in daylight the memory of that meeting, an audience with the dead in the park, at the feet of a soulless corpse leaking blood, could set a shudder fleeting through Paxton's bones. He'd spoken to Mark since, got to know him; even had a face for that voice, thanks to photos. But it was there, every time he switched off the light. A haunting manifesting only in his mind. Another psychological scar for the healing. *Thank God the psychological ones don't show ...*

His biggest worry was that there'd be another corpse cooling in the meantime. At any moment, Gardner and Stirling knocking on his door, asking for a few more moments of his time. As if enough hadn't already been wasted. He could just imagine what the sergeant would make of what they were planning. Hobnailing all over the law, adding threats and accusations to suspicion of murder.

For the first time since he'd left the Cock's Head, work was a release. While the world outside stood on its head, here — now that the press had departed — things stayed reassuringly familiar. Adam, more than familiar. Paxton had made the mistake of mentioning Lena to him on Saturday, and he was consequently as keen for details as Paxton's mother, only for vastly different reasons.

''Bout time you got laid, Pommy boy. Jesus, you can't get laid in this job there's something wrong.'

Didn't know the half of it.

With his own cheeky grin and permatan, Adam was never short an admirer or seven. It pissed Paxton off no end. Or had, until now. 'Hasn't made up for all that's wrong with you. From what I've heard, big tips, but sadly little ...'

'Bastard.'

'Now, now.'

IT was almost like a blessing, seeing her waiting there for him. Blessedly unaware that he was watching. It was a date he'd been praying for all day, and she hadn't stood him up.

She was sitting on the seat, knees together, staring off into the distance for the bus. Same bulging bag, same black case, different clothes as one might have hoped. Tonight she wore a long, dark green skirt beneath a roll-necked cerise jersey. With that auburn hair. Hopeless. No wonder she was doing something arty.

Well, so was he. He was nothing if not creative. Both in planning and in execution. Come someday soon he looked forward to making that pale cream skin turn all the colours of the rainbow. Red, blue, indigo, violet ...

He wondered if she was good at it, whatever she did, as he was. Would it be a tragedy, her loss, a terrible waste of talent? Would what he did have some impact, beyond her tiny world? He smiled to himself, in the dark.

Her name was Joanna Jeffries. Jo to her friends. She'd been invited to a twenty-first the following week. Would have been, anyway, if she'd got the invitation. In the event, she might be finding herself unavoidably detained.

He sat there, looking straight inside her empty little head. She really was the model student. Overdrawn on her tertiary account, almost a grand owing to Visa. Nothing exciting. CDs, campus lunches, clothes from no store he was familiar with. Explained a lot about her outfits. Income via Studylink — student allowance. She wasn't living at home. Nor, obviously, within budget. Deposits of cash appeared sporadically on her statement, whenever she hadn't spent it, suggesting a bit of tutoring on the side. Not enough for anything more interesting. He really *would* have been coming full circle.

A music grad student; so much he could have guessed. And a dedicated one, given the hours she spent at practice. Not quiet enough at home? She flatted with one bloke at least, possibly a couple, judging from the two other names on the invite. A Sam and a Lincoln. One of whom could have been her boyfriend, but surely not both. There'd been a bank statement for a Mr SE Wise as well. Didn't seem to live up to his name, if his finances were any indication. He sincerely hoped Sam wasn't doing commerce.

She scratched her knee, shifting uncomfortably on the metal seat, then crossed her legs, exposing a pair of brown boots. He could just make out the colour in the headlights of a car turning from Waterloo Quadrant. His mind drifted back into fantasy.

Would she kick him? Would she struggle?

Safer not to stray too far down that path. *Not* the appropriate moment. He forced himself to keep his hands at his sides. Focused on the changing of the traffic lights. He lowered the electric window a crack, letting in a sharp slice of night air. Indulgence could wait. He wasn't lacking in privacy, God knew, but what he needed was concentration. Later — was another matter.

The bus came, pulling up to the kerb as she stood and held out an arm. She gathered up her baggage and disappeared up the steps. He already had the car started. Three stages to Ellerslie. He knew the route by heart. Meet you at home, Jo.

As the bus moved into traffic, he was already several lengths ahead.

HIS receptionist tried to block them as they moved towards his office. She was a young thing in a short skirt, with an attitude that would have been more appropriate behind the bike sheds than a welcoming desk. Paxton had met these before.

'Do you have an appointment?'

'No. But I'm sure Uncle Colin won't mind.'

The receptionist's eyelashes flickered uncertainly. 'He said you were his friend's daughter.'

Colin. Getting stupid, he was. So he'd warned her not to let them through.

'It's complicated.' Lena swept by her, leaving the miniskirt gaping.

'He'll be in a meeting all day! I'm sorry —'

They ignored her. Lena knocked at Colin's office as reception hastily dialled his extension. She got through just as Lena opened the door.

'Hi, Colin. S'all right, only us.' Paxton closed the door after them. 'You can put the phone down now.'

Colin was furious. 'I thought I told you —'

'You're not really in a position to tell us anything.' Lena matched him glare for glare. 'You lied not only to me, but to Dad. My dad trusted you, more than any other person. Maybe even me; he knew you longer. Yet you suckered him out of money on false pretences. Do you know how that makes me feel?'

Colin's anger seemed sucked dry.

'Don't you think I have a right to know whether your betrayal was involved in his death?'

Genuine sadness filled Colin's face. The lines of his body sagged as if weighted.

'I'm sorry, Lena. I know … Look, you've been through hell. Mark was a truly great bloke, one of the best, and I wish to God they'd find whoever did this. I miss him too.'

'Would you ever have paid him back — or is that why he was thumped?'

Colin shook his head, closing his eyes.

'I swear to you, I was going to pay him back. I can't — I won't go into why I told him that little fib, but it wasn't why he was killed.' There was just the tiniest pause. 'It can't have been.'

'So it had nothing to do with Marcus?'

At the sound of the name, Colin's head jerked up. He stared at Paxton, with a look in his eyes Paxton recognised. Ah. He realised he'd been waiting for it for years, like an old friend long expected. That expression, half amazement, half fear. Fear of what he could do.

'That's why you're so afraid, isn't it, Colin? You think your son was behind it.'

Colin's eyes were still fixed on him, with such intensity he wasn't blinking. Behind his eyes he was falling. A man in a waking dream, plummeting into a deep well that had yawned open beneath his feet. The silence seemed interminable.

'Why would I think that?'

'To do with drugs, wasn't it?'

They had him. The refusal faded out from Colin's face, leaving only a pitiable, benevolent creature trying to understand the evil he'd never been taught. He went back to his desk and slumped into the chair, facing sideways where he'd left it, putting his head in his hands. He pushed them back through his hair, almost as if he were tempted to pull it out at the roots, and gave a deep sigh. He stared at the calendar on the wall as he spoke.

'He told me he was in trouble. Said a bunch of gang members had threatened him — if he didn't come up with the money, they were going to kill him.'

The words seemed alien in his mouth. He was plainly struggling to come to grips with what they meant. 'What else could I do? I'd already used up all my own money; he's been on shaky ground for months. He was trying to go straight, he told me, but all these people he's been mixed up with ...'

Lena stared at him, appalled. 'But I thought he was just small-time!'

'He was! But he just got pulled in deeper — they wanted more and more from him, and now he doesn't know how to get out. And I don't know how to help him ...'

'Oh, hell.' Lena skirted the desk and folded her arms around him awkwardly, chair and all.

Paxton stood frowning. 'Did you not think of telling the police?'

'He said they're bent. The gang's got insiders. I don't know. You can't trust them anyway.'

'So you're just going to let more people die?'

'James!'

'I'm sorry, Lena. But I have to be harsh. There have been three murders so far — that we know of — and I for one am keen to see there isn't a fourth.'

Lena's arms slipped away from Colin. 'Sorry, James. I forgot. This hasn't been easy for you either, has it?'

Colin looked puzzled. Paxton went on, with bitter weariness. 'I'm chief suspect, Colin. It's a very privileged position. It means that every time there's a new murder, I get to be hauled over the coals by a couple of detectives. Any day now I'm going to find myself in a cell, counting the skid marks in the loo bowl.'

'You? But why?'

'Usual reason. *I know too much*. And I know very well you haven't been straight with us about Marcus.'

Again that startled expression of wonder. All it took was a direct look in the eye and a bang-on instinct for the bluff.

'What do you mean?'

Paxton was getting sick of his hedging. A toddler could have seen through it. 'I *mean*, Mr Davenport, that you might be afraid for your son, but that doesn't explain what *one* person, not an entire gang of clomping thugs, was doing lurking in the park for your friend, and fatally bashing his head in.'

Colin swallowed, and Lena blinked quickly and went still. 'What have drug rings got to do with Mark? Where's the one link, Colin? Pardon me if this upsets you, but you're not just scared for your son, are you? You're afraid of him. You've been shit scared since the first time we walked through your door.'

Colin was fighting so many demons he needed an exorcist. He was visibly struggling. Against his will, Paxton felt sorry for him. 'Marcus wouldn't —'

Paxton walked slowly round to face Colin, who was still sitting side-on in his chair. 'Wouldn't corrupt schoolkids with illegal substances? Wouldn't have dealings with organised crime?' He came to a stop in front of Colin. Too close for comfort, letting the edge come through in his voice. 'That is indeed the question, Colin. What *wouldn't* Marcus do?'

'He's not a murderer. OK? I know my son; he'd never do a thing like that.' The desperation in Colin's eyes was sickening to observe. He didn't believe it any more than they did. But God he wanted to.

'Did you tell him Mark lent you the money?'

A couple of seconds passed.

'Yes.'

Lena closed her eyes. Colin threw out his hands miserably.

'I was trying to scare him! Thought if I told him I was out of money and Mark refused to lend any more, he might break away from this bad crowd of his. I lied to him — told him Mark said he'd rather see his godson out on the streets than help him buy more drugs. And then look what happened!'

He stared back at the wall. 'He was furious ...'

Chapter SEVENTEEN

'WHAT DO YOU mean, he hasn't come back from lunch? It's after half-past three!' Paxton wished he was as lucky. He was due at work by five, and he couldn't afford to be hanging round waiting for his rather less flexible employment to be terminated. Besides which, he was incredibly sick of office interiors by now. After only a few days of it, it probably explained why he'd never worked in one. He'd have been climbing the walls. Or partitions, or whatever.

The place where Marcus worked was your typical sort of setup, he imagined, if he'd been at all worried about the décor. Not bad, if you liked your prisons carpeted. Steel-grey for preference, with a water cooler in one corner, nice-sized desks with plenty of leg room and ergonomic chairs, and there was even a view of sorts over a busy street in the central city. For himself, he'd rather have had Albert Park. Better yet, Mission Bay. He had to admit, whenever he walked by a window in the bar he had one of the best views in Auckland City. A wide expanse of beach, real sand not horrible hard pebbles, pohutukawas that were smothered in red blossoms in the summer, the blue waters of the Hauraki Gulf stretching out to the almost perfect volcanic cone of Rangitoto and the islands beyond, all of it so unlike England, and so lovely, he had to give himself a mental pinch every time he saw it. It always took him by surprise, whenever he found a plus side to serving drinkers and wiping down tables.

At the moment it was hard to focus on the positive. The clock on the wall was sapping all his fluffy qualities.

He frowned at the man nearest him, addressed by the receptionist as Geoff. Dressed for the office in khaki cargo pants and a trendily faded t-shirt, he was semi-reclining in a chair that likely cost close to what Paxton earned in a week.

'Is this sort of thing normal?'

The other bloke gave him a look that could have been interpreted a number of ways. None of them flattering to the subject under discussion.

'For Marcus it is. Spends less time in here than the cleaners.'

Another voice spoke up from a workstation opposite. 'Yeah, and this floor is disgusting. There's chips in behind the copier. Mind you, I suppose even the rats steer clear of his kind of company.'

The speaker was a curly-haired woman about the same age as Lena. She gave them a curious glance. 'Why do you want to see him?'

The way she said *him* made Lena warm to her immediately. 'He owes us money.' It wasn't a lie so much as a half-truth.

Geoff made a derisive noise, shaking his head at his monitor. 'Sounds about right.'

'Tell you what, though. If he comes back in, we'll let you know straight away.' The woman smiled, with more than a little pleasure. 'It's the least we can do.'

'Jesus, he must be hell on wheels to work with.'

'Work with, talk with, share the same air with ...' The curly-headed woman stopped to consider her response. 'Let's put it this way. He's just a stuck-up arsehole, if you'll excuse me. Bit "cool" for our lot. Thinks he's God's gift to software developing, does most of his work from home — to avoid socialising with the likes of us, you understand — and whenever he is in here, even asking to borrow a pen usually just gets you this look as if you're the biggest moron to ever exist on the face of the earth.'

Geoff nodded. 'Problem is, there's lots of them like that. Eh, Sash? Not all of them are as arrogant as he is, but one guy I know, whenever he isn't visiting *Lord of the Rings* chatrooms or probably stalking Peter Jackson on his days off, won't even acknowledge you unless he worked with you at his last job. I mean, Christ!'

'What happens if you tell him you didn't like the films?' Paxton asked.

Geoff grinned. He glanced over to the far end of the long office, where another man was seated in front of a computer, his spreading backside making a mockery of the ergo chair. He didn't so much sit as hulk.

'Why don't you try it?'

'Uh. Not this time, thanks.' Paxton looked back at Sasha. 'But if you *would* let us know if he comes back. It's really important.'

'My pleasure. But he'll probably roll in late tomorrow morning. No knowing, though — his hours are somewhat erratic. Sometimes he'll come in at six and be here till seven at night. The boss lets him do anything.'

'Say this for him, he usually gets the job done.'

Sasha admitted this grudgingly. 'He is very good at his job. Unfortunately. What's your number?'

Lena gave her her cellphone number, though hopeless of success. 'Don't tell him we were looking for him, though, will you?'

Sasha widened her eyes, palms raised in horror. 'Lordy, Miz Lena, I wouldn't never presume as to speak to the Masser!'

Geoff looked at her dryly. 'Say that in his earshot and he'd probably ask you out. Just his kind of woman.'

Privately, Paxton wondered if the attitude was just what was keeping her safe.

THE rain was making vision difficult, sheeting down in torrents that turned the irregular footpaths of Symonds Street into lakes and streaming gullies. The road was awash with floodwater. He sat in his car, watching the lights cast reflections on the slick paths. Nearest the gutter, the bus lay-by floated, its reflections constantly moving with the passage of the water. Every time a vehicle cut through the lane, it set up a spray, like surf crashing against the kerb. Only one person huddled under an umbrella for the bus, half in and half out of the shelter. Male. It wasn't Joanna.

He checked the time again. Half-past nine. She wasn't coming.

He forced the rage of disappointment down, rising like the water fit to choke him. But rage was too old an emotion to get the better of him. He sat there moments longer, breathing steadily, drifting away into the rivulets cascading down his windscreen, one after the other, mesmerised. Then he blinked, and with the calm came clarity.

Wasn't this what it was all about, when it came down to it? Plotting her movements? Tracing a pattern? If there wasn't ever any variation, then where was the challenge? He remembered her instrument case, and the intermittent lump sums in her savings account. She could have been off giving music lessons all evening — her money had to come from somewhere. And university timetables were hardly nine to five, any more than his job was. The more he thought about it, the stupider he felt. Of course. Only real social write-offs practised late every night, no matter *how* talented they were.

For some reason he pictured her as gifted. She had to have something, if she'd made it to postgrad. He liked the idea. One artist hunting another. Steeped in historical tradition, really. All the writers, composers, painters and actors, backstabbing and poisoning from time immemorial. Some of them had even died. The great Mozart himself, if you watched the movie. Although the poncy giggling in *Amadeus* had really got to him. On the whole he'd preferred the same year's *Killing Fields*. Less horrible, in a way. The deaths of millions of faceless peasants, as opposed to the death of one who truly mattered. Honestly, which was more tragic, when you really stopped to think? But what a coup, to be the author of such tragedy ...

He started the car and headed for Ellerslie. See if she was home, and who with. Bit late for tutoring now, but the notion was spawning additional thoughts. The weekend was coming up too, when most people did sports or dancing or ... music lessons. If she did indeed give lessons, that usually meant in regular slots. And in private. His spirits rose as he got on to the motorway, hitting a hundred in seconds. He wouldn't think of this evening as wasted. All part of the process, wasn't it? Trial and error. He'd learn as much as he could, so whenever he felt like striking, he'd hold all the cards.

Last night there had been the red Toyota parked in the drive. He'd find out who that belonged to soon enough. Just a quick visit to the post office with the licence plate number. Then there'd be another name, another element to add to the mix ... The devil was in the detail.

COLD pasta and cold casserole he could handle, but tackling the hours-old schnitzel, congealing in gravy in the fridge, was the fucking limit. A retread would have been more appealing. Stirling had just spent a tedious, bone-wearying shift with Gardner, going over and over cold details that yielded nothing but more questions, listening to him froth on about Paxton and his being right all along — except for lack of real evidence — and his previously hollow stomach caved in at the sight of the jellied gravy, skinned over on its strip of vulcanised meat. He lifted it experimentally. The meat left an unchanging corpse outline in the solidified brown gel. It reminded him of things best forgotten. His appetite was now dead on the table.

He'd left messages with a number of contacts on the street, but hadn't had any hits. To the disgust of Gardner, Paxton's neighbours hadn't noticed a thing on the morning in question, and many weren't the sort to help out the police anyway. Some were perfectly law-abiding members of the public, to be fair, but others had rap sheets as long as your arm. Though even the long arm of the law would have had a job stretching that bloody far.

Kirkpatrick had all but given it up, according to Tony Rees. Interviews with the staff on the graveyard (aha) shift at Countdown and McDonald's Greenlane had yielded precisely nothing. Just like the initial canvass of Patteson Ave. The lab results were starting to come in. Startlingly swift because there was so very little.

Preliminary DNA tests on all three victims had found nothing. To be expected with Mark Bradley, who'd been struck from behind, but there were also no human skin cells beneath the fingernails of the two dead women. Stacey Ryan had been found in two feet of water, effectively washing her clean of evidence. However, toxicology revealed large quantities of alcohol in her blood. Hardly surprising given that her flatmate barely remembered the evening they'd both had. There were also cotton fibres under the nails on Gloria Tan's right hand — which could have belonged to any man, woman or child in the country. Tests were still underway, as much use as CPR on a skeleton.

There was still no murder weapon for the Bradley case. He'd almost lost hope of ever finding one. Could have been burnt, buried, dumped off the beach and washed away clean down the coast like a harmless bit of driftwood ...

Nicola came in from the bedroom, looking both relieved and pleased to see him.

He rounded on her, holding his untouched plate. 'Couldn't you have stuck it in the microwave? It goes all hard in the fridge.'

She blinked, and her pleased expression slipped. 'I didn't know when you'd be home! For all I knew, it was going to be there overnight. You didn't ring me.'

'I was busy.' He shook his head, turning away from her to toss the schnitzel and hardened greying potatoes into the rubbish.

She watched him go back to the fridge and pour a glass of L&P. 'You have a mobile. How hard is it to even send me a text message? Thirty seconds.'

She was right, and it wasn't helping. Stung and wrong-footed, he lashed back. 'You could have rung me.'

'I did. First time your phone was switched off — you might want to check it for messages before you open your mouth about *that*.'

Whoops. He'd been in a high-up meeting with the DI and a few of the other detectives most of the afternoon. All of them confessing to knowing absolutely fuck all.

'And then I left a message with reception, who promised to tell you to call me as soon as you were available. Did she not pass on the message? Or is it just that you're *never* available?'

That pinched a nerve. 'That's bullshit! Don't give me that guilt trip crap, Nics.' He put down the glass and strode past her into the hall. 'I really don't need it right now.'

'Good! 'Cause you're not bloody *getting* it right now. Or until you're ready to spend some quality time that doesn't involve me trying to talk while you've got your mouth full, ready to bolt. If it's not on your way to bed, it's on your way out the door! All I get to see of you is your back these days, and even your bum doesn't have the same appeal it once did, I tell you that now.'

Her worry had been feeding upon itself for hours, and now days of mounting neglect were spilling out like burst sacks of garbage.

He turned back to her, unaccustomed to such bitterness in her tone. She was usually so sweet and easy-going; it was disconcerting. Had he been wrong all the time? It came to him with a start of guilt. Had the smiles really been hiding all this?

'Hey —'

'I love you, Andy. But I'm beginning to think it's one-sided.'

'No!' He had to stop, trying to think of something to say that wouldn't come out sounding clichéd and insincere. His tired brain wasn't throwing up any winners. 'It's just work. You know that. Bloody Gardner ...'

'Did he tell you not to call me?'

'What?'

'Did he tell you never to talk to me whenever you're home?'

'Nic, don't be so bloody ridiculous.'

She was blocking the light from the kitchen, half-lit in the gloom of the hall. 'I realise you don't have the easiest job, Andy, but I *am* your wife, and the least you could do is share things with me if there's something on your mind. Or if you can't share things with me, then at least just let me talk to you, and don't shut me out and snap at me whenever I try to help you! Like I'm just Gardner in drag — that's how you're making me feel! Otherwise I'm not your wife, am I? I'm just some woman who helps with the rent. And I *hate* it.'

Shocked, he saw a tear splash on to the floor. In vain he struggled for words of comfort. Should he be putting his arms round her?

But he was too tired and guilty to move. He stood there looking at her for eternities, feeling a fool, unable to think of a thing. And feeling that if he ever did, it would have been too late. Too much time had gone past now since he should have spoken. He waited another beat, then gave it up. He turned around and kept going, into the bedroom.

ON such a shit of a Thursday night, the busyness came in odd patches. The restaurant was pretty full, sending a number of customers their way, but fewer people wanted to go out for a drink. They'd get wet enough just stepping outside. Paxton skulked at a corner of the bar, keeping an eye out for customers while he picked up the phone, though he needn't really have bothered. Adam was polishing the same glass for the third time, for lack of anything better to do.

'Give us a free one, Adam, I'm so thirsty!' Mel was a blonde waitress and hospitality student who worked one night a week in the bar, or whenever she was needed. Tonight she was on tables, and serving a family of gluttons.

'Sorry. I'm busy.' He picked up another glass and inspected it for dust motes.

'Smartarse. Come oooon. Just one, it's not like you're doing anything.'

'You're getting more tips than I am down this way. Why don't you pay for it?'

She gave him a filthy leer, trailing her finger along the bar. 'What would you like?'

'Get lost.'

'First I've ever heard of you being picky ...'

'Get lost.'

'Remember Kelly, James? We kept telling him off for letting dogs into the bar ...'

'Shut up. Go harass your customers.'

Paxton tried to stop sniggering, but it wasn't working. Adam watched her saunter off with a cheeky waggle of her bottom. 'Bitch.'

His tone was indulgent. Anything was a welcome distraction. Entertainment over, Paxton went back to his dialling. The number was for Marcus's apartment. He knew

Lena was somewhere around there already, watching out for his return. Every minute he half expected the phone to ring, but so far the silence had been absolute. He couldn't take the waiting anymore.

'Who are you calling?'

Paxton ignored him. The phone in the apartment was ringing. Once ... twice ... It got to three rings, and Paxton began to think his man wasn't home. How long could it take someone to reach the phone inside a shoebox? Four. Finally an answering machine cut in. The voice was the cruellest Paxton had ever heard. The mere sound of it was a splash of cold water to the senses. 'This is Marcus Davenport. Unfortunately I'm unable to take your call just at the moment, as I am out on a very interesting new project ... Please don't be offended if I can't get back to you straight away. I'm finding it rather difficult to squeeze everyone in.' There was the faintest breath of laughter on the other end. The finale was curt, arrogant and amused. 'Leave your message after the beep.'

The phone beeped. Paxton hung up, repulsed. He felt again those iron hands coiling round his throat. The bastard was *taunting* them! Damn him! *Flaunting* his own invulnerability, secure he wouldn't get found out. That everyone else was too stupid to be in the know ... It was an unpleasant reminder that even if he and Lena did track Marcus down, unless they got lucky they still wouldn't have any proof. What were they going to do? Threaten him? Secretly tape his confession while he sobbed with remorse in their laps?

This whole business was over his head, and he'd just be throwing himself to the cops if he went ahead with it. Then again, it could be his Get Out of Jail Free card, to clearing both himself and his hypersensitive conscience. It was a hell of a price to pay for Lena's company. But he had to admit to himself, the interest ran deeper than that. Knowing what he knew, he was in it to the death now — had been since the beginning if he acknowledged it. Where was the point of no return? Wasn't it fate, from the moment he stumbled across Mark on the grass?

For good or for ill this had to be seen through. He prayed to every deity there was that they weren't too late.

Chapter EIGHTEEN

DEPRESSING, THIS, THE march of metropolisation. This might have been almost any city in the world now, from where Paxton stood. The street was your usual drab commuter grey, unflattered by streetlamps, with fag packets in the gutters and a line-up of fairly undistinguished buildings. Some elderly by local standards but even these were younger than the public loos back home, and about as interesting. Britain was old, famous for having ghosts under every stone and hedgerow. Here everything was by comparison new. Not so many people, not so many ghosts.

Paxton realised he'd come to consider this place as his home, from which the uniqueness was fast disappearing. This collection of little islands, barely larger than his own Britain, but with an almost unpeopled landscape as varied as the accents from Cornwall to Inverness. He even felt affection for the locals' endearing habit of clutching at the skirts of any visitor and going, 'But do you *like* us?' then still waving a fist at the big boys of world politics whenever their vigorously upheld ideals were being shat on. It couldn't stay this way for ever, and Paxton realised with a pang that he regretted it.

The harbingers of change were cropping up like cold sores all over Auckland. High-rise apartment blocks, designed by architects and in Paxton's book consequently guaranteed pieces of shit. Those that didn't leak were still ugly. All wall and window and little grace, they were making accommodation in the central city cheaper as well as nastier. The worst of them reminded Paxton of council flats he'd seen in London, only here they were touted as trendy. Give him a garden any day.

He had to admit, though, that as apartments went, Marcus's wasn't too bad. They'd gone for the classical line rather than something that would date within ten years, and the bald concrete was softened by thoughtful detailing. Almost classy. There were even a couple of trees on the pavement outside. A user couldn't afford *this* bit of posh unless he was making more than small-time sales — or had a dad with deep pockets. Quite how Marcus was meeting the rent if he was so hard up was anybody's guess.

Paxton looked up at the balconied windows, some lit, some in darkness. He wondered which one was Marcus's. So many windows, all the same, but behind one of them lurked something rotten ... Like a children's game. *One of these things is not like the other* ... He felt a prickling on his skin.

'I haven't seen him all night. But if he's not home at this time of night, he's not coming home at all.'

Lena was plainly as twitchy as he, making a little more movement than necessary. She'd hung around the apartment all afternoon and almost all night until Paxton had come to join her, with only a brief break to grab dinner. She fumbled through her handbag, looking for imaginary keys while the residents punched in the admittance codes on the pad by the door. The first pair had kept their backs right in front of the keypad, totally obscuring the numbers. The second time was the opposite — the smart woman with the killer shoes had smiled straight at Lena while she entered her code, making covert surveillance impossible. And all the while Lena was fighting the urge to look over her shoulder, feeling terribly exposed every time she stood with her back to the door, fossicking for nothing through her bag. Feeling at any moment there might be a hand on her wrist, or a dig in her spine, and a familiar voice murmuring in her ear, 'Hello, Lena' ...

By the time she finally managed to get a look at the numbers without being seen, her nerves were shot to hell. She was, she admitted to Paxton, not cut out for the spying game.

Neither for that matter was he. He watched her key in the numbers, feeling that maybe for once he should have picked something up from the bar. But Jack Daniel's was more known for starting trouble than avoiding it. Before the night was over, Paxton might be needing those unfuddled reflexes ...

The light went green, and the doors unlocked. They stepped in-side.

Very nice. The lighting was on power-saving mode, but there was enough to admire by. Flooring looked like slate. The thoughtful pot plants and Pacific rim styling. And quite possibly its own resident murderer. The chill in here was less, but the extra heat did little for Paxton's nerves.

Lena glanced around rapidly, but her steps towards the lifts were slow. Everything echoed, even, Paxton fancied, his own breathing. Lena pressed the button for the lift, which opened at once. No one else was using it. What she saw inside gave her a jolt. A reflection stared back at her from the mirrored wall, with a man behind it. Her and Paxton. That was enough to scare the crap out of her anyway.

'It's two a.m. It's the height of rudeness. He's probably asleep. What if we're wrong, what if he really isn't the murderer? What the hell are we going to do then?'

Paxton gave her a look. 'The thing you should really be worrying about is: what if he is?' He let her think about it. About exactly what might be waiting. The lift door slid shut again as they watched.

'But we'll never solve anything unless we try, will we?' He muttered, 'You want to have fallen for a bouncer, not a frigging barman.'

She looked at him, then kissed him firmly on the mouth. She stabbed at the lift button. 'Come on, Paxton.' The door reopened. She got in and hit the button for the sixth floor.

'There's two of us, and I've been here all afternoon, so we might as well.'

He was fairly certain she was bluffing. He was damn grateful for it all the same.

He glanced at her as the lift ascended. Even the soft whirr got beneath the skin.

'You thought what you're going to say to him?'

'Constantly ...' Her expression was unreadable, and oddly vulnerable. 'But quite frankly I'll be lucky if I get "hello" out.'

She took up hardly any space in the lift. A fact of which she seemed acutely aware. Before Paxton could reply the ascent stopped, and the door opened on the sixth floor. Here too it was empty, and a great deal more enclosed than the lobby. Stepping out of the lift made little difference to the caged-in atmosphere.

They walked along the hall, reading the numbers on the doors. 6C, 6D, 6E ...

'Imaginative, this lot.' She gave him a small smile. His pulse accelerated as they reached 6F, then 6G, then finally, 6H. The sign of the beast.

'Here we go.' Testing, he turned the handle. Locked. As he'd expected. Nothing else for it. Before he could back out, he rapped his fist on the door.

They could hear nothing through the wood. The silence fell again thicker than blood.

Lena knocked on the door, more gently. 'Marcus! It's Lena. I just want to talk.'

Still nothing. They exchanged doubting glances. 'Maybe he really isn't home.'

'Maybe he's done a flit to his dad's. Wouldn't put it past Colin to be sheltering him.' He was still angry.

'He said he didn't know where he was. He was worried the gang might have got hold of him.'

'I'm more worried he's got hold of someone else.'

Lena met his eyes for a beat. She'd tried to ring Marcus herself, and heard that message. *I'm finding it rather difficult to squeeze everyone in.* Lena turned back to the door. 'No matter whether you're home or not, Marcus, I'm not leaving here until I've seen you. So if you are listening, be prepared to trip over me on your way to the gym, or the shops, or work or *wherever.* Sooner or later you're going to have to come out — and when you do I'll be waiting.'

They held their breath. But nothing happened. Marcus wasn't home. Paxton looked at Lena. Poor girl, all that effort. Keying herself up — for what? As for himself, he didn't know whether to be more disappointed or relieved.

'We'll have to c—'

A shoulder slamming into his chest arrested him mid-syllable. He fell backward into blackness, for several moments seeing nothing but stars as his head smashed into the wall. The pain was matched by the agony as he crumpled with all his weight to the floor, his ankle twisted beneath him. He heard Lena grunt as she hit the wall beside him, thrown aside by the shape barrelling through the door. Marcus was home.

And he ran ...

With supreme effort Paxton struggled to his feet, catching his breath in a hiss of excruciating disbelief as the pain turned his ankle to water. He wobbled, but kept his balance. Seeing the door swinging shut at the end of the hall — the door to the stairs. Lena was gone. Down the stairs, after a murderer ...

He forced his legs to move, wincing at every step, the blood in his head throbbing even more than the pain. He shouted, hearing his voice flung back at him.

'Lena! Don't!'

Behind him he heard a door open, and a female voice snarled, 'For Christ's sake, it's after two in the morning! Don't you have any fucking consideration?' He never even glanced back, driven on by a panic that overrode everything. He reached the stairs and crashed through the door, limping and unsteady, taking the stairs two at a time.

'Lena! It's too bloody dangerous!'

The man had killed three people at least, was someone whose strength had easily overpowered a fit young woman in her prime. Stronger than Lena.

The pounding of footsteps below him was getting further and further away. He wrenched his ankle again as he lurched down the stairs, bracing himself on the wall to keep from plummeting straight down. He gritted his teeth against the pain, nose stinging with tears. Fervently he prayed his ankle would hold up, throwing himself down faster and faster. The lighting here was dreary, like an underground bunker. Descending below the earth, into hell. He heard a woman scream, reverberating back up the stairwell.

'Lee!'

He was screaming as well now, but he didn't care. His breath sounded like a sob in his ears, enveloped in the gloom and the pain and the fear. He hurtled into the wall on a curve, striking his shoulder violently, and felt nothing. His feet were moving too fast for his body, out of control, reaching critical velocity. Somewhere close he could hear the sounds of a struggle, but it was too late. His feet fell away.

He tumbled forward, catching his forearms a vicious wallop on the next stair and rolling remorselessly downward to the bottom. He came to a jarring halt against the wall, at a sharp angle to the ground, his head spinning and every inch of him singing with pain. Only a few stairs kept him from the bottom, where just inside the door to the lobby, Lena was pinned to the floor, grappling against the man who was crushing her head into the ground. The young man with the dark hair, and the face flushing red with strain.

Without really knowing how, Paxton got to his feet, launching himself from the stair at Marcus's flank. He was almost incoherent, not even hearing what he was shouting.

'Get off her! You bastard, let *go*!'

The surprise and the momentum knocked Marcus off guard, and by sheer instinctive terror Lena stuck a knee in his groin. He curled in shock, spitting abuse like an insulted whore. With a final spurt Paxton flipped him on his back, trapping his arms, his breath grunting from his body. And Paxton was face to face with Mark's killer.

As he looked into those eyes, he *knew* ...

'It wasn't him.'

He could barely speak the words for want of air. Gazing down in horror at the man who wasn't a murderer. He felt dizzy and sick.

He glanced wildly up at Lena. She was staring back at him, her chest shuddering, eyes wide and uncomprehending.

He dropped his head back to Marcus, lying stunned and limp with exhaustion on the floor. All his strength suddenly left him. He felt weak as a child.

'It wasn't him.'

'I don't do much in the way of sales these days. Can't afford the risk.'

Marcus poured perked coffee into three matching cups. They were designer, like the rest of the place, and the type of drugs Marcus mainly dealt in. Painful to observe, the fucker certainly had taste.

The apartment was two rooms plus ensuite, and everything in it — from the glass-topped ironwork coffee-table to the chrome kitchen appliances to the original print on the painted feature-wall — contrasted sharply with the Garage Sale Collection gracing Paxton's own ex-state house in GI. There was not an article out of place, except for themselves.

Marcus seemed completely at home. His manner as he discussed his dealing was offhand, as if admitting he'd let his jogging slide. That he clearly hadn't; Paxton had to give him that. Paxton didn't usually bother much with what he looked like, which wasn't too bad, he supposed, but he was thankful that Lena was so pissed off with their host. Come to that, so was he. Vain prick. Wasn't so cute with that blossoming black eye.

'But I mean, Dad's rolling in it. He barely ever touches what he makes, and Mum's just the same. Golf subscription, the odd trip overseas, a nice car every ten years ...' He snorted. 'I couldn't believe it when he started coming down on me. I mean, what are they going to do with it all? They wouldn't know how to live if you marooned them on Ibiza.'

'So you thought you'd give extortion a go. Good one.'

'Look, don't start going all high and mighty on me, little Angelena. You can't take it with you, and they've both got years on the clock yet. What a waste! It's not my fault he's gullible.' He laughed, still disbelieving. Lounging back on the sofa facing them, one arm resting along the back.

'You really are an utter bastard, Marcus. You made him believe your life was in danger!'

'Dearie me, we are getting our knickers in a knot, aren't we?' Somehow he managed to take a sip of coffee without losing the insouciant grin.

Paxton glanced around at the spare furnishings in their tasteful colours. 'You've managed a nice apartment, I must say. Everything matches, doesn't it?'

'Gotta have co-ordination, James.'

'So how about another eye like that one?'

Marcus shut up.

'And anyway, wasn't it *nice* of Daddy to tip you off that we were coming?'

Marcus shrugged, no longer smiling. 'He has his good points.' They'd wormed the truth out of him while he was still off-balance after the chase. The answerphone message had been a nice touch. Typical of the little toe-rag. Didn't like the idea of giving up his money. Or more honestly, what he'd bought with it. He'd had a nice little scam running, emptying his father's pockets, and they'd been about to piss on his parade. Several aspects of his behaviour were best not brought to the police's attention. So in desperation he'd hid, and failing that, run. As he'd admitted, he wouldn't have tried *that* if he'd known Lena wasn't alone. He was perfectly open about his cowardice. But he wasn't the sort to stay down long. Like six rum-and-Cokes and a couple of pints of lager.

'It's his own fault he never taught me about saving. All the time growing up I had everything I wanted, never wanted for anything — and now he's going to cut me off? "Make me stand on my own two feet," he says. I don't think so, Colin. I work hard; don't I deserve a break? How'm I supposed to afford a holiday to the States if I've got digs like these to maintain? I don't even know what black looks like. You should see my Amex!'

He took an angry swig of coffee. 'He ought to thank me for not being stupid enough to try playing major-league dealer. How'd he like it if he ended up bailing me out of prison? That wouldn't go down well with the board, or Mum's friends at the City Mission.'

Lena smacked her cup down with too much force. Some of its barely touched contents slopped over on to the glass. Her eyes were narrowed with fury. 'I wish you'd been there, Marcus, to see the look on your selfish dad's face.' She grew sarcastic. 'What a loser! Dumb, useless Moneybags — who incidentally, is helping to support *you* and your pathetic existence — had the utter *stupidity* to be terrified out of his sodding brain that you were going to die! To lie for you, to me, and protect you even when he thought you were guilty of murdering his best friend! Damn, how do you put up with it?'

Marcus couldn't have looked less interested. 'Just shut up, Lena.'

Paxton knew of something that would interest him.

'Just one problem, Marcus. Mark got it in writing. About the money. It was in his organiser — with Colin's own signature. Lena found it this morning.'

Marcus looked rattled, his eyes shifting to Lena. She smiled with satisfaction. 'Should have remembered earlier. Never dropped an appointment.'

Paxton continued. 'Man of scruples, your dad. Shame it doesn't run in the family.'

'Be *awful* if the police were to hear about your little second business. Tax dodging, just for starters ...'

Marcus was in a corner, and he knew it. He rolled his eyes in disgust. 'All right. I've got a small stash in the bedroom. Once I get rid of that, I'll pay you back your money — and not a word to Colin.' He raised his index finger in warning, eyeballing them both seriously. 'Satisfied?'

'I wouldn't touch your filthy money, Marcus.' Lena got up. 'I wouldn't know what's been rolled up in it.'

Paxton leant over for a private word as she made for the door. 'Ever considered modelling, mate? Money's good ...' His friendly gaze shifted to Marcus's eye, which was colouring up nicely. 'And I hear heavy make-up's real trendy these days ...'

Chapter NINETEEN

THE PRINTER SPEWED out the results from the early testing, gathered from all the murder sites. The sum total of their knowledge so far, neatly tabulated by a detective. Ignorance documented in detail.

Extraneous DNA — none. Prints — none. Murder weapons — none. Clues — not a fucking one. Gardner screwed the printout viciously into a ball and hurled it across the office to the rubbish bin parked next to the copier. After striking off the wall it bounced from the rim and rolled several feet. Nobody moved to pick it up.

'I don't ... fucking ... believe it.'

Graeme Kirkpatrick watched the ball of paper slowly decompress, swelling and opening like a paper flower. 'I know. All that work, and nothing to show for it. Makes you sick, doesn't it?'

'It's been days now. Do you realise, this is the longest stretch since he started? We'll be seeing more bodies soon, no fear. And what do we tell the public when we do?'

Kirkpatrick shrugged wearily, intoning the official fob-off. 'We can't comment on that. We don't want to alert the suspects at this sensitive stage of the inquiries.'

Gardner hissed. 'Suspects! What suspects? There is only one. He's the only bloody link. All I need is for him to make one slip — just one! But he's being too damn careful. He knows we're on to him.'

'Then I guess you'll just have to wait for the next body to roll in.'

'Very funny, Graeme. I'm the one heading the investigation, not you. It's *my* head the press'll serve up on a plate. Not yours!'

A detective doing her copying hunched her head lower over the machine, struggling to hide a grin. As Gardner had his back turned, only Kirkpatrick saw. He sighed, walking towards the door. 'Just don't rush into things. Nobody wants a slip-up, I don't care whose name's in the news.' He reached the door and turned back: 'We *all* look like morons if the shit hits the fan. Government inquiry, you name it.'

'Don't stress yourself, Graeme. Call it a gut feeling.' Gardner broke into a shark-like grin. 'A sixth sense.' He followed Kirkpatrick down the corridor. 'Oooh! It's coming to me in a flash! I'm seeing — what's this? A man behind bars ...'

'Sergeant?' Both of them turned. It was a young DC whose name Gardner had forgotten. If indeed he'd ever known. The DC was looking both harried and excited.

'I've been looking for you everywhere. Been a report filed, sir.' He waited just a fraction longer than was necessary before dropping his bombshell. 'James Paxton's been accused of assault.'

Gardner's reaction was gratifying. *'What?'*

'You know the first victim, Mark Bradley?'

'Not fucking personally — what's he got to do with it?'

'His daughter was reported in connection with an attempted burglary-slash-assault last night. And Paxton was with her.'

'Come into my office.'

Gardner made the short trip almost at a run, with the DC and Kirkpatrick in his wake. Gardner grabbed for a pen, pulling a pad across the desk towards him and perching sideways on his chair. Kirkpatrick rested on the edge of the desk. There weren't any more seats, so the constable remained standing.

'Give me the details. Was *she* the assailant?'

'No. In fact, the guy who came in didn't want her involved at all. She was just mentioned as having been there at the time of the assault. Apparently she came with Paxton and tried to talk him out of it, when he grew violent.'

He paused, his face hopeful. 'You think this could be relevant to the inquiry?'

Gardner looked at his pad. He'd written the name Paxton and ringed it, without even noticing. Like a teenager in lust. 'I think it might well be. Thanks, er ...' Fuck it. 'Can you let me know the contact details of the guy who filed the statement?'

'Sure. It's a Marcus Davenport —'

'Hang on. Not the Davenport who ...' He'd blurted it out involuntarily, totally knocked for six.

'What?'

But Gardner had regained control of himself. His brain, however, roared on without braking, through all the signals. Marcus, not Colin. But the name could be no mere coincidence. 'Did he say how he knew the offenders?'

The DC checked a bit of paper in his hand. 'Says here the woman is a friend of the family, and James Paxton is her boyfriend.'

Bingo. Different man, same family.

'All the details on that?' Gardner nodded at the paper in the DC's hand.

'Yeah.'

'Let me have it. We'll waste less time.' He snatched it before the DC could respond. 'Cheers.'

The DC looked a bit at a loss as Gardner focused on the paper. Kirkpatrick gave him a look of approval. 'Thanks, mate. Well done.'

The younger man gave a watery grin and vanished. Kirkpatrick gazed at the carpet, pensively thwacking a heel against the floor. He straightened unconsciously as Gardner looked up at him, a smile like an oil slick over his face.

'We've got our arrest, Graeme.'

NICE apartment, this Marcus Davenport had. Had it all set up so he could work from home. Lucky for some.

'Excuse me a moment while I clear this away.' Marcus fiddled with a few keys on the Mac that rested on the flash little glass table, then shut the lid and took it into the other room. Gardner took a good look around as he sat. Rees took up almost all of the tiny sofa, leaving him a sliver to squeeze into.

He'd chosen to bring Tony Rees this time, seeing as no one was overly busy chasing up leads. He'd had a strong reluctance to bring DC Stirling. Young Andy didn't seem too happy about abandoning his pet and facing the facts. His mood of late had been less than pleasant. No doubt if he'd known what Gardner was up to he'd have been ripping his blanky. Let this be a lesson to him, then.

They got the introductions out of the way quickly. Gardner could hardly wait to get into it. 'So, Mr Davenport. Before we start, can I just ask what relation you are to Colin Davenport?'

'He's my father. Was it you who spoke to him then?'

'That's right, I did, as a matter of fact. Very nice chap. I didn't know he had a son.'

Marcus grinned engagingly. 'He was so impressed with the service I thought I'd give it a go.'

Gardner smiled. Rees kept his face deadpan. 'Just make sure we don't charge you for it.'

Gardner cleared his throat, frowning, as it got a laugh. 'Speaking of which ... Can you go through what happened last night? I know you've already given a statement down at the station, but this is part of a separate investigation. I know it's a nuisance, but it's important.'

'I'd heard about that. You're talking about Mark's murder, aren't you? And those other women?'

'That's right. Although this may have absolutely no bearing on that whatsoever. We just have to investigate every possibility, as you can understand.'

'I'll do what I can to help. I truly *hope* this has got nothing to do with it.' Marcus spoke slowly, his manner troubled. 'Thing is, Lena has been really upset since it happened. Of course. It's only to be expected. But — I'm worried for her.'

The two detectives waited. Rees had his pad out, ready to take notes.

Marcus's brow was creased, and his words burst out with all the force of feeling. 'She's just so fragile! I'm really afraid ... he's got some kind of hold over her. I don't know where on earth she met him. But he's masquerading as a psychic or something, is that right? That's what my dad said. Personally, I'd say his only visions would come from bad trips, not spirits.'

Gardner leaned forward, blinking. 'What makes you say that?' Marcus looked uncomfortable. 'I don't know if I should be telling this to a couple of cops. I used to do drugs, back in high school. I've been clean for years; you can check this apartment if you like. But Lena hasn't seen me in aeons. I wouldn't blame her for thinking I was still the same guy. Some of my old mates still are. Why I don't see them now, I suppose ... Anyway, when I saw this guy — James — the first thing I thought was: drugs.'

'You think he was after drugs here?'

'It's the most logical explanation I can come up with. I mean — what else would explain behaviour like that?'

'What did he do, Mr Davenport? What happened?'

'I went outside for a bit, to get some air. I'd been hard at my software programmes all day and I needed to stretch my legs. It's convenient, but it's not exactly palatial in here. Anyway, so when I came back from my walk —'

'And this was?' Gardner wanted this watertight. A coffin without any leaks.

Marcus thought. 'About two? I often work late. Anyway, I saw a couple of people outside my door. This guy was trying to break in, and a girl was fighting with him, trying to pull him back. Looked like he was hurting her. So I yelled out from down the corridor and ran towards them. When the girl turned, I saw it was Lena, and I was so stunned I didn't know what to do.'

Rees's pen was scribbling fast along the paper. Marcus took a deep breath and went on.

'By then I'd almost reached them. While I was sort of slowing down, staring, he grabbed me —'

'Mr Paxton grabbed you?'

'That's right. He just attacked me! Right in the middle of the corridor. Lena screamed at him to stop, but he just wouldn't. He went berserk, yelling at me. I'm sure the neighbours must have heard him. Anyway don't ask me how, but I managed to break free of him, and ran off down the stairs. I was so scared I couldn't think.'

He paused for a minute, lining up his thoughts. 'He followed me, and Lena chased after him trying to stop him, and when he finally caught up to me, he gave me this black eye.'

The bruised eye had been visible from the moment they'd entered the room. Gardner found himself staring at it. It almost struck him as beautiful. Beautiful, God-given proof. Staring him in the face, so to speak. What Marcus didn't tell them was that it actually came from Lena. She'd smacked him one while they'd been struggling on the floor.

'You might also want to check out my ribcage.' Marcus raised his shirt, displaying a purpling row of ribs that made Gardner wince just to look at them. Marcus focused on the damage. *Anything* to keep from laughing. He wanted to see that Pommy git mouth his way out of this one.

Sadly he shook his head.

'I still can't believe it. Dad said he was rude to *him* as well. But I never thought —'

'We should talk to your father again.'

Marcus's reply was swift. 'No. That's OK. It wasn't anything major. He just wants to forget the whole thing.'

'Well, if we have any further questions we'll get in touch.' Gardner rose with a little difficulty from his tight space beside the detective.

'Thanks. I appreciate your quick action. Nice to see you're taking it seriously.'

'We always take cases of assault seriously. They often lead to more serious things ...'

Marcus nodded, and shook hands. Rees gave him a civil nod in return, then opened the door. As he shut it behind them, he carefully scrutinised the lock, bending down to inspect it. He rubbed his fingers over the keyhole, questing.

'What are you doing?'

'Checking out his story. Just doing my job.'

Gardner was irritated. He knew he ought to have thought of it. Knew likewise that there wasn't any point.

'Can't see any signs of a break-in ...'

'It was just an attempted break-in. He probably didn't have time to do damage.' Gardner strode back towards the lifts. Uniform were dealing with the neighbours.

Rees gave it one last look, then unfolded to his considerable height. He nodded again to himself, with a noncommittal shrug. The thing he liked least about all this was the thought that someone would have to tell Andy.

PAXTON sat on his couch, watching *The Mummy* on DVD. The player was another essential purchase — though he ought to have thought of a comfortable sofa. He couldn't face the idea of reading a book at the moment; turning the pages was too much effort. Good old-fashioned mindless entertainment was what he really needed.

Well, no, change that. What he *really* needed was a time machine that would take him back to last Wednesday week and ensure that he never got out of his damn car. Fantasy or science fiction — pity they were both a load of bollocks.

He paused the DVD as the badly decomposing High Priest Imhotep tried to stick his tongue down Rachel Weisz's throat. Lucky bloke.

Lena had gone out with a bunch of workmates and friends from university. The ones from the funeral, he was guessing. Retail therapy, the female's way out. He'd have asked her to join him here, but he knew that time apart was probably in their best interests. It wasn't as if Paxton had dazzlingly positive associations. She'd laughed when he told her what he'd said to Marcus, but they'd both been pretty quiet on the way home. Saying things for the sake of it, just to fill an awkward silence. Then about halfway into the drive they'd both shut up, without even noticing the change. When he glanced over at her in the passenger's seat, she'd almost looked asleep with her head resting against the window. Oblivious to the chill of the glass.

He'd wanted so badly for Marcus to be the murderer. So badly for it to be *over*. He'd cut off every damn corner that didn't fit, just to jam the piece into the slot. The thought brought him up sharp. Who did that remind him of? For the first time he felt a dawning of sympathy for Gardner. He could see how easy it was to get carried away by the desire for closure. Blaming Marcus to make it all go away ...

He shunted the comparison aside. They were still a pair of cunts. End of story.

No wonder he was hungry. It was almost two. He went into the kitchen and opened a tin of baked beans. He tipped the contents into a saucepan and put on some toast, then fried up an egg. Comfort food. Bright red beans, sunny-coloured yolk. My, wasn't he Mr Analytical today? Piss easy to cook was the answer. He was a fair-to-middling cook at most times. Days of mediocrity, and periods of sheer brilliance, like the time he'd experimented with soaking blueberries in red wine, then stuck them in a chocolate pudding and served the lot with brandied cream. One of his proudest moments; but rare was the occasion he couldn't eat at least half of it. Even so, he'd rather have slept with Nigella than imitated her. That brought back thoughts of Lena.

He poured the beans onto the toast and dumped the saucepan in the sink, full of water. As usual, the breakfast dishes were still waiting to be done. He'd get to them later. While away another half hour once the film was over. He dropped back onto the sofa and unfroze *The Mummy*, then stuck his knife into the egg, watching as the yolk oozed into the tomato sauce. Paxton made a face. Probably shouldn't have paused it while Botched Skin Peel was on the screen.

The doorbell rang, just as Paxton was drying the last of the dishes. The logical first thought was Lena. He couldn't think of anyone else who'd ever visited. He wiped his wrinkled hands on the tea towel and went to the door.

A couple of coppers stood on the step. One stood military style, his arms behind his back. The other one also seemed to have pinched a leaf out of *FBI for Dummies*.

'Are you James Paxton?'

'Yes. Where's DS Gardner — off sick today?'

'We'd like to ask you to come to the station with us, please.' Paxton felt the egg and beans scramble inside his stomach.

'What? Am I under arrest?'

‘Not at the moment, sir. We’d just like you to come with us.’ Again he had the strange sensation that someone else was operating his mouth by remote control. ‘But what *for*? I’m going to miss work!’ While his mind suddenly spat out: *Marcus.*

God. The fucking bastard. They’d nail him for it this time.

‘Best if you accompany us to the police station, sir. It’ll all be sorted out then.’

Chapter TWENTY

STIRLING STARED AT the steam curling off his coffee, wafting uselessly away. Somewhere in the midst of nutting out theories he'd drifted. He was wondering what Nicola was doing. Devising marketing strategies for home furnishings? On the phone with clients, probably. Or possibly laughing at some dirty email she'd been sent by a colleague. She frequently sent them on to Stirling. The ones with H Dorbeck as the origin were always tasteless, off-colour and fast-forwarded through CIB within minutes. Nicola Stirling was very popular with the crew. But there'd been nothing in his in-box today but an internal memo to please return any glasses to the Barracks, as they were running low again. The policemen's bar was always hardest hit by petty theft.

The ringing of his cellphone unfogged his head. He made a grab for it in his pocket.

'Hello?'

'DC Stirling I presume?'

The voice was familiar, a grumbly, thick Kiwi joker accent that called up the image of an honest man of the soil and very little brain. None of it was even remotely accurate.

'Harry?'

'Give the boy a prize.' There was a rumbly laugh over the phone. 'Tell you what, I'll cut you a deal on a blonde dancer.'

'Pole-dancer?'

'Ballet, son. Thought you'd want a bit of culture.'

'Cheers, but I'm sorted for that, thanks.' Or used to be, he thought sadly. 'What can I do for you, Harry?'

Old Harry, as he liked to be known, had nicked his name off Harry Houdini. But whereas Houdini had performed all his own tricks, it was Harry's pretty assistants who did all his, as Harry loved to point out. Harry had grown rich off the backs of numerous women. Literally.

The name fitted in so many ways. Stirling had heard of him by reputation before he'd even laid eyes on him, and had thought immediately of Hatchet Harry from *Lock, Stock and Two Smoking Barrels*, except that this Harry had never been known to take an 'atchet to anybody. He wasn't a betting man; he simply dealt in whores' flesh. Dirty Harry was another name that sprang all too easily to mind.

He was one of the sharpest men Stirling had ever met. Harry had had his knuckles rapped for a few minor incidents, but by and large he was a fish too slippery for the force to reckon with. While still on the beat, Stirling had patched up one of his ladies after some drunken knob-heads had failed to understand the concept of 'off-duty', and taken her to hospital without a word. Two weeks later he'd found another higher than her hemline, with a snap-lock bag of what was probably half Panadol she'd just bought from a spiky-haired youth in a club. He'd questioned her, found out where she worked, and gave her a note for her boss as a warning. He'd threatened her with arrest if she didn't pass it on, and she was so spaced out she'd have believed she was the Virgin herself if he'd said so, despite the see-through blouse with no bra and the almost non-existent skirt.

The next time Stirling had patrolled K Road, Harry had come. Shorter than Stirling, but solid as a brick, what Harry's figure lacked in grace it made up for in muscle. He had a plain, no-nonsense face you could pass a thousand times without ever noticing, somewhere between forty and fifty. He wore discreet, dun-coloured trousers and a Line 7 shirt, the epitome of smart-casual, and with nary a gold chain or carpet of chest hair in sight. He strolled up to Stirling's car as Stirling eyed a group of pissed-up teenagers trying to figure out which foot was which.

Politely he motioned for Stirling to wind down his window. Silly him. Stirling had guessed he was looking for help finding his daughter in one of the clubs.

'Evening, Officer. Remember passing a note to one of the ladies a few weeks back?'

Stirling tried not to look too startled. The other man ignored it, supremely unperturbed. His earthy, uneducated drawl was oddly out of tune with his vaguely preppy appearance. Like hearing the Queen do Ali G.

'I got it, thanks. I had you pointed out. I wanted to come over and chat.'

The pimp's security could have whipped the force's any day. Stirling had debated radioing for back-up, but Harry's demeanour had been disarmingly friendly, in a blunt sort of way.

'Firstly, thank you for telling me about Trix's problem. I appreciate it.'

'Trix? Nice ...' Bet the clients got a kick out of doing Trix more than she did.

Harry smiled slightly. 'Well, well. A smart copper ... She didn't even get it till some kind fuck explained it to her.'

He was regarding Stirling with interest, as if holding auditions for another slot. 'She's clean now. I saw to it. I won't have my workers so out of it they can't defend themselves. This business is dangerous enough as it is.'

'You're not selling?'

Harry's lips hitched up in amusement. 'Oh yes, I am. But not drugs, son.'

That laconic attitude had walked straight off a Speight's beer ad. But this was bent as hell. Stirling felt a sense of the unreal.

'You new to the force?'

'Not quite. I've been on it a year.'

Harry chuckled, deep and chesty. 'Better watch out for *you*, Inspector ...'

Stirling could have kicked himself for an idiot.

Harry held out a hand. 'Old Harry. That's all you need to know.'

Stirling was reluctant to take it, feeling like he was indeed making a pact with the devil. The name wasn't the only reason. But he shook. 'Andy Stirling.'

Harry released his hand. 'Well, Inspector, stay in touch ... I shall watch your career with interest, young man.' With a nod that effortlessly took the piss behind his poker face, he walked away down the street. He'd been Stirling's contact ever since.

Even so, it was a shock to hear that gravelly voice on the phone. 'I think I have some information for you, mate.' It was the first time he'd ever called Stirling 'mate'. There was no ribbing in the pimp's voice now, only a plain-spoken directness. 'Can you meet me in the café on Ponsonby Road in half an hour?'

'Is this about the murders?'

'I think it might be related. I'll stick to that for now.'

'See you in ten minutes.'

DESPITE the vagueness of Harry's description, Stirling knew where he meant. They'd met there a few times before, near the K Road intersection. A small place, and trendy. Not somewhere you'd expect a cop to meet with his informant. When Stirling saw him now, he was dressed in his usual spic-and-span attire, dark hair with its few strands of grey curling gently over the collar of his beautifully ironed shirt. He was already halfway through a bottle of Phoenix mineral water. He waited until Stirling had ordered his latte before acknowledging him.

'Busy day at the office?'

'Flat tack, Harry. Had to drop everything when you rang.'

'You're bullshitting, but I'm honoured.'

Stirling didn't reply.

'I've been following the news. All that stuff about collecting evidence and interviewing more witnesses ... You fellas don't know dick.'

'But we have him down for questioning.' Stirling gave a sigh of pure, uncut fatigue. 'All right, Harry. This isn't a social call.'

Harry took another gulp from his Phoenix, emptying the bottle and plunking it down in front of him. 'I always enjoy my chats with you, Inspector.' He took a beat, decided to drop it. 'But I really think this time you would be doing me a favour ...'

Stirling had never seen him so preoccupied. That, more than anything, made him feel that what was coming next would be important.

'Some of my girls are scared. You know what it's like. Murderer on the loose, chances are he's already frustrated and fucked in the head. All the more likely to be one of our clients. What worries me, given the public nature of a lot of the killings, the boutique home delivery services are getting more of the business.'

'Sorry, Harry, but my sympathies on this matter are a little strained.'

Harry shrugged. 'It's all right. Shop's doing OK.' The place was on quite extensive premises, only part of which was open to the casual public. Stirling had only ever seen a brief glimpse of the rest through the doorway, which had resembled a respectable gentrified villa but for the unconventional choice of art and rather more creaking than you usually found even in houses of that vintage.

'I wouldn't have told you, mate, but it's getting out of hand. Call it public spirit if you like. I've always been a big one for safety ... Fact is, I think he was one of our clients. Back in June. Two of the girls were found strangled.'

The barista chose that moment to arrive with the lukewarm coffee. Right when Stirling's thirst had completely disappeared. He waited till she was out of earshot before firing off the question.

'And you never reported it? How the hell did that get past the coroner?'

Harry looked vague. 'Couldn't possibly say, mate.'

Nothing should have surprised Stirling any more. Undertakers on the take. Harry slouched back in his chair.

'Anyway, I didn't want to scare people. Death is a bit more over the edge than the clientele tend to like. Doesn't matter if it's not your fault, the shit sticks any old how. Not good for business, is it, knowing there's a murderer about on your patch? Kind of puts you off your stroke. If more of the girls had known about it, they'd have gone on strike. Just like they're doing now …'

'So it's not just public spirit then?'

Harry glowered. 'No. No it fucking isn't. Not when half the staff are resigning because it's got out that a serial killer might be a patron.'

Stirling frowned, while his mind went: *Ah*. 'I'm going to need more than that, Harry. What happened?'

'You going to drink that?'

Harry's face was closed. He was telling this story. Stirling pushed his untouched latte across the table to Harry, who took a sip. 'Ugh, this is cold.' He shrugged it off. 'It was free. Anyway, as for your dates, remember the twentieth of June, and the third of July. A Friday and a Thursday. Both busy nights, and no one had time to stand round gawking. We thought the first one might have been an accident …'

He tilted his cup, as if to check if there was coffee lurking anywhere beneath the foam. But it might just have been a convenient way to avoid Stirling's eye.

'She was tied up, you see. One of those kinky jobs. There was a leash around her throat. We thought the game had gone wrong, and he'd got scared.'

They weren't anywhere near the door, but Stirling felt a chill on his neck. Harry was frowning into his coffee.

'But even then ... It was strange. It's usually the client who wears the choker ...'

Stirling forced himself to answer calmly. 'What time was this? And where? In the back of the shop?'

'Yeah. Upstairs. Sometime between 9.30 and midnight, we think. But no one saw him leave. She's supposed to come down, you see, and let us know there's a room free.'

'And no one saw him?'

'No one saw him *leave*, son. But Larissa — she was front of house on the night — she saw him arrive.'

'Shit, someone *saw* him? What did he look like?'

'In her words, "Tall, dark and handsome, the kind I go to work for." Lying bitch, of course she only ever works for the money ... But she's not sure it was him. She just saw him pick out Carla. And then Carla was found dead three hours later.' He shrugged. 'Someone else could have come in and done it after he'd left.' They both knew that was crap.

Stirling thought: *Paxton works late on Friday nights. And he's only average height* ... Without making himself too uncomfortable about it, he'd rate Paxton as reasonably good-looking, but definitely well short of being an underwear model. Nothing to stick in your memory, unless what usually came through the knocking-shop door was really so incapable of getting laid elsewhere. 'So how come she didn't see him go?'

'Ladies' bladders, son. They're a bloody nightmare. And there is a fire exit. As I said, we run a safe house.' There was an acerbic rasp in his voice now. 'Could have walked out any number of ways, and we'd know nothing about it.'

'All right, tell me about the next one. July the third.' Stirling had given up all pretence of being neutral.

Harry sighed. 'Carla might have been an accident, but not Gene as well. Short for *Geneviève*, by the way. Looked like Gene Hackman the way she wrote it. Tits to tadpoles her real name was Jenny; she was common as muck ... Anyway, Rach saw a man pick her up off the street in a red Holden and leave for her flat. No room at the inn that Thursday.'

'Did Rachel see him?'

'No. Tinted windows. Didn't notice the plates either.' That would have been too much to expect.

'Then what?'

'Then she got herself dead. No leash this time thank God — but it was pretty apparent she didn't kill herself off.' For once even Harry's composure slipped. He scowled at the table. 'Fucking cock-sucker ... He'd got hold of one of her lipsticks. Wrote HO HO HO all over her chest ...'

Yet another game. There was no doubt left in Stirling's mind. He stood up, holding out his hand. 'Thanks a lot, Harry.'

'You find this bastard, Inspector.'

'Next time you tell us, all right? No more cut-price burials at the expense of the taxman. I'm probably speaking to the wrong man here, but it's not decent.'

'There's decency and there's decency, son. Just you tell us when you've caught him.'

Harry and his presence left without a backward glance, subtly parting the pedestrians on Ponsonby Road like a barrel rolling through in slow motion. Stirling dialled Gardner's mobile as soon as he was out the door. It cut straight to the messaging service.

HAD the entire room been drenched in disinfectant and the furniture burnt, Paxton would still have scented coffee leaching from the walls. It hung in the air, the ghost of interrogations past. Thankfully the emotional residue wasn't quite so detectable. The pungent, slightly burnt aroma of coffee and cigarettes was infinitely preferable to the stink of fear.

Gardner stood to one side, leaning slightly against the wall. *You're nicked, son* was scrawled large across his face. Paxton had never seen him happier. Though that wasn't saying much.

'Mr Paxton.' He nodded with faultless politeness, slipping from the room as Paxton was brought in.

'Hang on, Sergeant.'

Gardner turned, his forehead creasing into three parallel lines of false surprise.

'What's this all about? Aren't you going to be interviewing me?' Paxton could barely contain his fury, but fear kept him from acknowledging it. For the first time, he began to be really afraid. He of all people knew what fear and ignorance were capable of.

Gardner smiled, letting his disappointment show. 'Sorry, Mr Paxton. I realise it'd be nice for you to have a familiar face, but this isn't my case. However, I'd like to pop in and have a chat later, if you wouldn't mind.'

He glanced over at another cop sitting behind the interviewing table, his eyebrows gently raised. The uniform nodded, just once, in deference. Gardner smiled again. With a nod of farewell to Paxton, he left.

Paxton stared at the black box at one end of the room, with what looked like two video recorders silently taking down everything. No way Gardner would be missing this. There had to be a live feed somewhere.

There wasn't any real evidence to prove he'd killed Mark; it was all circumstantial and he knew it. But all the same ... Men had been hanged for less.

The uniformed sergeant had a round, inexpressive face and flat brown hair. His manner resolutely gave nothing away. Paxton recognised him from every kid's alphabet chart. Letter P, for Plod. Just missing the hat and the truncheon. He'd still have been recognisable at a naturists' resort.

The sergeant spoke. 'Good afternoon, Mr Paxton. Could I just get you to say your full name for me, please?' Paxton turned his head and spoke directly at the camera.

'James Alan Paxton. *And I want my lawyer.*'

DUNCAN Knowles could, it seemed, break free of the shackles that bound him to his desk. Paxton hadn't known who else to call, but as soon as Knowles entered he knew he'd made the right choice. The solicitor walked very composedly into the interviewing room, grey of hair and of suit, as unshakeable as stone. Paxton was surprised at the power he radiated. He'd gone from dry old stick to divining rod. 'Could I get a cup of coffee, please? I was supposed to be going home at four.' He gave the barest glance at the clock on the wall, hung in full view of the camera. It pointed to twenty-four past.

'Make that two please.' Paxton wasn't thirsty, but he urgently needed something to do with his hands.

The sergeant's eyes touched on him for half a second. Knowles slapped his briefcase on the table.

'Just a dash of milk, one sugar, if you wouldn't mind.'

The sergeant shut his mouth, which had only got half open.

'I have two sugars in mine,' said Paxton.

The sergeant didn't even bother looking his way. 'Would you like some time with your client?'

'I think that would be a good idea, don't you?' Knowles's smile was brisk, like his words, and the cop quietly beat it. The lawyer had him by at least twenty-five years. When the camera was off and the door had closed, that quiet, penetrating gaze was turned on Paxton.

'Well, Mr Paxton. We do seem to meet in unfortunate circumstances.'

'And ones not of my making.' Paxton met his gaze and held it. The solicitor watched him again for a short moment, thoughtful, then nodded. He sat down in the chair the sergeant had occupied across the scored, badly tagged table.

'Now, what have you told them? You say you've been accused of assault.'

'I'm pretty sure that's what it is. For now. I *hope* so ... But I haven't said anything yet. I wanted to speak to you first.'

'Good. You may have behaved like a fool once, perhaps, but I'm glad to see it's wearing off.' The door swung open, and the coffee came in. 'Ah. Thank you.' He took just a sip, then waited till they were again left alone. 'Right, go on.'

'Thanks for coming, by the way.'

Knowles scoffed dismissively. 'No, not at all. It's my job.'

Paxton looked embarrassed. 'I actually thought you'd pass me on to one of your colleagues or something. I never expected you to come yourself. I thought you just dealt with deceased estates and conveyancing ...'

Knowles seemed faintly amused. 'Now I do. But only because so few of my clients seem to end up in these situations nowadays. Makes a change, I must say ... In previous years I've drunk more watery coffee than I care to remember.' He looked with distaste into his cup and took another sip. He bared his teeth, pained, and pushed it out of his way.

'Well, you wanted my advice. So my advice to you, Mr Paxton, is to tell the truth. It's the only way that will see justice served.'

Paxton gave a laugh that was a half-sneer of bitterness. 'Really? I admit I tackled the little weasel —'

Knowles gave a sharp look at the black box, then an admonitory glance at Paxton. Paxton shook his head.

'But that's not the whole story, Duncan. They're trying to fit me up for murder. One sergeant's been after me for weeks. He's convinced I killed Mark Bradley.'

Now Knowles looked surprised. 'On what evidence?'

'None. That's just it! I can only guess that Marcus Davenport dobbed me in to the cops for pulling him off Lena — and *that's* what happened — but they're going to try to hold me. I know it.'

Knowles shook his head. 'They can't. From what you've just told me, they can't even arrest you.'

It was what Paxton had believed all along, but it was such a relief to hear it from the elderly solicitor. Hope was flooding back. The door handle creaked, and the sergeant returned, his slightly bovine face business-like.

'Ready to begin?'

Knowles nodded. The sergeant bent over the recorders, pressing a button.

'Sergeant Dan Cressey, returning' — he checked the clock over his shoulder — 'twenty-five to five.'

Knowles relinquished his seat and came round the table to sit on Paxton's left. Throughout the interview he said nothing, and made no move, but Paxton could sense from him a steady sort of comfort. The questions were rather more probing than Paxton had expected, and Cressey returned to some of them several times, from different angles. His particular favourites seemed to be: *Why did you feel the need to visit Mr Davenport at that time of night?* coupled with variations on: *Are you usually about at that time of the night?* As soon as he heard them Paxton knew the man had been receiving directions from Gardner while he'd been gone.

It turned out the neighbours had readily backed up Marcus's story, complaining about the shouting and thumping noises in the hallway. The grumpy bitch from 6G — who else was there? — had apparently been more than willing to make a statement, and her description of Paxton was uncannily accurate for someone supposedly just out of bed. Perhaps it wasn't sleep they'd been spoiling.

Paxton admitted nothing, offered to submit himself for drug-testing, and suggested that his interviewer might wish to probe a little more carefully into the credentials of his accuser, as well as his connections in various nightclubs around central Auckland. When all the questions were exhausted, Cressey looked a little out of his depth. That he was surprised was perfectly obvious.

He stood. 'If you'll excuse me for just a moment ...' He walked out, rather quickly.

When he'd gone, Knowles showed expression for the first time since questioning began, rolling his eyes up to the dingy, smoke-stained ceiling. Paxton broke into a broad smile, and a faint returning smile appeared on Knowles's face. Neither of them said a word. Knowles got to his feet. 'Excuse me, I really must see about getting a decent cup of coffee.' He picked up his cup, scowling at it. 'Like warm milk in a dirty mug. If I can find the kitchen, I'll make it myself.'

'This is a cop shop. See if you can find some doughnuts as well.' That arid smile.

'Try not to say anything while I'm gone.'

Knowles shut the door.

To while away the time Paxton went over various plans for murdering Marcus. Just how stupid was he? Clearly, with his usual arrogance, he believed that in a my-word-against-yours contest, Paxton's status as chief person of interest in a murder investigation was going to swing things heavily in Marcus's favour. Paxton fantasised about swinging heavy things in his direction. After several minutes it got old. Knowles still had not returned. Paxton began to wonder if he had actually left the building in search of a café. The room was beginning to seep into his clothing, marking him with its own smell. The solid black box squatted metres away. This was not a room for happy contemplation. Malevolence and misery passed through it daily.

In an attempt to keep his mind off his surroundings he read the markings inscribed on the table. Some inked, others just crude scratches that Paxton speculated had been gouged out by car keys. They weren't terribly edifying. The usual illiterate tags were enlivened by the occasional 'Death II Pigz', 'Southside' and 'A-dog in da house '02'. Not far from Paxton's elbow some enterprising poet had incised a homage to Dr Seuss: '1 PIG, 2 PIG, DEAD PIG, SCREW PIG!!'. Either the original artist had spent a lot of time alone in the room, or someone else had inked it in.

Paxton checked his watch against the clock on the wall. A minute fast. Still no sign of Knowles. At that moment the door re-opened. Paxton looked up expectantly. Instead of refreshments, it was Gardner. Paxton's sense of humour vanished.

Gardner checked the recorder was off. 'While you're here, Mr Paxton ...'

'My lawyer's not here. *Sergeant.*'

Gardner motioned facetiously to the door. 'We can go out into the hallway if that would be better?'

'Sorry? I don't speak bastard.'

'What was that?'

Paxton wasn't fool enough to enlighten him. Gardner loomed closer, every hair in his nose visible. 'I just want to know whether you think it makes you innocent, meddling with the law? This money you say Mr Davenport owed Mr Bradley. That wasn't the only reason you went round, was it?'

Paxton's jaw was glued shut. He wouldn't respond. It didn't seem to bother Gardner in the slightest. He was inching closer still.

'Think you're above the law, don't you? Immune to it ...' He glared down at Paxton, who stared stolidly at the scratches on the table-top, ignoring him completely. Gardner's voice got even lower. 'You think it'll never get you, don't you? Well, boyo, I've got news for you. It will.' Every syllable was sharp as a paper cut. 'We'll get you ...'

The door opened, and Knowles came in with a waxed paper cup full of coffee. Gardner straightened ever so slightly, smiling pleasantly.

'Afternoon. Don't worry, he hasn't said a thing.'

Knowles smiled in return, looking much chirpier for the addition of caffeine.

'Uh — Sergeant?'

It was Cressey, looking deeply worried. He beckoned Gardner over, and they held a furiously muttered conversation. Gardner looked sick and livid.

'What?'

His tone alone was enough to make Paxton inebriated with relief. Gardner stood there, shaking his head, as Cressey came over to Paxton. 'I'm very sorry, sir. You're free to go. The charges have been dropped.'

Gardner had to turn away, so no one could see his face. Watching himself in front of the lawyer.

Paxton watched the lawyer himself. 'What in hell's name could have caused him to do this?'

Cressey answered, looking harried. 'He admitted he wasn't being entirely honest with us, sir. And what he said backed up your version of events. That's all I can say.'

It said fuck all to Paxton. Knowles spoke up, seeing his bewilderment. 'Shall we talk in the car? I'll give you a ride home.' Going back to work was out of the question — Paxton had already rung in sick.

Knowles started walking off, without checking to see if Paxton was following. In a stupor of disbelief Paxton hurried after him, half jogging to catch him up. He risked one glance at Gardner as he went, and saw the detective sergeant look up at him walking free, then turn his back on the sight. His lips were almost invisible, sucked into his bloodless face.

By the time they were two streets away, Paxton's limited patience had expired.

'Do you know something about all that?'

Knowles smiled, his eyes on the traffic lights. His voice, as ever, was tinder dry. 'I may have placed a quick phone call to Miss Bradley, to tell her her boyfriend was with the police. I thought it only decent. I didn't want her to worry if she couldn't get through to you.'

Paxton stared at the little old solicitor with something approaching awe, as the penny dropped. He gave a burst of laughter. 'Holy ... Shit ... She rang his dad!'

The lights changed. Knowles glanced over.

'Now, just to change the subject for a moment, where am I going?'

'THE ... *bastard*! I can't *believe* he tried that on!' Lena was flushed and ranting, unable to sit still. 'I bloody gave Colin what for, I can tell you! I'm pleased to see he's shown *some* signs of reason. At long last!'

Knowles had brought Paxton here to her place, at Paxton's request. Her embrace had well-nigh put him in a body cast. In her first almost unintelligible gush of words, amid the anger he'd read the unmistakable outpourings of guilt. She couldn't forgive herself for drawing him into her campaign against Mark's killer, thus putting him squarely in Gardner's sights. Unspoken was the fact that Paxton's arrest would have removed yet another person close to her heart.

'I owe you a beer for this one,' he said.

That brought a smile to her face. 'Bastard. I should have left you to your showers with the Mongrel Mob.'

'Hmm. I didn't think I'd shared that fantasy with you ...'

He leaned across and kissed her with a teasing grin, and then, unthinkably, burning curiosity took over. He sat back.

'What did you say to him? Colin, I'm talking about.'

'A bit of a gamble, I admit ... I made an appeal to his conscience.'

Conscience. Yes. Paxton doubted Colin could have handled another toxic dump of guilt on his already crushing load.

'Guess he didn't fancy his son as a perjurer any more than a murderer.'

'No ...'

Lena drew her knees up under her on the sofa with an unhappy expression, finally coming to rest.

'He said: *You can't blame me for wanting to protect my son, can you? You ought to know, a father would do anything for his kid.'*

She bit her lip.

'I feel bad now. He meant well, I shouldn't have said it ... I said to him: *Yeah, well mine did. But what you should be asking yourself, Colin, is, would your kid do anything for you?'*

She squeezed her eyes shut. 'Then I just hung up ...'

Chapter TWENTY-ONE

THE NIGHT WAS fine; with the clouds and the mists of rain dispersed, he had a clear, unimpeded view of the seat on the corner. The empty seat.

He was more philosophical about it tonight. Perhaps she hadn't stayed late at Uni. Never mind that. He knew where she lived.

Should he go? In the moment between thought and decision, a tap came at his window. His head jerked. So intent was he on watching for *her* that he hadn't looked out for himself. The uniformed security guard stood at his driver's door. He had to duck his head, retinas popping, as a torch beam shone at his face.

'Could you wind down your window please, sir?'

The watchmen were hired by the university, as campus security. Protecting their assets — bit optimistic really. But he remembered now. The guards would occasionally patrol the bus-stop area, in case of late-working students. Very occasionally.

Kind of a buzz. This was like running into a species long thought extinct.

Rent-a-goons like this one weren't allowed weapons. They barely allowed them to cops. He pushed his finger on the button for the electric window. His hair ruffled in the draught as it whipped in.

'How can I help you?'

'You're not allowed to park here, sir. You can see the signs.'

'Umm ...'

The *Titanic* would have been invisible at six feet in the Stygian lighting down the drive.

'OK, sir. I realise it's dark, but you've got headlights and I'm sure you're aware of it. I'm going to have to ask you to move on, or you'll get towed.'

He gave a sheepish grin. 'Sorry. Yeah, I know I shouldn't be parking here. But I'm waiting for my wife. She said she'd only be a few minutes. She's sorting out some youth group programme at the church.'

He nodded amiably at the stone wall in front of them.

'You could have parked on the road, you know. It's free at this time of night.'

He grimaced, acknowledging the hit. 'Yeah. I know. But I didn't think there was any harm. It's closer here, and it's not as if I'm blocking anyone. Am I? Hadn't seen anyone around until you scared me.'

The guard grinned. 'Sorry about that. Guess it *would* give you a fright, me bashing on your window like that.' He hesitated a second. 'How long do you think she'll be?'

'Shouldn't be long. I hope. Though that's what she keeps saying whenever she's on the phone. And *that* always means hours ...'

The guard gave a chuckle. 'Tell me about it.' The official manner had completely vanished now. 'Well, just so long as you don't do it again. I won't tell for tonight.'

He gave a smile of sincerest gratitude. 'Thanks, mate.'

'No worries.'

The guard shambled off, back into the darkness. God it was cold. It was about to get colder.

THERE was a click as a car door opened behind him. Abruptly the torch was ripped from his grasp, coming crashing down on his head. One of those solid industrial jobs that could be used as a weapon. Only *he* was the one supposed to be using it.

The irony was lost on him. All that filled his brain was pain. The sheer, excruciating agony of blow after blow, raining down upon his skull, without reprieve. Even when he was on the ground, moaning incoherently for anyone to hear him. Someone did. A thick boot slammed hard into his face, with a crack that belonged to nothing on this earth. A mercy, of sorts. He could no longer feel the pain. Seconds after unconsciousness came, death followed. His killer made sure of it.

Pity the bloke hadn't been a real parking warden. He'd always wanted to do that to one of those.

He half dragged, half kicked the body further back from the road, by the feet to avoid messing his clothes. Heavy work. Man probably doubled as a nightclub bouncer. Thankfully it was downhill. Breathing harder than usual, he left the dead guard between the church and the cheap, prefabricated offices that sprouted behind it. Practically sacred ground. Rest in peace, chubby.

There was blood smeared all over the torch, laced with strands of dull brown hair stained red. He ran a finger through it thoughtfully, wiping it off on the stone of the church before it could dry. Rubbing it every which way to leave no clear print.

It was the car that worried him now. With Joanna, there was never any issue of being traced. Who would link a car at the university with a girl murdered miles away? But *this* was different. He might have been seen. Just as the dead man had seen him. His heart was going full trot. The night air was sharp in his lungs. His mind even sharper.

This was what he was born for. Oh God yes.

He got into the Holden, bringing the torch with him. Might as well. Wasn't doing the other bloke any good. He rested it carefully on a gym towel down on the floor. Wouldn't do to leave stains.

Should he head off to Joanna's now? He considered a moment, but his thoughts were sweeping along too fast to catch in the flood of adrenaline. Nah. He wanted time to soak this one in. Revel in it. Plot how much better the real one was going to feel. Like a kid with his first skin mag. He felt a silent laugh bubble up in his throat. He didn't think he'd sleep at all tonight.

THE alarm had woken Julie Mehra at half-past five that morning, and her head still didn't seem to have stopped buzzing. So much bloody work to get through. A pile of critical analyses left to mark, the ones she hadn't been arsed missing Graham Norton for. Monday's lecture to prepare. A conference with guest lecturers from the UK and America beginning at ten — on a *Saturday*. A new proposal to draft in response to yesterday's disastrous meeting with the rest of the department. Tentatively entitled: Why I Am Excited About Teaching Yet Another Course For No More Pay. And the bastards wanted her to up her research output. She'd have been better off going into primary teaching and mopping up puddles on the floor. Plus as usual her damn publisher was going on about the deadline for her new study on ritual in Early Modern Europe. Every time she heard a student whine about work overloads she was tempted to slap them.

She pulled into her assigned slot in Carpark Number 9. At least she could be grateful for that. Staff had died on the waiting list for spaces. It had only taken her four years. The crust of frost had melted from her windscreen on the trip, leaving her with a clear view.

The church was a stone's throw away, blending in a monochrome with the overcast sky. Some hues, on the other hand, stood out. Beneath a rusty brown smear on the bluestone, a khaki form was lost in a vivid pool of red. Julie had a sudden, powerful reluctance to open her door. When at last she did, she could hardly feel her feet make contact with the ground under her. She'd lost all sensation or control.

Walking down the path now, towards the church. Seeing nothing but that shape, lying in its splash of horrid colour.

Unable to stop, she got closer. Looked down at what had been a face.

And Julie Mehra didn't get any work done that day at all.

'STILL no clear prints! It's *unbelievable*. Whoever coined the phrase "like getting blood out of a stone" was a right smart-aleck bastard.' Even Rees was unable to keep a hint of exasperation from his voice. It always seemed to be his shift.

'Unless DNA proves it's the killer's ...'

Kirkpatrick didn't sound too hopeful. He, Rees and Stirling were clustered together in his office, temporarily escaping the embarrassing pile-up of cases. Gardner had been in conclave with Woodward and the sergeant in charge of the latest murder most of the morning. 'Yeah right. It's just as likely to be O. J. Simpson's.' Stirling had a right to be sour. That morning, he'd learned from a mate still in uniform about Gardner's little run-in with Paxton. Furthermore, Stirling's interview with Harry had fallen on deaf ears. Gardner had been in a stinking temper all morning, dishing out vindictive little retorts every time Stirling had opened his mouth.

'How many red Holdens do you suppose there are in this city, Andy? You been out to West Auckland lately? I can't believe you're so desperate you've stooped to believing a pimp and a prostitute!' It was the only time all day Stirling had seen him laugh, and he acutely wished he hadn't.

It got even nastier later. When Woodward had suggested the new casket case was linked in with the existing investigation, Gardner had just about hit the roof. The idea that the *fucker* had done it, *right* after he'd let him go ... He knew it was improbable, and it was therefore impossible. He refused to believe it was even connected.

'We haven't got the manpower for this.' Kirkpatrick was swivelling in his chair, fidgeting away excess stress, as was his wont. 'We're going to have more bodies than men.'

Rees cleaned his glasses on his shirt. 'I was talking to Vicky just before she went in with Ray and Willy. They're still not sure it's him. Guy's shirt was all rucked up at the back — he'd been dragged by the legs.' It was for this precise reason that no one had found him. His colleagues had assumed he'd done a bunk; they hadn't thought to check behind the church. 'Sure, Blundell's one, the Ryan woman, she was moved too. But not the other two. Then again, the bashing's a lot like the Bradley one. Fucked if anyone's got a clue ...'

Stirling grunted. 'And there's your link right there.'

HE had no idea whether she'd be there. He was only guessing. She might well give lessons — if she even gave lessons at all — at other people's houses. He gazed out the windscreen at the Saturday sports-going traffic, strangely content. There was no need for him to even be here today, but he was drawn like a blowfly to a corpse. Breeding suspense. He was getting slowly beneath her skin, becoming a part of her life without her even knowing it, before he took that life away. An invasion in every sense. Developing a taste for his prey. Better, far, far better, than the quick smash and grab jobs so far.

Could no one honestly see it in his face? The days of waiting, of watching her and imagining, were building an anticipation so intense he almost wondered it didn't make him spontaneously combust. Now the nervousness and inexperience had worn off, he was enjoying himself more. Developing his technique. It was just like sex. The slower you took it, the more pleasure you got. Or so he'd heard. Sex was never about pleasure for him; not in that sense. Not too many women enjoyed the sort of things he went in for. The less they liked it the more he paid them.

The very reason he'd never really had a 'proper' girlfriend, truth be told. He wasn't into kiss and tell.

A bright red Toyota flashed past him as he was parking down the street. Lincoln's Toyota, so the post office said. The third flatmate. And look! The man himself, getting out of the driver's seat. Talk about timing.

But what happened next had him hanging his mouth open. Leaning closer, unable to believe his eyes. Lincoln's passenger was a young man with tight blond curls. As he watched, he saw the young man casually reach out and give Lincoln a squeeze on his backside. Fucking hell. Had that really just happened? He sat there in his car, his stomach puckering, feeling like he'd just witnessed someone spewing up their own appendix in the street. Fucking poofs!

And *look at him*. Lincoln was smiling. He was carrying a small bag of groceries in his left hand, and now he switched hands to slobber on the other guy's cheek. They had an arm slung around each other as they walked up to the door.

He wanted to kill them both, then and there. Flaunting themselves like that, *in public*. What if children had been watching? Fucking sick. That's how he was feeling. He'd been in a gay club, once, just from pure curiosity. Naturally he hadn't stayed long.

Nauseating, it had been. Grown men crawling all over each other. A camp striptease. Gays and transvestites and fucked-up faux-mosexuals trying it on with him while he'd sat with his drink, trying not to look. Impossible not to. Like standing at an intersection, watching two cars approach at speed ...

The entire experience had been utterly humiliating. He'd soon realised he'd made a mistake, but what a wuss he would have looked just leaving. Before he could chicken out he'd gone over to the bar and ordered tequila, just to shut the whole thing out. Tequila was good like that. Still, much as he'd tried to avoid eye contact, several of them came over and tried to chat him up, sidling up next to him on the stool. Could they not see he wasn't one of their type? He had his back to them, for Christ's sake.

'Shy, are you? Don't worry — none of us has anything to hide here!'

'You certainly aren't hiding anything, Dom. Could you possibly be any more obvious?'

'Shut up, bitch. Get your own.'

The old memories came back then. His room at home. Tormenting him. The dread. The pleasure. The shame. It had felt wrong. Worse still — it hadn't felt bad.

After half an hour, he'd had enough. He'd sculled the rest of his drink and left, feeling like a burn the brush of a hand against his rear as he'd cut through the dancers to the door.

He realised now his hand had curled into a fist as he watched Lincoln and his bum buddy mince inside the house. Had they just been out for milk and toast bread, or had they both stayed out all night?

Three in one household? There'd be a big question mark over that one. No, he'd love to, but he'd made his plans. They'd be carking it soon with AIDS anyway. Raving homos; didn't matter what kind of pricks they liked to stick into each other.

As the door opened the soft ripple of a flute spilled out, which helped to cool him down. Music soothes the savage beast. Or was it breast? He couldn't remember. Breasts weren't the appendages on his mind. His flesh was tingling cold with the memory. Then the world came suddenly upright, and he realised what the music meant.

Jo was home. Right now. And giving flute lessons by the sound of it. Damn he was good. Revulsion flicked over to anticipation like a switch in the current of his body.

From this angle he couldn't see. He'd have to get closer; and thus risk being seen himself. Well, so be it. She'd see him before she died, wouldn't she?

He pictured that. Squeezing the sinews of her neck as her pulse raced away against his hands, the light dimming in her eyes as he stared straight into their depths, watching the life be extinguished ...

He strolled past the living-room window, just some guy off to the corner dairy. Bored, looking around for the source of the music as he went for his *Weekend Herald*.

She was in there. With a young girl, standing almost with their backs to the window. It was the pupil who was playing, some piece he'd never heard full of long trilling passages that went nowhere. Sure as fuck wasn't Mozart. It stopped and started, and re-started, with every cock-up, each break in the rhythm, setting his teeth on edge. Her orangey bun bobbed as she dipped her head to the music. He wondered if flute players knew how rude they looked to anyone who happened to be passing.

He did a proper job of it, as he always did, actually going to the shop and buying a paper. Paid to be thorough. He read the IT section as he sauntered back past the house. She was still playing the same piece of crap as before. Presently she fudged a note and broke off. Thank God it didn't start up again. He'd only got three pages in before she appeared in the doorway and scurried to a station wagon waiting just up from the drive.

Another carrotty woman in it. Hadn't even looked up from her book as he'd passed the car. She'd be pissed when she had to find a new tutor. He turned the page.

The flute music started up again, but the difference in quality was so marked it could never have been mistaken for just another schoolkid. He waited a few more minutes, but no more students showed up. Sitting back in his seat, paper spread out on the dashboard, he listened for almost an hour. Difficult to imagine a better way to start off a Saturday morning.

Dreamily he wondered what they'd play at her funeral.

Chapter TWENTY-TWO

GUILT WAS CAPABLE of great things. The day after Paxton was cleared of assaulting Marcus, Lena got a phone call from Colin. He wanted to repay the loan. Debts owing, he said.

'I could set up a direct debit, if you like. But I'm afraid the instalments won't be terribly big at the moment ...'

Lena tried to get over her initial shock. 'No! God, Colin, no. Thanks very much, but honestly, I don't want it. It was Dad's to give, it was never mine in the first place. Let's just let it drop, OK?'

'Thank you very much; that's very generous of you. Thank you. But I can't. I borrowed it, Lena, and I always pay back what I owe. God knows I've not been a spectacular godfather up till now ... I couldn't sleep if I —' There was a long pause over the phone. Lena knew something was coming.

'I worried him, I knew that. When I asked for the money. I've often asked myself, what was it that meant he couldn't sleep that night?'

He sounded so unhappy Lena couldn't stem a sudden rush of appalled affection as she understood.

'Oh *no* ... Colin, you can't —'

'What if in some way I *am* responsible for —'

She cut him off. 'Colin, you can't blame yourself. It just happened! He often had trouble sleeping, for no reason at all.'

'You've never asked that friend of yours?'

'No. And there's no need to. Colin, it's not your fault, believe me.'

There was a heavy silence. 'I'm sorry, Lena. And tell your friend I'm sorry too, for what's happened. I hope he won't — I hope he won't be too angry ...' He seemed to give himself a mental head-shake. 'Take care. I'll post you a cheque tomorrow.'

Before she could protest, he'd clicked off, leaving her staring at the phone.

IF she'd really wanted confirmation that things had changed, the second phone call was it. It came on Sunday morning, as she was in that state between finishing breakfast and debating whether or not she could be bothered getting up to do the dishes. The ringing of the phone across the kitchen decided for her, and as she scurried to answer it she intensely regretted ever plugging it back in.

'Hello?'

'Hello, Lena, it's me. I'm really sorry I didn't call earlier but I've been very busy. We had to go to New York, and everything took ages. So much mucking around ... How are you?'

Elke spoke in English, but with a flawless Swiss-German accent that breathed her exasperation. Lena used to get wild whenever anyone mocked the German accent as harsh and cold. Listening now to her mother's slightly high-pitched voice, thin and crisp as alpine air, she couldn't help thinking that stereotypes were based on something.

Still, she was her mother and Lena couldn't help but love her. After all, Mark had loved her once too. Elke had been young when she'd married, and not at home in her transplanted country. Going back to Switzerland had been a fresh beginning, an attempt to reverse her mistakes. Lena believed she truly did feel remorse for the pain she'd caused. Elke's way was simply to lock it away in a vault and pretend it never happened. The policy had worked well for her country both before and after the 1940s.

'I'm fine, Mutti.' She used the diminutive word, as she always had — in German it didn't sound quite so bad as saying 'mummy' at the age of twenty-four. 'I mean, it still hurts. Of course; I miss him terribly. But I'm OK.'

Her mother sounded relieved. 'Good. I'm very glad. He was a good man, your father. I — was not happy to hear that he had gone.' Her voice was softer, more tired than Lena had often heard it. 'Do you want to come and stay with us for a while?'

'No. Thanks, but I'm all right here. I've got ... someone.'

'Oh.' Elke sounded surprised. There was a slight hesitation. 'Is he a nice boy?'

Lena debated mentioning to her mother that he'd been hauled in for questioning by the police.

'Yeah. Very nice. His name is James. He's English.'

'Oh.' Now Elke seemed even more uncertain. 'Well ... perhaps, if you ever go to visit his family, you might come and stay with us. Are they still living in England?'

'Yeah, they are. That'd be great.' There was another brief moment of silence. Lena asked about her stepfather Peter and the rest of them, and got the usual automated response. After that her mother seemed at a loss.

'Would you like to speak to Stefan? Sophie's out with some friends at the moment, but I'm sure Stefan would love to chat. He's not in bed yet.'

Lena's half-brother was fourteen. There was no chance in hell he'd be in bed by 9.30. Not while there was an X-Box hooked up to the plasma-screen TV in the lounge and his seventeen-year-old sister was out having fun with her mates.

'Yeah, all right, if he wants to.'

Lena exchanged a few words with her brother, this time in German, and was forcibly reminded of her own school days in Switzerland between the ages of eleven and fifteen. Stefan was regretting having insisted on their local school, because the girls in his class were all bitches. Also, did she realise what a *Scheisse* English was to learn? And had she met anyone from *The Lord of the Rings*? Eventually she let him get back to his X-Box. He offered to put Elke on again, but she’d left the room. Lena told him not to bother.

Chapter TWENTY-THREE

JO JEFFRIES HUMPED her bag higher on her shoulders, wincing as the textbooks inside promptly yanked it earthwards again. Settling like lead weights — or student debt. She'd blown over a hundred bucks she couldn't afford on chiropractors' visits already, and vowed never again. The way her joints were cracking now she could have been a strip-dancer for the blind.

At the bus stop she gratefully dumped her bag onto the concrete, rotating her shoulders to get rid of the ache. She didn't usually mind the darkness; the traffic was normally fairly dense, even at this time on a Monday. Safe as houses. But last week's discovery of a worked-over corpse in the driveway almost directly behind her went an awful long way toward making her want to wet her pants. It was nerve-wracking just standing here in the one place. She turned as far towards the church as she could without completely losing sight of the road and any approaching buses, little liking to have that well of darkness at her back. Her back felt somehow twice as cold as her front, and not just in the patch where her bag had been. It didn't help that she believed in ghosts.

Another security guard walked past along Symonds Street, the second she'd seen since she left the practice room. The Student Association had insisted, and for once there'd been little resistance from what her council friend Kyle called the Scrooge McFuckers in Property Services.

'Hi.'

'Hey.'

And that was the sum total of their conversation. The khaki-clad guard didn't seem any happier about being here than she was. There was no line of defence between madmen and guards.

Blame Lincoln and Sam. Complaining her practising interrupted their Monday night TV; God only knew why it mattered. What were they watching anyway — re-runs of *Hercules* with buff young men in leather and open-necked shirts? Jo had nothing against that, but she was playing with the APO in a few months, for Christ's sake.

In reality, she knew it was her fault. Linc and Sam were good guys — they'd have understood. They'd even offered to pick her up in fact. Lincoln in particular was stressing worse than her mother at the thought of her being alone after dark in *that* place.

'Look, you silly cow, are you mental? Are you *actually* mental? Someone just died! As in, like, dead body? I'm picking you up if I have to drag you from the bumper.'

But it came down, in the end, to this. She hated inconveniencing anyone, even friends. She'd rather have slept on the sofa in her clothes after a late night than risk waking anyone by creeping down the hall with its creaky floorboards. Just-Me Jo, Lincoln had called her once, laughing at her fondly. *Don't worry about what I think, it's Just Me*. She would have died rather than make them go out of their way for her and her stupid little anxieties. It wasn't like a lucky Lotto shop — the odds of lightning striking in the same place didn't increase with every customer whose numbers came up. Probably just drugs.

Shivering a little in the cold, and from the feeling of death between her shoulder blades, she waited.

'Freezing tonight, isn't it, miss?'

Yet another guard, with one of those regulation monster torches hooked to his belt. He was rubbing his gloved hands together against the bite of the air, his dark eyes sympathetic.

'I'll say.'

He frowned, stopping. 'You shouldn't really be out here at this time of night. After what happened last week. Isn't someone picking you up?'

'My flatmates are watching TV.' She rolled her eyes, palming the blame. 'Pigs.'

'You should have a word with them, then. It's not safe out here anymore.'

'I'll be fine.' In the face of his concern she grew brave, rising to the challenge of an audience as she always did. She gave a toss of her head, beautifully blasé. 'Still lots of traffic around. And all you guys to watch out for me.'

'One of us every five minutes. I've timed it, it's true.'

'Impressive.' She matched his smile. Now that he was up close she noticed he wasn't in uniform. 'You one of the extras they hired?'

He nodded again. 'That's right. Making the streets safer.' He coughed into his hand, with camp modesty. She laughed. From this distance his eyes were clearly hazel, not brown, and lit up with a green light when he smiled. Whew ... If he *had* been in uniform ... He nodded towards the black case in her hand. 'So what's in the case? You been practising music?'

Jo smiled, pleased he'd noticed. 'Yeah. I play the flute — there's a recital on at the Town Hall that I'm preparing for.'

'Town Hall?' He raised his eyebrows, clearly impressed.

'Just for an hour and a half. Nothing too special.' She almost grimaced at the falseness of the statement.

'Well, I still say it's crap of your mates not to support you. Ring them up. Haul them away from the TV — tell them their brains'll shrink to resemble their willies. I dare you.'

'Noooo ... I couldn't. I've already told them I'm fine.'

He could hear the hesitation in her voice.

'Go on. I can't stay here watching you all night.'

'But you don't have to! Honestly, the bus will be along in a minute.'

He looked down the hill. Nothing came around the curve but a sole speeding Mini. He smiled at her, folding his arms.

'And then you've got to walk home from the bus, right? In the dark?'

'It only takes me a few minutes.' Jo hated the dark. All at once she remembered what they'd found in the darkness behind her, and she shivered.

The guard kept his arms folded expectantly. A small smile was on his lips. 'D'you want my mobile, or are you going to use yours?'

She looked at him. An unexpected wave of relief hit, breaking out of her in a laugh. 'No, I've got one.'

She rummaged through her bag, tipping out several textbooks she was reading for her dissertation. The same old routine. Whenever it rang she had to upend her bag to find the damn thing, and it almost inevitably went to voicemail as soon as she did. But at least it wouldn't get stolen, if no one could find it.

At last she located the phone in the bottom corner, rattling around in a nest of old bus tickets and Kit-Kat wrappers. It was amazing now how desperate she was to call them. The phone book was already on Home.

'Hi Sam, it's me. Look, my bus isn't coming and I'm getting really cold and tired. Sorry, but do you think you guys could pick me up after all?'

The expected complaints filtered through from the receiver.

'I know ... I know.' She glanced at the guard and saw him give her a wide grin and a triumphant shake of his fist, mouthing *You go, girl*. Her guilt vanished instantly.

'The bus stop. Yeah — but I'm not too tired for a drink, if you want one. What? Of course you're bloody dressed! You girl, I'm in my uni clothes ... OK. OK — see you soon. Bye.' She hung up.

'Is that both of them coming?'

'Yeah. Lincoln's the only one with a car, and Sam gets off on riding in it. It's a little red homo-bile.'

He gave an odd little grin that was almost a sneer. 'So, you feel better now?'

'*Much.* Thank you.'

'My pleasure, Jo.'

He was picking up her bag and the flute case. Her smile suddenly faltered. She looked up into his face.

'Hey, how did you ...?'

He pulled her close with one arm, his grip like a shackle round her elbow. Her heavy bag dangled off his shoulder as if full of feathers.

'If you scream or make any sort of sound *whatsoever*, I'll do to you what I did to that other guy last week.'

Her already wide eyes went round with shock. The light in them guttered like a snuffed candle as she looked into his own, and saw no light reflected there, only the darkness looking back. It wasn't behind her after all ...

'On second thought, I'm not happy with you waiting here. I'd rather give you a lift home myself.'

The breath seemed stopped in her lungs as she stood there, pale and lifeless as a waxwork in the Chamber of Horrors. They lurched on, a grotesque death march, one foot after the other. She scarcely heard him talk, whispering orders, walking alongside her like a lover, arm wrapped around her shoulders. Lovingly pinning her own arm to her side.

She was barely aware of any of it. She shivered uncontrollably. The cold had finally got her.

He shepherded her through the twisting guts of the History Department, an up-and-down labyrinth open to all weathers. The wooden stairs between the rooms rang deadly like a gangplank beneath her feet. All was impossibly dark, no contrast between light and shadow. Here it was all shadow. She couldn't even see her feet, though the sounds were all around her.

How fitting to die here, in this place. She knew with vivid certainty that she would. Blood dripping through the timber treads, pooling on the concrete. Seeping into history, the very substance of which history was made ...

But they kept on. Down, through the narrow, concrete-walled tunnel, chill as a morgue, that gave onto Wynyard Street, the hidden little access road to the university buildings and the marae. Further along was campus security. The irony was excruciating.

She prayed they'd meet someone; anyone, though she hardly knew what would happen if they did. Some part of her registered the hideous flow of gibberish that had set into her brain without her knowing.

If you feel like calling out to anyone, remember who's closest. They might be able to get you away — but not before I've broken your neck.

She could just make out a car ahead of them, parked in the lee of Ancient History. It was, she felt instantly, their destination. It pulled them closer. She felt her terror rising.

Please, oh please, don't let us stop.

More than anything, she didn't want to reach it, willing this march to go on and on, forever, even like this, just so they would never get to the car.

But they were already there. He had a silent alarm; it made no sound as he set down her case and pressed the button in his pocket.

A flash car, it was — a Holden, new, and red as Lincoln's Toyota.

Grief detonated suddenly in her brain. He seemed to feel the sob welling up within her, for with an abrupt jerk he twisted her wrist. The gasp of pain it tore from her seemed to satisfy him.

'Get in.'

He opened the passenger door and actually lifted her inside, slamming the door shut before she could react.

He'd already locked it. Quickly she went for the driver's door, pushing up the lock and grabbing at the handle while he threw her case and the bag into the back. She got the door open, putting a leg outside, screaming so hard the inside of her throat felt torn. In the same second he pushed her back inside, throwing her across into the passenger's seat. She landed awkwardly on the gearstick, feeling it jab into the small of her back as her head thumped against the door. Desperately Jo canted round, her hand stretching for the door-handle. A fist smashing into her temple cracked her skull against the glass. She reeled, her whole head filling with pain and tears.

'I thought I told you to shut up.'

He was beside her, starting the car. The roar of the engine split the silence, and loud music filled the car with a heavy bass, intensifying the stabbing in her head. With shaking hands Jo put her fingers to the blossoming bruise, but it hurt too much. She covered her face instead, giving in to choking, shuddering tears. Her throat had closed over. She couldn't have screamed now if her life had depended on it. The most terrible thing of all was that it did.

'Put your seatbelt on.'

Jo ignored him, locked inside her circle of grief. He peeled one hand away from her face, and she stared at him stupidly.

His face got very close to hers, his breath hot against her skin. '*Put* your fucking seatbelt on, or I'll kill you right here.'

She shivered again, though his voice was barely a murmur. Reflexively she did what he said, then snapped her hands back into place. If you can't see the monsters ...

'Don't want any cops to stop us, do we?' Through her hands she could tell he was smiling. He called cheerfully over the thumping house music. 'Well I don't.'

He was in a good mood all the way along the motorway. She realised dully that the windows were slightly tinted and, it being night-time, no one was likely to notice if she waved at them. Now she understood the reason for the music. It would cover up any attempt to scream.

It was all academic at this stage. He frightened her too much for her to try it. He was likely to drive into the cliffs that edged the motorway. Her side of the motorway.

Her body would be broken beyond recognition, and he'd calmly walk away, still smiling ...

Her eyes were fixed on the oncoming traffic, a game to distract herself, examining every car to see if it was a red Toyota. Was *this* them? Was this them? Lincoln and Sam, coming to rescue her. And finding her not there. If she hadn't already been weeping she would have then.

'Why are you doing this? Don't you have *any* feelings?'

'Hmm?' He glanced at her, only half hearing. She didn't have full control of her voice, and the music could have heralded the Apocalypse. 'Why am I doing this?'

That smile again, which somehow frightened her more than anything. 'Man's got to have a hobby.' He laughed.

She didn't ask him anything more.

He took the Greenlane off-ramp. She noticed that his eyes moved past the traffic at the roundabout, gazing further into the distance, off to the right. The way to Cornwall Park and, closer at hand, the twenty-four-hour McDonald's she'd once been to at two a.m., blind drunk and throwing up in the restaurant toilets.

His face had carved itself in half with a delighted flash of teeth. He shook his head, as if he'd just spotted a coincidence. Jo wondered what it could be. She didn't think she wanted to know. Longingly she thought of her mobile, in the back seat. Out of range.

He'd turned left, towards the racecourse. As they drove past the palings it clicked, and her fear shot up another level. She hadn't thought it possible, but there didn't seem to be any limits.

'We're going to my place. Aren't we?'

'Ding ding. She's not so stupid!'

'How did you know where I live?'

He glanced at her. 'Same way I knew your name was Jo ... Miss Jeffries.' He smiled again.

'Stop it!' Her voice was so sharp it almost splintered. It startled even her.

He seemed surprised, and horribly, pleased. All of a sudden she had to say something, it didn't matter what. 'As soon as Linc and Sam see I'm not there they'll call me. And if I don't answer my phone they'll know something's wrong.'

'And?'

'I have neighbours. Someone's bound to see something. Plus I give music lessons on Monday nights — I'm expecting my pupil to be there soon. She always comes early.'

'Always?'

'Always.'

'And which pupil would this be, Jo?'

'Which ...? Lisa.'

'Oh yeah?' He sounded amused. 'Promising student, this Lisa? Good embouchure and all that?'

'How do *you* know about embouchure?' He was always catching her off guard.

'I've done my homework, Jo. I looked up flutes on the Internet. Never even heard of embouchure before that, to be honest, let alone how to pronounce it.' He tasted it in his mouth. 'Om-buh-sher. Nice ring to it.' He beamed widely.

She stared at him. Her stomach swam with ice.

'Oh, did you not recognise the car? Sorry, my manners. I thought you'd have been clever enough to twig by now ... I've been following you, Jo. I've been following you all bloody week. In fact — Christ, it's a new week now. You're a bit slow.'

He was damn well *laughing* at her again. Nothing he'd said struck her as remotely funny. Nothing he'd said struck her as remotely *real*. The gears of her mind were slipping as if waxed.

'You've been planning to kill me for a week?'

'Who said I was going to kill you?'

She stopped, thrown. A tiny flicker of joy flared into life. It died the next moment, on his lips.

'Well, you're an honours student. Guess you can't be *all* stupid.' He was toying with her, amused. She was cold again now, inside as well as out.

'Stop calling me stupid.' It came out as a whisper, to herself. Over the music he couldn't have heard.

'Thing is, Jo, you're screwed. Your sick gay buddies are going to be too late — *far* too late — to help you. You don't even *teach* classes on a Monday night ... and I've got absolutely no idea whether this Lisa's a real person or not, but either way she can't help you either. This is a private session.' His grin was ear-to-ear.

Tell them their brains will shrink to resemble their willies. When had she told him her flatmates were male? She tried to think. No point. There was nothing that he didn't know.

He'd called her bluff. They were almost home. He pulled into her street, and then into her driveway. Any hope she might have had that he was wrong faded on the instant. He wasn't wrong. He never made mistakes.

As he switched off the ignition, the music cut off. She drew a breath to scream, and screamed only into his hand. He gave her a violent twitch, hissing into her ear.

'One sound and you're fucking dead.'

She was dead anyway, and she knew it. The thought, insanely, gave her courage. She tried to bite his palm, but he dug impossibly strong fingers into her arm, causing another jab of pain. He pushed her towards the door, and, atheist that she was, she prayed again to who ever there was that someone might see.

Not a curtain moved anywhere.

When had he taken her keys? With a shock she saw him fish them from his pocket with a familiar jingle. *Her* keys. He pressed his frame against hers, crushing her bodily into the door to prevent escape while he dealt with the lock. She wriggled angrily, but he could literally kill her with one arm behind his back. She might as well try jogging Everest as breaking free.

As the door opened, he shoved her inside and shut the door behind them, snibbing it locked. He threw the keys into the lounge. Then he reached into his pocket again and pulled out a travel pack of tampons and the spare pair of knickers she kept in the front part of her bag, and gave the knickers a sniff. As she craned her neck to see, he made a considering face.

'Hmm. Could do with a wash. Get something fungal if you wore those.' He dangled them in her face, then as she grabbed for them, flung them after the keys.

Her cheeks were flaming red with humiliation. At that moment she felt the desecration was worse than the murder.

What would he do to her first? Do the same thing to the knickers she had on? Smile as he stripped away her clothes, then her worth, then her sanity ...

He was relaxed now, certain of his goal. The door was locked behind her — he had her exactly where he wanted her. No way out but horizontally. In a freezer bag, with no more identity than a roasting chicken. Corpse Number 9. Frozen stiff. Plucked bare of all that made her human.

He was laughing again, so smug, so Mr *fucking* Untouchable ... She wrenched her hands free, and jabbed at his throat.

She'd surprised him. The look on his face was pure astonishment, alloying her muscles like steel. She kicked him in the soft bits, dimly hearing the solid *thwack* and the howl, but didn't stop to assess the damage. She fled. To get to the front door she'd have had to pass him. She sprinted for the back, breathing like she'd covered a mile in those meagre ten paces. She had to get out, had to make people see ...

She made it as far as the kitchen door.

Fingers curled around her wrist, yanking it so hard her shoulder dislocated instantly. She screamed, a shrill sound of pure agony, until her head smashed into the wall a split second later. She hit on the site of the existing bruise, and the pain almost made her vomit. Lights flashed before her eyes, unbalancing her.

He dragged her into the lounge, half by her hair, ripping at her skirt as he pushed her savagely to the floor.

'Don't!' She was wailing it over and over, almost chanting, like a terrified Hail Mary. God forgive the unbelievers, for they have no one to pray to ...

'Don't what? Rape you?' He clawed again at her skirt, anchoring her to the worn grey carpet with his knees. Under the sheer unbearable weight of him she felt as if her fragile bones would break. The skirt gave with the shriek of rent cloth.

'Violate you?' He was breathing hard, hurling the fabric aside and reaching for her throat, his face twisted and ugly, all teeth. The cruellest face she had ever seen. 'You don't like that, do you?' She could feel his breath again, brushing her face, invading every pore as if the evil could leak in like poison. And he was smiling. Salt tears slid into her gasping mouth, mixed with the snot running down her face.

In her own home, the place where she felt safest ...

At the pit of her stomach she felt this was the point. He'd crossed the line.

Lashing out like a cornered cat she got his brow-line, scratching her stubby nails down his cheek just millimetres from his eye. If instinct hadn't made him turn his head at the last instant, she'd have gouged the socket. Red lines scored the side of his face, like blood painted on with a fork.

He seized her hand, crushing the fingers so hard she could hear them snapping. She screamed higher than she thought her voice could go. Her voice choked off abruptly as he yanked her up by the throat and threw her head back into the floor with the ease of cracking an egg. The back of her skull felt shattered.

'Bitch.'

Dazed and dizzied by the pain she wilted, spent, her breathing ragged with sobs. Then she couldn't breathe at all, as his hands began the death squeeze. Tightening round her windpipe, hot with sweat and excitement.

God, this is it, this is it ... Strange, that of all things she could think of at this moment, the first thought was of her mother. With it came a wrenching sorrow. *I don't want to die ...*

The sounds she made now were less than human, strangled still-born by those fists around her throat. She could no longer scream, though she tried. The sound of it was deafening in her head.

The pressure was increasing, harder and harder. The dancing pinpricks in her vision grew blinding. Her own hands were clamped around his, straining to pull them away, but they were made for mu-sic, not for strength.

With this most intimate of gestures, her hands holding tight to another's, Joanna died.

Chapter TWENTY-FOUR

THE PHONE SHATTERED what semblance of sleep Paxton was enjoying. He'd drifted off somewhere between three and four, and it felt like no time at all. As if to pay him back for pulling a sickie on Friday, he felt a cold coming on. On Monday even a glass of water felt like he was drinking acid. Swallowing experimentally now, he found with relief that the sharp agony had gone. Instead he realised he'd been breathing through his mouth in his sleep.

He caught a blurred glimpse of the red digits on his alarm clock as he reached to pick up the phone. 8:53 a.m. He never slept past eight.

'Have you listened to the radio this morning?' It was Lena, her voice subdued. 'There's been another murder — in Ellerslie. Some girl, a student, they're thinking it might have been a rape this time, but they're still running all the tests. Strangled, the same as the other women. Only this time it was in her own home. They found her in her own *house*, James.'

'You what?'

There was a pause. 'James, are you OK?'

'Yeah. Yeah ... Sorry, I just woke up.' He rubbed the crusts of sleep from his tear ducts, and swept off the covers, swinging himself upright. He might have been more awake but he wasn't any less weary.

'I'm getting sick of this, Lena. When's it going to end?'

'I'm beginning to think never. And if those arseholes try to put you in jail again ...'

'They can't.' He said it firmly. And as he did he remembered the boiling anger on Gardner's face, when he'd watched him walk free ...

Lena seemed to read his mind. 'It won't stop them trying.'

Paxton reflected for a minute, looking down at his toes. Another morning, another murder. Maybe a rape.

'There's one piece of luck. At least with them watching I'm not able to talk to the girl ...'

HE had a long career ahead of him, full of God only knew what horrors. But Andy Stirling knew he'd never forget this one. Pinned to the board in the incident room were the photos, the most hateful, cruel acts of deviance elevated to art. In Stirling's mind he could still see the real thing. He'd spent last night with his eyes open, not liking what appeared whenever they were shut. Was this something that would pass given time and experience? He hoped so. But at the same time ... How terrible.

When you could shut your eyes to this.

Many of the details had not been leaked to the press. When the call had come through last night, he'd felt instinctively they were dealing with their man. Coppers have a sixth sense all of their own. The uniforms were already retching at the scene when he'd arrived with Rees. He had to step over a pool of vomit to reach the doorway to the room where the body lay.

A young girl, barely if at all out of her teens, stripped naked on her living room floor. As he stepped in from the numbing air outside, the first thing that crossed his mind was: *how cold*. All that pale bare flesh, exposed to the chill ...

Then he registered what he was seeing, and the goosebumps broke out in earnest.

One of the contamination-suited scene-of-crime officers was speaking. 'Can't tell yet if she's been raped. But —'

Rees gave a slight nod. Under the circumstances it didn't really matter. The sounds of sobbing, almost screams, mixed with someone being violently sick, came from down the hall.

A printed note in block lettering lay in the middle of the carpet, written on a sheet of manuscript torn from a pad: WHAT'S LONG AND HARD AND GOES IN THE WIND SECTION?

Jo had been violated all right. The flute case lay open on the sofa, empty, near the corpse lying skewed on its stomach. Blood congealed down the backs of her stiffly splayed legs. Her wide eyes bulged sightlessly at the wall, blue lips frozen open in a silent scream ...

Stirling felt his stomach clench, and abruptly turned away, feeling the room spin with him.

'Jesus Christ ...' Rees muttered.

At the bottom of the note was printed: KEEP PRACTISING YOUR FINGERING BOYS.

As Stirling fled back into the cold to lose his guts, the sound of howling followed him.

'HE'S getting more cocky. He's on a bloody power trip!' Gardner's hands were flexing convulsively, looking for something to fasten around.

'Really, sir? You think.'

'If you can't handle the stress, Tony, go home.'

Rees shook his head and stared at the floor. His eyes were like stones cased in glass.

It was in the morning's paper, and on breakfast TV. *East Auckland Serial Killer. Police still hunt for clues as slayings enter third week*. Gardner's temper was stretched to snapping. Elevation from the ranks of drones was looking further away by the hour.

There'd been a press conference at eleven that morning, and he'd been hard pressed to make up leads to feed the baying media. There'd been only one, and not very helpful. A sighting of a red HSV possibly leaving the victim's house, reported by an envious neighbour just arriving home. Not much with which to placate the press or an increasingly anxious commissioner. Not to mention Wooden Willy, to whom Gardner was having to report hourly. DI Woodward, displaying the hard balls he was known for, had shrewdly insisted on giving Gardner 'full credit' as officer in charge of the investigation. In other words, Gardner was marked by the media. All day he'd been fixated by the sight of his name on the page, placed in the driver's seat at the time of the crash.

'*Damn* them!' Gardner smacked his hand down on a desk. 'If they'd only let us hold him this wouldn't have happened!'

They were back in the briefing room, all the usual suspects. Stirling tried hard to hold back an expletive. 'Sarge, since when has James Paxton owned a red HSV? He's got a crap and very dark *grey* Nissan!'

'That's up to you to follow up. We haven't got the plates — it could have been stolen. Assuming it *does* have any connection.'

'I don't believe this. I told you about the Holden before — the hooker saw it, remember? And that thing with the lipstick was just like Joanna Jeffries. He likes to play games. You can't just blame Paxton every time someone is killed! We had to let him go for a reason — there's no bloody proof!'

Gardner pounced on him. 'And *you* were left out for a reason, Andy. You're too bloomin' soft. I don't know what your wife's been telling you ...'

Stirling's blood was rising like a flash flood. Nearing danger level. 'Leave my personal life out of this. *Sir.*'

Kirkpatrick was on his feet, looking worried. 'Hey. Come on, fellas. We're all upset. Leave him alone, Ray.'

Gardner glared down at Stirling, in the seat across from where he stood. 'He deserves to be left alone. He's got no place on a good team.'

The others were all squirming uncomfortably in their seats. DC Coleman seemed grateful it wasn't him this time. Stirling stood.

'Are you saying I'm incompetent, Sergeant? Because as we both know that's defamation.'

Kirkpatrick frowned tightly. 'Sit down, Andy.'

Gardner was grinning at Stirling, nasty. 'The truth isn't defamation, matey.'

'Ray, that's enough.' Rees was no longer slouching.

'Come on, Ray. Back to the job, mate.' Even Little John Blundell was joining in. 'Sit down, Andy.'

'Not until I've received an apology, John.'

Gardner sneered. 'Then you can damn well stay standing while the rest of us send your buddy down for life. And if your arse gets itchy while you're up there, remember it only needs *one* hand ...'

His hands were the very things Stirling was focusing on at that moment.

Kirkpatrick raised his voice, ignoring them both. 'So. We've agreed that we're looking at the same offender. The killing bears all the hallmarks of his usual style, but even more vicious. He's growing more confident, as Ray said. Unusual — he's slowing down instead of speeding up ...'

'Except if you count the security guard,' said Blundell.

'True — which would tend to place Mr Paxton in the clear.'

Gardner bristled. 'You can't count the security guard! Where's the evidence of strangulation? The MO's not even the same.'

Coleman spoke up. 'His first one, the Bradley bloke — that was similar. There wasn't really any strangulation to speak of there, either.'

Kirkpatrick nodded his agreement. 'MOs can change, Ray, you said it yourself. Look at the timing. It's hardly regular. I'd say these were the two he wasn't planning. Plus they were both men — a whole lot iffier strangling a male. He probably didn't want to risk it. Fact is, he's our best match at the moment.'

Gardner huffed in disgust, shaking his head. 'Not even in the same area.'

Stirling fixed him with a sub-zero stare. He hadn't sat down. 'Did you get a statement from the two flatmates last night? 'Cause I did. When one of them had stopped crying enough to speak, he told me he was meant to have picked up the victim from the bus stop right by that church. He even got a phone call from her to say that's where she was waiting!'

Gardner remained stonily silent.

'It's in the *notes*.'

At the tone of Stirling's voice, the room seemed tensed, waiting. No one else even seemed to be breathing. He'd been awake since six the previous morning, and oh was he tired. It was now two on the second afternoon. He hadn't exchanged one word with Nicola in the last twenty-four hours.

'Did you even bother to read them before you called this meeting?'

'I read them.' Gardner shrugged idly.

Stirling was in utter disbelief. 'But you don't *care*, do you! You won't even look past —'

'Andy ...' Kirkpatrick's voice was a growl.

The pressure of words in Stirling's throat was so great it physically hurt to force them back. His breathing sounded stentorian in the still room.

'*That's* why you left me out of the Paxton thing, wasn't it, Sergeant? Not because you thought I wasn't up with the play, but because *you knew I was*. You didn't have a scrap of evidence to cover your arse with, and pardon me, you couldn't face being exposed! Well, well done sir! You did that all on your own.'

Stirling was hearing himself speak from somewhere else, in a ringside seat while the man who wore his skin offered himself for sacrifice. He didn't know who that man was any more, but the words were surely not his. And he had as much power to stop them as he did to reverse the earth's orbit.

Gardner came to stand directly in front of him. His eyes smiling, goading.

'Anything else to say, Andrew? It's been hugely entertaining, but ...' He pushed his face closer. 'If I were you, I'd just shut my little baby's bum face, and *sit the fuck down*.'

Stirling smashed him across the nose. His fist struck out with a satisfying crunch, possessed by a force outside the bounds of mastery. He saw Gardner reel, almost falling into the wall behind him, blood streaming from his nose. He wasn't smiling now. Then Stirling felt Rees grab him, pulling his arms behind his back.

'Bastard!' It was a plea, to Rees.

'Shut up, Andy. That was fucking stupid.'

Gardner winced as he gingerly touched his shattered nose. He dabbed at his mouth, where his lip had split open. Blood stained between his teeth. His voice crawled at the base of Stirling's spine as he looked up at him, thrumming with barely suppressed fury. 'I'll do you for this, boy. You're out. And I'll fucking well be laying charges, too.'

A crimson bubble of spit popped as he formed the F. Stirling felt sick, knowing he meant it. What had he done?

'*Not* your best decision, Andy.' Stirling had never seen Kirkpatrick look so furious. 'Come on, mate. Let's get you cleaned up.'

He led Gardner away, half supporting, half dragging him from the room. Blundell followed, without once looking in Stirling's direction. As they went into the hall Gardner turned his head and caught Stirling's eye. He shook his head, his mouth a bloody slit, and drew his finger silently across his throat. It left a tiny trail of red, from where he'd touched his nose.

'Come on, Andy.' Rees gave his shoulder a solid whack. Though stinging, the slap seemed as much congratulation as reproach. The big man said nothing, which for him spoke volumes. When Stirling looked back, the other DCs' eyes held a wary mix of awe and admiration. He should have taken heart, but he didn't.

He felt like the walking dead.

IN an odd way, his last brush with the law had made Paxton feel better. He no longer felt he had to get involved — the police saw to it that he couldn't. What was he really achieving, at any rate? They'd copped on to that slimy little thug Marcus who, if karma existed in this world, would end up face-down in a junkies' toilet. But the real killer was too careful. All Paxton's past attempts at discovering him had got him nowhere.

For all he'd found out, it could have been virtually anyone. They were hardly distinguishing characteristics, maleness and dark hair. How in the hell had he ever expected to find that one poison ant among the whole nest? Thinking about it now, it beggared belief. He wasn't risking his freedom for that again. While the thought of Gardner still made him uneasy, the sense of release was heady.

And there was Lena. Until tomorrow, when she went back to work, the time was all theirs. There was still a small amount of packing to do but it wasn't urgent. One weekend she'd get around to having the house valued and put up for sale. Tonight they'd abandoned the lot to go to a movie, taking advantage of the cheap Tuesday tickets. Celebrating their freedom. By some unspoken assent, they both knew they weren't going near the murders again. It was over. Life went on.

Lena surprised him by picking an action flick over a comedy, but they'd both laughed the whole way through at the crappy one-liners. The bloodshed and gore weren't personal — they were happening to someone else, in a place far removed from reality.

After the movie they'd gone back to Lena's place, where they'd just polished off a huge dinner of tortellini and red wine. Lena swore she could make it from scratch, but this came from a packet. The sauce was fresh off the shelf. It tasted damn good to Paxton, although his sense of taste was somewhat impaired thanks to the oncoming cold. Pasta was usually his favourite, but tonight he was talking so much that the taste was far in the background. They'd also kissed a fair bit while it was cooking.

What with the Italian food and the extraordinarily good company, he didn't know when he'd ever felt happier.

He belched gently as he put his empty wine glass down on the coffee table and settled down on the sofa. 'Ooh.' He touched a fist to his mouth. *'Scusi.'*

'Great, so do I have to look forward to you breaking wind next?' She was in the corner by the stereo, sticking on a CD.

'Nah, that's only with Indian.'

She gave a proper belly-laugh, that wonderful dirty chuckle Paxton couldn't get enough of. He felt his muscles totally relax, sinking in to the sofa cushions.

'God this is good.'

Glen was curled up in his favourite spot — directly in front of the heater. The CD was one of the *Lazy Sunday* compilations, cruisy chill-out music that caught the mood perfectly. Lena pulled at her hair tie, letting her hair fall loose, messing it up with her hands to get rid of the kink. She drifted back to the dining table and scooped up her wine glass between two fingers, returning to join Paxton. She set down the glass beside his.

'I thought I owed you *one* day, at least, when you weren't sorting my problems.' She curled up against him on the sofa, basking in the warmth that managed to escape from around the sides of Glen's body. She smiled up into Paxton's face.

'Hmmm ... Communicating with dead people. Bashing up my — god-brother. If there's such a word. *And* getting pulled in for murder! Goodness me. How frigging high-maintenance can one woman get? I don't know why you haven't chucked me.'

Paxton smiled. 'You think you've got problems. I'm a habitual loner with a history of difficulty forming relationships, plus I'm suspected of multiple homicide. I'm a real catch, me. You want to make the most of me before it comes out I really *am* him and I'm put away for fifteen years less parole.'

Lena laughed again, and he kissed her before the smile faded. 'You sure you don't mind my cold?'

'Bit late now, isn't it?' She nuzzled against his jaw, resting her face in the angle where it met his neck, as he leaned back into the sofa. 'Anyway, relationships are all about sharing.'

'That's OK. I really don't want your cramps.'

He felt her breath heat his skin as she laughed, and the weight of her against his chest. The laugh turned into a sigh. 'I was going to say I wished my dad could have known you. But I guess he actually does ...'

Paxton was silent a moment. 'Would have been nicer to have met under different circumstances, wouldn't it?'

My name is Mark Bradley. Please listen, something awful has happened ...

He refused to recall his promise. Some promises were best never given.

'Is he here with us now?'

'Possibly. I'm off duty.' He closed his eyes, absorbing the music and the scent of her hair. Mark and murder had no place here now.

'At least he seems to like you. He talks to you.'

He pulled his head away slightly to smile at her, deliberately breaking the melancholy draping them like a damp cloth. 'Don't let that sway you. People talk with lawyers all the time.'

'Come on! If there's one thing you're *not*, it's a pathological liar with a complete lack of conscience.'

'Sure? Ten-thousand criminal profilers can't be wrong.'

'After everything you've done for me, James, they bloody well can.' He was surprised to hear the intensity in her voice. She shook her head. 'All I've put you through, and you're still here ...'

She was gripping his hand. He gave it a little tug, making her look at him.

'Hey. Course I am.' She met his eye, and at last she smiled. He looked back at her gravely. 'Now. Do my eyes look close together to you?'

She gave a disbelieving cackle of laughter.

'Well, if we're going to play How Big is My Neurosis ...'

She kissed him, hard, and he tightened his hold on her, pulling her close against him. As the kiss broke he whispered into her mouth, with the faintest of smiles. 'Sure this isn't just gratitude? Filling the void?'

Her mouth was warm and soft against his as she kissed him again, breathless. 'Post-traumatic stress disorder.'

'Grief and loneliness ...'

She was straddling him now, sitting across his lap, their bodies and mouths pressed tight together. He traced the outline of her bra through the back of her woollen top, sliding his hand down via the curve of her breast to the warm skin above the waistband of her suede pants, radiating body heat. Her palms pressed against his shirt, moving up to encircle his neck, pulling him closer still. Her lips skimmed his ear as she murmured hot into it, 'I'm sorry James, I'm afraid this is nothing but pure, uncontrollable lust ...'

Then her mouth went to the pulse in his throat, throbbing out of control. From there to his collarbone ... Her legs wrapped around his waist as he stood, brushing a kiss against her cheek, her neck, her mouth, whenever he felt sure enough of his direction. When they reached her bedroom, he met the edge of the bed a little earlier than anticipated, bumping into it with his knees. With Lena hanging from him, albeit slight, he overbalanced. He crashed down on to the bed on top of her, and they both dissolved into helpless giggles, which rapidly melted back into ardent kisses as their gazes caught. He slowly glided her top up over her head, and with unpractised but willing hands proceeded to unclothe the rest of her. Fumbling a bit with her bra, until she gave a breathless laugh and guided his fingers to the catch. She seemed to have no trouble at all undressing him ... It wasn't till hours later they remembered the heater still going full blast, when Glen climbed up on the bed and jolted them awake.

Chapter TWENTY-FIVE

AT WORK HE couldn't help his thoughts straying back to the last kill. The last taut, shuddering throes of death before she'd gone limp and died beneath his hands. And afterwards, *the pièce de resistance,* going out to the car in full sight of anyone who might have been watching. Calmly taking the flute case and the bag from the back, just as if he were nothing but a pupil turning up for a lesson. Then doing that to her, the final invasion, what was probably the crowning moment of his life so far. Sending a message to those rectum raiders she lived with. He'd almost wept from the magnificence of it. Even during the light of day with a computer screen in front of him he wanted to break out in a smile at the mere remembrance. But as always, he never let on.

It never ceased to amaze him — none of them *knew*. Not a single one of them understood anything. At times he would have given anything to be able to tell them, to get up there on his desk and shout out the truth: *I Fooled You! Look at what I've done! All I've achieved! And did any of you even have an inkling of who walked in your midst, and shared your coffee mugs, and left them there draining beside yours in the sink? Do none of you cretins even realise who I am?*

But that would have given away everything. And he was never giving this up. No way.

No bloody way.

IT sat on his chest as soon as he opened his eyes, and Stirling knew that this day would be, past imagining, the worst of his life. Today the hammer would fall. As he'd promised, Gardner would have him.

Nothing in all Stirling's previous career would have given any indication of something like this. Young Andy Stirling was a good team player, a favourite drinking buddy with colleagues — never drank too much, though — and also a crack independent thinker. Respectable and respect*ful* to his elders. Responded to hazing with a laugh. He played by the rules, never cracked under stress. In fact, he hadn't taken a proper holiday in three years.

Stirling stared at the ceiling. Seeing the speckles of fly dirt. Crapped on from a great height. He'd sweated his way up the greased rungs of the police career ladder, putting in the hard yards as a beat cop, taking the hard knocks on the street and worse, in the station, and now just when he'd got past halfway, those rungs would vanish. Leaving nothing but a greasy pole, all the way down ...

Nicola had already got up and left for work. He'd stayed in bed, feigning sleep, until he'd heard the shower shut off, then the sound of her heels on the doorstep, and the muffled slam of the front door. When the silence returned Stirling felt a guilty rush of gratitude. He didn't want to break now and blab the truth. Last night he'd circumvented the issue by hardly speaking at all, escaping the reality of his life through so-called reality television. There was a programme for people like him, wasn't there? Something called *Faking It*.

Nicola had tried getting him to open up. She'd come up to his chair and rubbed his shoulder, her face creased with worry. 'I'm sorry I had a go at you earlier. I don't mean to stress you out ... Are you OK?' There'd been a plaintive thread in her voice. He'd wanted to tell her, so badly.

But not speaking at all was better than the truth. Stirling imagined what she'd say when he finally told her. After all this time he didn't think he could predict her response. Somewhere along the way she had become the enemy behind his own lines, to be dodged until all had blown over, a creature with whom he'd shared his life but not, he now realised, his problems. The everyday run-of-the-mill niggles he'd blown off like steam, but the larger ones, the dark spectres that got in the way of sleep, he just interred in an unmarked grave. Buried they were voiceless, dead. But, Stirling reflected dully, even the dead are remembered.

A muscle was spasming in his leg, with the flickering irregularity of a half-blown neon sign. He massaged it to no avail. The erratic pulsing made it impossible to think. In defeat, he got up.

They came to meet him as soon as he got to work. As he'd known they would. With their grim carven faces, about to read him his rights. Woodward was at the head of the bunch, followed by Kirkpatrick and, hovering in the background, an impassive Rees, who'd probably got here early just to make sure. Rees's face said nothing, but his bearing would have sobered up any urine-soaked P-brain down at the watch-house if they'd seen him coming. Or made the horrors much, much worse.

A few others had surreptitiously drifted into the frame. Working in a building full of detectives was like being surrounded by purse-lipped elderly curtain-twitchers, who watched the road when the *Street* wasn't on. Not a lot that went down was missed.

'Come into my office, Andy.'

At least it wouldn't be hanging over him all day. Woodward waited for him to go first. Kirkpatrick followed them, by some pre-arranged request.

A shrink was already sitting at the desk. All part of the service. They were a stock component of every team, the official alternative to boozing yourself numb. That didn't stop most cops preferring the booze. Woodward nodded a greeting in her direction.

'I thought you'd better have a talk with Diane, Andy. I think we all know why, don't we?'

'Yes, sir.'

Woodward nodded. Stirling felt like he'd been called up in front of the headmaster, looking anxiously for a signal to indicate the depth of his disgrace. Woodward's face would have cleaned out the house at poker.

'Give us a yell when you've finished — I'll give you about half an hour. All right? Then we'll all have a talk.'

More nodding, from Stirling. In the general spirit of co-operation. 'Yes, sir.'

It was hellish.

The police psychologist, whose name was Diane Priestley, was an untidy-haired woman in her mid-forties, though her dark lipstick made her look older. She wore a long-sleeved blouse, striped white, tan and chocolate, and a brown calf-length skirt, also brown, which made her crossing her legs beneath the desk somewhat less of an event. Neither fat nor slim, she rested somewhere comfortably in the middle. For some reason she reminded Stirling of his mum. It lulled him into a false sense of security.

She'd obviously learnt the same interview techniques they did — but she'd been around longer. The silences stretched out until they became filled with the sound of Stirling's own breaths and swallows. Interview psychology was so much easier to understand from this side of the table. Unable to curb his natural obligingness, he talked. He made the mistake of mentioning Nicola, and her interest palpably spiked.

His worst nightmare started. She fired off the questions one after another with bewildering irrelevance. Why didn't they have kids? Was Nicola OK with this? How did he know? Was Nicola OK with the job? How did he know? When was the last time they'd talked — and actually listened? Steering between truth and lie, Stirling tried to turn the conversation back to his problems with Gardner, and finally succeeded, but not until he felt like a cigarette butt ground under the high heel of her boot. He came out hating psychologists more than he had before he started. They could twist the evidence worse than any crook lawyer, smelling the shit but never the roses.

At the end of it, she went out to chat with Woodward. Stirling could hear their voices through the office wall, the tone but not the words. Finally Woodward opened the door, with Kirkpatrick in tow. Woodward came to park the edge of his bum on the desk, facing Stirling.

'Right. Well, what do you think? Was that useful?'

As a paper umbrella. 'Yes, sir.'

'I could recommend ongoing counselling, if that's what you'd like.'

'That's all right, sir. I think we got to the bottom of it.'

Stirling almost saw him smile. 'She says you've been under a lot of pressure, and I think we'd all agree with that. Plus, just between you and me, certain people aren't the easiest to work with. I've had a word with Ray too.'

Stirling said nothing, deeming it wisest. The not-quite smile was undetectable now.

'You'd be best not to listen to Ray, Andy. He has his own technique, which gets him his great results, but don't let him put you off yours. All right? We can't have this sort of behaviour among our crew — I'd expect to see it out on Queen Street, but not in here. You'll just have to harden up. Otherwise we might have to send you somewhere else.'

Stirling nodded again. Kirkpatrick spoke up from his corner. 'I've told the Inspector what happened, just so he's heard it from someone else. Ray's been encouraged *not* to press charges.'

Stirling picked up a note of sympathy in his voice. Woodward went on.

'But all the same, this has to go on your record. And I'm sorry, but I'm taking you off the case. You'll be stood down till Monday, and when you come back, you'll have nothing to do with Operation Werewolf. Is that clear?'

'Yes, sir.'

It was a mere slap on the wrist. To Stirling it seemed like the end of the world.

TWO weeks today since it all began. To Paxton it felt more like years. He was no longer so haunted by that miserable voice, echoing into his head from the darkness, or by the weight of obligation. On the contrary, whenever he thought of what that obligation had entailed, he grinned like an idiot. He'd heard of people meeting their partners in strange circumstances, like catching the wrong bus, or having their dinner spilt into their lap by a stunning klutz, but this would have to take the cake. Lena was far and away the highest point in a life not noted for highlights. Hell of a macabre way to start up a romance, but he couldn't help feeling like the world had suddenly become a lot less shitty.

She'd had to go to work early — Murphy's law dictated that the very first day she went back would coincide with a colleague's attack of the flu, so she had to help out in the multilingual gift shop on the premises until teaching started. But not before they'd managed the best breakfast in bed Paxton had ever had. A lot of toast had gone cold.

Tonight after Paxton finished work they were stopping by the reserve. Another of Lena's ideas. It would be their final farewell, a literal attempt to lay the ghost. Paxton checked the clock on the wall. Only two hours to go. The chattering hordes of boozers who'd characterised that other Wednesday night had not materialised, and for once even Adam was quiet. A friendly Tuesday touch game in someone's back yard had turned into an all-night party with too many salted potato chips and a fridge full of beer. Adam had lost the game, but not the results.

Paxton blinked again, and winced, suffering the only ill consequences of last night. He'd fallen asleep with his contacts in, and they were playing merry hell in retaliation, despite the rest he'd given his eyes in the afternoon. It felt like he had sandpaper under his eyelids. He hated glasses; he refused to wear them, no matter what the cost. He didn't know if his watering eyes were the reason his nose was running, or whether it was his cold. To distract himself from the torment, he pictured Adam's response if he could see into his head and get an action replay of *his* night ...

In the same instant, Adam looked over. 'What are you grinning at?'

'Eh?' Shit. He wasn't the only one with psychic powers.

'You're grinning like you just heard a really dirty joke, man.' A corresponding grin sidled over Adam's face. 'So come on. Spill.'

'No, it's nothing. Just had a funny thought, that's all.'

'Yeah, like what?'

'You're a nosy bastard, Adam.'

Adam stopped, taking a good, appraising look at his face. 'Ohh-hhhh ...' He nodded knowingly, his leer stretching further.

Paxton's face was probably going redder than a Bloody Mary, to match his burning eyes and nose. He wished he could damn well stop smiling, but the grin was still firmly fixed to his face by sheer embarrassment. He was bloody well *beaming* with mortification. He was thankful that Brent was busy with punters.

'Guess *one* of us scored last night.'

'Just shut up, you bastard,' Paxton muttered.

To his relief, Adam did, but it seemed to have cured his fatigue. There was a twinkle in his eye every time he looked at Paxton for almost an hour afterward, which he kept up just to embarrass him.

Paxton kept overshooting his hand and skimming coins onto the floor all through cash-up, so impatient was he to be gone. He rang Lena as Brent was spinning the dial on the safe, to tell her he was on his way.

Brent gave the handle of the safe a couple of experimental tugs to check it was locked, then set the alarm. They slipped on their jackets and went out to the carpark. The night was beautifully clear, and could have frozen the balls off a snowman. It never snowed in Auckland, but it was a damp sort of cold, with the promise of more rain. Coming from England he shouldn't have complained, but like a true Englishman, he would anyway.

As he wound up Patteson Ave towards the park, he saw Lena's Honda in the lay-by, waiting for him. As he drove up behind she got out, rubbing her hands in the cold and stamping her feet.

'Bloody hell. Even with the heater on, it feels like my nose has frozen solid. It'd probably just snap off.'

'Mmm ... Snotsicles.' The thought reminded him to blow his nose.

'Should you have been serving drinks? Don't mean to be rude, but you look like Rudolph the Red-Nosed Reindeer.'

'Least it's not Snotty the Green-Nosed Reindeer ...'

He took her hands and rubbed them between his for warmth. Then still holding her right hand, he led her into the park. Although they were reasonably far from the houses, he kept his voice to a low murmur as they drew close to the spot.

'How was work today? All right?'

She looked at him, surprised by the question, then frowned critically. 'Not too bad. Good to be back, really.'

Paxton nodded, and the conversation petered out. This wasn't the time. They'd reached the place. Though it was pitch dark, Paxton scarcely needed to check his bearings.

Lena shivered. 'Me and my urge to be dramatic.'

'Brings it all back for me, I have to admit ...'

She looked at him seriously. 'It would.'

'I'm all right.' He nodded his head slightly, indicating the dark. 'He'll hear you. Go on.'

She faced the darkness again, then looked down at her feet. Searching for the right words.

'Goodbye, Dad. I love you. You can hang around as long as you like ...'

Paxton smiled.

SO did the other man, watching. He guessed he wasn't any different from any other killer after all, in that respect. Returning to the scene of the crime. He wanted to laugh. He'd always, always return to this one. His first time. The hookers were nothing; this was the real dummy run. The first public airing. And no one had seen a damn thing.

He watched the woman walking beside the bloke, back towards their cars. His view wasn't distinct, but he guessed from the way she walked she was quite young. Perhaps even a girl. No older than the nurse had been — or the blonde bimbo. Man, for someone so fit she'd weighed a hell of a lot being dragged down to the water. Boobs probably outweighed all the rest of her. Especially her fucking brain.

He felt an itching in his palms again, to have them round a smooth, warm throat. No more farting round. Let *her* do the waiting for a change ...

Jo had been mind-blowing. Fucking *fantastic*, no question about that. But he already had better plans for the next one. This time it would be no game, over in minutes. This time it was going to be the real thing. Hour after hour of pleasure, strung out dark and beautiful like a twist of black licorice, until finally she snapped. And he'd have her, again, and again, and again … Tearing that soft skin, inhabiting her flesh, turning her against her own body, before at last she was begging to die. Willingly offering up her very will to live. Begging him, please, please to end it. And after that — *long* after that — he would oblige.

And why couldn't it be *her*? Seeing as she'd turned up for the part. He gazed out at the mystery woman. She cut such a sweet and fragile figure, reaching up to plant a kiss on her boyfriend's cheek as they parted for their separate cars. A grin spread across his face, slow as treacle. She'd do nicely.

The man turned his face towards him for the first time. Impossible to see the features, but there was something vaguely familiar about that outline he just couldn't place. As if he'd seen him before somewhere. Possibly he was a frequent visitor to the park. Anyway. Whoever he was, the man drove off in the same direction as the chick — he was going to have to be careful.

But the first part was a piece of piss. He kept pace with them easily, from streetlight to streetlight across the eastern suburbs. Into the dark and out of it. They didn't go far. A small house somewhere in Glendowie. He made a note of the address on the back of a business card. Shit, he was going to need a little black book. He caught a glimpse of her as she waited in the driveway for her boyfriend. Her face was mostly in shadow, turned to the darkness of the street, but enough of it was illuminated to show that she was very pretty. Wavy dark hair, good bone structure … Recognition zapped through him. It was *her. His* daughter. Number one. He sat in his car, just staring, feeling the stars locking into place above their heads. There was something inevitable about it. Something final. It almost scared him, until the overwhelming *rightness* of it all brought out the smile on his face. This would be the one to remember, and relive forever.

A car door slamming brought him out of it. The dude in the Nissan went inside after her, a Rorschach inkblot of black against the light on the doorstep. What the hell was that he was wearing? Poor bastard, looked like he worked in a morgue. He smiled to himself. Would that make it easier, then? After. He wondered if they allowed conjugal visits ...

But Loverboy would have to wait for that. And wait ... And wait ...

Chapter TWENTY-SIX

STIRLING SHAVED BECAUSE it was part of the routine, but he didn't linger in front of the mirror. After an initial fatalistic glance to check whether he really looked like the piece of shit he felt, he was sick of the sight of his own face. Shaving off the stubble did nothing to improve his appearance. It only meant his sallow complexion had more room to shine. Or not in this instance.

Nicola had been taken aback when, without a word, and still in his pyjamas and dressing gown, he'd made her pancakes and coffee. A guilt offering. He couldn't eat a bite of it himself. When she kissed him goodbye he was a little more passionate than usual, clinging on for longer than he had to. Nicola was pleased. She thought she was seeing a return to his old attentive self. She'd tasted sweet, like syrup and toothpaste. When the door closed it felt horribly like goodbye.

Stirling stared at the clock on the microwave. Mere hours from now she'd come home again, and find him still here. There'd be no more lying then. He'd have to tell her.

There was a backlog of books on his shelf, waiting for his next free moment. He couldn't remember which Christmas they were from. He picked one up, just to take his mind off. A crime novel. Typical formula — who paid these people? Even on half concentration he had it figured out inside thirty pages. He flipped to the end. He was wrong.

He stuck it back on the shelf. He'd ruined it now anyway.

It felt ghastly sitting here, on home detention, wondering how the investigation was going. Powerless to do anything to help. And Gardner, was that arrogant fucker crowing about his success? Sneering at him down his bandaged nose?

He went into the kitchen and opened the cupboard door, restless.

Stared at the unappetising packets of instant noodles and vegetable soup, and tins of spaghetti and sweetcorn. Invalid food. He shut the door again, and tried the fridge. He could have eggs, cheese on toast or cold beer. Fuck it. He wasn't even hungry.

He wandered through the house. What if Gardner was right after all? What if it was James Paxton? Or what if Paxton just walked straight back into his wide-open trap ...

When the digits on the microwave glowed 4.57 he gave up. She was due home in twenty minutes. Stirling grabbed his keys and went for a drive.

SHE was home. He could see her shadow moving past the drapes in her lounge as he eased into the kerb. The rain was javelining the car window like the start of Agincourt, making it difficult to see. Even the heating was barely holding its own against the cold.

He depressed the little button on his watch, illuminating the face in eerie blue. Should he go in now? No. Still too early. It was just past the rush hour. A little risky, even for him. The street was a bit busier than Jo's.

Still, it was getting harder and harder to wait these days.

He sat back, letting his eyes unfocus at the curtains, and set his imagination loose.

'OI, James. Phone for you.'

Brent held out the phone to Paxton, who took it in surprise. 'Hello?'

He heard Brent speak again behind him. 'Don't be long, because it's getting rather busy.'

Brent's voice was drowned out by the sound of his mother. 'Hello, Uncle James! Guess what, your sister's just had her baby!'

Paxton was torn between confusion and astonishment. How in God's name had they found him here? 'What? Say that again?'

'I know. Almost a week early. That's common with the first one, though. I tell you I'm bloody knackered; I'm still at the hospital. We tried you at home, but when you didn't answer we guessed you'd be at work. Good thing you told us where it was. I got Dad to check on the Internet after you rang.'

Paxton was mute with amazement. Whether it was because they'd remembered the restaurant and bar or the fact that his dad had used the Internet he couldn't have said.

'Thanks ... Thanks so much for telling me. Um — love to Nat. She's OK?'

'Yeah, she's fine. Exhausted, though. Almost as much as I am. Eight pounds, ten ounces.'

'Oh yeah. Any ideas what to call him?'

'They thought Henry. Henry Bryan, after Hamish's dad, but with a Y.'

Paxton silently grimaced into the receiver. Fuck. Poor kid. 'Henry? I know ironic kids' names are in at the moment, like Mavis or Bertie, but I thought Hamish would have put his foot down.'

'Actually it was his idea. He wanted to pronounce it the French way, after that footballer Thierry Henry, but I told him they'd look stupid.'

Ah. He should have guessed. Gunners man to the death, was Hamish. If — God forbid — Arsenal should ever be relegated, he'd swallow his nail gun.

'Tell them congratulations.'

After a blow-by-blow account of all thirteen hours of labour, and a scathing appraisal of the coffee in the caff, Cathy Paxton rang off.

When Paxton hung up, he felt suddenly restless. He scanned the bar for Brent and saw his back was turned. Quickly he picked up the receiver again, and dialled Lena's number.

THE porch light coming on snapped him fully awake. He was sitting in full darkness now, and the traffic had all but ceased. TV dinner time. But there'd be no capitalising on the lull. The Bradley girl appeared in the doorway, dressed to go out. She dressed herself well in actual fact. Dark, charcoal pants, a cream top, and a bronzey-coloured scarf under a long charcoal coat. Nice boots too. He approved. Had a bit of class, this one. He hoped they were off somewhere nice.

She got into her Civic and drove off, the way he'd seen her come earlier. He gave it a few seconds then followed. Didn't pay to be too careless. They'd put a notice in the paper asking the owner of a red HSV to come forward, as a witness in the Jeffries case. Sure ... Come and get me, dipshits.

The Civic was still in sight when he rounded the corner. They cut through St Heliers, down to the waterfront, then westward through Kohimarama. He had a sinking feeling that she was heading for the city, but when she reached Mission Bay she turned into the carpark by the beach. Circled it slowly until she found a space towards the back. In an optimistic mood, he noticed there was still room for him. Score. He liked Mission Bay. Nice setting, and the choice of restaurants was good. Although most were overcrowded on weekends, it was a great place to get lost and just to watch. In this weather people kept their heads down, not out for the view. He could stick by her all night and she'd never notice. What was it to be, dinner or a movie?

He visualised following her into the cinema. Slipping into a seat behind her in the dark. Then leaning forward as she sat there engrossed in the movie. Casually putting an arm around her shoulders. And one hand over her mouth. Hooking his elbow round and pulling his arm back until she choked, flailing against the padded seats, her death drowned out by the Dolby Surround. Then calmly exiting with the rest as the credits rolled, leaving her to be collected with the stale popcorn on the floor …

But no. That was murder for beginners. He wouldn't even get to see her face. And she'd doubtless be with that guy, the familiar one whose face he couldn't quite pick. Sooner or later, though, he'd get her alone …

It wasn't to be the cinema after all. She walked into a restaurant. One of those places with a bar attached, and in fact one he'd been to a number of times before. Anubis. The dog-headed Egyptian god stood impassively to one side of the entrance. The food here wasn't too bad, and the décor was pleasant enough. They'd had the sense not to thrash the Egyptian theme; being surrounded by sarcophagi and bare-chested pharaohs was somehow a little more Ponsonby. A slight hieroglyphic motif on the walls was about it. There was a dimly lit softness about it as he entered that was strangely welcoming. The ambience was spoiled only by the old cloakroom whiff of wet umbrellas and drying clothes, and the rugby on the TV in the bar. The bloke who ran it saw the world in black and white. Or blue, if the Super Rugby was on.

He spotted her chatting to one of the barmen, who had come out from behind the bar. It was him. Her boyfriend from the park. He was struck again by that odd sense of familiarity, but trying to pin it down was like grabbing at shadows.

Just a coincidence, probably.

'HI, Uncle James.' Lena gave Paxton a kiss on the cheek, mindful that he was working.

He couldn't help smiling. 'You sound like my mum.'

'How does it feel to be an uncle?'

The regret was back. 'Bit crap, actually. I can't exactly afford to go over and see them.'

'No ... How long has it been?'

'More than five years ... Mind you, now probably isn't the best time. Give it a while, till he's out of pooing his nappies and sicking up all over anyone who holds him.'

'Good thinking.'

Adam gravitated towards them, having finished pouring beers. 'Ah, so you're the one who did this to James. Used to be such a miserable bastard till he met you. I'm starting to worry.'

'Oh, don't worry. He's still a bastard.'

'Thanks.' Paxton retreated behind the bar, wiping down the counter as they sniggered. It was truer than they realised, what he'd said. He wasn't feeling the greatest at the moment. A queasy feeling had developed at the pit of his stomach.

Adam was grinning. 'I like her already.' He wiped condensation-slippery hands on his pants, holding one out for Lena to shake.

'Hi, I'm Adam. I run this place.'

Paxton scoffed. 'Run this place? You barely work here.'

'Shut up.'

Lena laughed, shaking hands. 'Nice to meet you. I'm Lena.'

'Lena? That's a pretty name.'

Paxton rolled his eyes. 'God, here we go.'

'What? It is ...'

A couple came up to the bar right beside them, and Paxton's attention was momentarily diverted. When he returned to Adam and Lena they were discussing Switzerland. Adam looked wistful.

'You're so lucky. I'd love to go to Europe, but I don't have the money, eh? Don't know my rellies either. My poppa never kept in touch.'

'Your granddad was from Europe?'

'Great-granddad. He was German. They used to own Samoa, up till the First World War.' He gave another one of his grins. 'Give them a fright if I went back there now, eh? *Guten Tag, palagi. Youse got any Kokosnusskuchen?'*

Paxton's elbow just about slid off the bar. 'You speak German?'

Adam shrugged. 'Sort of.' He looked at Lena. *'Ich sehe wahrscheinlich wie ein totalles Arschloch aus, oder?'*

Lena looked delighted. 'No! That was great!'

'Shit. So that's how you do it ...'

'I'm thinking of starting up a pub quiz, fellas. First question, how much do you get on the dole?'

Both men gave a guilty start as Brent loomed up behind them. 'Sorry, mate. I was just introducing Adam to my girlfriend. Lena, this is Brent, the manager.'

Lena gave Brent such a sweet smile that the bar manager was almost looking for hair to smooth over. In the kitchen he was lost amid the chrome. Another pair of customers came up as he and Lena were shaking hands.

'I'll get it.' Paxton went to serve them, only to find that they were complaining about the lack of vodka in the woman's drink.

'It's supposed to be a double measure, and I can't even taste one!'

'I'm very sorry about that, but the recipe does only say one shot, and I'm sure I put it in there. I have a set order.'

'The place next door does two.'

The place next door also served minors, but Paxton didn't say it. 'Must be using a different recipe there, then. I can put in another shot if you like.'

'Are you going to charge me for it? Because I swear you haven't even got a single in here. It just tastes like water.'

You're on your third, you stupid tart, that's why. Paxton was most definitely not in the mood for this. 'Would you like me to taste it?'

Her glare increased. 'I want a new one if you do that. You sound like you've got a cold! You could give me meningitis or something.'

There are quicker ways of getting you to hospital, Paxton thought. But he merely added another shot without wasting his breath, and sent her on her whining little way. Lena caught a look at his face when he turned towards her again, moving a little slower than usual.

'Are you OK?'

Paxton paused, frowning. 'No. Not really. Feeling a bit yuk, to be honest.'

'Oh no. What's brought that on? Is it your cold?'

'Don't quite know ...' He shook it off. 'I'll be fine. Not a major. Sit down, what can I get you?' He bent closer, darting a glance towards Brent. 'Make it look as though I'm working ...'

Lena arched at eyebrow at him, her eyes dancing. 'You up to a Sex on the Beach?'

Paxton consulted his watch. 'Well, I've got a few hours to go yet. And isn't it a bit we—'

'All right. A Pineapple Teaser then.'

'I can think of a crack about prickly things and Teasers ...'

''Scuse me!' came a voice.

Paxton shot up straight, his heart beating double-time, until he saw Adam's smugly grinning face.

'Oh it's you. This is like the start of a bad joke: an Englishman, a Samoan and a Swiss walk into a bar ...'

'I'm a Kiwi,' said Adam and Lena in unison.

'Jeez, all right.'

Lena lightly punched him on the arm. Adam watched them indulgently. 'You make a cute couple, you know that?'

Lena smiled. 'Thanks.'

'Hey, how'd you two meet, anyway? Didn't think he went out.'

Lena flicked a glance at Paxton and looked away. Suddenly the good mood was gone. Paxton filled the awkward gap that followed. 'Tell you later. It's got to do with what happened a couple of weeks back.'

Adam got it, not fully understanding but realising he'd made a mistake. 'Ah, sorry. I didn't know ...'

'You're all right. Well. Best do some work ...' Paxton gave Lena a smile and returned to the bar to fetch her drink. He set it down in front of her.

They didn't get much of a chance to talk afterwards. Activity in the bar was picking up rapidly. As soon as she'd finished her drink, Lena weaved through the tables to Paxton.

'I'm going to be off, I think.'

Paxton nodded, kissing her cheek. 'OK. I'll see you tomorrow. Thanks for coming.'

An impish little grin appeared on Lena's lips, and her eyes had a devilish glint, but she refrained from commenting. Paxton got it anyway. She reached up and gave him a swift kiss on the mouth.

'Any time ...' She gave Adam a wave as she went out the door.

IN the corner a dark-haired man drained his glass and made his way from the room.

He followed her back to the carpark, strolling harmlessly in a crowd of people milling from the restaurant. Lena. A lovely name indeed. Engrossed in her conversation with the two young men she hadn't even noticed him ordering a drink not five feet away. Just the way he wanted it. They jaywalked across Tamaki Drive in a gap in the traffic. The lights sparkled off the road in the reflective sheen of rain. She was gazing out to sea, totally oblivious to his presence. Walking past the tiny, prefabricated community constable's office, shut tight till the following morning. In the distance, off to the left, the fountain where beachgoers waded in summer was lit up blue against the dark, like liquid ice. Looking at it, he felt a deep calm. It was so perfect ...

The people immediately surrounding him reached their car, and fell away. She was scrounging through her handbag now, grappling with her umbrella, searching for her key. He walked up, without haste. As though he were just going to the next car. She glanced up as she heard him, aware of the dark.

'*Hi*,' he said.

She seemed surprised but not displeased to see him. 'Oh — hello!'

'Need a hand?' Teasing, he held out his hand for the umbrella. Automatically she gave it to him.

'Thanks.' She half-turned back to her car, palming her keys, a smile still on her face.

With a sudden sharp blow, he struck her across the head. She dropped instantly, as if someone had removed her knees. He caught her as she sagged against him. Calmly supported her towards his own car, shielding her with the umbrella, looking for all the world as if he were giving his girlfriend a hand after she'd had a few too many. She weighed less than nothing at all.

PAXTON couldn't remember the last time he'd felt so crummy. If he didn't know better he'd have called it PMS — general shittiness with no rational explanation. It wasn't just that the work seemed twice as boring with Lena gone. The tar-laden exhaust from the smoking tables had never got to him this way before. It flitted across his mind that the illness might be psychosomatic. Or more accurately, psychic. Residual discomfort from Natalie's childbirth, shared between siblings? It was the only thing he could think of, little sense though it made. *Her* bloody suffering was over. And the time she'd broken her leg skiing he'd actually laughed, till he realised it was serious.

Anyway, his was less a physical pain than a chronic kind of unease, going as deep as the soul. And consequently totally unshakeable. He started clearing the tables of glasses to keep himself busy.

'There's another one by the door.' Brent nodded his head. Paxton's hands were already full. He deposited his armload on a tray and went back for it. A beer glass on an empty table, solitary in a ring of condensation. He picked it up.

The moment his fingers made contact, there was such an almighty shout of evil that he staggered back. Voices crowded into his head, sonic bursts of half-captured speech, as if the whole room were suddenly thronged with the dead.

He screwed me, and then he screwed me over ...

... said he was in pain ...

... trapped, I couldn't get free.

It's my fault, I was lusting after him ... I was unfaithful ... ... but they didn't come ...

Someone was sobbing, *'Don't don't don't don't don't don't ... Please ...'*

The voices were rising to a shout, stripping away all resistance. ... *why? Why* me?

... please! ...

... whacking me, over and over and over, I ...

'Deus, *boy, go after her*! *Go, for God's sake, GO*!'

'James! You OK, man?'

Paxton looked up, realising he was bent almost double over the table, gasping as if his head had been held underwater.

Adam was standing beside him, staring in appalled concern. Paxton stared back, right through his head.

'I've got to go.'

'And I thought you were pale before ... Gimme that glass, man.' Paxton didn't move. That voice. A voice he hadn't heard in more than ten years, exploding in his head with the roar and fury of fermenting wine kept bottled in the cellar. Smashing down everything in sight. *'I've got to go.'*

He looked down at the glass in his hand, and saw it was shaking. He thrust it into Adam's grasp and fled.

HE didn't even use the steps. He flew straight from the top to the ground, hitting the footpath at a dead run. The traffic was stopped at the lights, and he slalomed through the bumpers with reckless abandon, racing for the carpark. He stared into every corner, between the cars, fearing to see something he didn't dare imagine.

Then he saw a familiar umbrella, skating in a gust of wind across the tarmac. And there was her car, right at the end of the carpark. Empty. An icy hand reached into his chest and stopped his heart. Frantic, already soaked through, he turned almost three-sixty, whirling to catch any glimpse, any sign.

His eye lit again on the traffic waiting at the intersection. No. Oh no.

He ran full pelt back towards the road, eyes straining towards every car, wishing so much it hurt for that one power he did not possess, the power to see. Then, in the same instant, he did. She was there, head lolling back in the passenger seat of a red HSV, her face too dim to properly distinguish the features. But it was her.

'Lena!'

He sprang for the door-handle, as the driver looked over and saw him. A man with dark hair, and eyes that were not at all mad, but all the more frightening for that. He knew exactly what he was doing. Just as he had that night at the park. *It was the neighbour's chatty friend.*

He looked startled to see Paxton there, but then a shock of recognition seemed to strike. His eyes looked straight into Paxton's, and he smiled. Paxton wrenched fiercely at the handle, teeth clenched with the effort. It didn't give.

'Lena, wake up!' He pounded on her window, screaming with bursting lungs, but she didn't open her eyes. He smashed at the solid glass, but it wouldn't break.

Then the light turned green. The driver gave him a little wave, which changed into a single upraised finger, and the car slid out from beneath Paxton's clutching palms. He was trapped on the spot, as cars surged off all around him. The HSV roared ahead, along Tamaki Drive.

Almost crying out aloud in frustration, Paxton sprinted for his car as soon as he could move again. He had to force himself to slow down so he could line the key up with the lock. The Japanese engine whined as he floored it from cold. Its little old lady previous owner had never driven it like this. He actually did a wheel-spin on the wet road as he pulled out onto Tamaki Drive. He sped back through Kohi and St Heliers as fast as the traffic would allow him, gritting his teeth when a Mitsubishi got in his way.

'Come on, come *on*!'

He overtook on a double yellow, on a road known for fatalities, reckless of the cliffs to one side and the water to the other. Twice he had to brake for oncoming cars, swerving back onto his own side of the road after a blind corner as their headlights flashed in his eyes. His own death was the least of his worries now.

At last the cliffs cut him off, and he could go no further. No sign of the HSV. Paxton slid to a stop, staring at the wall of earth in front of him, his mind racing. Which way now? They could have taken any side road, been anywhere by now ...

He tried to push aside thoughts of the last girl, the end that had awaited her. Kidnapped in that very same car, killed where she'd thought she was safest ...

Rapidly Paxton did a three-point turn, and took off toward Lena's house.

The drive was empty as he sped up. The road too was bare of cars save a little silver Laser. The sound of an engine reached his ears. He swung round in his seat. A Mazda 6 was turning into the street. Paxton felt his senses dying, one by one. He fell out of the car and flew to the door. All was dark and silent as he rattled the doorknob back and forth like a wild man. He pummelled on the door, shouting. Knowing it was useless.

'Lena!'

At once, a muffled barking started up from within the house. Startled from sleep and frightened, Glen was roused from his usual placid amity. The barking grew louder as he rushed to the door. There was nobody there.

Paxton slumped against the wood on the other side, crushed by the sheer helplessness. Were he ten years old again, he would have sunk onto the step and cried. For all his 'special' abilities, for all his *fucking gifts*, he could do *nothing*. With unimaginable cruelty, they had tuned him in, then abandoned him, powerless to stop it. A punishment for turning his back. The only sound in his head now was the barking.

He tried to block it out, shivering violently. His clothes were plastered to his skin. He hadn't even stopped to collect his jacket. He hammered on the door again, giving a guttural cry of rage. *Think*, Paxton, *think*!

And then it hit him. The barking, the darkness, the cold and the fear ... All of these he had known before. He was *there.*

Dear God. *The park.*

He turned and ran to his car. Back to where it all began.

Chapter TWENTY-SEVEN

THERE WAS NO need for questions; he knew it like he knew his own name. They were in the park, or nearby. The man's name came to him suddenly — Jason. And he was clever. His route along Tamaki Drive was just to throw Paxton off while they doubled back. It was lucky Paxton wasn't pulled over — the speed limit wasn't the only rule of the road he was totally ignoring. He could kiss his freedom goodbye if Gardner ever found out about his driving. But when he got back to Patteson Ave, he slowed to a positive crawl. The delay almost had him screaming, but he had to keep his eyes peeled every second for a flash of red. It could be in any garage. Behind any infill house on a big section …

In his rear-view mirror he saw the headlights of another car, forced to slow on the treacherously wet road, unable to get past. Paxton didn't give a damn. He was waiting for that spark of intuition, that inner Yes when he'd found it. It never came. He drove past the park, peering into the shadows. Seeing absolutely nothing, till he was at the bottom of the hill and staring at the empty sea.

But he wasn't wrong, *he wasn't wrong*. Gritting his teeth, he did a U-turn and went back. Doubt was there on the edges, threatening to break his will. On the other side of the park, in the street running behind? Or not here at all? Every second he couldn't decide was another second Lena didn't have. She might already be dead. *No. That* of all things he would know, surely. But he might well drive round and round this street, going out of his mind, until the signal came. The agony was unbearable.

'Fuck! Where are you?'

He wiped his face, wet from his streaming hair. Nearing the top again, and here was the reserve. There were more lights than on that other night two weeks before. It was earlier, and the neighbours were still up. A mad idea blazed through his brain. He didn't even give it a moment's thought. Didn't have to. He was shit out of alternatives.

He pulled up at the house from last time, leaving the engine running as he sprinted to the door.

Again it was the woman who answered to his knock. A look of surprise, and not a little alarm, fleeted across her face as she laid eyes on him. He was probably the last person she'd have expected or wanted to see. He didn't give her the chance to speak.

'Sorry, I'm doing it again, but I *have to know*. Does anyone round here have a red Holden HSV?'

'Ummm ...' She didn't seem to know how to respond, no doubt feeling even more alarmed now. Her kids, two boys under the age of twelve, had come out to stare at him behind her. They took one look and left, not much interested. But at the word 'HSV', her husband also materialised over her shoulder.

'What was that?' He caught sight of Paxton, and his eyebrows shot up. 'It hasn't happened *again,* has it?'

'Who was that man you were talking to?' Paxton virtually shouted it at him. 'The night of the murder? He drives a red HSV.'

They both stared at him. The man said, 'You mean Jason?'

'Yes! That's him!' Paxton felt a thrill pass through him. *They knew who he was*. And that meant ...

'Doyouknowwherehelives?' It came out as a single word, all syllables blending into one.

The wife looked at her husband, out of her depth. 'He lives just up —'

Paxton's stomach jack-knifed at his response.

‘Two doors up, yeah.’ He stabbed a thumb up the hill. Paxton could see the house from here.

He turned back to face them, every word crystal-clear. ‘Right — I want you to call the cops. Do you hear me? Because yes, it is happening again. *Right now*. And they’d damn well better be quick, tell them. He’s got another girl in there ...’

He was already off and running across their lawn, tearing up the sodden grass beneath his feet.

There were two houses on the section, the older one in front. Lights were on in neither.

He saw it just the same. It was parked round the corner behind the first house, invisible from the street. He did wonder for a second about the owners of the house behind, but a quick glance revealed everything. All the blinds were drawn, and the carport was empty. There was a curling homewares catalogue on the doormat, its plastic wrap getting wet. Away. No one would have seen a thing.

He was close enough to see the number plate on the red HSV. It was the car.

Now, for the first time, he hesitated. Surprise only got you so far. He was just one man, whose chest was already hurting, against a guy who’d already killed at least five. There hadn’t really been time for a game plan. He stared at the blank windows and thought of Lena, alone, scared, in pain. Dead.

Fuck the game plan. He grabbed the doorknob. When it didn’t turn, he smashed a window and hurled himself through.

He hurt his shoulder as he landed, but luckily escaped injury from the glass, that he could feel. He uncurled, gingerly rising to his feet. He was in the kitchen. A watery gruel of moonlight hinted at various surfaces. No knives, no promising objects in sight. Nothing to help him that could be used as a weapon. Everything was squared away tidily. Sterile. The house was all in darkness, shuttered, eerily still. As if the hush of death lay over it already. Paxton knew better. It was just waiting.

He groped as silently as he could through a cupboard, his hands lighting on a frying pan. Stainless steel, not cast iron. It felt light as air. It could only slow the guy down. But there wasn't time to hunt for more. He'd have his back to the killer while his skull was cracked open. He crept through the blackness of the rest of the house, moving away from the light, still clutching the useless frying pan. It would have to do.

The sound of his own feet as he stepped into the next room made him cringe. Careful as he was to be quiet, there was no carpet, just wood, underfoot. It amplified every clomp and squeak, as well as the cold blasting through his bones.

A tiny shuffling, an infinitesimal change in the air current, alerted him to the killer's presence.

Slowly, very slowly, Jason came through the door into the lounge. With a sudden movement he flicked on the lights, catching Paxton like the proverbial possum. The light gleamed off the polished floorboards, except for where a large rug lay in the centre of the room. It was almost like Marcus's apartment, the same modern style, but with much more ostentaion. A little too ostentatious for Paxton's taste. It seemed a mockery of sense, that a man so flawed should live in a house so clean and unstained. Bright colours in place of the darkness within.

The man himself stood at the opposite end of the room. His hand holding a large kitchen knife. The knife held at Lena's throat.

Lena's face was set with terror, which seemed only to increase on seeing Paxton there. He could see it in her eyes. She wanted to tell him to leave her, but she couldn't do it.

Jason's gaze landed on the frying pan, and he gave a laugh. 'Sorry, is it time for breakfast already?' He was relaxed, apparently enjoying himself. He might have been offering drinks, except that his eyes warned subtly of poison. 'I didn't hear you knock.'

Paxton stared him down. 'Like me to smash the window in again?'

A glimmer of something that might have been laughter appeared in the other man's eyes. 'That's leaving a bigger mess for the authorities to clean up, isn't it?'

Paxton wanted nothing more than to drive that knife right through his heart. 'I've already called the cops. They're on their way.'

'We'll have to make this quick, then ...' He spoke in Lena's ear, his voice a hiss. 'Won't we?' His eyes never left Paxton's face. He smiled again. 'You really don't want to piss me off. Because I'm not some terrorist you can negotiate with — I don't have a nice agenda. I'm just doing this for fun. So the moment *I* get mad ...' He laughed, and Paxton's stomach turned.

'If you move, I slit her throat. If the cops come, I slit her throat. Gee, well fuck it, I'm doing it anyway!' He was smirking. 'Fast or slow? Please choose slow — no one ever does.'

'You arsehole, you strangle, you don't cut. Where's the fun for you in that?'

He looked almost lazy. 'I get my kicks from variety ...'

Paxton took in his yellow-white knuckles gripping the knife, the fingers clenched on Lena's shoulder. For all he knew, the cops would be here any minute. Or they'd got his car's registration. He wasn't nearly as calm as he seemed. Neither, for that matter, was Paxton. Psychology never had been his strong suit. He suspected you'd need a long time swotting for this final ...

In desperation, he did the only thing he knew how — he did what they did on the telly. Rule number one: Keep The Fucker Talking.

'So what was it? The great excuse? Mum run away as a kid? Eat too many pies, or did you just have really bad BO, er …? I don't think we've been introduced.'

'I beg your pardon! Where are my manners? Name's Jason.' He glanced down at Lena, then back up at Paxton. 'Now, do you want me to gut your girlfriend now, or would you prefer to watch while I fuck her first?'

'Go fuck yourself.'

It was the first time Lena had spoken. The blade left her throat in a flash of silver, slashing a trail down her arm. Lena's breath hitched in a throttled scream of pain and shock. The sleeve of her coat was in two ribbons. No hope that Jason was more sloppy with his sharpening than he was with his dusting. Paxton had involuntarily taken a step forward, but the knife was already back at Lena's throat, its tip now stained with blood. A warning. Jason curved his face round, pressing a kiss on Lena's cheek.

'I'd rather have you do it …' He hadn't even broken a sweat.

He was too smart to have his buttons pushed. He was just pushing right back. Sick and reeling, Paxton felt his knees shivering beneath him, almost as much from anger as from the cold. Goose-bumps crawled all over his skin. A sudden sneeze shook him. He saw his dripping clothes making a mess of the polish.

'*Gesundheit*.' Jason was smirking again. 'Although, doesn't that mean "good health"? Not really appropriate, is it?'

Paxton looked him dead in the eye, clutching at straws, saying anything that came into his head.

'Funny. I didn't think you usually raped yours either. What with this lovely clean house and that big, shiny, compensating-for-something car, here I was thinking you were going to screw me.'

He saw a flicker of something then, igniting behind the smugness. Was that it, then? Was *that* what the fucker was repressing?

He went for it like a shark, scenting blood in the water. 'Actually, you're kind of cute ...'

'Shut up.'

'Ooh ... Can I go first, big boy?'

Jason put his hand on Lena's injured arm and squeezed it hard. She screamed as the blood soaked through her sleeve. It pierced Paxton to the heart.

'Suicidal as well as psychic, are we — James? May I call you James?'

Paxton froze. Lena's eyes were on him, full of tears. He saw her throat working, trying to hold them in, and recoiling as the blade dug into her skin at every swallow. Another faint smile was playing round Jason's lips.

'What do you think we've been doing all this time? Drinking tea? I know *all* about you, my friend. And you don't scare me ...' He was getting closer. Pushing Lena before him, the blade still hard against her throat. 'I wondered where I'd seen you before. And then it hit me. You were there — in the park. I just caught a glimpse of your face for a second when one of the policemen got you with his spotlight.'

He hooked a thumb over his shoulder towards the window, but Paxton didn't take his attention off the smugly grinning face for a moment.

'You have *no* idea how much I enjoyed that. Better than TV! Dumb fuck — didn't he know it's dangerous to go walking in the park at night?'

'Did you rape him too, before you killed him?' Lena's voice was thick with tears, and colder than death.

His grin hardening, Jason made a swift movement with his hand, making for her arm. But before he did, his right hand, the one holding the knife, moved the tiniest fraction. The unconscious instinct of a right-handed man. Quick as a flash Lena braced her feet against the floor, throwing herself back against him. Sending him off balance. Her teeth sunk deep into the tender veined flesh of his wrist. He gave a howl and his fingers relaxed on the knife. She knocked it from his hand as she burst free of his grip, fleeing towards Paxton, only to have Jason lunge forward and grab her again. She squirmed in his hold, sobbing and howling with fury.

'You bastard! You *bastard*!'

His arm locked fast round her throat. Paxton seized hold of the knife, which had skittered to a halt near his feet. He was still holding the frying pan in his other hand. He charged at Jason, who stepped back a bit, looking uncertain what to do next. With a sudden movement, he seemed to make up his mind, sending Lena sprawling with a vicious thrust of his arm. She hit the hard wooden floor with an audible thump. Face down. Her body still as an old heap of rags.

Half mad, Paxton swung at Jason with the frying pan. It had a longer reach than the knife. That didn't make it a good weapon. Jason deflected it easily, sidestepping and holding up an arm. He'd have got no more than a slight bruise from the stainless-steel pan, which made a small, ineffective dink as it hit his forearm. Looping his arm round, Jason grabbed the pan and wrenched it out of Paxton's hand. He swung it hard at Paxton's face as Paxton teetered forward, pulled along with the pan, but Paxton ducked just in time and went for Jason's knees.

They tumbled to the floor, and the frying pan went clattering across the bare wood as it flew from Jason's grasp. He grabbed Paxton's wrist, the one holding the knife, and began twisting it in an agonising Chinese burn. His strength was more than a match for Paxton's. Struggling, Paxton tried to hit him, but he simply blocked the blow and held on to Paxton's fist, while almost breaking his other wrist. He was going to get the knife. Paxton could feel Jason's weight tilting to the side; he was going to roll Paxton beneath him, destroying the only advantage Paxton had. In that event, it would be game over.

His teeth grinding together against the pain, Paxton slammed a knee into Jason's gut. It missed his bollocks by centimetres. It was too low to wind him, too high to render him permanently impotent, but the brief moment of lowered resistance was all Paxton needed.

With a sudden jerk he swung the knife arm down, wrist still twisted backward in Jason's lock-hold. The blade cut through the shirt above Jason's left breast with a sound of tearing, and he saw the sudden well of blood. He followed up instantly with a second knee to the stomach in exactly the same place as before, abruptly cutting off the yell of pain. Blessing his bare arms, slippery still with rain, Paxton pulled himself up out of Jason's hold and went for the finish. He stamped a foot hard in Jason's midriff, with the thick black boots he always wore to work, just as Jason went to rise from the ground. Jason crumpled back on the floor, his frantic struggle for breath sounding like a death rattle. Paxton felt a vicious spurt of pleasure. Now the bastard knew how it felt.

He scrambled to the window and hurled the knife through it, hearing it strike against the fence. He didn't trust himself to keep hold of it in another rumble. Best not to leave it to chance. As he turned, his eye lit on Lena, still motionless on the floor, her dark hair spread out like a shroud. Then another sight sent a fresh hit of panic through him. Jason was up. Already.

There was no pretence at urbane calm now. Paxton had blooded him, and he was angry. They'd turned round in the struggle, and he was blocking the way to the kitchen, the way out. The window was one of those security jobs. How wonderfully ironic. It wouldn't open far enough to pee from. He could have smashed it, could have got free ...

And left Lena all alone with Jason. He might as well have thrown himself head first from an upstairs window. If there was any chance she was still alive, he was damn well going to make sure she got it. On numb legs Paxton fled through the other door, into the hall.

Perversely he prayed that Jason would follow, that he wouldn't stay behind in the room with Lena. The horrible images came crowding after him.

But Jason followed, his painful breathing ringing loud as his footsteps on the timber floor. With each breath he sounded stronger. Paxton was operating on sheer panic and instinct alone. A dozen different options scrolled through his head, almost too fast to be comprehended. *Front door that way — leave Lena. No. Kitchen that way — knives, forks and heavy crockery. No. Stairs over there — only idiots in horror flicks go up the stairs ...* But the time for decisions was past. Jason was right behind him. It was the stairs or nothing.

As he pelted up, he formed a vague, hopeless idea of barricading himself in, calling the police if Jason hadn't already disconnected the phone. Finding a weapon and venturing out if things got a little too quiet. A still of Lena's limp body flashed into his mind again, just as he tripped on the next stair, missing the tread in the dark.

He almost went down on one knee, grabbing the banister to stop himself. He heard a grunt of triumph on the stairs below. Jason threw himself forward in a full-length tackle, his hand latching on to Paxton's leg, fingers vicing in. Paxton kicked out backwards like a shying horse at a blacksmith's, feeling his boot connect with Jason's chin in the wild swing. Teeth clacking together, Jason went down with a thump, off balance, but as he scrambled up the stairs Paxton knew it wouldn't stay him for long. Sure enough, it was only moments before he heard those feet once more pounding after him.

At the top of the stairs now, but which way? A dark hallway, with doors to both sides. All paths, he knew it now, were one way. Jason was too powerful, and on his own turf. Only luck and adrenaline had kept Paxton alive so far. But if he delayed it long enough, till help arrived, till Lena could wake ... If waking now were possible.

He ran left. His steps in any case were loud enough to announce his direction to anyone in the house. There was no hiding. It was only a matter of time. He ran through a door at the end of the hall, pulling it open and slamming it shut after him. A bedroom, the master by the looks of things, with a big queen-size bed in the middle. The Venetian blinds were shut, closing out all light, making a detailed survey impossible, but as he swivelled his head he spotted a TV cabinet in the darkness off to his right. He instantly dove for it, frantically straining his back to drag it across the floor. There was a rug beneath it, which made it easier to slide, but the TV was a large one, its owner measuring more than one thing by inches. The cabinet was solid wood and glass and slow to move despite the rug. He'd barely got a sliver over the doorway before the edge of the door smacked into it with a deafening bang. Paxton's insides went to liquid.

He tried to pull the cabinet further across, but now the door was slowly pressing inward, pushing the cabinet back into the room. Paxton tried to push back, but it continued to give. Jason was by far the stronger. Paxton desperately turned his back, bracing his legs, heaving himself against the cabinet to stop its progress, but now the rug had turned against him, simply slipping inexorably over the smooth wood. His chest was all over pain, filled with ground glass in place of blood and air.

At last the door was free. It flew open with such force that it shivered as it smashed into the stopper, nearly swinging shut again on the rebound. Paxton hastily backed away as Jason stepped through. He felt the backs of his knees hit the bed. He moved round its edge, glancing at it.

'Must be convenient for you, this. Should have brought a bottle of wine with me.' He could barely get the words out between breaths, but he wasn't going to take death lying down, no matter which way up that was.

'Shut the fuck up, you sick piece of shit.' Jason flicked on the light by the door. Sweat was mingling freely with the blood soaking through his shirt, his breathing an unhealthy rasp. Now that he was aware of it, Paxton realised with a shock that his own sounded exactly the same. In the light he could look out for a weapon, and his eyes chased every which way, searching …

Nothing, unless he sprayed Jason in the face with his cologne. It was meticulously, ridiculously, tidy.

'Come here, fucker.' Jason was advancing on him, wiping his forehead. Backing him into the corner he'd stupidly chosen. But there had been nowhere else to go. 'Think you're hot shit on toast, don't you? When really, you're just cold fart on bread.'

Paxton pulled open the walk-in wardrobe, which must have been added during renovations. It didn't belong to the period. He was greeted by racks of hanging shirts and pants, and neatly paired-up shoes. All of it totally useless.

Jason was half-smirking now, knowing he had him. 'I guess this is a good career move for you, isn't it, *fucker*? Moving closer to the suppliers. Really I'm doing you a favour. You'll go from mere piss-arse medium to friggin' well done …' He laughed.

Paxton leapt on him. He managed to land a good one on his jaw before Jason pushed him back against the bed, gaining the ascendancy before yanking Paxton up again by the shirt collar and banging his head against the bedside table. Pain mushroomed inside Paxton's skull. He fastened his hands on Jason's throat, but another cracking blow off the edge of the table robbed his fingers of their strength. He heard himself scream. He managed to pull Jason down off the bed, both of them tumbling to the floor. Paxton was crushed beneath Jason's falling body. Every part of his anatomy registered its own unique level of pain. Now Jason's hands were round *his* throat, the pressure increasing mercilessly inside his windpipe as well as his head as Jason knelt on his legs, pinning him like a butterfly specimen. Just as fragile, just as surely dead.

But still he struggled on, trying to move his legs, to kick, to wrest those hands from his neck … Struggling right to the end, his pulse beating audibly in his ears like rising footsteps. Getting closer now …

'Get off him, right now!' A furious roar, from somewhere over Paxton's head.

The pressure miraculously lifted. Air blasted back into Paxton's aching lungs, almost choking him. Sending him into a fit of coughing, saliva flecking his lips. He raised his head with a tremendous effort, and the room spun painfully round. But the figure in the doorway was clear enough. Detective Constable Stirling, outlined against the dark.

From the floor Paxton saw Jason rush towards him. Saw Stirling take a step back. Bring a large object from behind his back. And swing.

He missed.

With excellent reflexes Jason ducked out of the way, twisting the wrist holding the weapon. Stirling bellowed with pain, caught unawares. But he wasn't giving it up without a fight. Paxton could hear them grunting, grappling like a pair of wrestlers in a death match. Although tired, Jason was still strong. Stirling's face clearly showed his strain, distorted into something animal by effort. His fingers seemed to be loosening on the weapon.

Paxton forced himself to get up, pausing as the room whirled at a speed that nigh emptied his stomach. He saw Stirling kick Jason's legs from underneath him with a wide sweep of his leg. Both men went down together. Paxton could feel the vibrations underfoot as they hit. The object was jarred from Stirling's hand, making a dent in the wood as it landed.

Jason was ready for it. The instant his back met the floor he rolled, using the same tactics as before. Now Stirling was the one beneath. Jason pulled back a fist and punched him in the face, and Paxton saw blood stream bright from Stirling's mouth. Paxton took two steps forward, then another. Jason drew back his fist for another blow.

The scraping sound warned him, but it wasn't enough. Clutching the fallen object, Paxton swung it hard at the back of his head.

It seemed to take forever. In a state of dazed unreality Paxton watched Jason drop, out cold, as the object met his head with a sound not dissimilar to a cricket bat hitting a ball. Saw Stirling sit up, gasping, pushing Jason off him. He checked the pulse, then whipped Jason's belt from its loops and cinched it tight round his wrists. That done, he looked up at Paxton. Paxton glanced down at his hand. At last he registered what it was he held. A marble paper towel dispenser. Lifted from the kitchen.

'That's bloody pessimistic, isn't it? Sending corpse-control instead of uniforms ...' His voice was a rusty croak. It hurt to speak.

Stirling sat down on the edge of the bed and closed his eyes, breathing too hard to respond.

AFTER fully a minute of silence, Stirling reopened his eyes. They travelled back automatically to the prone figure on the floor. An expression of wonder came into them. 'How the *hell* did you find him?'

Paxton shrugged, fighting back the crushing agony in his skull. 'Psychic.'

For the first time, Stirling smiled. Before Paxton could ask the obvious, there was a loud rap on the door downstairs, and a shout.

'Police! Anyone there?'

Stirling wiped his mouth, and strode out to lean over the banister. 'Yeah, up here, mate!' He started down the stairs at a trot. Paxton trailed more carefully after him, seeing two cops in uniform step puzzled through the front door as Stirling unlocked it. They stared at the detective with matching frowns.

Stirling raised his eyes to the ceiling. 'It's all right, I'm a DC. There's an injured woman through there who needs attention.' He waved towards the lounge. The policewoman quickly skipped through, as Stirling and her partner climbed the stairs.

Paxton diverted course after her. The constable was kneeling over Lena, two fingers at her wrists. She clocked the worry on Paxton's face.

'She'll be all right. Breathing's fine, and her pulse is steady. What happened?'

The relief, more than anything, almost did Paxton's head in. 'I'll let DC Stirling do the talking.' He sank to his knees to take Lena's hand for himself. And because his legs were still a bit unsteady. He felt the warmth of her palm, reassuringly alive. He kissed it, and wrapped it in both hands. He heard the sound of footsteps descending the stairs, and Stirling came into the room.

'Bloody hell — I can't believe it. Good luck explaining this one.' He rubbed a hand over the bits of stubble he'd somehow missed while shaving. The blood had crusted at the corner of his mouth. He also appeared to have given up sleeping till he could track down his comb. Paxton was in no mood to be critical. He knew he looked like he'd been thrown from a speeding car then backed over twice. He studied Lena's pale face, noting the red patch on her forehead where a horrific bruise was due within hours. He kept his eyes on her as he spoke.

'That reminds me. As long as I owe you, Constable ... Could you do me another really big favour?'

Stirling raised his eyebrows, deep troughs of exhaustion marking his own forehead. 'Well, I'm not sure what powers I've got at the moment, but I'll try.'

Paxton glanced up at him, with a look that encompassed everything in the room. 'Could you ... stick this up your boss's arse? From me?'

Stirling went very still. He gave a slow, despondent shake of his head. Quietly he said, 'Can't help you there, I'm sorry.' A small grin leavened the grimness on his face. 'If I do, it'll be all from me.'

Chapter TWENTY-EIGHT

PAXTON SAT IN the hospital chair beside Lena's bed all night, not caring about the cost to his health or his spine. She'd come to as they were loading her into the ambulance, and he'd used his own wounds as an entry pass. Thankfully they'd decided not to stick him in a ward as well. She'd smiled blearily up at him as they pulled out of the drive, siren wailing.

'Idiot. I'd still have dropped in for a chat ...'

Paxton glared. 'Say that again and I'll kill you myself.'

On doctor's orders, he talked constantly to keep her awake, despite the rawness in his throat, battling the stupefying effects of the pills he'd been given to stave off pneumonia. The police had already been in for a statement, and to bring him dry clothes. A little after they'd gone, Stirling came in. Noticing, Paxton turned his chair a little towards the door.

'Still got him?' he asked.

'Yeah. You didn't kill him. More's the pity. He's claiming self-defence. He doesn't know our girl here's come through ...' Stirling smiled at Lena. 'You OK?' He included the two of them in the question.

Paxton spoke for them both. 'Yeah. Thanks to you.' He watched curiously as a fleeting smile spirited across the DC's face, then died out again. 'But you're not, are you?'

Stirling pushed his hands into the pockets of his trousers, his shoulders hunching. He let out a long, considering breath. 'I don't know.' He glanced at Paxton. Bone weary, he didn't have the resources to hold back the truth. 'Truth is, I'm on stand-down at the moment. I punched Detective Sergeant Gardner.'

Paxton stared at him in shock. He thought briefly of thanking the DC again, but that would have been a little insensitive. 'When?'

'Few days ago.'

'So — *how* ...?'

Stirling shrugged, looking a little sheepish. 'I had a lot of time on my hands, didn't I? So I staked out your restaurant. I figured ... if a murder took place somewhere else while I was with you, then I might have been able to dig Gardner's head out of his arse and get some work being done to find the real killer. And even if I saw you with your hands round someone's throat, I'd at least have been doing my job.'

Paxton's jaw fell open. 'Hang on ... Does that mean you were following me? All that way —'

'Lucky I wasn't on duty. That was some pretty hairy driving you were doing.'

'But —' Paxton thought back, aghast. Then memory tapped on his shoulder. Of lights, always behind, in the rear-view mirror. 'Do you — you wouldn't drive a Primera?'

'That was me.'

'Jesus ...' Paxton bent forward, exhaling, resting his elbows on his knees. He felt overwhelmingly light-headed. 'Thanks, mate. I mean that. Don't know if those other two would have been there in time.'

Stirling frowned. 'What do you mean?'

'The regular police. You responded quicker than they did.'

Stirling was giving him a strange look. 'You called them?'

Paxton's own certainty was fading at the look in his eyes. 'The neighbours did. I asked them.'

Stirling slowly shook his head. 'I called 111 myself. It was the first they'd heard.'

Paxton sat back, suddenly wide awake, the reality sobering as cold coffee. There never had been anyone coming. Except for Stirling.

'I'd been driving round for a bit first. Before I caught up with you. I just arrived down at the waterfront to see you bashing on the window of the Holden. Course, I twigged *then* what was happening. Then after I saw you run inside the house, and I was wondering what the hell to do, I heard her scream. So I called the cops. They said to wait outside for an I-car. But then I heard this loud bang.' The door hitting the cabinet. 'So I came in. And saw Miss Bradley on the floor ...'

His eyes drifted to Lena, propped up on her pillows. His gaze turned inward. 'Anyway. I just wanted to check in with you, make sure you were both all right. Best be getting home now.'

He held up a hand in farewell and made towards the door. Lena called to him as he turned his back. 'Thank you!'

He gave another distracted wave, his other hand in his pocket. He had his mobile out before he even reached the door. As he went down the hall Paxton heard him talking softly into it. Cradling it at his ear.

IF it weren't for the guilt, Paxton thought, he'd have felt better. He coughed again, a hacking cough that made his chest ache and his throat raw, slumping forward on the sofa. He stared at his woollen-socked feet, feeling the raging in his throat to be less than what he deserved. He'd spent almost the entire week in bed, the legacy of his cold and his wet shirt. It gave him plenty of time to think. He couldn't help but linger on the honest truth — if he'd just let the reporter and his two companions come up to him at the park ... Gone up to Lena at the funeral, shaken hands with her friends, looked Jason in the eye ... He knew it wasn't his fault, but he'd live with it all the same. It was a gift, what he had, no mistaking. But for him it would never be a blessing.

Except, Paxton considered, for Lena. She'd been around every night bringing food and blankets, given that he was unable to go out for himself. For one reason Paxton was almost grateful for his incapacitation. Adam had called, wanting to visit, but Paxton had warned him, off citing contagion. He didn't want to face Adam just yet, with an explanation he didn't much fancy giving. Bullshit wouldn't fool Adam for one second.

The biscuit packet rustled as Stirling helped himself to a Tim Tam from the coffee table. They were all here at Lena's, a week to the day after their hospital visit. It was questionable which of them showed the least damage. There was a small healing scab at the corner of Stirling's mouth, but at least he'd shaved. Broken veins spidered Paxton's nose, and he looked more pallid than ever. Lena, lucky her, had been discharged from hospital the night after, and was now in perfect health, except for the mustard-coloured bruise on her forehead, livened by patches of startling purple. A mutual liking and respect had developed between the three of them. Stirling had rung to check on them both, and promised to keep them in the loop.

He swallowed his mouthful of chocolate biscuit before he spoke. 'Well, where do you want me to start, folks? His name is Jason Mercer. Network designer; nothing but glowing references from his employers. Gifted, apparently. Quiet, but a great sense of humour.'

Paxton nodded. 'Yeah. He'd have been wetting the swivelly chairs at Microsoft ...' He coughed again.

'He's still living in the house he grew up in with his parents.' Stirling dusted the crumbs off his trousers. 'An uncle used to live there too, for a bit, till they locked him up in Paremoremo. Got done for raping a thirteen-year-old schoolgirl. There were more, apparently, girls and boys. But they couldn't get the others to testify.'

All three of them were silent.

Stirling sucked the smudges of chocolate off his fingers. He was lucky to be back on the case, and he knew it. Woodward had hauled him over the coals for his unauthorised proceedings, but he was being let off with a reprimand. It wouldn't have looked good in the papers, the saviour of the eastern suburbs being discharged, all because of a workplace tiff. After all, he'd only hit a copper.

The team at CIB had clapped and whistled as he walked into the building, rolling out all the fraying old jokes.

'Three cheers for Handy Andy!'

'Well done, mate, you really cleaned up!'

'Ha ha.'

Strait-laced DS Vicky Nielsen slapped him on the shoulder as he passed. 'Sterling work, Andy.' He hadn't realised she even knew who he was.

But that wasn't why he was smiling now. Gardner had been passed over for promotion. Instead, they'd decided to honour another bloke with the title of detective senior sergeant. Former DS Graeme Kirkpatrick.

'It was beautiful,' said Rees. 'He was shouting, "But the wanker couldn't tie up his own shoes, let alone an inquiry!" Then he saw that Graeme had come in, and he went red as an Amsterdam street-light. I've got to hand it to Graeme. He just eyes up the bandage on Gardner's face and goes, "Nose out of joint, Ray?" Dammit, I wish I'd had a camera.'

Celebrations were otherwise a long way off, as Stirling admitted to Paxton and Lena.

'The case against Mercer is building, but forensics could take months.' He frowned. 'It's a bit frustrating. They had a break-through on his car. Cigarette butt in the passenger-side ashtray. He's a non-smoker; he never thought of cleaning there. There'll be DNA on that. But there'll be a long wait for the body.'

He thought he knew who it belonged to. They'd gone back to Harry's, to visit the two witnesses. Rachel, the one who'd seen Gene get into the car, had recently left to study anthropology, but they got directions to her flat. And she confirmed it: Gene had always had a ciggie in her mouth. Likely she'd stuck the butt in the ashtray while he'd been watching out for witnesses. It was only his second. He'd have been nervous.

The problem was getting hold of the body. The mechanics of the job aside, exhumation was a messy business. The laws were still so arcane the corpse had to be dug up at daybreak. Furthermore, the undertaker had understandably been reluctant to co-operate with the investigation. Gene had been buried along with an elderly woman, in the same coffin. They had to get permission to exhume both bodies, and the woman's appalled family were dragging the chain.

The whole inquiry was a mass of breakthroughs and setbacks. There was of course the red HSV, which alone meant sweet FA. However, a single auburn hair had been found clinging to the upholstery, on the passenger's side. They'd also found a torch in the boot next to the emergency puncture kit, engraved 'CAMPUS SECURITY' — scrubbed clean of blood, hair, or prints. On the plus side, Mercer lived in East Auckland, where the crimes were focused, directly opposite the scene of the first. There was the testimony of Paxton and Lena, and Mercer's favoured method of dealing with them both — blows to the head and strangulation. Finally there was Larissa, chatelaine of the knocking shop, who'd had one squiz at a line-up of photos and IDed Mercer as Mr Tall, Dark and Handsome.

Exhaustive searches of the house had failed to bring up any murder weapon for the Bradley inquiry. Out of curiosity, Lena rang Ngaire Alexander, her father's colleague at the clinic. As he'd claimed, Jason Mercer was on file. Astigmatism requiring contact lenses — he'd made a visit to Mark himself just the previous March. It was chilling, but it wasn't proof. Mercer defied the police to find any, while still denying he was guilty of anything. He seemed above even arrest.

THE phone call came out of the blue.

Paxton was sitting watching a DVD with Lena — at his place, because despite everything his was the better TV. Lena still hadn't decided whether to move into her father's place or stay where she was. The house at Mission Bay felt too large, too empty. On the other hand she wasn't sure she wanted renters in there, wrecking the place. It was her childhood home. And then there was Glen, off-limits at her flat, and used to a large back yard ... A decision would have to be made soon — but not now.

The movie was a disappointment, and both of them were yawning. Paxton was gearing up to suggest bed — and not necessarily sleep either. He looked down at the top of Lena's head, resting against his chest, and planted a kiss on it. She looked up at him, seeing him watching her absently.

She gave him a dreamy smile. 'What?'

'Ich liebe dich.'

A spark lit in her eye. She brought her face bewitchingly closer, her nose almost touching his. 'Who's Dick ...?'

The phone went, startling them both. Creakily Paxton stood to answer it, reluctantly depositing Lena on the cushions.

'Hello?'

'Oh good, you're home.' The DC's voice was curiously keyed up. Paxton waited, feeling his irritation subside. 'Lena with you? I tried her number first.'

'Yeah she is. Why?' Seeing him glance in her direction, and sensing news, Lena straightened. He rejoined her on the sofa, holding the cordless phone.

'I think she might want to know this ... Although I never told you.'

Paxton felt a familiar prickle of anticipation. 'Understood. What's up, Andy?'

'Funny you should put it like that ...' The DC gave a grim little chuckle, at some private joke even he didn't find all that amusing. 'Jason Mercer is.'

'Eh?'

'Or was.'

Paxton froze.

'They found him two hours ago. Dead in his cell. He'd hung himself.'

Paxton was paralysed with astonishment. Too startled to point out that the correct term was 'hanged' ...

'Seems Gardner had had a word with him. Trying to dig up some credit. *He* wanted to be the one who cracked Mercer. I listened to the tapes ...' Stirling was silent for a moment. 'We like to joke, occasionally, about the pretty ones. You know. How popular they'll be in jail ... Sometimes it makes them snap, see?'

Paxton did see. And so it had.

'He never said a word to Gardner — no screams, no curses, no begging. Not a single word. He just went silent ...'

Stirling saw in his mind's eye that long, fluorescent-lit, concrete corridor, with its smell of stale urine. The grates in the floor where the hoses sluiced down the piss and vomit and raw excrement from the holding cells. And surrounded by cops, plainclothes and uniform, one of the cell doors standing open. A gruesome hanging ornament filling the doorway ...

'I didn't think he was a suicide risk. He never seemed bothered at all.' The watch-house officer stood at Stirling's elbow, gazing into the tiny room as if trying to get answers from the corpse. 'It was just when I couldn't see him ...'

He held up a key, with its special blade attachment, indicating the shattered glass emergency panel set near the door. 'I went to cut him down. But then I opened the door, and ...' He stared at the occupant of the cell. 'Didn't seem much point.'

A torn blanket stretched from Mercer's neck, bound tight to the viewing grille in the door at its other end. Eyes bulged from their sockets, shot with red, a contrast to the stiff ugly blue of his lips, framing ivory teeth. Set in a horrible rictus of death, that might almost have been a smile …

PAXTON held Lena close, staring at the blank TV screen.

'You know what the biggest irony is, he said? Ultimately, he strangled to death …'

Epilogue

STRANGE, THE GOOD that comes out of bad things. Kids, who were set down as retarded, finding out it's their eyesight that's all to cock instead. 'You're not thick, son, you're just half blind.' They're always so delighted ...

Her memory of me's scabbing over now. And so it should. I mean, no one could cope with that raw kind of grief forever. I know I couldn't. I'm dead, and she isn't. No use pretending otherwise.

And I like to think, in some way, that's done her some good. The saying really is true: as one door closes, another opens. Exit me, stage right, and lo and behold, what — or rather who — should pop up through the hidden trapdoor ...? I mean, seriously, if it hadn't been for what happened to me ...

The good from the bad. You see?

I'm sure there has to be some kind of neo-transcendental, karma ... pyjama ... meaning in that somewhere. And to think I was apologising. Christ.

But to be perfectly honest ... it is a comfort, in a way. I've thought about it, a lot. Fair bit of time these days.

My own personal Meaning of Life. Or death, to be more accurate ... Ha.

I couldn't have thought of a better one myself.

TAKE care, sweetheart ... I'm watching. And I love you too.

Printed in Great Britain
by Amazon

50691800R00187